THE Ballroom GIRLS CHRISTMAS DREAMS

JENNY HOLMES

PENGUIN BOOKS

TRANSWORLD PUBLISHERS
Penguin Random House, One Embassy Gardens,
8 Viaduct Gardens, London SW11 7BW
www.penguin.co.uk

Transworld is part of the Penguin Random House group of companies
whose addresses can be found at global.penguinrandomhouse.com

Penguin
Random House
UK

First published in Great Britain in 2023 by Bantam
an imprint of Transworld Publishers
Penguin paperback edition published 2023

Copyright © Jenny Oldfield 2023

Jenny Oldfield has asserted her right under the Copyright,
Designs and Patents Act 1988 to be identified as the author of this work.

Lyrics on p. 71 from 'I Won't Dance' written by Oscar Hammerstein II,
Otto Harbach, Dorothy Fields and Jimmy McHugh.
Lyrics on p. 84 from *My Gal Sal* written by Paul
Dresser, Ralph Rainger and Leo Robin.
Lyrics on p. 117 from 'Strip Polka' written by Johnny Mercer.
Lyrics on p. 157 from 'Winter Wonderland' written by
Felix Bernard and Richard Bernhard Smith.
Lyrics on p. 172 from 'Pack Up Your Troubles in Your Old Kit-Bag'
written by Felix Powell and George Henry Powell.
Lyrics on p. 254 from 'Mamãe eu quero' written by Vicente Paiva and Jararaca.

A CIP catalogue record for this book
is available from the British Library.

ISBN 9781529176544

Typeset in 11.75/14pt Baskerville by Falcon Oast Graphic Art Ltd.
Printed and bound in Great Britain by Clays Ltd, Elcograf S.p.A.

The authorized representative in the EEA is Penguin Random House Ireland,
Morrison Chambers, 32 Nassau Street, Dublin D02 YH68.

Penguin Random House is committed to a sustainable
future for our business, our readers and our planet. This book is
made from Forest Stewardship Council® certified paper.

MIX
Paper | Supporting
responsible forestry
FSC® C018179

For Eve, Kate, Evan, Jude and Lola – always.

CHAPTER ONE

November 1942

Bernie Greene's train approached its destination. Lost in thought and leaning back against the cushioned head-rest, he scarcely registered his fellow passengers or the condensation trickling down the windows of the crowded carriage. Daylight was fading fast, wheels rattled rhythmically over steel rails – *nearly there, nearly there, nearly there*.

'No high jinks for Guy Fawkes last night, worse luck,' the woman in the seat opposite remarked to no one in particular. 'Mr Hitler has put paid to that.'

'Remember, remember the fifth of November.' A man in a trilby hat and belted raincoat who was in charge of two high-spirited lads took up the theme. 'In the good old days we had bonfires all along the coast, as far as the eye could see. Catherine wheels, jumping jacks, sky rockets. Gunpowder, treason and Lord knows what.'

'Not during this rotten blackout,' the woman said with a sigh. 'Show one chink of light after dark and the blessed wardens will nab you, sure as anything.'

A weary Bernie closed his eyes. *Nearly there*. A canvas kitbag containing his shaving kit and pin-striped suit was perched in the luggage rack above his head. Pearl had told him not to bother bringing a change of clothes; she'd rather he showed up at the church in his army uniform, but he'd brought the suit just in case. Forty-eight hours' home leave before a possible posting to North Africa – that was all he had.

One of the boys tripped over Bernie's thick boots, polished to perfection, as he lunged towards the window to wipe away the condensation with the sleeve of his school mackintosh. 'I can see the Tower!' he crowed.

'Can't!' the second lad argued for argument's sake.

'Can!'

'Can't!'

Bernie opened his eyes. Sure enough, they were within sight of his home town's most famous landmark. The 500-feet-tall construction of iron and steel soared skywards; a metal finger standing out against a background of heavy grey clouds, signifying that his long journey from the west coast of Scotland to Lancashire was nearing its end. He reached for his kitbag, keen to be the first to leave the compartment, to be out in the corridor waiting for the train to grind to a halt, to fling open the door and step down on to the platform where, fingers crossed, Joe Taylor would be waiting. Bernie slid down the window and leaned out. The air smelled of smoke; steam belched from the funnel and brakes screeched as his train entered the glass cathedral of Blackpool North Station.

Not far away, in a room above Ibbotson's tobacconist shop on North View Parade, Pearl Scott watched Sylvia Ellis put the finishing touches to the cream silk dress that Pearl would wear for the most important day of her life.

'I don't know what's wrong with me,' she'd grumbled

as she'd handed her needle and thread to Sylvia. 'I'm all fingers and thumbs.'

'You've got the wedding jitters, that's what's wrong.' Sylvia made tiny, neat stitches in the gown's delicate fabric – one inherited from her dance instructor mother, passed on first to Sylvia and now to Pearl. It had a narrow waist and a full skirt, a scooped neckline and long sleeves: ideal for petite, dark-haired Pearl's bridal outfit.

'What if Bernie changes his mind?' Pearl voiced her worst fear. *Where is he now, right this second? Is he a bag of nerves like me? Oh Lord, why ever did I say yes?*

'Don't be silly; I've never seen a man more head over heels in love than Bernie is with you.'

'But what if his leave is cancelled?'

'It won't be.' Sylvia had almost finished hemming the shortened skirt; she was a good three inches taller than Pearl – hence the adjustment.

The bride-to-be refused to be comforted. 'But the way things are in North Africa, his regiment could be sent there at the drop of a hat.'

'Unlikely.' Sylvia prided herself on keeping up to date with the news. 'Monty's got Rommel on the run from El Alamein. It's been heading in that direction since the end of October.'

'All right, Miss Clever Clogs.' Sulking, Pearl peeked around the side of the blackout blind to view the gloomy shopping street below. Though dusk had already descended there were no street lamps to light people's way home. A tram without headlights stopped and offloaded its passengers. 'Here comes Joy with the bouquets,' she reported to Sylvia before dashing downstairs to greet their friend. 'Quick – come in and close the door before you catch your death. Sylvia's upstairs.'

'Is the dress finished?' Joy had rushed straight from the florists with three bouquets of pink roses: one for the bride and one for each for her bridesmaids. 'Have you tried it on?'

'Not yet.' Pearl led the way upstairs then stopped short on the landing outside Sylvia's rented flat. 'I still can't believe it's really happening. I'm thinking of all the things that can go wrong – from Bernie's train breaking down in the middle of nowhere to him getting cold feet . . .'

'It's not going to happen, silly!' Joy swept ahead then carefully deposited the armful of flowers on the nearest flat surface – a green baize card table standing in the bay window. The living room was small, with an old leather sofa taking up most of the space. Colourful cushions, china ornaments and a standard lamp enlivened the otherwise utilitarian effect, as did red velvet curtains (one of many donations from Sylvia's mother). Bright posters advertised recent productions at the Grand Theatre: Sadler's Wells had performed there with Margot Fonteyn and Frederick Ashton, as had the Old Vic Company with Jean Forbes-Robertson as Portia in *The Merchant of Venice*.

Sylvia looked up from her sewing with a knowing smile. Her fair hair glinted in the firelight and her wide-apart blue eyes sparkled with amusement. 'Don't tell me – Pearl's been regaling you with more imaginary catastrophes. Lovely flowers, by the way.'

Pearl had no idea what the word 'regaling' meant but she got the gist. 'Maybe we should have waited.' A new train of thought steamed into view as she hovered, pale-faced, in the doorway. 'People will wonder why Bernie and I are rushing to the altar. They'll say it's a shotgun affair – my dad is marching Bernie down the aisle in order to make a respectable woman of me.'

4

'But you're not expecting,' Sylvia pointed out as she approached Pearl and held the dress up against her. 'Are you?'

'No!' Pearl was adamant. 'But the gossip doesn't end there. You know what they say even if there's no baby in the picture – "She's only getting hitched so she can claim the soldiers' separation allowance or the widow's pension if the worst were to happen."'

Handing the finished gown to Joy, Sylvia used her fingertips to gently wipe away the tears that had begun to trickle down Pearl's cheeks. 'There, there,' she murmured. 'This isn't like you. You're the fun one of our little trio, the live wire who jitterbugs and jives her way through life with a smile.'

'Oh!' Pearl covered her face and sobbed helplessly. 'Oh, oh, oh!'

'Here; blow your nose.' Joy handed her a handkerchief. 'It's only natural for you to have butterflies, but there's absolutely no need. Everything's in hand.'

'Flowers, for a start.' Sylvia gestured towards the bouquets.

'And the special licence is in place, thanks to your mother charming the socks off the vicar at All Saints,' Joy continued. 'Joe has the ring and he's organized a car to take you from Empire Street to the church. Your dad has borrowed a camera and film for the photographs. We've begged and borrowed enough food coupons to feed an army in the church hall afterwards. A leg of ham, pickled eggs, butter, bread, jam – it'll be a feast, I promise you.'

'And we'll have plenty of records to get people in the mood for dancing,' Sylvia chipped in. 'Victor Silvester, naturally. Joe Loss, Maxwell Stewart, Jack Parnell – you name it and Mother has loaned it to us.'

'Yes, you're right.' Pearl blew her nose noisily and made an effort to pull herself together. 'Sorry, I don't know what on earth's got into me.'

'That's better.' Joy smiled encouragingly. 'Now for this beautiful wedding dress – are you ready to try it on?'

Yes, she was ready. Pearl took a deep breath. *So silly.* She couldn't thank Sylvia and Joy enough. Off with her cardigan, blouse and slacks, on with the cream silk dream of a dress, zipped up by Joy, creases smoothed out by Sylvia while Pearl covered her eyes as directed before allowing herself to be led to the wardrobe mirror in Sylvia's bedroom.

'Open your eyes,' Joy breathed.

A vision, a magical transformation had taken place – from hard-working live wire who ran Great Scott's North Shore Amusement Arcade to shimmering, glowing, dainty, fairy-tale princess. Pearl gasped and stared. She turned this way and that. The fabric swished and swayed. 'What do you think? Will Bernie like it?' she whispered.

'Like it? He'll love it!' Sylvia sang out in sheer delight at the result of their handiwork.

'If not, he's an idiot,' Joy beamed. 'Tomorrow will be perfect – just you wait and see.'

Joe was waiting on the station platform as arranged. Bernie shook his hand then the two friends made their way through the jostling crowd, past porters unloading mailbags from the goods wagon, through clouds of steam and smoke.

'I almost didn't recognize you,' Joe confessed when they reached the Morris Oxford that he'd borrowed for the weekend. 'The uniform and the short back and sides had me fooled.'

6

Bernie took out a packet of cigarettes and offered one to Joe. He'd been gone for six weeks of basic military drills at his Primary Training Centre but in that short time his horizons had been transformed. The routine of running Henry Scott's North Shore Arcade with Pearl had vanished, replaced by endless drill, rifle and pistol shooting, gas training and map reading from dawn until dusk. Was Bernie even the same person as the carefree youngster who had swept his fiancée off her feet on the Tower Ballroom floor and romanced her into his bed?

'What's up?' Joe asked as the two men leaned against the side of the car, staring up into the darkening sky and inhaling deeply. Joe was unaltered, the same easy-going market trader that Bernie had known since they'd started school together. He wore his cap at a jaunty angle and his dark hair curled on to his collar – a reminder for Bernie of his best pal's lifelong dislike of the barber's chair.

Joe's house on King Street was where tomorrow's bridegroom would spend his last night of so-called freedom. 'What do you mean?' Bernie blew a spiral of smoke out of the side of his mouth. 'Nothing's up.'

'So why the long face?'

'Nothing; forget it.' Bernie ground the stub of his cigarette beneath his boot then slung his kitbag into the car and sat in the passenger seat, waiting for Joe to join him. People swarmed out of the station on to trams and buses. Someone shouted a harsh warning to watch out as a taxi lurched out in front of a young girl on a bike.

'Aren't you going to ask me how Pearl is?' Joe ventured as he got into the Morris and slammed the door.

'I know how she is – she writes to me practically every day.' Each lovey-dovey word was committed to Bernie's memory and all her letters were stashed away in his metal locker. Sometimes, after a day of relentless target practice and rifle maintenance, he would take them out and reread the heartfelt vows – the endless 'I miss you' and 'I'm lonely without you' messages, the rows of kisses and the tear-stained signatures – 'Your ever-loving Pearl'. At first the daily missives would make Bernie's heart soar, but lately his thoughts had grown darker and he would often go to sleep trying but failing to picture her dear face with its ready smile and startling green eyes. She belonged to a different life. He was a soldier now; not the quick-witted, jokey young fairground worker that she'd fallen for.

'Don't you at least want to know if everything's sorted out for the big day?' Joe threw Bernie an anxious glance.

'It is. Just drive, Joe – all right?' Bernie ignored his surroundings – in any case, it was too dark to make anything out. King Street was a ten-minute drive along the breezy promenade, located in the maze of terraced streets behind the Tower. The night air smelled of smoke, seaweed and salt water. Every sound was familiar: trams rattled, drunks lurched along the prom and shouted incoherently, wind gusted, strains of music and laughter drifted through the open doors of pubs and dance halls.

'Cheer up – it'll soon be done and dusted.' Turning off the prom to negotiate the narrow streets, Joe tried again to get more than a few reluctant grunts out of his glum companion.

'Don't mind me,' Bernie mumbled. 'I'm worn out – that's all.' *What the hell am I doing, getting hitched in a mad rush? And for God's sake, why?* Nothing made sense. His legs felt weak as Joe parked and he got out of the car. 'This isn't King Street,' he remarked as he took in features of his old stamping ground – the shadow of the Tower building

8

and the semi-derelict Mason's Yard, with the Black Horse pub just beyond. 'We're in Empire Street.'

'That's right, Bernie lad.' A shove from Joe set the reluctant bridegroom in motion towards their local. 'You're a bundle of bloody nerves, but I reckon a pint of best bitter will take the edge off those jitters. Follow me.'

Pearl lay in bed, staring at her wedding dress. It hung from a hook on the door of the bedroom that she shared with Elsie, her eight-year-old sister. Though it was scarcely light, the luminous hands of the alarm clock told her that it was a quarter to eight. Her big day was dawning.

'Pearl, are you up?' Pearl's mother, Maria, called from the bottom of the stairs. She tapped the banister impatiently then sent Elsie to turf Pearl out of bed. 'Tell your sister she'll be late for her own wedding if she's not careful.'

Elsie, dressed only in her vest and knickers, tumbled through the door, almost knocking the bridal gown off its hook. 'Mum says you have to get up.' She snatched at Pearl's slippery green satin eiderdown and pulled it off her bed. 'Get up! Get up!'

The bride-to-be clutched at the top sheet to keep it in place. 'Leave off, you little pest.'

'You'll be late.' Elsie tugged Pearl's pillow from under her. 'Why won't you get up? Come on, breakfast's ready – get up!'

'Tell Mum I'm on my way.'

'Now!' Elsie insisted, fists clenched and eyes glaring. She hadn't forgiven Pearl for not making her a bridesmaid, choosing instead her grown-up friends, Joy and Sylvia, who would wear beautiful royal blue satin dresses as they walked down the aisle. Now, as far as Elsie was concerned, the sooner they got through the boring church bit, the sooner she would be able to gorge herself on sausage rolls and ham sandwiches at the party afterwards.

Pearl swung her legs over the side of the bed. She'd scarcely slept. Breakfast was the last thing she wanted. Oh, the nerves!

Elsie plonked herself down beside Pearl. 'What's the matter? Don't you want to marry Bernie?'

'Yes, course I do.'

'Why aren't you smiling?'

'I am – look.' Pearl forced a grin then quickly relapsed into pale-faced seriousness.

'That's not a proper smile.' Elsie grew uneasy. 'I like Bernie – I want you to marry him so he can be my sort-of brother.'

'Pearl, for the last time!' Maria called again.

'Coming!' Prodded and poked into action, Pearl reached for her dressing gown.

Elsie scooted downstairs ahead of her. 'She's coming!' she reported, followed by, 'She doesn't want to get married, I can tell.'

Their twelve-year-old brother Wilf glanced up from his toast and jam. The subject was of only passing interest and by the time Pearl put in an appearance, he was once more engrossed in the Rupert Bear strip cartoon in the *Daily Express*.

A quick glance at Pearl's ashen face told Maria what was the matter. 'Sit down,' she ordered. 'Don't worry; there's not a girl on this earth who doesn't get butterflies before she walks down the aisle. Let's start with a nice cup of tea followed by a slice of toast.'

Pearl sipped obediently at the tea. Soon her other brother Ernie appeared in a blast of cold air, flinging down his newsboy's delivery bag and snatching the last piece of toast from the table. 'I saw Bernie sitting on Joe Taylor's front doorstep,' he reported between mouthfuls. 'All by himself, smoking and biting his nails.'

Pearl took a sharp intake of breath. 'You actually saw him?'

'Unless he was a ghost.' Ernie chomped happily. 'He had his uniform on and everything.'

'You see,' Maria soothed. 'Bernie arrived safely. Nothing's going to go wrong.' Married to Henry Scott at twenty and with four offspring to their name, Pearl's mother could nevertheless remember the stomach-churning agony of her own wedding day: a helpless mixture of dread and excitement. 'Now eat your toast, there's a good girl.'

Maria was in charge as usual. Henry knew his place – he'd put on his double-breasted suit, crisp white shirt, blue tie and gold tie-pin and cufflinks then left the house, determined to keep out of the way until he was needed. Ernie and Wilf had orders to smarten themselves up then head off to All Saints on their bikes, ready to act as ushers. Elsie clamoured to be allowed to put on her crimson velvet dress and have her dark hair plaited.

'Stop pestering me,' Maria scolded. 'I'm busy helping Pearl.' By her calculations, she would have fifteen minutes at the most to get herself ready – mother of the bride in a mauve two-piece and matching hat with a light veil concealing the top half of her face. Her finishing touch was a luxurious collar fashioned from an old fox-fur stole.

Pearl's hands trembled as she slid her dress from its hanger. It was soft and smooth to the touch, its bodice elaborately trimmed with lace. Stepping into it, she saw again that the skirt skimmed the floor and swished as she moved. *Thank you, Sylvia's mother!*

Maria fastened the zip, helped Pearl on with her short veil then stood back with a satisfied nod. 'You'll do,' she said before retreating from the room.

There was half an hour to go before Joe arrived with the Morris Oxford. Time to get Elsie kitted out. Only minutes for Maria to put on her make-up, style her jet-black hair into a French pleat, then on with her outfit before the taxi for her and Elsie arrived. Where was Henry, for goodness' sake? Trust him to cut it fine.

In her bedroom Pearl adjusted her veil and reached for her bouquet. She heard the front door open and her father's booming voice demanding to know where the hell Joe Taylor had got to. Her mother answered him calmly as she and Elsie left the house.

Pearl descended the stairs to find her father waiting in the front room, looking a million dollars in his dark blue suit and silk tie, like a leading man in a Hollywood film: a Humphrey Bogart or a Joseph Cotten. He had the full showman swagger; Mr Blackpool off to a tee.

'Blimey, you look grand,' he said as he took in the apparition in white. Neither he nor Maria had ever been ones for overblown compliments.

'You don't look bad yourself,' Pearl teased.

A car horn sounded. 'That'll be Joe.' Henry offered an arm to his daughter, puffed out his chest and led her on to the street.

Neighbours who had known Pearl ever since she was a tiny girl in short skirts and white ankle socks stood on their doorsteps to wave them off. My, but Maria Scott's eldest was a beauty now! How had she conjured up that spectacular dress on the meagre clothes coupons she was allowed? As for Henry Scott; he looked pleased as Punch, as well he might! So, good luck to them.

All was a blur – the Tower building, the promenade, Blackpool's three piers striding out into the sea, which was blue for once under a crisp, late-autumn sky. In the back seat of the Morris Oxford, Pearl straightened her skirt then stared straight ahead. Her heart raced despite her attempts to stay calm as they reached the church. She could see Sylvia and Joy in their blue satin dresses, standing in the porch. Somehow, with her father's help, Pearl got out of the car, lowered her veil then walked to join them.

'Beautiful!' Joy whispered, letting best man Joe slide by to take his position in the front pew before stooping to arrange the folds in Pearl's precious dress.

'Is he here?' Pearl whispered to Sylvia who nodded.

Pearl's unreliable heart skipped several beats as the organ began to play.

No turning back now! Inside the church, Bernie stood stiffly to attention, arms clamped to his sides and staring up at the rich reds, greens and blues of the stained-glass window behind the altar. He'd made it thus far thanks to Joe, whose prediction about a couple of pints steadying Bernie's nerves had been proved wrong. The jitters and doubts had only got worse as the night had worn on. Somehow a dazed Bernie had managed to get up this morning to shave and put on his uniform in time for the ceremony. Now, with rich organ notes ringing out to the church rafters and beyond, there was definitely, once and for all, not a hope in hell of getting out of tying the knot with Pearl. With mounting dread, Bernie turned his head to look up the aisle.

CHAPTER TWO

When Bernie saw his bride in her long white dress, gliding towards him on her father's arm – 'Off-white; or cream, to be exact,' Sylvia corrected him when he recalled the heart-stopping moment later that afternoon – he knew in a flash that getting married was the right thing to do. Pearl seemed to float like a swan rather than walk; all grace and mystery behind her veil, carrying pink roses, turning her head to smile at him as he joined her and they approached the vicar together.

'It just felt right,' he confessed to Sylvia and Joy once the eating part of the reception was over and chairs and tables were being pushed to one side of the church hall, ready for the dancing to start. 'Like it was always meant to be.'

'You should've seen him last night,' Joe cut in. He'd loosened his tie and undone his top button, ready to claim the first dance from chief bridesmaid Sylvia. 'Talk about the jitters.'

'Yeah, what an idiot.' In that moment of revelation, Bernie had sloughed off all doubt and had gone on to pronounce his vows with enthusiasm. God, he'd forgotten how beautiful Pearl was, and she'd been shaking like a leaf through the whole performance, poor lass. 'Do you, Bernard Greene, take this woman . . . ?', 'Do you, Pearl

Maria Scott, take this man . . . ?' He'd fumbled with the ring and almost dropped it, making her giggle. That smile, those eyes! 'You may kiss the bride.'

Her face still glowed and her eyes shone; even now, after the speeches were over and Wilf was put in charge of the gramophone –'Big mistake,' Ernie predicted grimly. None of it mattered. Bernie was married to Pearl and he was the happiest man alive.

Across the room, Pearl basked in compliments. 'Breathtaking', 'stunning', 'a perfect bride'. The warm praise felt like the sun's rays on her face and she soaked it up. Nothing had gone wrong after all. She'd been a fool to worry. She and Bernie were married and all was right with the world.

Close by, her father preened and strutted while her mother supervised the moving of furniture.

'Pearl definitely gets her looks from you.' One of the guests, Terry Liddle, laid it on thick for Maria's benefit. As a relative newcomer to Blackpool, he hadn't seen mother and daughter together until now. 'In fact, you two could be sisters.'

'Get away with you.' Brushing away the compliment, Maria handed him a tray of leftover sandwiches. 'Take these into the kitchen for me and put a clean tea towel over them to keep them fresh.'

'If you promise to dance with me later on.' Terry – a Cary Grant lookalike – charmed his way past Maria's no-nonsense defences as only he could – unabashed, devilishly handsome, tall, long-limbed and never taking no for an answer. He winked and took the tray away as Victor Silvester started proceedings with 'You're Dancing On My Heart', chosen by Sylvia's mother, Lorna Ellis.

'Mr Silvester recorded this last year with Monia Liter on

piano, Alfred Campbell on lead violin and Ben Edwards on drums.' Lorna spoke with her usual air of authority. She looked glamorous as ever in a slim-fitting, silver-grey two-piece with an embroidered velvet collar, with her fair hair swept up to show off her elegant long neck. After all, as the owner of the Lorna Ellis Dance Academy, the premier ballroom dance school in town, she had standards to maintain. 'It's a quickstep, which anyone can attempt, provided they know the basic rules.'

Wilf had lowered the needle on to the record while Ernie had rolled his eyes and stuck his hands in his pockets. You wouldn't catch him doing a quickstep – or any other type of daft jigging about, come to that.

The smooth sound of violins filled the hall. 'Come on, Ernie – dance with me!'

Heck; some daft woman in a pink flouncy frock – he had no clue who she was, but she was probably one of Pearl's dancing pals – dragged him into the middle of the room before he could object.

'Just run, jump and skip in time to the music. Follow my lead and you'll be fine.'

Ernie gave in with a groan.

Meanwhile, the floor filled with couples in formal ballroom hold. Joe swept Sylvia in a snappy diagonal across the room, mixing running steps with hops, skips and graceful natural turns.

'Not bad,' she acknowledged with a tilt of her head. They skimmed past Joy and her beloved Tommy, recently arrived from a matinee performance at the Tower Circus where he was a whiteface clown – the one in a dunce's hat and spangled pantaloons who played the trumpet while all kinds of knockabout chaos reigned in the ring.

Joy loved the rapid, syncopated steps of the quickstep.

16

'My, Mr Silvester is simply the best!' she breathed in Tommy's ear.

He wiped away the smudge of white greasepaint that had transferred itself from his cheek to her lips. 'Did the wedding go off without a hitch?' he murmured above the swell of the orchestra.

'It was perfect,' she replied. It had been the ceremony that every girl dreams about: beautiful, blushing bride; tall, broad-shouldered groom looking pleased and proud; a pink rose bouquet tossed over the bride's shoulder and caught by a triumphant Mavis Thorne, who was, like Joy, a member of the Tower Ballroom cleaning team, now firmly on course to be All Saints' next blushing bride.

'I'm sorry I missed it,' Tommy said.

'Never mind – you're here now.' Keep the feet parallel; heel lead followed by two steps on the balls of the feet – it came as naturally as breathing to Joy. Tommy threw in a lock step, crossing one foot behind the other. He held her close and they made a pivot turn – right foot forward for the lady, quarter turn to the right, left foot back and slightly to the side.

Observing them with her expert eye, Lorna was pleased with what she saw. Since her daughter Sylvia's dramatic split from Eddie Winter, Joy and Tommy were her current star pupils and she had high hopes for them. Even now, in this party atmosphere, among the bumping and jostling, they were head and shoulders above the rest.

The music ended and Wilf chose another record from the pile – a Latin number this time, much to Lorna's disgust. Latin dances were all bounce and swivel out of hold, with wild shaking of the hips and shoulders and high kicks that inevitably displayed too much leg; downright vulgar, in Lorna's opinion.

Meanwhile, in the short gap between numbers, Ernie escaped from the frilly woman's clutches and Terry cajoled Maria into fulfilling her part of the bargain – the leftover sandwiches had been duly covered with a tea towel and now it was time for them to jitterbug and throw caution to the winds. Sylvia took the opportunity to excuse herself from Joe with a polite thank-you. She wanted to talk to Eddie, who lingered by the door, as if on the verge of making a quick getaway.

'I didn't see you at the church,' she said by way of greeting as she noted a change to the parting in her old partner's wavy, fair hair and his new, expensively tailored suit: padded at the shoulders and with stylish, wide lapels. He really was a good-looking man, there was no denying.

'I was there.' Eddie had sat in the back pew, coolly observing as usual. 'I thought it went splendidly.'

'Poor Pearl; until the very last minute she was certain that something dreadful would happen.'

'An unexpected spanner in the works?'

'Something like that.' There was an awkward pause. 'I don't suppose you'd like to dance?' Sylvia volunteered.

'Not to this.' Eddie had intended to ask her to do the quickstep with him for old time's sake, but best man Joe had beaten him to it. Eddie was a traditionalist so rotating his hips and swivelling his feet didn't come naturally. Besides, he and Sylvia hadn't danced together for months; not since she'd gone over to Latin and joined Cliff Seymour's rival academy on North View Parade. 'I'll have a drink with you, though.'

So they went to the trestle table and picked up a glass of lemon squash apiece before making their way outside and sitting on a bench that overlooked a small cobbled yard adjoining the graveyard and All Saints beyond. The clock face on the squat, square tower told them that the time was half past three.

'You're sure it's not too chilly?' Eddie asked, courteous as ever.

'No, I'm glad of the fresh air.'

'You look lovely, by the way.' When did Sylvia not? 'That shade of blue suits you.' Thanks to a bargain she'd made with Cliff that she would eat more to keep up her energy, she was doing her very best to regain her curves after a period of almost starving herself; there was colour in her cheeks now, too. Not that it had been easy. Often she'd had to force herself to swallow down larger portions of potatoes or bread in order to keep her side of the agreement.

Sylvia brushed away the compliment with a quick dip of her head. 'Have you found a permanent partner yet?'

'Yes: Mavis Thorne. She was your mother's choice.'

Ah, Mavis: the sharp-elbowed catcher of the bride's bouquet. 'And how is it working out?'

'I've yet to find out.' Eddie picked at the dry skin close to his thumb nail. 'We have our first lesson together on Monday. Mavis is roughly the same height as you so there doesn't need to be any adjustment of hold, length of stride, and so on.'

Hearing the dry analysis, Sylvia raised an eyebrow. 'Mother will soon knock you into shape,' she promised.

'I hope so – she intends to put us forward for the first round of the Allied North of England Championship in January,' he informed her.

'So soon?'

'It's a fair amount of pressure,' he admitted. 'Tommy and Joy will enter too.'

'There's kudos in it for Mother if you four do well. The Academy will benefit. How do you feel about it?'

'Nervous.' *Missing you with every step I take,* is what Eddie didn't say. The conversation drifted on while strains of energetic jive music reached them from inside the hall.

'You – nervous?' Sylvia gave a light laugh. 'You've been entering dance competitions since the age of fourteen.'

'Always with you,' he reminded her, clasping his hands together then leaning forward to rest his forearms on his knees.

The gap between them yawned wide. A cold breeze combined with Eddie's pointed reminder of their broken partnership caused Sylvia to shiver. 'Perhaps we should go back inside,' she suggested.

'Of course.' He offered her his arm as the music changed to a slow, old-fashioned waltz (a sign that Lorna had taken over the reins from Wilf). 'Well done you for helping Pearl prepare for her big day,' Eddie said as they re-entered the hall.

'Joy and I did it between us. Look at Pearl now: waltzing with Bernie – the two of them together couldn't be more perfect.'

'And you'll dance this one with me?' Eddie looked Sylvia in the eye, his gaze questioning and intense.

There was a slight hesitation. 'One waltz and then I must go,' she decided briskly. 'I promised Cliff that I'd teach his Paso class at five. He and Terry are having a meeting with their landlord over an increase in rent so I'm afraid there was no getting out of it.'

The waltz wasn't Pearl and Bernie's favourite dance. Give them the lindy hop or the cha-cha any day of the week. But on their big day they glided across the floor in ballroom hold, upper bodies leaning to the left, swaying on the first beat of each bar then rising high on to their toes into a natural turn without having to think. Bernie led, Pearl followed, with her skirt billowing and her eyes gazing deep into his.

Bernie's serge battledress felt rough to the touch but he wore it with pride. It was the new pattern: the blouse was stripped of its pleated pockets, fly front and brass buttons, and its close fit gave him a sleek outline. Training had added muscle to his torso so he knew he cut a decent figure on the dance floor. He could tell from Pearl's doting gaze that she thought so too.

Two quarter turns followed by a reverse turn – one-two-three, one-two-three – Pearl was in heaven, with Bernie's right hand resting lightly against her shoulder blade. It was as if he'd never been away. 'Happy?' she murmured as they spun on.

'Need you ask?' His beaming smile said it all; pre-wedding nerves consigned to oblivion, never to return.

'It feels like a dream.' Bernie's proposal of marriage had come unexpectedly, soon after his conscription letter had arrived and only days before he'd started his training. Until then they'd had a high old time competing against Joy and Tommy and Sylvia and Eddie at the Tower Ballroom. Pearl's lively spirits and Bernie's jokiness had been the hallmarks of their courtship. Never still and rarely downhearted, she'd enticed him on to the floor by dangling the carrot of cash prizes: ten bob here, a quid there. At first he'd met resistance along the lines of 'only sissies get involved in that ballroom malarkey', which had led to explosive confrontations between Bernie and his older brother Mick, who had ended up in prison. But that was another story.

Then came the moment when friendship had turned into something deeper. It had crept up on Bernie first, with Pearl sailing gaily on, to the point where, one day during a walk along the beach, he'd had to spell it out – in a rare moment of seriousness he told her that she meant more to him than she realized. He wanted something other than friendship. In fact, he was in love with her and did she feel the same?

'Yes!' Pearl had cried after his words had sunk in. 'Yes, yes, yes!'

He'd bought a ring from Hartley's: a ruby with two small diamonds to either side. They'd vowed to love each other for ever and to write every day.

'A dream is what it is.' After a long pause and a sequence of smooth turns, Bernie picked up on Pearl's earlier remark. 'Someone will have to pinch me and wake me up.'

Instead, she leaned in and planted a soft kiss on his cheek. The waltz music ended with a dying fall of violins, replaced by a foxtrot that had them skipping across the floor at ragtime speed. 'I probably shouldn't admit to this,' Pearl warned as they danced on, 'but last night the dream nearly turned into a terrible nightmare.'

'What about?'

'"There was I waiting at the church."' Trying to make light of her fears, she whispered the words of an old music hall song. '"When I found he'd left me in the lurch . . ."'

'"Lor', how it did upset me!"' Bernie lifted Pearl clean off the ground and spun her round. 'You daft thing; I'd never do that!' He set his bride down then walked her to a quiet corner. 'Listen, I might have had a touch of the collywobbles on the train down here,' he admitted. 'God knows why; you're the best thing that ever happened to me.'

Pearl drew him close. 'Being hundreds of miles apart didn't help. Neither did reading about the war in North Africa and dreading that you'd be posted there.'

'Hush – nothing's certain yet!' He put a warning finger to her lips. 'What will be will be, and besides, thousands of others are in the same boat.'

'I know.' She sighed. His hand was warm and it gripped hers tightly. *Stop the world; let this moment last for ever.*

Their wedding guests danced on or stood to the sides of the hall chatting. Henry Scott had stepped in with a flourish to reclaim his wife from Terry the erstwhile gigolo. (What a first impression the man had made – girls had fallen at his feet like skittles. Little did they know!) Lorna had resumed control of the gramophone and Ernie and Wilf had disappeared into the kitchen with Elsie, no doubt to scoff leftovers. Joy and Tommy waited between records for the next dance to begin. It turned out to be a tango, full of drama and passion.

'Well, Mrs Greene,' Bernie said to Pearl as they took up position in the centre of the floor, 'what do you say we show them how it's done?'

Eight hours of bliss. Once the reception was over, Pearl and Bernie retreated to the spare room in Joe's house where they would spend their wedding night.

'I can't remember a single detail about the church ceremony.' Pearl stood by the bed while Bernie unzipped her dress. It slipped from her shoulders then fell around her feet in soft, billowing folds. He turned her towards him. 'Did we really go through with it?' she asked.

'I think we did.' He raised her left hand to his lips. 'There's a ring on your finger to prove it.'

She absorbed the silence of their surroundings. The

blind was down and a small lamp lit the sparsely furnished room – not much more than a narrow single bed, a chest of drawers and the bedside table. There was a rug by the bed and Joe, bless him, had seen to it that there were clean sheets and a freshly laundered pillow case for the newly married pair.

The evening silence was precious after the excitement of the day. Pearl closed her eyes and rested her head against Bernie's shoulder. His skin was warm and his heartbeat strong and steady. They stood for a while, neither wanting to rush the moment when they would sink on to the bed.

'Remember how this feels?' he murmured. The long, drawn-out breaths, the brush of her soft hair against his chest, knowing what was to follow.

Pearl didn't reply. The weeks apart had dimmed the memory of their first time together but now it shone bright and clear; that heady mix of uncertainty and longing, of knowing that she wanted him and he wanted her. *Are you sure?* he'd asked. *Yes*; she'd never felt more sure or more ready to prove her love.

Now Bernie swayed her gently towards the bed. She stepped clear of the folds of cream silk. 'I can't say half of what I feel in here.' He placed her hand on his heart. 'You know that, don't you?'

'I do.' Words were tame, trite little things that didn't do justice to the depth of their feelings. Proof was in their kisses and the tenderness of their touch that grew in urgency as they lay together, limbs entwined.

'Even though letters aren't a patch on this, we'll still carry on writing?'

'As often as we can.' Bernie would most likely be out there in the burning-hot desert, fighting the enemy, while

Pearl would be wrapped up in layers of warm woollen clothing, preparing the end-of-pier amusement arcade for a short burst of pre-Christmas business. 'Whenever I feel lonely I'll remember this day,' she promised.

Bernie couldn't bear to look too far ahead. He wanted them to exist here, in this moment, so he kissed her cheeks, her lips, her neck, and she folded herself into his embrace, there in that quiet room, while the world turned but nothing mattered except the closeness of their bodies, all fears banished and swept away by love.

The next morning Pearl and Bernie stood on the cold station platform, arms clasped around each other, unable to speak. He was in his army uniform, clean shaven and clipped, she wore an everyday red jacket, matching beret and black slacks. The grey light stripped them of the last shreds of wedding-day bliss – the smoke and steam, the brutal hulk of the engine and its gleaming steel wheels and the barking cries of porters brought home their impending separation. But they must not break down, they must not weaken.

He kissed her long and hard then bent to pick up his kitbag.

She gathered every ounce of willpower she possessed. 'When?' she murmured.

'When what?'

'Will your next leave be?'

Bernie shrugged. Doors slammed. The stationmaster stood by with his whistle and flag.

'Before Christmas?' Pearl knew the answer before he shook his head.

'No; not that soon.'

'I'll count the days.' She would cross them off on the

25

calendar as November faded into December and winter took hold. Every morning she would race downstairs before breakfast, impatient for a letter in the post, and would endure an endless, aching longing to see her husband's dear face again.

The stationmaster made an irritable gesture for Bernie to board the train.

'I have to go.' *No choice. End of story.*

Helpless and heartbroken, Pearl stepped to one side. Bernie slung his bag over his shoulder and without looking back he stepped from the platform into his carriage. The shrill sound of the whistle pierced her chest like an arrow. Bernie was at the window, leaning out with a hundred other passengers waving their goodbyes. The train edged slowly forward. The distance between them grew. Still he waved. She waved back. Steam enveloped them, hiding their tears. He was gone.

'At this rate I'll be out of business by Christmas,' Cliff Seymour complained to Sylvia and Terry. 'Nicholson knows I can't just up and move studios; not after all the money I've poured into this one. Our damned landlord's got me over a barrel and he knows it.'

Sylvia busied herself by sorting through records for Monday's six o'clock jive class – for this session she needed lively tunes with a syncopated rhythm and plenty of bounce. Outside it was already dark but inside the studio the lights were bright and inviting, as was the new sign above the entrance – 'Learn to Dance with Cliff and Sylvia – Live in Your Dreams'. It was a sleek, modern space with a beautiful sprung floor and floor-to-ceiling mirrors, plus expensive equipment, including a brand-new gramophone and a rack containing the most up-to-date

26

dance records. Photographs of Cliff's glamorous life in Berlin and London were displayed above the rack: Cliff in top hat and tails, looking for all the world like Fred Astaire, with the same twinkling smile and slicked-back hair; Cliff wearing a black silk shirt with wide, high-waisted trousers and a red cummerbund, standing in the centre of a chorus line of girls dressed in tight corsets and fishnet stockings.

'Chin up,' Terry told Cliff. 'Think of all the handsome RAF recruits flooding into Squires Gate.'

'And the GIs,' Sylvia added. 'You can't keep them off the dance floor, even if you try.'

'That's all very well, but where are we going to scrape together the extra rent?' Cliff remained gloomy. 'I'm already up to my ears in debt, paying off the bank loan I took out for renovations to this place.' It had been a gamble from the start: returning to his home town after years spent working in cabaret in Germany's capital city, before the first rumblings of war had forced him back to England. A few months in London, hobnobbing with a wealthy, high-society crowd, had seen money trickle through Cliff's fingers like water, and now here he was in Blackpool, back where he began, setting up in competition with Lorna Ellis's academy on King Alfred Street and struggling to make ends meet.

'I'll get a job,' Terry suggested half-heartedly before laughing at himself. 'Yes and look how that worked out the last time I tried.'

'You can pay me a reduced rate for teaching your classes.' Sylvia jumped in with a more realistic offer. 'That would help a little. And surely we can drum up more custom by distributing leaflets around town – at the Tower, for a start, and out at Squires Gate and Warton Aerodrome.'

Cliff rallied a little. 'You're right – more advertising could do the trick.'

'And Terry, if you're serious about getting a job you could audition for parts in musical theatre,' Sylvia pressed on. Pupils would soon be arriving and she was keen to brighten the mood before they appeared. 'Tell him he's ready to do that,' she urged Cliff. 'And the build-up to Christmas is the perfect time of year – all the theatres are scouting for new talent.'

'You're more than ready,' Cliff agreed. 'I've taught you everything I know, dance-wise; all the Latin dances and tap routines to boot. And look at you; who could resist?'

'Not you, apparently.' Terry basked in the warmth of Cliff's praise. The two men's love affair was no longer a secret – they'd been out in the open for a few months now and the majority of people had accepted it, except for the odd backward-looking die-hard who still found it unnatural, against the law and so on. This being the reason that Terry had lost his summertime job at the lido, he and Cliff still had to be on their guard against those few.

'Sylvia hit the nail on the head,' Cliff conceded. 'You've got natural ability by the bucket load. Start at the top by auditioning at the Grand or the New Opera House and work your way down from there.'

'I'll do it if you will.' Sylvia's offer was unexpected. 'Don't look so surprised,' she told Cliff. 'You're not the only one who's struggling to pay the rent. And don't suggest going cap in hand to my mother.'

'I wouldn't dream of it.'

'No, I'll do it my own way,' Sylvia insisted. 'So how about it, Terry – shall I make enquiries about auditions at the Opera House?'

The first pupils trickled in, features pinched and

reddened by a fierce wind blowing in off the sea. They wore scarves and gloves and carried bags containing dance shoes as they made their way across the studio.

'Okey-dokey.' Terry murmured a reluctant agreement.

'That's the ticket.' Sylvia began a headcount – eleven, twelve, thirteen pupils so far: seven bashful-looking men and six excited girls. 'Well, look who the wind's blown in!'

Pearl hovered in the doorway, blinking in the bright light and clutching the collar of her jacket as if in two minds.

Sylvia hurried to meet her. 'Come in, come in. Take your coat off – we're about to start.'

'I'm not sure what I'm doing here,' Pearl faltered. She'd rushed straight from North Pier after closing the arcade, having kept herself busy all day in the hope that it would take her mind off the recent painful goodbye. The tactic hadn't worked: every rattle of a small ball falling into a metal cup in the dozens of slot machines had reminded her of Bernie's absence. Playball, Chip or Bust, Lucky Star; you name it – all the best Allwin machines had drawn in the punters as usual but the hours had dragged, and now here Pearl was at the studio door, without a partner, feeling lovelorn and bereft. 'Perhaps I'll give it a miss after all,' she said in a choked voice.

'You'll do no such thing.' Sylvia helped her off with her jacket. 'Stay – it'll do you good.'

'Will it?' Pearl gazed around the room at the motley array of men: civil servants in home-knitted jumpers and creased trousers, with a couple of incredibly young-looking, off-duty RAF men thrown in – some of them scarcely out of boyhood and yet prepared to risk their lives in the lethal skies over France, Italy and Germany.

'Of course it will.' Sylvia wouldn't take no for an

answer. 'Terry will look after you. Terry, come and dance with Pearl.'

No sooner said than done. Sylvia clapped her hands to gain attention while Cliff lowered the needle on to the record she'd selected. 'Everyone, choose a partner,' she instructed over the introductory bars. 'Jive is like jitter-bug only faster; forty-one bars per minute, made up of moves from salsa, swing and tango. Are we ready? Then let's begin.'

CHAPTER THREE

Joy gazed down at the circus ring as she walked along the corridor towards Tommy's changing room. Every square inch of the walls and ceiling was intricately tiled in blue, red and gold, following a Moorish style that transported members of the audience into an exotic world a thousand miles away from Blackpool on a chilly November afternoon.

She'd finished her afternoon cleaning shift in the Tower Ballroom and said goodbye to the group of young women whose task it was to sweep, dust and polish until every surface gleamed. They took pride in their jobs and often had fun while they worked, whistling along to tunes on the Wurlitzer played by the great man himself. Even during rehearsal, Reginald Dixon's lilting music would soar across the vast ballroom with its tiered balconies, crystal chandeliers and arched ceiling resplendent with frescoes of maidens dressed in flowing pastel robes as they floated on sunlit clouds high above the heads of the humble cleaners below.

'Bye-bye, Joy – I'll see you in a little while,' Mavis Thorne had called at the end of their shift as Joy had headed off to the circus next door. 'We're due at the academy,' she'd reminded her. 'Half six on the dot for our joint session with Madam Ellis – don't be late.'

'I'll be there,' Joy had replied. It would be the first time that she and Tommy had shared a dance lesson with Eddie and Mavis under Lorna's eagle eye. They were to learn the Viennese waltz and rehearse, rehearse, rehearse in the build-up to January's championship. Joy wondered how the new partnership would get along; no doubt Eddie would be polite and patient, but whether or not newcomer Mavis could rise to the challenge remained to be seen.

Joy waved at Alina and Irena, two Polish acrobats who had bounded into the ring to rehearse their routine. She breathed in the smell of fresh sawdust and the faint aroma of animals housed in the underground stables – horses and elephants, lions, pumas and tigers that rarely saw the light of day, poor things. Joy studied a garish poster as she approached the dressing-room door. It advertised Cavalini's Canine Comedians and beside that there was a black-and-white picture of the grand circus finale: the Enchanted Cascade featuring the famous Valmar Trio. 'Get a move on, Tommy,' Joy muttered out loud. At this rate they'd never make it to their dance lesson on time.

Truth to tell, she was feeling a definite anticlimax after the highs of Pearl and Bernie's wedding, where all had been bright and cheerful and everyone had taken to the dance floor determined to ignore the fact that bride and groom had less than twenty-four hours in which to enjoy their married bliss. Joy couldn't imagine how hard yesterday's parting must have been for them both.

'Uh-oh, why so glum?' Tommy emerged from his dressing room with a theatrical flourish that faded when he saw his sweetheart's serious expression. He slipped his arm through hers then whisked her through the nearest exit and down some broad stairs leading to a wide, lavishly decorated entrance hall lined with more posters for both circus and ballroom.

'I was thinking about Pearl,' Joy admitted. 'Saying goodbye to Bernie can't have been easy.'

'Have you spoken to her since?'

'Not yet. I haven't had a chance.'

Tommy grew thoughtful as they exited the building then walked along the promenade. A faint glimmer of evening sunlight rested on the horizon, allowing them to make out Central Pier with its cluster of buildings at the far end: a theatre surrounded by cabins selling candyfloss and ice cream next to a row of fortune tellers' booths, skittle alleys and amusement arcades. 'Pearl just has to accept what she can't alter,' he concluded as they passed the lifeboat station next to the pier. 'She and Bernie knew better than anyone that they wouldn't have long together, thanks to this rotten war.'

'But remember how upset your mum was when they carted your dad off to the Isle of Man.' Tommaso Rossi senior was Italian by birth and had been declared an enemy alien. He was destined to sit out the rest of the war in a POW camp, despite never having put a foot wrong. Lucia had been inconsolable on the day that the police had swooped in to arrest her husband, prompting Tommy junior to swear he would quit the circus and take charge of the family's ice-cream business for her.

'No; there's no need.' Knowing how much her sweetheart loved clowning and making people laugh, Joy had stepped in with a solution. She would be the one to help Lucia in the ice-cream parlour, fitting in cleaning shifts wherever she could. It had meant she would be busier than ever but it would be worth it if Tommy could keep his job.

'Yes, if you agree to leave your lousy digs in Silver Street and come to live with us,' Tommy had declared on the spur of the moment. 'There's a spare room above the café, looking out to sea. It's yours if you want it.'

It had been decided in the blink of an eye; to heck with the proprieties surrounding whether or not sweethearts Tommy and Joy should live in the same house without being married or even engaged. This was wartime and rules were there to be bent or broken.

Now, as Tommy and Joy walked hand in hand in the fading light, she felt her mood lighten. An invigorating breeze flicked one end of her woollen scarf against Tommy's cheek and made them smile and draw closer. They strode in harmony past a reserve water tank, one of many constructed in case of bomb damage to nearby reservoirs, then on past the deserted Pleasure Beach, with the soaring outline of the Big Dipper silhouetted against the dusk sky. Fun House, Ferris wheel and Grand National – all were closed and boarded up for winter.

'How about we buy three tickets for a Christmas show to cheer Pearl up?' Tommy suggested as they drew close to South Pier and Rossi's Ice Cream Parlour. 'One for Pearl and one each for you and me. *Sleeping Beauty* will be on at the Winter Gardens. Or we could go ice-skating for a change, or to the flicks; whatever Pearl fancies.'

'That's a lovely idea – if you can get the time off.' They waited for a tram to pass before crossing the wide road then pausing under the parlour's green-and-white-striped awning. Here they snatched a kiss and a cuddle before going inside. Joy sighed over the soft touch of Tommy's lips against hers and the feel of his thick, wavy hair as she cupped her hand behind his head. The temptation to linger was broken by an air raid warden's faint cry of

'Put that light out!' and the sound of an irate resident answering back: 'Keep your hair on, why don't you?'

'Let's go in and grab a quick bite to eat,' Joy murmured. 'It'll be time for our dance class before we know it.'

Tommy sneaked one last kiss.

'I hear you, *due piccioncini*!' Lucia's rich voice sang out from inside the café.

'What does she say?' Joy whispered as she and Tommy broke apart.

'Two lovebirds,' he said with a grin as they stepped inside.

'Correct technique is everything.' Lorna went back to basics for Mavis's benefit. 'It's not simply about learning the steps for the Viennese waltz – it's about musicality and moving across the floor without apparent effort.'

Mavis grimaced at Joy behind their teacher's back. She'd arrived for her first lesson incorrectly dressed, according to Lorna – in trousers and a tight sweater that showed off her slim waist and hips.

'Next time wear something more appropriate,' had been the curt instruction. 'Perhaps a skirt with pleats that will flare out as you turn.'

'Yes, miss,' Mavis had said under her breath. *Prim and proper, or what?* In her opinion, trousers suited her better than a skirt; after all, she kept up to date with fashion, styling her shoulder-length, fair hair in soft waves that framed an oval face and emphasized her brown eyes. Her fashion-model slimness drew admiring looks wherever she went and gave her the confidence to pull off the latest look.

'Mavis, dear; please pay attention.' Lorna caught the tail end of her pupil's sideways glance in Joy's direction.

'I recommend that you visit the town library and borrow a book entitled *How to Become a Good Dancer* by Arthur Murray. There you will learn the importance of poise and posture.'

Prim and proper. Poise and posture – all the Ps. Suppressing a rebellious smirk, Mavis pulled herself upright and squared her shoulders.

'Relax,' Eddie said under his breath. 'Remember, Lorna's bark is worse than her bite.'

'Thanks.' Mavis smiled back at him. How was her teacher to know that Mavis didn't possess a library ticket? Her family weren't readers – they were too busy scraping a living; her father at the Vickers Armstrong factory, where orders for Wellington bombers had skyrocketed since the start of the war, and her mother serving in a shoe shop in the centre of town.

Mavis herself had been a bright pupil, but had left school at fourteen without qualifications and taken a poorly paid job as a cleaner at the Tower and thrown herself into leisure activities that suited her lively, physical nature. She'd become a star player in the local netball team and a leading member of a League of Health and Beauty group, until at the age of eighteen she'd developed a passion for ballroom dancing.

A few coppers had bought a ticket to a church hall hop or Mecca dance hall, where she'd thrown herself into the latest craze with any partner who came her way. 'You're a smashing dancer' would quickly follow on from, 'Do you come here often?' as the couple joyously jitterbugged or jived their way around the room, finishing in close hold for a final slow waltz and then the obligatory necking session outside on the pavement and a quick 'Cheerio, see you next week' before Mavis fled the scene.

'*How to Become a Good Dancer*.' Lorna repeated the title of the book that would steer Mavis away from the bad habits she'd already picked up. There was to be no more flat-footed shuffling or swinging of the hips – from now on Mavis would maintain an elegant, upright ballroom frame at all times.

Eddie smiled encouragingly as he took Mavis in hold, while Tommy and Joy stood close by, ready to begin.

'The popularity of this classic dance has declined for a very good reason.' Lorna got into her stride. 'It resembles the modern waltz but it's more than twice as quick: fifty-eight bars per minute instead of twenty-eight. And the frequent turns are too complicated for many amateur dancers. That's what makes it an excellent choice for January's championship.'

Once again, Mavis looked to Joy for support. It was one thing to dance the night away at the Mecca, quite another to train for a big, regional competition.

'Copy me,' Joy suggested under her breath. It was unusual to see Mavis thrown in this way – away from the dance studio she gave off a confident, fancy-free air and had a reputation for being a bit of a flirt.

'Poise is everything,' Lorna continued, without picking up on Mavis's unease. 'You must travel smoothly across the floor with the correct body alignment – no gapping is permitted.' How many times had she made this introductory speech, she wondered? She thought back to the early nineteen twenties, to her training with the ISTD – the Imperial Society of Teachers of Dancing – and before that to the big competitions she'd entered. The Star Competition in London and the Gaumont British Trophy had been her highlights; she recalled those wonderful, walking-on-air moments when judges had pronounced her and her partner the winners. Lorna hadn't thought to question the rules and had never been tempted into the Latin shenanigans of that degenerate decade – the Charleston, in particular; so un-English and vulgar. Now, without further ado, she lowered the needle on to the record and gave the instruction for her two couples to begin.

No gapping. Mavis didn't mind this part of the Viennese waltz. Eddie held her close, leading her into a quick natural turn and out again, his strong movements giving her no option but to follow. His face was turned away as required but at the corner of her vision she could make out his angular jawline and handsome profile. Not bad at all for a stuffed-shirt type who sat in an office all day and went to the opera on his nights off.

Lorna lifted the needle. 'Joy, you must turn your head a fraction further to the right, with your gaze directed towards the ceiling. And execute the moves with a touch more optimism, please. Tommy, place your hand higher on your partner's back. Mavis, we require less rise and fall but your frame is generally good. Again, please.'

On it went, through sixty dizzying, relentless minutes, until Lorna was satisfied and both couples were exhausted. As their teacher closed the lid of the gramophone then slipped records back into their paper covers, the four dancers exchanged comments.

'It turns out you're a natural for the Viennese waltz,' Joy assured Mavis.

'You think so? All that "spotting" while we turn has given me a splitting headache.' Her feet were killing her, every muscle ached and she was damp under the armpits, but overall she felt satisfied with her progress.

'Yes; Tommy and I had better be on our mettle.'

The two couples chatted easily as they laced up their outdoor shoes.

'Are you walking home?' Eddie asked Mavis.

'No, I'm taking the tram,' she replied over a reminder from Lorna that their training would have to continue through the Christmas and New Year period, come what may.

'There will be no slacking because of the festivities,' Lorna insisted. 'It will be essential for you to work extremely hard, Mavis, if you're to reach the required standard for the competition.'

'I'll accompany you to your stop, if I may,' Eddie ventured. Mavis wasn't the least like Sylvia in many respects but he'd convinced himself that this was just as well. It would mean he wouldn't be forever looking back to past glories. And after all, Mavis had charms of her own, including a cheeky spontaneity that Sylvia lacked and a determination to succeed despite her status as a beginner.

'Champion!' Mavis replied with a wide smile as she linked arms.

Joy and Tommy followed them out of the studio. Each knew what the other was thinking but neither said a word until Eddie and Mavis had stepped on a tram together then rattled off along the prom.

'Well,' Joy commented with raised eyebrows.

'Well,' Tommy echoed. 'Fancy that!'

All blinds were down and there was no sign of life as Lucia's lovebirds approached the ice-cream parlour. Using the side entrance, they were surprised to find Tommy's mother sitting pen in hand at the kitchen table.

'I write to Tommy's father,' she explained in her thick

accent. 'I tell him the war finishes *presto* – soon. And we are together again, me and my own Tommy, *il mio amore*.'

Joy noticed the effort that Lucia made to hide her sadness behind a brave smile. Her plump, round face bore signs of the strain she was under because of her husband's imprisonment. There were shadows under her eyes and her healthy glow had faded with the summer sun. She sat in her dark blue dressing gown and slippers, her greying hair contained beneath a hairnet. 'My Joy, I fill hot-water bottle for you?' she offered, then, without waiting for an answer, proceeded to place the kettle on the hob.

Meanwhile, Tommy chatted to his mother in rapid Italian, giving her an account of the afternoon's run-through of a new routine; how he'd played the trumpet while Doodles the Clown cavorted around the ring in his outsize boots, complete with pratfalls and collisions with the other performers, until he'd sent Tommy reeling backwards, trumpet and all, into the arms of a stooge sitting in the front row. They expected this to cause gasps of concern all round until he leaped to his feet again. 'Tomorrow we give our first proper performance in front of an audience,' he told her.

The kettle soon boiled and two hot-water bottles were filled. One accompanied Lucia up the stairs to bed. She came back down two minutes later. '*Momento*,' she told Tommy and Joy, who had been locked in an embrace but who broke apart as soon as they heard her footsteps. '*Una lettera* – I forget,' she apologized as she drew a crumpled, dog-eared envelope out of her dressing-gown pocket and handed it to Joy. 'And so *buona notte e dormi bene*,' she said as she ascended the stairs once more.

Glancing at the envelope, Joy saw only her first name

scrawled in pencil. No surname, no address. The letter had obviously been hand delivered but she didn't recognize the writing. Assuming that it couldn't be important, she tucked it into the waistband of her skirt.

'Aren't you going to open it?' Tommy asked, drawing her towards him to continue their goodnight kiss.

'Later,' she answered as their lips met. There was a tingling temptation in this moment that they never talked about, though both felt it. It came of living under the same roof in a house where every footfall caused floorboards to creak and the opening and closing of every door could be heard. Each night Tommy and Joy would kiss and part: Tommy to his room overlooking the yard at the back, Joy to her room next to Lucia's at the front. They would undress and slide between the cold sheets, listening out for movement, each imagining the other as their heads sank against the pillow.

'How do you resist?' Pearl had asked Joy during one of the three girls' cosy chinwags in Sylvia's flat above the tobacconist's. 'Come to that, how does Tommy manage to control himself?'

'You're assuming he does,' Sylvia had cut in tartly.

Their eyes had bored into Joy, making her blush and stammer.

'He does,' she'd said loud and clear. 'We agreed; no funny business – it was a condition of my moving in.'

'She calls it funny business!' Pearl had rolled her eyes. 'Me and Bernie, we couldn't keep our hands off each other and we weren't even living together.'

'Everyone's different,' Sylvia had said in Joy's defence.

'For a start, Tommy's mother is in the room next to me.' Joy had put her case. 'Anyway, we both believe in waiting until you're married.'

41

'Don't say a word!' Sylvia had raised a warning finger at Pearl. 'It may be old-fashioned but I happen to agree.'

Pearl had thrown up her hands in disbelief. 'Are you telling me that you and Eddie . . . ?'

'Never.' It had been Sylvia's turn to blush. 'The situation simply didn't arise.'

Pearl hadn't known whether to feel smug or embarrassed. In fact, she was nonplussed; surely she wasn't the only girl in Blackpool to hold these modern views.

'What if it hadn't worked out between you and Bernie?' Sylvia had pointed out the major pitfall. 'Wouldn't you have wished you'd saved yourself until you were certain he was the one?'

Pearl had stuck to her guns with a simple, 'We *were* certain.'

The conversation had made Joy uneasy. She didn't judge Pearl for falling into bed with Bernie, but a strict Methodist upbringing held her in its grip. She might long to give way to temptation and creep along the corridor into Tommy's room in the dead of night, to take that feeling of longing a step further, for them to come together in the dark and experience what Pearl and Bernie had known before they were married. But though Joy dreamed of it, she was too shy and inexperienced to act out her fantasy. Instead, she and Tommy would kiss goodnight in Lucia's kitchen, among the shiny pans and crockery, with the blind down and the faint sound of waves breaking on the shore.

Upstairs in her room, Joy removed the scruffy letter from her waistband and was about to put it to one side when she had second thoughts. The untidiness of the handwriting and the crumpled state of the envelope bothered her. Who among her acquaintances was so slovenly? It could hardly be a written request to increase her hours from one of the half a dozen ladies who employed her to clean for them. Puzzled, she opened the envelope and took out a sheet of lined paper ripped from a spiral pad.

She read the first, scrawled word, written in large capitals:

HUSSY!

Joy gasped and recoiled, letting the note slip from her fingers and flutter to the ground. She stooped to pick it up with trembling fingers then read on.

I know what you and your fancy man get up to in those rooms above that café. You're a tart and a tramp.

The writing sloped off the line and the letters tilted backwards and forwards, as if formed by a child.

I KNOW YOUR DIRTY LITTLE SECRET and soon the whole of Blackpool will as well!

Filled with disgust, Joy screwed up the note and threw it on to the bed. *So nasty, so unfair!* Not a word was true but how could she prove it? In a fury she rushed at the ball of paper, took it up and tore it to shreds then trampled it underfoot, as if to make the vile insults disappear. But they were engraved in her mind – *Hussy – tart – tramp*. She felt herself go hot then immediately cold. No child could have written this. It must have come from an unknown rival or enemy, but who? A fellow competitor in the dance world, perhaps, or a girl she cleaned with at the Tower – not

Mavis but any one of the others, including her supervisor, Ruby Donovan. No, surely not generous, fun-loving Ruby – she was the person who had encouraged Joy on to the dance floor and into Tommy's arms in the first place.

What to do? Joy bent down to gather the trampled remnants then without thinking she rushed downstairs and used the poker to thrust the scraps of paper into the embers of the kitchen fire. She watched them flare yellow and blue then disintegrate to ash. Dashing back upstairs, she found Tommy waiting at his door.

'What's the matter?' he whispered.

'Nothing.' She willed herself to invent a plausible excuse. 'I left my door key in the lock, that's all.'

'I'll say goodnight then?' he said in a concerned voice that rose higher towards the end of the sentence.

'Yes, goodnight.' Joy left him wondering and closed her door on the lie. *Hussy – tart – tramp.* Joy pressed her hands to her ears as if to shut the words out. *Forget about it, pay no heed;* she knew in her heart that she was none of those things. But the insults crept into her system like poison and kept her tossing and turning through much of the night. When she got up next morning and went down to breakfast she was sure of only one thing: Tommy and his mother must not find out.

CHAPTER FOUR

My dearest wife, my Pearl,

How are you today? All is fine here, except my sergeant major had a go at me for poor timekeeping, also for my unmade bed, untidy locker, cheeking a superior officer — there was a list as long as your arm. You can bet your life I'm not his favourite recruit. The lads here have seen the photo I keep of you in my top pocket — it fell out when I reached for my packet of Player's. They call me a lucky devil and a jammy bugger, excuse my French. Just think, it's exactly a week since we tied the knot. Can you believe it? How's business in the build-up to Christmas? Are the new Spitfire and Dawn Patrol games pulling in the punters like we hoped? And is young Ernie doing his bit? It's nice to hear that Tommy and Joy are planning to give you a treat to cheer you up — good for them. What's the weather like down there? It's grim up here — the cold gets into your bones and it's only the middle of November. Lord knows what it'll be like when December comes, if I'm still here and not sweating it out in the desert. Sorry to go on like a miserable devil; you must be wondering where your old, cheerful Bernie has gone. I can't say much regarding what's going on with my regiment — against the rules, careless talk and all that. I'm sitting up in bed writing this before I get some shut-eye, wondering where you are right this minute and what you're up to and wishing I was with you. Don't do anything I wouldn't do, wink-wink. I'm looking at your picture. You're my ray of sunshine, did you know? I can't wait to see you again but in the meantime keep smiling.

SWALK, your ever-loving Bernie xxxx

Pearl read the letter three times, cherishing every word, before she went downstairs for breakfast. Bernie wrote in the way that he spoke – breathless, rambling and going off at odd tangents. Unmade bed, untidy locker, cheeking an officer – this was Bernie all right. His ray of sunshine – she liked that. She pictured him sitting up in bed, probably in need of a shave, with his hair ruffled and two fingers on his right hand stained with nicotine. He smoked too much – she would encourage him to ease off the Player's next time she wrote.

'It's breakfast time.' Elsie burst through the bedroom door in helter-skelter fashion. She was dressed in a thick red jumper, a tartan kilt, long grey socks and black plimsolls, the spitting image of Pearl at the same age, with her tomboy way of darting about and her thick, dark hair cut short. 'Mum says to hurry up or else.'

Pearl folded Bernie's letter and carefully put it back in its envelope. 'Or else what?'

'Or else!' the whirlwind declared as she shot back out of the room.

Another day, another dollar. Sighing, Pearl put Bernie's latest missive in the shoebox with the two previous ones. Three in one week was some going. Sliding the box under her bed, she followed her sister downstairs to the kitchen where she found her mother sending Elsie off on a Saturday-morning errand.

'Fetch half a stone of spuds and three onions from Joe's

market stall,' Maria ordered. 'Tell him I'll settle up next time I see him.'

Elsie cannoned into Pearl on her way out. Maria greeted the latecomer with a frown. 'Make your own toast,' she muttered, pointing with the bread knife and wearing a tea towel tucked into her waistband as an improvised apron. 'Then make yourself scarce before your dad gets back from the paper shop. You're cutting it fine if you want to open your arcade on time.'

So much for life as a newly married woman – still under the thumb of her ma and pa! Pearl said she would skip breakfast, ta very much.

'Please yourself. But I need you back here straight after you've finished on the pier – to make a shepherd's pie for tonight's supper.'

'Sorry, I can't.'

Pearl's shirty reply brought a frown to Maria's face. 'Don't tell me you've made other plans?'

'Yes, as a matter of fact I've arranged to meet Sylvia and Joy and a couple of other people at the Tower for our regular Saturday-night shindig.' The chilly atmosphere dropped to below freezing. 'Don't look at me like that – it's not a crime, is it?'

'That depends. Which people, exactly?'

'Cliff and Terry, if you must know. We arranged it earlier in the week.'

Maria nodded slowly. 'Do you know who Terry Liddle reminded me of when I danced with him at the wedding reception?' She went on without waiting for Pearl's reply. 'Cary Grant; that's who. Tall and dark, with a way of looking at you as if he can't quite work women out.'

'I don't suppose he's had much practice in that area.' Pearl threw in a cheeky grin and a wink. 'But he and

Cliff are good company and they're the best dance partners going. So you see, tonight's outing is all perfectly innocent.'

'Hmm.'

'Hmm – what?'

'Have you told Bernie that you're carrying on with the dancing lark?'

Pearl was about to flounce off but Maria caught her by the wrist. Pearl tried to pull free. 'Let go of me.'

'I take it the answer's no. But don't you think you should – tell him, I mean? Innocent or not, tongues will wag if people see a married woman out on the town, enjoying herself.'

Pearl prised her mother's fingers from around her wrist. 'Ruby Donovan does it all the time,' she pointed out. 'And her Douglas has been off fighting Herr Hitler for two whole years.'

'You're not Ruby and Bernie isn't Douglas,' Maria insisted. 'Remember how Bernie got into a scrap with Terry because he saw you two together?'

'How can I forget?' North View Parade had turned into a miniature battleground, with Bernie and Terry engaging in full-blown fisticuffs and half a dozen others joining in. As it happened, Terry had come off worst. 'It was all a misunderstanding – Bernie said he was sorry and that was that.'

Maria's tone softened as she backed away. 'I'm not saying you're doing anything wrong – I think you should keep your husband informed, that's all.'

'I will – I'll write to him tomorrow.' All week Pearl had tied herself in knots. *Why not carry on dancing, for goodness' sake? It will help keep my spirits up, and Lord knows, I need that. I might not show it, but every day, every hour, every minute I'm without Bernie is a struggle, knowing what he and his regiment might have to face. I can't bear to listen to the wireless or pick up a newspaper – anything to do with the war sends shivers through me. It's like standing at the edge of a cliff, not able to step back from the brink. I dream of falling, falling, falling on to the black rocks below.*

She knew full well that such fears could not be expressed; rather, they must be hidden behind a keep-calm-and-carry-on façade.

'I'm sorry,' she whispered to her mother.

'It's hard for you,' Maria acknowledged as she eased the tea towel from her waistband and used it to wipe her hands. 'I know you'll do the right thing by Bernie and that's what counts.'

'Thanks, Mum. I'll have time to make the shepherd's pie before I go out,' Pearl conceded. It would be a rush to get ready afterwards then reach the ballroom on time but she could do it if she got her skates on.

'Right.' Her mother gave a satisfied nod.

Stay busy, keep smiling, carry on dancing – that was the ticket.

'Here are a few facts and figures to help calm the nerves.' Cliff sat with Terry and Sylvia at a café table in the light, bright arcade that linked the two main entrances to the Winter Gardens. Palm trees lined the glass-roofed walkway; an art deco masterpiece to rival the luxurious facilities offered by the Tower building close by. 'This new Opera House was opened three years ago by none other than Jessie Matthews. It's a three-thousand-seater, with the biggest stage in Britain.'

'Stop,' Sylvia pleaded. 'You're making things worse.' She and Terry were here for their audition for *Sleeping Beauty*, sticking to their plan of aiming high then working their way down to less prestigious venues if necessary.

'Take no notice,' she advised her fellow hoofer. 'All we have to do is go in there and do our best.'

Terry looked at his watch. 'We're early – there's still time to look in on the Empress Ballroom that I've heard so much about.'

'Re-floored eight years ago.' Cliff proved to be the fount of all knowledge as he and Sylvia followed Terry out of the café. 'Pretty fancy, even by Blackpool's standards.'

Sylvia paused at the entrance to the ballroom – part of the Winter Gardens complex of bars, lounges, exhibition spaces, theatres, dance halls and cafés – to admire the art nouveau decor. There were gilded balconies and mirrors lining the walls. The gold ceiling glinted in the light of three enormous chandeliers and there was a stage at the far end with a clam-shell proscenium arch.

'Twelve and a half thousand square feet,' Cliff informed them, 'designed by Magnall and Littlewood in 1896.'

'I've changed my mind – I don't want to go ahead with this audition.' Overwhelmed by his surroundings, Terry meant what he said. 'There are dozens of other productions we could try for; at the smaller theatres like the one at the end of Central Pier.'

'I'll pretend I didn't hear that.' Cliff led them back to their table, where they finished what was left of their morning refreshments – buttered crumpets with a pot of tea for three. He was his dapper, sophisticated self in a double-breasted blazer, white shirt, blue tie and grey slacks. 'I'm pinning my hopes of financial survival on you, love,' he reminded Terry. 'And the odds are in your favour – the Opera House employs the biggest dance troupe in town.'

'But still . . .' Terry wasn't convinced.

Cliff waved away his objections. 'You're skilled enough

50

to beat the competition into a cocked hat, so just go in there imagining you're Fred Astaire in *Holiday Inn*.'

'Again; you are definitely not helping.' Sylvia noted that it was time for her and Terry to go through into the Opera House auditorium, where they would wait to be called forward. 'Wish us luck,' she said to Cliff as she led the way.

'Sylvia Ellis and Terry Liddle, here to audition for the chorus line in *Sleeping Beauty*,' she told the attendant on the door.

'Whose bright idea was this?' Terry continued to grumble as they shuffled forward. The theatre was vast and every bit as intimidating as he'd feared. Row upon row of crimson seats spread out before their eyes, with half a dozen self-important, casually dressed people sprawled across seats in the front row. Armed with pen and paper, they invited dancers to come forward four at a time, observing and making quick notes before summarily dismissing them from the stage.

'I suppose we can blame Joy for this.' All of a sudden Sylvia dropped the bright and breezy act and admitted to feeling the strain.

'How do you work that one out?'

'Remember, she was the one who first came up with the idea of auditioning for the theatre – back in August when you lost your job at the lido and I decided against going to London.' Since Joy had made her suggestion, Cliff had worked hard to broaden Terry and Sylvia's dance repertoires. All three knew that financial pickings for amateur ballroom dancers were slim, whereas wages for chorus-line dancers were significantly higher. 'But frankly, my dear, I'm not sure it's my cup of tea, so I'm mostly here to give you moral support.'

'Now she tells me!' Terry's panic increased. 'Sod's law

is that they'll want you but not me.' Determined to down-play his chances, his stomach lurched as his name was called.

'Good luck,' Sylvia whispered as she gave him a gentle shove.

Terry made his way down the centre aisle, past the empty orchestra pit then up some side steps on to the stage, where he joined three other male dancers waiting to audition. Blinded by the glare of the footlights, Terry was unable to make out the choreographer, musical director and various assistants in the front row.

Come on, Terry – you can do it. Sylvia crossed her fingers as music blared through loudspeakers: 'Begin The Beguine', a jazzy Cole Porter number from *Broadway Melody*.

Dance your heart out; show them what you're made of.

Concentrate! Terry did his best to control his jitters. He and Cliff had been to an Odeon cinema in the West End of London to see this film. Eleanor Powell and Fred Astaire's spirited dancing had taken his breath away. Now the fa-miliar, liquid clarinet notes soared above brass instru-ments and drums, smooth and swinging.

Sylvia watched Terry glide into action – loose limbed, rhythmical and undeniably magnificent. He drew atten-tion like iron filings to a magnet, as if he was alone on the stage. Graceful, self-assured and smiling, without a trace of nerves. *Well done, well done!*

'Thank you, gentlemen!' The music faded and a female voice called from the front row.

The dancers shuffled off-stage while four other hope-fuls took their places.

The same voice read from a list. 'Arthur King – sorry but no thanks. Billy Morris – it's another no. Jim Evans – no again. Terry Liddle – you're hired.'

Blimey, he's only gone and done it! Sylvia's eyes opened wide in amazement as Terry disappeared into the wings. She gave up her place by the entrance and ran to find Cliff sitting at their table under the glass roof. 'Terry was brilliant!' she crowed. 'They offered him a job!'

'Naturally.' Nonchalantly brushing an invisible speck from his jacket lapel, Cliff acted as if it had been a foregone conclusion. 'Now the hard work of rehearsals begins,' he warned his protégé when a breathless, red-in-the-face Terry joined them.

'It's your turn,' Terry reminded Sylvia as he collapsed into his chair. 'You'll lose your place in the queue if you don't watch out.'

Sylvia shrugged. 'That's perfectly fine by me,' she said with a coy smile. Let other girls audition for the high-kicking, Busby Berkeley numbers while she celebrated with Cliff and Terry. 'I've decided that chorus work isn't my style after all.'

Keeping secrets didn't come easily to Joy but the burning shame she'd felt when she'd read THE NOTE (in her own mind capital letters gave the unwelcome missive the importance it merited) prevented her from telling anyone about it, not even best friends Pearl and Sylvia.

Twice during the week she'd been on the point of spilling the beans: once when she and Sylvia had shared a cup of tea after a Viennese waltz lesson at the Lorna Ellis Dance Academy. Lorna had sent Joy up to the flat with the throwaway remark, 'I never know when that daughter of mine will favour me with her presence but she's up there now, expecting you.'

'Come in and sit down; you look worn out,' Sylvia observed as she presented Joy with a much needed cup of tea.

'Your mother is a hard taskmaster.' Aching over every inch of her body, part of Joy simply wanted to go home to bed but instead she flopped down on to the sofa and kicked off her shoes.

'What's up? You don't seem your usual self,' Sylvia observed as Joy sipped her tea.

Joy felt the sudden, sharp prick of tears as the words in THE NOTE flashed back into her head. 'I'm fine, thanks.'

'You stole my line,' Sylvia teased. 'That's what comes out of my mouth whenever I have something to hide. I can get away with it but you're a rotten liar.'

Hussy, tart, tramp. Fancy man, dirty little secret. The insults and the threat to blacken her name stuck in Joy's craw and stayed there, unspoken. 'I'm fine,' she insisted.

'As you wish.' Unable to draw Joy out, Sylvia moved on to admit to the knot in her stomach she felt at the thought of flirty Mavis paired up with Eddie for the Viennese waltz. 'Here am I, sitting reading a magazine, listening to the music in the studio, not knowing what to do with myself. Tell me, how are Eddie and Mavis getting on?'

'Mavis is still finding her feet.' Joy looked closely at Sylvia. 'Is that why you invited me up here – for me to give you the lowdown on her and Eddie? You're asking me to be your spy?'

A defiant Sylvia flicked her hair back over her shoulder. 'In a word: yes.'

Joy popped her lips and shook her head. 'Sorry, no can do.'

'Why ever not?'

'Because it's not fair and you know it. Let me ask you a direct question and I want an honest answer.'

'Am I jealous of Mavis?' Sylvia predicted as she toyed

with her empty teacup. 'Not jealous exactly – well, perhaps a teeny bit – but mostly I feel sad.'

'You miss dancing with Eddie, even though it was your decision to make the break?' This came as no surprise to Joy, who waited for her friend to make a clean breast.

'Yes; it's my own fault,' Sylvia admitted, standing up and pacing the room. 'I didn't realize how much a part of my life he's always been; someone to turn to when things went wrong or to share the good times with when they went right. I took it all for granted and now that I can't do that any more, I do miss him.'

'And there's no way of changing that?'

Sylvia sat down next to Joy with a heavy sigh. 'I don't think so; do you?' Her appeal was frank and stripped of all pretence.

'No, I'm afraid not,' Joy replied softly. 'I know it's not what you want to hear, but there really is no turning back the clock.'

The second time that Joy had been tempted to share her own woes was when Pearl had dropped in at the ice-cream parlour to talk through the pros and cons of carrying on dancing without Bernie.

'What would you do if you were me?' Pearl asked Joy as they sat in the dimly lit, empty café with the blinds down. 'If Tommy was the one who'd gone off to war, would you still consider dancing and entering competitions without him?'

'Oh, I don't even want to think about it.' Joy shuddered at the prospect.

'I know it's not the same,' Pearl acknowledged. 'For one thing, you and Tommy aren't married. And for another, you're much younger than me.'

'Nearly eighteen,' Joy reminded her with a smile.

'Exactly – still in the first flush of youth. You have every right to go out and enjoy yourself. I turned twenty-one last month.'

'Oh yes, you're well past your prime.'

They laughed and Pearl won Joy's approval for her decision to dance her cares away, so long as she was honest with Bernie about it.

'That's exactly what Mum says.'

'There you are, then; the oracle has spoken.'

'It's all right for you: you're an open book.' Pearl's well-meant comment brought a blush to Joy's cheeks. 'I expect you tell Tommy every darned thing that goes on in that pretty head of yours.'

'Not quite everything,' Joy objected. Now was the perfect time to open up about the mysterious note but she hesitated and before she knew it the opportunity had passed.

'Still, my ma was right, darn it – it simply won't do to hide my decision from the man I'm married to.'

So Pearl went away with her mind made up and Joy reached the end of a difficult week still weighed down by the secret knowledge that some unknown person wished her ill. Who on earth could have taken a scrappy piece of paper and scrawled the cruel message? She went on racking her brains to identify someone who might bear a grudge but no name came to mind.

'*Allora, a cosa stai pensando?*' Lucia asked as she and Joy cleared tables in the café on Saturday afternoon. Trade had been slow – few people bought ice cream on a cold November day when waves crashed against the sea wall and a fierce wind whipped spray on to the promenade.

'A penny for my thoughts?' Joy's Italian was now almost

on a par with Lucia's English. 'They're not worth it,' she said with a shake of her head.

'*Sei triste* – you are sad today. I watch, I see.'

'I'm tired – *molto stanca* – that's all.'

'Come.' Lucia put down her dishes and offered to give Joy a hug. 'You stop work,' she said. 'You rest.'

Joy sank into kind-hearted Lucia's warm embrace. When she broke away she broached the subject that had bothered her all week. 'You remember the envelope addressed to me – the one that came through the letter box on Monday?'

'*Sì, sì – la busta.*' Lucia shooed Joy out of the café into the hallway. 'Go – sleep.' She mimed the act by putting her palms together and resting her plump cheek against her hands.

'But the note – did you see who delivered it?' Joy was desperate for any scrap of information. 'The person who brought it – did you see?'

Lucia shook her head and continued shooing Joy up the stairs.

'You're sure?'

Tommy's mother was obliged to give the question more serious consideration. 'I remember – I hear this noise.' She turned to rattle the flap of the letter box in the front door. 'I am up in my room. I look down from my window. The street is busy – there is a tram; many people step down, three climb on.'

Joy nodded eagerly at this first hint of a lead. 'The three who got on the tram – did you recognize any of them?'

Lucia shook her head. 'One woman and small girl, crying: boo-hoo! One man *con le stampelle* – with sticks, like this.' She imitated a person using crutches, struggling to mount a step. 'I see him and I feel sad.'

57

Joy's brow creased into a deep frown as she pictured the scene. Perhaps the man with crutches had been a soldier, invalided out of the army. Such a sight wasn't uncommon. 'Anything else besides the sticks?'

Lucia concentrated hard to add extra details. 'Small man, *magro* – thin – wearing cap like this.' She pulled an imaginary peak low over her face. 'This is all.'

A thin man on crutches, his face obscured by a cap. Joy stored the details for future reference.

Lucia's interest was piqued. 'The note – what does it say?'

'Nothing. Never mind.' Joy smiled thinly as she brushed away the question. 'Thank you anyway.'

'And so rest, *cara mia*.' Lucia ushered her towards the stairs. 'Later, you go dancing with my Tommy. You are young people in love – enjoy!'

'Look at us – the Three Musketeers!' Pearl quipped as she joined Sylvia and Joy at the entrance to the Tower Ballroom. She gave a swashbuckling swish of an imaginary sword. 'One for all and all for one!'

'Dressed up to the nines and without a partner between us.' Sylvia wrinkled her nose in a show of dismay. She'd teamed an off-the-shoulder, peach-coloured blouse with black trousers, while Pearl had made every effort to overcome her missing-Bernie blues by choosing a cherry-red, knee-length skirt and white silk blouse. Joy, modest as ever, was in a short-sleeved lilac dress with padded shoulders and a mid-calf-length skirt.

'No Tommy tonight?' Pearl asked Joy.

'No, he has to work.' Much to her disappointment, he'd made a last-minute telephone call from the circus to tell her he'd been obliged to stay on for the evening performance, worse luck. 'One of the other clowns cried off with a case of the flu so Tommy agreed to step in.' Joy glanced up and down the unlit prom. 'Cliff and Terry are set to join us,' she reminded the others. 'Shall we wait or go in without them?'

'Go in,' Sylvia decided. 'We can save them a place in the queue.'

'Buck up, girls – let's get in out of the cold.' Pearl marched ahead to join an untidy line that snaked through the entrance hall with its sea-green tiles featuring dolphins, starfish and other sea creatures. The queue extended up the wide staircase to two ticket booths on the first floor. 'Do I smell of onions?' she checked with the others.

Joy took a sniff of her outstretched hands and set her mind at rest. 'No; I got a whiff of talcum powder, that's all.'

'Good. I had all on to get here on time after I'd finished making shepherd's pie for the hungry hordes. Look at this queue – it goes on for miles. Does anyone know what the competition dance is tonight? Fingers crossed it'll be Latin of some kind.'

As Pearl chatted on, Sylvia watched the queue inch forward, picking out half a dozen potential partners in GI uniforms – so much smoother and smarter than British Tommies in their rough serge battledress – and the usual gaggle of excited shop girls ready to fling themselves into a night of glamour and romance.

'I hear it's a lindy hop.' Joy guessed that Pearl would be pleased. 'That's more up your street than mine.'

Pearl gave a wave to some chums ahead of them in the queue. 'I was hoping for jitterbug or jive. Lindy hop's getting to be old hat.' She, Sylvia and Joy were still waiting for Cliff and Terry to join them when they reached midway on the stairs with a clear view of the box-office booths. Pearl dug Sylvia in the ribs. 'Still, lindy hop involves plenty of bounce and swing; far better than boring, no-rise-and-fall foxtrot, eh?'

Sylvia was staring up at the high ceiling with a fixed expression.

'Yoo-hoo!' Pearl snapped her fingers close to Sylvia's face.

'Sorry.' Sylvia blinked then inhaled deeply. 'Look who's at the front of the queue,' she hissed.

Pearl and Joy stood on tiptoe and craned their necks to see Eddie at one of the ticket booths with Mavis at his side. They saw him take his change then offer Mavis his arm before walking her into the ballroom.

Pearl raised her eyebrows but said nothing.

'It's a new partnership,' Joy reminded them. 'I suppose they need to practise every chance they get.'

'Practice is for the studio – under Mother's supervision.' Sylvia took another deep breath. The way Eddie had crooked his elbow and Mavis had slipped her arm through his, the way she'd smiled at him and inclined her head; Sylvia had been caught off guard. They looked good out and about together, damn it.

Unaware of the chat between Sylvia and Joy earlier in the week, Pearl couldn't resist poking fun. 'Someone's complexion is turning a fine shade of green as we speak.'

'Don't be ridiculous,' Sylvia protested. 'Eddie's a free agent. He can do what he likes.'

'But ouch! Up until a few weeks ago that was you having your ticket bought by him, gliding into the ball-room, queen of all you surveyed.'

'So it serves me right.' Sylvia had the grace to blush. 'I deserve to be taken down a peg or two. And I'm better off now, living an independent life, teaching at Cliff's studio, helping Mother out when she needs me.'

Pearl brought her up short with, 'No need to go on; you're preaching to the converted.'

Taking the hint, Sylvia quickly changed the subject. 'By the way, did I tell you that Terry auditioned to dance in *Sleeping Beauty* at the Opera House?'

'Did he get in?' Pearl asked.

'He did,' Sylvia confirmed, her mind lingering on Mavis, whose purple halter-neck dress had attracted much attention. Men's heads had swivelled to follow her progress into the ballroom – slinky and slender, with a mesmerizing swing to her hips as she walked. Was that Eddie Winter's new partner now that the old one had given him the heave-ho? If so, he'd fallen on his feet and no mistake. Girls in the queue were fascinated. What was her name and where did she spring from? What happened to Eddie's old partner: Sylvia What's-her-name?

When Pearl caught sight of Cliff and Terry hovering uncertainly in the entrance she waved both arms and called their names. 'Cooee; up here!'

Sorry – excuse us – thank you. The two stylishly dressed newcomers eased their way towards the middle of the queue. 'Sorry we're late,' Terry apologized. 'His nibs here couldn't decide which jacket to wear.'

'But you're here now; ready to put us all to shame with your paso and your samba.' Pearl was eager for the night to begin. *'My darling Bernie.'* In her next letter she would be open with him and hold nothing back. *'How I wished with all my heart that you'd been at the Tower with me and the girls last night, dancing our favourite lindy hop.'* She would tell him how much she missed him and worried about him and she would remind him about smoking less and looking

61

after himself better. But for now she would reach the front of the queue and pay for her ticket. She would leave her coat in the cloakroom and cast care to the winds, swinging and spinning until she was dizzy; swept along by the music, free as a bird.

CHAPTER FIVE

Nothing compared to the Tower Ballroom; not even the much-vaunted refurbished Empress Ballroom in the Winter Gardens. Ordinary dance halls up and down the country were half the size and not nearly so splendid; no wonder Blackpool's jewel was dubbed The Wonderland of the World. Every surface shone and sparkled. The parquet floor was polished to perfection, reflecting a thousand lights from crystal chandeliers suspended from the vast painted ceiling. It was almost too much for the senses to take in – gilded balconies, marble pillars and vibrant ceiling frescoes vied for attention, while the stage at the far end was draped with crimson curtains and displayed a painted backdrop depicting a sunny Mediterranean scene of white villas bordering a curved blue bay. Filigree screens concealing the loudspeaker system bordered the as-yet empty stage.

Sylvia, Joy and Pearl linked arms to make their grand entrance while Cliff and Terry headed for the bar that ran along one side of the ballroom.

'This feels odd,' Sylvia admitted, as the girls found seats under the balcony opposite the bar. She could count on one hand the number of times she'd come here without a partner.

'Chin up,' Pearl told her. 'You'll soon have blokes queuing up to dance with you.'

'Likewise.' Sylvia returned the compliment as she placed her handbag under the table then glanced around to see if she could spot Eddie and Mavis – pretending not to be looking, of course. *Tra-la; what do I care who Eddie Winter dances with? I'm here with my two best friends, looking forward to dancing the night away.*

Seeing through her subterfuge, Joy and Pearl exchanged knowing glances. *Who's she trying to kid?*

'Well, well – look who's here.' Joy's cleaning supervisor, Ruby Donovan, wasted no time in seeking them out. Her striking auburn hair was swept high on her head and held in place by two glittering diamanté clips. She'd spared no effort in the glamour department – her carmine lips and polished nails matched her low-cut dress and the effect was finished off by silver, strappy, high-heeled shoes. 'Hello, Joy – where's your Tommy tonight? Busy entertaining the masses, I expect. Now then, Pearl – congratulations; I hear Bernie made an honest woman of you at last. I see it hasn't stopped you from putting on your glad rags, though.'

Pearl patted her hair – an awkward gesture that betrayed a sudden attack of nerves. No need to worry, she realized, given that Ruby Donovan was an enthusiastic advocate for married women to keep on tripping the light fantastic regardless.

'Good for you, love. No sense in you turning into a hermit just because your hubby is away serving king and country.' Ruby's high spirits were infectious. She beckoned over a bunch of friends who began to compare dresses and bemoan the shortage of eligible dance partners. 'They're thin on the ground so far,' Ruby agreed. 'But wait; things are looking up. Here comes the American contingent.'

No sooner said than Ruby and her pals set sail across the floor to position themselves in a brightly lit spot close to the stage where they could be seen to advantage. At their backs the mighty Wurlitzer rose into view with Reginald Dixon at the keyboard. The first notes of his theme tune, 'I Do Like To Be Beside The Seaside', drew excited applause; let the revels begin!

Who could resist the swell of organ notes that filled the vast space? Not Eddie and Mavis, for a start.

'Shall we?' He held out his hand with a smile and a slight dip of his head.

Mavis sprang to her feet and accompanied him on to the floor – one of the first couples to step out.

'Quickstep,' he informed her. 'Four/four time and fifty bars per minute – extremely quick, as the name implies.'

It was Mavis's turn to nod calmly and respond like the expert she was. 'One of my favourites,' she assured him. The dance was everything she liked best – a good old standard that combined foxtrot and ragtime, where the challenge lay in the speed of the dancer's footwork rather than the intricacy of the steps. Conscious that they were attracting attention, she assured Eddie that quickstep was second nature to her. 'I'll keep up, don't you worry.'

She was nothing if not blasé. Taking her in hold, Eddie counted them in. They broke straight into a run combined with smooth chassés and then a hop and a skip that took them to the very edge of the dance floor, right under the noses of Sylvia, Joy and Pearl. Swiftly Eddie guided Mavis in a half turn that took them back across the diagonal with a series of rapid syncopated steps in which their feet seemed scarcely to touch the ground.

'Show-offs,' Pearl muttered. Was it strictly necessary for Eddie and Mavis to rub Sylvia's nose in it? More couples came on to the floor, creating a swirl of bright colours as skirts flared and the volume of the organ increased. Soon Eddie and Mavis were hidden from sight. 'Mavis knew everyone was looking at them and she was lapping it up.'

Joy defended her cleaning comrade. 'Leave her alone,' she tutted. 'Mavis is a decent sort.'

'Yes, let her have her moment in the sun.' Sylvia once more hid her true feelings with a bright, dismissive smile. She was on the point of suggesting that they go over to the bar to seek out their drinks when Cliff appeared.

'There was a mighty long queue at the bar,' he told them. 'Terry volunteered to wait while I asked one of you to dance. Joy, how about it?'

'Me?' She looked at Sylvia and Pearl to make sure they didn't mind.

'Yes; we can't have a budding competition winner sitting this one out,' Cliff flattered. 'The quickstep is your cup of tea.'

Joy accepted with a shy smile then encountered some funny looks from a group of men congregated in a shadowy area beneath the balcony. They leaned against the wall with pint glasses in hand and seemingly passed snide comments about her and Cliff before breaking into unpleasant laughter.

'Ignore them.' Cliff was used to the 'funny look' treatment and assumed the ribald comments were directed at him. 'It's water off a duck's back to me.'

Joy shrugged off the uneasy suspicion that it was in fact her who had been the object of the men's derision before launching into the quickstep – heel lead then on to the balls of the feet then a series of lock steps smoothly led by her professional partner – tricky and light, breaking out of hold to kick sideways to the right side then kick across the body with the left and so on across the floor.

'I'd almost given up on the drinks front,' Terry admitted as he deposited the laden tray on the table then approached Sylvia when the music eventually segued from quickstep to a slower Latin number with an insistent beat. 'Would you care to dance, señorita?' he asked her. 'Rumba fits you like a glove – tease and run is the name of the game.'

'I'll pretend I didn't hear that,' Sylvia made a show of taking offence before accepting the invitation, having checked in with Pearl, who would be left sitting alone at their table.

'Yes; go ahead.' Pearl was happy to play the wallflower. Really, it would be amusing to witness the attempts of wet-behind-the-ears local lads to impersonate the required Cuban bravado and sex appeal of this dance, swivelling the feet and rotating the hips in a figure of eight. The rhythm was tricky, too – the fourth beat in the bar carried the strongest accent, carrying over to the first beat of the next bar. If you missed out a preparatory sideways step, all was lost. There was much overbalancing and stepping on toes as the dance got underway.

'Sorry – let's try again,' followed by a swift, 'If you don't mind I'd rather not.' Pearl watched her friends Ida and Thora leave their gormless partners in the lurch.

'Hi there.' A figure in GI uniform came between Pearl and the entertainment. 'Care to dance?'

'Why not?' That was the reason she was here. Before she knew it, Pearl was on her feet and in close hold with an American soldier dressed in an olive-brown, belted jacket that sported sergeant stripes. His khaki cotton shirt was complemented by a black woollen tie, his dark hair was cut short on top as well as on the back and sides, and his features were small and neat, with wide blue-grey eyes that lent his face an open, friendly feel.

'Errol Jackson,' he introduced himself as they took their first tentative steps – straight leg, direct lead through the ball of the foot then swivel.

'Based at Warton?' Her partner stood well over six feet, with the erect posture of a well-trained military man – head up, shoulders back. Even under the bright lights and in the dead of winter, his skin seemed to have retained an all-year-round tan.

'Yes, ma'am. I'm a sergeant in the Engineer Corps; proud to serve.'

'And where's home for you?' Pearl executed an underarm turn to the right before being led into a cucaracha – three steps: side, replace, close – smooth as you like. My, this man had rhythm aplenty!

'Fayetteville, Georgia, just south of Atlanta City,' he began, as if she would know the area, then corrected himself. 'I'm from the southern part of the United States, ma'am, where the peanuts grow.'

'Peanuts?' She cocked her head to one side.

'Yes, ma'am, peanuts and cotton. It's pretty hot where I'm from.' Side chassés in hold – slow and sensuous, but taking care that their bodies didn't come into contact.

There was a tension in the air, created by the slow rhythm and the side-to-side sway of their hips. Pearl was aware of the light touch of her GI's palm cupping her shoulder blade as they stepped forward then back then into a side chassé, making a spot turn before coming back into hold. 'No one has ever called me ma'am before,' she confided.

'What name should I call you by?'

'Pearl.'

'Pleased to get to know you, Miss Pearl.' The music faded but neither made any move to leave the floor. When the famous organist continued the Latin theme with a strong, staccato tango, they took up hold once more.

Joy walked by, escorted by Cliff. 'This isn't the dance for me,' she mentioned. 'See you at the interval if not before.'

Terry and Sylvia were faced with the same choice. 'Stay or go?' Terry asked in the deep mumble that was his trademark. 'You decide.'

'Stay.' Sylvia realized that there would be more space to show off their talent. She also noticed that Eddie and Mavis had retired to the bar area. 'Posture,' she reminded Terry. 'Move like a cat. Right shoulder lead.'

'Yes, miss.' He grinned before launching into the tango walk – no rise and fall this time, but everything with the foot flat to the floor: sudden kicks and flicks and quick changes of direction.

In the centre of the floor, Errol complimented Pearl. 'You're pretty good at this.'

Quick, quick, slow for the reverse turn, locked at the hip. She stretched out her right arm and stared straight ahead for the promenade that followed. 'Decent of you to say so, Sergeant Jackson.'

'I mean it, Miss Pearl.' Bending his knee, flicking his foot between her legs in time to the clipped notes of the organ, he threw in an enigmatic question. 'So how come?'

Pearl told herself to keep looking straight ahead and not make eye contact. 'What do you mean?'

Errol tapped her ring finger. 'How come you're not dancing with him?'

Pearl took a short, sharp breath but tangoed on without missing a beat. 'He's in the army.'

'Gotcha.'

No more was said. Sylvia and Terry swished by in a closed promenade, knees flexed. Sylvia shot Pearl a questioning look that Pearl chose to ignore.

The tango ended and was replaced by a swing number that invited an energetic jive.

'Now you're talking!' Errol embraced the new dance. No question about it – he and Pearl would carry on dancing together. He kicked and shook his shoulders, swung her out to the left and then the right. This took him back to his high school prom and the dance madness of those fun-filled years when the kids had outraged their elders with displays of freestyle dancing that had no rules, when they'd leapfrogged and somersaulted, perspired and kicked at the ceiling of every dance hall in Fayetteville.

'Enough!' By the end of the jive Pearl was breathless. Her heart raced, her palms sweated; she was done in.

Errol laughed as he ran a broad hand over his army crew cut. 'Thank you, Miss Pearl – that was the most fun I've had since I stepped off the ship back in September.' Sliding his arm around her waist, he escorted her to her table where Sylvia and Joy were already seated. As Pearl collapsed on to her chair he gave a small bow and a click of his heels then backed away. Within seconds he was swallowed up by the crowd.

Joy and Sylvia raised their eyebrows but passed no comment and when Reggie Dixon calmed things down with a sedate waltz that didn't appeal, Sylvia reached for her handbag. 'Come along, girls; time to get another drink before the interval rush for the bar.'

'Good idea,' Joy agreed.

'Wait a sec – let me catch my breath.' Pearl's head was

still spinning and a tingle of exhilaration ran through her from head to toe.

'Now!' Sylvia grabbed her hand and pulled her to her feet. 'Before your handsome GI swoops again and sweeps you off your feet.'

'"I won't dance – don't ask me!"' Terry sang the first line of a popular Fred Astaire number as Pearl entered the studio on North View Parade the following morning. He wore an open-necked shirt and a pale blue pullover, teamed with navy blue slacks and black patent-leather tap shoes. 'Dancing leads to romancing, don't you know?'

'Ha-ha, very funny.' For once Pearl wasn't in the mood. She'd come to meet up with Sylvia, as arranged.

Terry executed a few dance moves, leaning in to each series of tip-tappety steps with a flourish then ending in two full pirouettes, perfectly spotted. '"I won't dance – da-da-dah!" Who *was* last night's American hunk, may I ask?'

'His name was Errol.' Pearl hovered by the door. 'Trust you to notice the best-looking man in the room.'

'Pot – kettle – black! So what the heck were you thinking, turning the poor chap down when the lindy hop came along?' Terry had been on the dance floor with Sylvia when the MC had announced the competition section of the evening. He'd been surprised to witness Pearl's refusal. 'You two would have had a good chance of winning the damned thing.'

'Why set tongues wagging more than they already were?' Pearl had been tempted but had managed to resist. Her sergeant had retreated with his tail between his legs and she'd seen nothing more of him all night. In the event, Sylvia and Terry had won the competition and set different tongues in motion. 'That's not fair – they're professional dancers – what chance did we poor mortals have against the likes of them?'

'"I won't dance . . ."' Terry teased again as the door opened and Sylvia came in.

'There you are!' Pearl's back was turned but she caught sight of her friend's elegant reflection in the enormous mirror – purple mohair jumper and black slacks, with her hair falling softly around her face – and turned to greet her with an irritated frown. 'We said we'd meet here at nine o'clock. It's ten past.'

Sylvia didn't see what the fuss was about. 'What difference does ten minutes make?'

'You know very well that I have to open the arcade at half past.'

'Sorry, girls; gotta run.' Terry made his excuses as he changed from his tap shoes into an outdoor pair then scooped up his belongings. 'There are *Sleeping Beauty* rehearsals to attend, dance routines to learn.'

'Good luck,' Sylvia and Pearl called after him as he rushed from the studio.

'What's eatin' you, Miss Pearl?' Sylvia mimicked an American drawl as she finessed her hairstyle in the mirror.

'You know what's eating me.' Pearl had been expecting Sylvia to display more sympathy when they'd arranged this short get-together for a post-mortem on the previous night's events.

'You had fun with your GI – I know that much.'

'He's not *my* GI,' Pearl protested, before jumping to the crux of the matter. 'But that's exactly what's bothering me.' Her next letter to Bernie had hung over her head like a heavy grey cloud, causing her a sleepless night. 'It's not that I give a fig what the gossips say . . .'

'Good, because you shouldn't. Go your own way as you've always done.'

'But am I going to mention the Yank to Bernie when I write to him later today – bearing in mind everyone's advice about being honest with him?'

'Dear girl, what possesses you to come to me of all people for marriage guidance?' Sylvia's silvery laugh echoed through the empty studio. 'But seriously, if you really want my opinion, I'd tell him that you've kept up your Saturday-night routine of going to the Tower with me and Joy but not much else. In other words, no specific mention of the hunk in GI uniform. What would be the point?'

Pearl nodded thoughtfully. 'He – Errol – noticed my wedding ring. I didn't hide the fact that I was married.'

'And also you chose not to dance the lindy hop with him – so, not guilty, m'lud!'

'You're right.' Pearl felt the dark cloud lift. She tilted her head back and squared her shoulders. 'I've done nothing to feel bad about.'

'Hip, hip, hooray, I've got the old Pearl back!'

'And thank you.' It was time to leave – the arcade was calling. 'My turn to dash – there's money to be made, slot machines to feed . . .' And, with this echo of Terry's parting shot, Pearl hurried off in her black slacks and green windcheater, with a clear conscience and with her red beret perched at an angle on her dark, glossy hair – smiling again.

'That's right; face your fears.' Pearl praised Joy for venturing along North Pier late the next day. Business had been slack so Pearl had already made the decision to close the arcade early when Joy unexpectedly dropped by. Now she put up the 'Closed' sign then busied herself by emptying coins from the rows of Playballs and Little Mickeys. She spoke over the rattle of pennies as she filled her metal cash box. 'What is it about you and piers exactly?'

'I don't like the gaps between the boards and the fact that you can see the sea below your feet,' Joy confessed.

'Bless you; it never even crosses my mind.' Pearl smiled as she placed the box of coins in her bag then switched off all but one of the lights. The idle slot machines glinted in the half light – Jackpot and Fill 'Em Up, Chip or Bust and What's My Line? – shiny red, yellow and silver slot machines, all designed to tempt unsuspecting school-boys and drunken uncles into Great Scott's North Shore Amusement Arcade. 'So this visit must be important?' Pearl guessed.

They ventured out on to the pier, where Joy blew on her hands and stamped her feet while Pearl closed the shutters and locked the door. Three men, wrapped up in Army and Navy Surplus overcoats, scarves and balaclavas and surrounded by baskets, reels and other tackle, were fishing from the end of the pier, hoping for a bite before dusk descended. Two gulls perched on a railing, watching every whip-like flick of the men's lines. 'I've been stewing over something for days,' Joy admitted. 'Going round in circles and getting nowhere. I feel as if I'll burst unless I tell someone.'

The two girls set off towards the prom, where blackout regulations meant that not a single street lamp was lit and all car headlights were dimmed.

'So spit it out – what's eating you?'

'A letter.' Joy sighed deeply. She held her collar tight under her chin against the biting wind. 'Actually, a note.'

'Who from?'

74

'I have no idea. It wasn't signed.'

'And what did it say?'

'Oh Pearl, it wasn't very nice – there were insults – about the kind of person I am . . .' Joy's voice trailed off. *Pearl is your broad-minded friend – you can share anything with her!* But the shameful insults stuck fast in her throat.

'Ah!' Pearl's exclamation didn't register surprise so much as recognition. 'You mean the nasty gossip about your and Tommy's living arrangements?'

'There's gossip?' Joy gasped. It struck her forcibly that all this time the poison had been spreading, working itself into the minds of others without her knowing.

'My friend Ida picked up a few iffy comments from the usual suspects. She passed 'em on to me,' Pearl admitted. 'And by "suspects" I mean members of the shady crew who never set foot on the dance floor but spend their time propping up the bar instead. But don't worry; I tore Ida off a strip for lowering herself to their level.'

'Oh!' Joy's head dropped forward and she sank on to the nearest bench. The situation had run beyond her control, like the black water lapping against the legs of the pier and foaming beneath her feet.

Pearl sat beside her. 'Now tell me, word for word, what was in this note?'

Still she couldn't repeat the words. 'It called me horrible names that I don't deserve – cross my heart – and it threatened to reveal what it called my dirty little secret.'

'There, there – don't get upset.' Pearl had once shared with Bernie her theory that Joy had been born into the wrong century. 'In a different era she might have entered a nunnery and devoted herself to prayer and good works,' she'd remarked.

'How's that?' Bernie had prompted.

'Joy is honest and kind to a fault and innocent too,' Pearl had explained. 'It's only on the dance floor that she shows a different side. It's there that she truly blossoms.'

'And you've kept this note business close to your chest?' Pearl asked Joy now.

Joy nodded miserably. 'I asked Lucia if she knew who had delivered the wretched thing but I'm afraid she wasn't much help.'

Pearl thought for a while. 'And does Tommy know about it?'

'No, I couldn't bear for him to find out.'

'Why ever not?'

'I'm afraid it might spoil things between us.'

'I'm hardly one to talk – but wouldn't honesty be the best policy here?' Before Joy could object, Pearl shared her reasoning. 'Listen, if Ida got wind of the gossip, how soon will it be before the whole town hears? You know what Blackpool's like. And Tommy's work at the circus puts him at the centre of things. It won't be long before he picks up an off-colour remark here, a snigger there.'

Realizing the truth of this, Joy drew a jagged breath then pounced on what she saw as the only possible solution. 'I'll go back to my old lodgings!' she cried. *Leave my lovely, cosy, safe room and kind, loving Tommy and Lucia. Live alone and prove the note-writer wrong.*

'Hold your horses.' Pearl had other ideas. 'No – what you should do is tell Tommy everything then the two of you can tackle it together.'

'But what if . . . ?'

Pearl pulled Joy to her feet and spoke earnestly. 'Listen to me, you idiot; he loves and respects you and would go to the ends of the earth to keep you happy. This is a tiny hiccough – you'll be over it in the blink of an eye.'

The two friends stood awhile, until dusk closed in and the wind chilled them through.

'Well?' Pearl prompted.

'I want so much to believe you,' Joy said in a faint voice. She formed her hands into fists and grew more determined. 'You're right,' she decided. 'I'll tell Tommy tonight, the moment he gets home from the circus.'

CHAPTER SIX

My darling Bernie,

How long a week seems when you're missing someone as much as I miss you. The days since we parted have dragged by and I've thought of you almost every minute of every hour of every day, except when I'm asleep, of course – and sometimes you're in my dreams too.

Pearl perched on the side of her bed with her pen hovering over the pad that rested on her knees while Elsie sat cross-legged on the other bed, writing her letter to Father Christmas.

'Isn't it a bit early for that?' Irritated by the lack of privacy, Pearl tried to oust her little sister from their shared room. 'Wouldn't it be better to wait a while?'

'No. Father Christmas needs to know what I want now.' Determination sparked from Elsie's eyes. 'Wilf says we won't get any presents this year if we don't send our letters early. The bloody war means there'll be no toys left at the North Pole if we wait any longer.'

'Don't say bloody.'

'"Dear Father Christmas".' Elsie ignored Pearl's reprimand and spoke every laboriously written word out loud. '"Please can I have some roller—" Pearl, how do you spell skates?'

'S-K-A-T-E-S.'

'"Skates and a—" How do you spell hula hoop?'

'For crying out loud!' Unable to stand any further interruptions, Pearl took herself off to the airing cupboard on the landing where there was just enough room beside the copper boiler to squeeze in among the clean towels and sheets and continue her letter to Bernie in private.

I've moved to the airing cupboard [she wrote]. *How about that? It's the only place in this blessed house where a girl can find some privacy. As for those long days I mentioned – as I explained in my last letter, I've been busy running the arcade with a bit of help every now and then from Ernie or from Dad when he's not at the pub or running our other arcade on Central Pier. Takings are not what they were in the summer months, naturally, and since there are no Illuminations again this year, what with the blackout, I can't see things improving before next spring when, God willing, the war will be over and you'll be back here in Blackpool with me, safe and sound.*

Pearl paused and waited for the royal-blue ink to dry so she could continue on the reverse of the sheet. Her fountain pen had leaked on to her forefinger and she resisted the temptation to wipe it on her trousers.

'Bedtime, Elsie!' Maria hollered from the bottom of the stairs. 'Pyjamas on and brush teeth, quick as you can.'

It's pandemonium here as usual so it's not easy to concentrate and write what I really feel. Dearest Bernie, you seem so far away. I don't even know if you're still in Scotland or if they've moved you on to join the rest of your regiment, wherever that is now: Egypt or somewhere else entirely. You could be heading to the Far East to fight the Japs, for all I know. The not knowing is the worst part so write to me again as soon as you're able. Even if you can't say where you are, at least let me know that you're safe and if there's anything that I can send to you in a parcel — more socks, underwear, a bar of chocolate, even a home-made Christmas cake; whatever you need and are allowed and will help to keep your spirits up.

Pearl's hand trembled with intense yearning and she was forced to pause again. Elsie's light footsteps sounded along the landing and down the stairs as she rushed to brush her teeth at the kitchen sink.

I'm considering making some alterations to my wedding dress and wearing it to go dancing in.

Pearl chose an indirect route into the thorny topic that had bothered her all week.

Yes, that's right — Joy and Sylvia dragged me out to the Tower Ballroom last night. No time to sit and mope with those two around, believe you me! As for the dress — Sylvia says I can keep it as it's too short for her now. I thought I might dye it a nice shade of pink or lilac; I haven't decided which.

Another pause was accompanied by a long, drawn-out sigh. *There, I've come clean as Ma, Sylvia and Joy all said I should.* With this niggle out of the way, what else was there to write to the man whom Pearl loved with all her heart?

It's time for me to finish now, my dearest. You know that I love and miss you more than I can say. Keep my photo with you always, wherever you may be. I wear your ring and it reminds me of your love for me and my love for you whenever I look at it. Our two hearts will soon beat as one again as they did on our wedding night. Until then, I'll dream of our next meeting,

Your ever-loving wife, Pearl

*

Lorna liked to make sure that everything in her apartment above the King Alfred Street studio was just so. Cushions were plumped, ornaments on her mantelpiece repositioned to best effect and a signed photograph of Victor Silvester hanging on the chimney breast was tweaked until it sat perfectly straight. Needless to say, there wasn't a speck of dust to be seen.

'Knock, knock!' Sylvia tapped lightly on her mother's sitting-room door before entering. 'I hope you don't mind my popping in.'

'Hello, dear. I wasn't expecting you.' A slight frown creased Lorna's brow. 'Anyway, to what do I owe the pleasure?'

'Does there have to be a reason?' Sinking on to the sofa, Sylvia unbuttoned her coat and removed her hat and gloves. 'I was at a loose end – Terry's rehearsing for *Sleeping Beauty* and Cliff is out drumming up extra business, so I thought I'd spend an evening with my dear mama.'

'Very nice too.' Lorna wished she'd been given advance notice. 'Except that I'm expecting visitors.'

'So that's why you're all dressed up.' Sylvia wasn't surprised. Her mother loved to play hostess – often to Eddie's father, Maurice Winter: a widower and local GP whose suave manner and sophisticated tastes suited Lorna down to the ground.

Lorna repositioned a cushion that had been shifted by Sylvia. 'You look well,' she conceded. 'Cornflower blue brings out the colour of your eyes. I take it there's no more nonsense about losing weight?'

81

Thrown off balance as per usual by the thorny topic of her eating habits, Sylvia resisted the urge to bite back. 'No, Mother; you'll be pleased to know that I grow plumper by the week, like a turkey in the run-up to Christmas – all thanks to Cliff.'

'Nonsense – you're not plump.'

'That's a matter of opinion.' Convinced that the four pounds she'd put on since September had sent her on a downward spiral from which there would be no recovery, Sylvia avoided looking in the mirror – she was all too aware that her cheeks were fuller and her hips more curvy, with – God forbid! – the suspicion of a tummy bulge developing; but what could she do? Cliff's one condition when he'd offered her part-time employment had been that Sylvia would stop starving herself unnecessarily – otherwise, no deal. 'Anyway, which visitors are you expecting?'

'Edward is calling in for a glass of sherry and a chat.'

'By himself?' Sylvia picked up a guarded edge to her mother's reply.

'No. Mavis is coming too. I want to run through the Viennese waltz with them – Mavis is having a few problems with her frame but I feel sure we can iron them out.'

'I see.' *Drat!* Sylvia experienced an unwelcome flashback to the moment at Pearl's wedding when Mavis had made a netball player's leap to catch the bride's bouquet – elbowing fellow guests aside and rising high in the air. She quickly dismissed a sharp pang of envy by reminding herself that it was a stupid superstition when all's said and done. 'Well, I wouldn't want to be in the way.'

'There's no need for you to take umbrage, dear.' Lorna hovered by the door to listen out for the doorbell. 'Half an hour or so should do it then after that we can have a nice little chat.'

Sylvia reached for her hat and gloves. 'No, really – I'd rather not stay.'

Too late. The bell rang and Lorna hurried down the stairs. She came back up with Mavis and Eddie – Mavis in her winter outfit of tweed jacket teamed with dark brown trousers and a narrow-brimmed hat with a feather trim that gave her the incongruous air of someone dressed for a day on the grouse moor. Eddie followed behind and was caught off guard when Sylvia stood up from the sofa to greet them.

Drat again! Sylvia struggled to keep control of her expression. *Smile as if you couldn't care less, damn it!*

'Hello, Miss Ellis.' Mavis shook her hand before glancing at Eddie for reassurance.

'Call me Sylvia – please. Won't you both sit down?' Sylvia offered the sofa to her and Eddie, who avoided eye contact.

'Sherry!' Lorna said brightly. Three glasses and a decanter were already set out on a small round table in the bay window. 'Edward, dear, would you care to do the honours? You'll find an extra glass in the drinks cabinet.' She took Eddie's place next to Mavis, leaving Sylvia to choose between two armchairs placed to either side of the marble fireplace.

There was an uncomfortable silence broken only by the gurgle and plop of Eddie pouring the sherry and then by a nervy question from Mavis. 'Did anyone see *My Gal Sal* at the Odeon this week? Rita Hayworth is one of my all-time favourites. I wasn't keen on Victor Mature, though – his Adam's apple is on the large side.'

'*My Gal Sal?*' Lorna repeated the title as if trying to place the film.

'Yes, it's a musical set in the time when ladies all wore

crinolines. You know: "I'm the toast of the town but I hope to settle down . . . tra-la-la."'

Mavis's childlike lilt and unaffected manner made the corners of Lorna's mouth twitch. 'A musical, you say?'

'Lovely dance numbers, beautiful costumes – it really took me out of myself.'

'It's what we need in this day and age.' Eddie came to Mavis's rescue while Sylvia sat in isolated silence. 'We've all had enough of Herr Hitler's "Deutschland Über Alles" to last a lifetime.'

'And now we're told to follow the Potato Plan,' Mavis rattled on. 'Eat potatoes instead of bread, would you believe? I'm not kidding – it was in this week's *Gazette*. We're meant to eat spuds for breakfast as a pancake with sausage meat. Spuds, spuds, spuds with everything!'

'That's the Ministry of Food's bright idea.' Eddie handed out the drinks. 'We'll all end up looking like a Jersey Royal if we're not careful.'

Everyone smiled and took a few polite sips of their sherry before Lorna decided it was time to get down to business.

'Now, Mavis dear, I've brought you and Edward here in order to go through your ballroom frame with you. You have developed an unfortunate tendency to raise your shoulders, which has the effect of shortening your neck and gives a less graceful appearance. Edward, if you would take Mavis in hold, I'll explain in more detail. That's correct – close contact, no gapping between your bodies. Mavis, shape your left hand thus and rest the tips of your fingers on Eddie's shoulder, with the little finger cocked. Your right arm should be extended to the side with the elbow slightly bent and your hand placed on his left palm. It's vital that you are aware of every detail. But there: you see that you've automatically raised your shoulders. Consciously lower them and lengthen that lovely neck – that's better.' Lorna made small adjustments to Mavis's posture as she spoke while Sylvia picked up a magazine and pretended not to pay attention.

Inside she was tied up in the usual knots. The snob in her had reared its ugly head when Mavis had prattled on about Rita Hayworth and Victor Mature. Surely Eddie could see how lacking in sophistication his new partner was? Next thing they knew she would be babbling about *ITMA* on the Home Service, repeating Tommy Handley's feeble jokes. As for the potato nonsense!

Sylvia pursed her lips then gave herself an imaginary slap on the wrist before turning her irritation against her mother – so pernickety in her teaching methods, stuck twenty years in the past. She flicked through the pages of her magazine without taking in a single word of what she read. Then, after ten minutes, when Lorna seemed satisfied with Mavis's progress, Sylvia flipped the magazine down on to the coffee table, stood up and pointedly drew Eddie to one side. What did he think about a recent opinion piece in the *Gazette* in which the editor had adopted the tally-ho battle cry of the RAF for his headline and described how the British lion was sharpening its claws in the frozen wastes of Russia as well as the deserts of Northern Africa? 'Is it merely sabre-rattling or are there genuine grounds for optimism?' she asked.

'Who knows?' To some extent, Eddie's office job at the Vickers factory kept him abreast of events – he was aware, for instance, that government orders for Wellington bombers showed no sign of dropping off and that yet more men had been recruited for training in photographic reconnaissance at Squires Gate. In fact, he'd made enquiries about the role, only to find that his health status as a severe asthmatic debarred him from applying.

'Stick to your desk job, son,' had been the recruiting officer's curt response. 'Applicants with your condition are of no use to the RAF, even in this capacity, and that's the way it is at present.'

'The Kimberley Hotel and the Imperial are bursting at the seams with civil servants, if that's anything to go by.' With her back turned to Mavis, Sylvia continued in the same vein. 'Mainly from the Department of Health and the Pensions Office, apparently.'

'And have you seen the RAF boys doing their physical jerks in the Tower Ballroom?' Mavis muscled her way into the conversation. ''Cos I have. They run those classes while I'm doing my cleaning shift and it's a sight for sore eyes if ever there was one. Just ask Joy – she'll tell you. Afterwards the boys go for a shower at the Derby Baths. My pal Joan works there as a lifeguard and we both say the same thing: what an awful waste!'

A startled frisson passed between Sylvia, Eddie and Lorna. As if to distance herself from the unpatriotic implication of Mavis's remark, Lorna collected up the sherry glasses and carried them into the kitchen.

'It is, though, isn't it?' Mavis barrelled on. 'I know we're not supposed to say it out loud but deep down we all think it. How many of those lovely RAF trainees come back from bombing raids over Germany; that's what I'd like to know. Hardly any. And then you have the likes of Cliff Seymour and Terry Liddle and men of their sort who never run the slightest risk of getting called up . . . Oops, sorry; I forgot they're friends of yours.' She gave an apologetic grimace in Sylvia's direction then carried on regardless. *In for a penny . . .* 'Not that I have anything against either of them. They're perfectly nice chaps and good dancers, too; only it's not fair, is it? Why, I've heard that some blokes even invent being queer as an excuse to get out of fighting, when really they have a wife and two or three kids tucked away.'

Eddie, mild mannered as ever, interrupted Mavis's flow with, 'Best not . . . don't you think?'

'Oh dear; have I gone and put my foot in it?'

'Yes, actually.' Gathering her outdoor things, Sylvia made a beeline for the door where she paused. 'Anyway, as Eddie will be the first to tell you, there are lots of other reasons not to be fighting on the front line and it's nothing to be ashamed of.'

'I know − me and my big mouth.' Genuine regret turned Mavis's face bright red. 'Me and Joan feel sorry for those young pilots, that's all. And Eddie did explain to me about his asthma and how they wouldn't let him train to take photos for the RAF because of it.'

Sylvia's eyes narrowed as she swung round to face him.

'It's true,' he confessed. 'It was a reconnaissance role but I was told no − for now, at least. Meanwhile, I'm thinking of volunteering for a Civil Defence job instead − as an ARP warden or a driver for a first-aid party; in fact, anything at all. At least then I'd feel I was of more use.'

Sylvia felt a band of pressure tighten around her chest, causing her breathing to grow shallow and rapid. Volunteering as a warden or a similar role was tantamount to putting oneself in harm's way. 'You're of use now at Vickers,' she insisted. 'They've put you in charge of ordering parts for the Wellingtons and making sure the workers have everything they need to keep production going.'

'I could do more.' Yes, his job at the factory was

important but as the bombers rolled off the production line and he saw them flying out of Squires Gate with their courageous, idealistic young pilots at the controls, his heart grew sore in the knowledge that his own wings were drastically clipped. It had preyed on his mind for long enough; surely, surely he could contribute more directly to the war effort!

'Does Mother know that you intend to do this?' Sylvia asked.

'No, nothing's definite yet.'

'What's not definite?' Lorna's return coincided with Sylvia's blunt question. She was on high alert, expecting the worst.

'Don't worry, Mrs Ellis, there's nothing to know.' Eddie gathered his own belongings and gestured to Mavis that she should do the same.

'Surely you're not . . . ?' The worst, the very worst as far as Lorna was concerned, would be for Eddie to back out of the Allied North of England competition. It would be so calamitous that her ability to form a complete sentence abandoned her. 'January . . . the championship?'

'Oh no, no,' Eddie quickly reassured her. 'I won't let you down as far as that goes. I'll continue to work hard with Mavis. We'll do our very best to win the trophy for you.'

Lorna's sigh of relief filled the room. 'Dear Edward, I know you will. And you too, Mavis – I have no doubt that your freshness and natural ability will impress the judges.'

Freshness and natural ability! Sylvia managed a strangled goodbye then rushed down the stairs ahead of Eddie and Mavis. 'I can't bear it,' she would tell Joy and Pearl the next time she saw them. 'Yes, you're right – I am green with envy!' she would declare. 'Joy knows that I've been a complete fool as far as Eddie is concerned and now it's too late to remedy it. I simply have to stand on the sidelines and watch him and Mavis dance into the sunset, scooping up prizes as they go.'

'Where's Joy?' Tommy demanded of his mother as soon as he stepped over the threshold. His coat hung open despite the raw temperature outside and he flung his cap and gloves on to the kitchen table in a show of exasperation. 'Is she in her room?'

'No, I'm here.' Joy had been tidying shelves behind the counter in the ice- cream parlour when she'd heard the bang of the door followed by her sweetheart's raised voice. She hurried into the kitchen, fearing the worst. 'What's the matter?'

'Everything's the matter!' He was fuming, almost unable to speak.

Joy's heart fluttered madly. Tommy had heard the rumours – no doubt about it. Why else would he be so upset? She sat down weakly on the nearest chair.

'*Calmati*.' Lucia pulled out another chair. 'Sit. Be calm, my Tommy.'

Ignoring his mother's advice, he paced the room, from doorway to the sink then back again. 'Today I came as near as dammit to punching a fellow in the audience smack in the chops. How dare he talk about Joy like that? He was sitting in the front row, mouthing off at the top of his voice. I tell you, it's a good job he didn't hang around after the performance; otherwise I'd have gone over there and knocked him flat.'

'Tommy, please . . .' Joy caught his arm as he passed but he pulled free.

89

'Laughing as if it was a joke, spreading filthy lies . . .' Running out of steam, Tommy paused by the sink to draw breath.

'My Tommy, what is this?' Lucia pleaded.

Joy knew that she must speak up – Tommy's mother was agitated, patting her chest and growing breathless. 'I think I know how this has happened,' she said as calmly as she was able.

'How do you know?' Tommy turned with a puzzled, accusatory look.

'It's because of the note.'

'What note?'

'*Ancora una volta la nota!*' Lucia cried, wringing her hands. Again the note!

'A horrid one, calling me names – it was pushed through the letter box on Monday,' Joy explained.

Tommy struck his forehead with the heel of his hand. 'And you didn't think to mention it? Instead you let me overhear cheap comments from a chap in the audience, sniggering behind my back?'

Joy drew a sharp breath. 'I meant to tell you – tonight when you came home. Pearl convinced me that I ought.'

'You've discussed it with Pearl? Bloody hell, Joy . . .'

'My Tommy, *per favore* . . .'

He hushed Lucia. 'Who else have you told?' he demanded.

Joy steeled herself to offer a full explanation – Tommy deserved no less. 'Not a single soul, I swear. I'd reached the end of my tether, wondering what to do. I burned the note and hoped the problem would go away, but in my heart I knew it wouldn't. The writer warned me as much.'

'For God's sake!' Tommy groaned and shook his head. 'Was there a threat?'

Joy nodded, desperate now to have everything out in the open.

'What did he say – I'm supposing it was a he?'

'He used horrid words.' Her lips trembled and hot tears stung her lids as she stumbled on. 'Hussy, tart, and such-like – because he said I was living in sin with you. And in a way, it's true—'

'Never!' With a sudden switch of mood, Tommy rushed to the table and crouched beside her. 'We both know nothing could be *further* from the truth; I think far too much of you to take things faster than you want. Listen – I'm sorry I was angry. Please don't cry.'

Joy succeeded in stemming her tears. 'The truth doesn't matter. If I've learned one thing this week, it's that what counts is how a situation looks from the outside.'

'But does it – really?' Tommy demanded. 'What's it matter if a few rotten beggars try to spoil things for us? What people say isn't important – it's how we feel.' He emphasized the final two words by clasping her hands between his.

Joy shook her head. 'Don't you see: it's not that simple? When I was growing up my parents took me to chapel every Sunday and my mother taught my sister and me that it's far worse for a girl to lose her good name than it is for a man.'

'And you believed it?'

'I still do. It's always been the way – you men can shrug off any whiff of scandal by claiming to be playing the field before you settle down. We women can't.'

'My Tommy, my Joy – *dica pure* – tell me!' The height-ened emotion between the pair was too much for Lucia.

'It's nothing, Mamma. Everything's going to be fine.' Tommy drew up a chair close to Joy. 'We'll soon find out who's behind this,' he promised. 'We'll make the letter-writing swine take it all back. The slate will be wiped clean and we can go on as before.'

Joy closed her eyes to shut out the sight of Lucia weeping. 'Perhaps it would be simpler if I moved back to my digs on Silver Street,' she whispered. 'At least until the fuss dies down.'

'Over my dead body.' Tommy grew angry again. 'No – tell me more about the dratted note so we can set about finding the culprit.'

'It was written in pencil in capital letters then stuffed into an envelope and delivered by hand – no date or anything and of course it wasn't signed.'

'Swine!' Tommy said again, a deep frown creasing his brow. 'Anything else?'

'I don't think so.' The sequence of events had begun to blur in Joy's mind, distorted by the wave of anxiety that had practically knocked her off her feet and left her fighting for breath. Keeping her eyes tightly shut, she strove to remember more details.

'*Sì, sì!*' Lucia contradicted. 'I tell Joy I pick up note then I look out to the street. I see man with sticks.'

Ah yes, a man with crutches getting on to the tram. 'We may be clutching at straws,' Joy warned.

'Describe him,' Tommy said to Lucia.

'Small, thin, *trasandato*.'

'Scruffy,' he translated for Joy.

'With sticks,' his mother insisted.

'Crutches.' It was Joy's turn to explain. Opening her eyes wide, she brought herself back to the present.

'A cripple with a grudge against you.' Tommy kept firm hold of Joy's hand. 'Who do we know who fits that description? Wait a second!' Her mention of Silver Street set the cogs of his brain grinding into action. 'Iris Grigg – your old landlady. Her son is Sam Grigg.'

No; surely not! Then again, now Joy came to think of it, Sam Grigg had been among the group of shady characters who'd sniggered and made off-colour remarks as she and Cliff had walked on to the ballroom floor the night before.

'Think about it,' Tommy urged. 'Sam got badly injured during the attack on Cliff and Terry a few months back.'

'Yes, that's right.' Joy shivered at the memory. 'Thanks to Mick Greene, Sam fell under the tram wheels.'

'The docs had to amputate his right foot. He spent weeks in hospital before he went back to his mother's house.'

'He lost his job and everything.' She rubbed her temples as if to erase a bad memory then looked up at Tommy. 'You think it could be him?'

'Sam's not in a good way, by all accounts.' Tommy thought it through. 'He still blames Bernie and me for siding with Cliff and Terry on the night of the fight. What if it's a grudge against me, not you?'

'So he's using me to harm you?' Joy turned to Lucia, eyes alight with fresh hope. 'Do you know who we mean? Would you recognize Sam Grigg if you saw his face rather than his back view?'

'*Lo riconosceresti?*' Tommy urged.

Lucia shook her head. '*Mi dispiace.*' Sorry.

'But it would be Sam's style,' Tommy insisted. 'He's a bitter little bugger, always propping up the bar at the Black Horse, bad-mouthing people. I'd bet my life he's behind this.'

'But how can we be sure?' Joy asked. It was one thing to suspect Sam of writing the note, quite another to prove it. 'He's never going to admit it, is he?'

93

'Maybe, but then again maybe not.' Tommy's frown deepened. 'But I'm damned if I'm going to let it drop; not after what he's done to you – to both of us.' Pulling Joy to her feet, he held her in a close embrace.

'I go now.' Lucia dabbed her eyes with her apron. Though she didn't understand all of what had gone on, the hug had reassured her. '*Buona serata, miei cari.*'

'Good night,' Tommy and Joy chimed.

They were alone with only the rustle of embers settling in the grate and the sound of their own soft, slow breathing. Joy felt Tommy's heartbeat strong against her chest. The familiar faint smell of greasepaint lingered on his skin. He kept his arms around her, held her tight.

'There is something else we could do to kill the gossip.' Between kisses he breathed the words into Joy's soft, silky hair.

She pulled away with a questioning look. All was well; it was as if there had never been an argument or any secrets between them. And he was her lovely, straightforward Tommy again, smiling and leaning in to kiss her lips.

'Don't you want to know how?'

She kissed him back then nodded. 'Go on – how?'

'We could get married.' In a slow, soft murmur he uttered four simple words that would transform their lives.

CHAPTER SEVEN

'Pack up your troubles in your old kitbag, eh?' Private Arthur Allen laid out his cotton shorts, aertex shirt and ankle boots on the bed next to Bernie's.

'What troubles might they be?' Their standard tropical battledress – Khaki Drill or KD as it was known – had been issued earlier that morning and their sarge had informed them that they'd be on the move by midday. No one knew where to. Tobruk was the most mentioned destination; a sweepstake had been set up and bets taken.

'Search me.' Arthur was a wind-up merchant who liked to have a dig at Bernie whenever he caught him penning what Arthur called his lovey-dovey letters to Pearl. 'All I know is, you've had a face like a wet weekend ever since you received wifey's last letter. She hasn't gone and ditched you, by any chance?' He noted Bernie's sour expression. 'Uh-oh; bull's eye!'

'Give it a rest, pal.' Bernie didn't lower himself to reply. After making a final search of the empty metal locker then checking under the bed for any stray items, he tightened the drawstring around the top of his duffel bag. Then he felt in his top pocket for his packet of fags, without success.

'Here, have one of mine.' Arthur tossed him a cigarette. 'Catch,' he added, chucking a lighter across the gap between their beds. 'I must say, a drop of sunshine won't come amiss,' he admitted as Bernie sat on the edge of his bed, lit up then threw the lighter back. 'I'm browned off with the weather up here in the wilds of Scotland – it's as bad as the bloody Arctic. Seriously, though; what's eating you, Private Greene?'

'Seriously? Nothing.' *Only the fact that Pearl's been out on the town without me.* The bombshell in her last letter about going to the Tower had hit hard and no matter how many times Bernie tried to convince himself that it was a bit of harmless fun, still the picture of her dancing the night away in some other bloke's arms continued to rear its ugly head. *Don't be daft – it's Joy and Sylvia's fault for dragging Pearl there in the first place. They're three girls having a laugh, that's all,* followed inevitably by a gut-wrenching, *What if some red-blooded chap comes on strong to Pearl? I know I'd be in there like a shot, looking the way she does.* Round and round he went in ever-decreasing circles.

'Nothing, as in "I hit the nail on the head."' Arthur's glib remark coincided with him lighting a cigarette and sitting down next to Bernie. His actions were smooth and unhurried and his know-it-all expression never wavered. 'She mentioned something in the letter that you didn't like, that's for sure.'

'So you're a mind-reader now?' Bernie knew that sharing confidences with Arthur Allen wasn't a sensible option – the bloke had a reputation for being leakier than a sieve.

That's me,' Arthur confirmed. 'What you're going through with your girl makes me glad to be single and fancy-free.'

'You don't say.' Bernie deadened the business end of his fag between pinched fingers then slipped it into his pocket, saving the rest for later.

'Yes – at least I won't have to worry about what my other half gets up to while I'm sunning myself in foreign parts.'

'Five minutes, lads!' A skinny private with a brutally short haircut and ears that stuck out from his head appeared in the doorway. His warning echoed across the otherwise empty Nissen hut, where regimented rows of bare mattresses retained the impression of bodies that had dropped on to them like stones, dead to the world after a day of mindless square bashing – left-right, left-right, present arms! 'Sarge's orders are to report to the parade ground at eleven hundred hours.'

'Get lost, Wing-nut.' Giving the messenger the two fingers, Arthur put his feet up on the bed and rested his head against the wall while blowing smoke rings into the air. 'Have you written back to her?'

'Who?'

'To wifey, of course.'

'Get lost yourself, Arthur.' Of course Bernie had bloody well written back! Yesterday, as a matter of fact; short and sweet.

Dear Pearl,

Just a quick note from yours truly to inform you we'll be on the move tomorrow, sailing out of Greenock to God knows where. Ours is not to reason why. By the way, I enjoyed reading more news about the arcade and tell Ernie from me that he has to pull his weight, or else. As for sending me socks, Christmas cake, et cetera: better to hang fire for now. I love you and miss you and think about you all the time.

More soon – your Bernie xxx

He posted it, knowing that what he'd left out spoke volumes.

Arthur took a last drag on his cigarette before flicking the butt under the bed, getting to his feet and shouldering his kitbag. He used the toe of his boot to prod Bernie into action.

'Get lost, Arthur. I mean it.'

'Ooh, touchy!' A laugh and another prod. 'Shift yourself, Romeo – it's time for us to go and fight the Hun.'

Time flew by without Sylvia finding any opportunity to share her ongoing Eddie-and-Mavis woes with Pearl and Joy. Her days had been crammed with lessons in the studio on North View Parade, teaching beginners not to tread on each other's feet as they practised samba whisks to the left and promenades on the diagonal. Each morning she would smile ironically as she passed beneath the sign above the door – 'Learn to Dance with Cliff and Sylvia – Live in Your Dreams!'

Fat chance, she thought. Most of her pupils displayed an abundance of enthusiasm but zero talent – shop girls from Woolworth's and clerks from the Ministry of Food spectacularly failed to master the samba bounce, and when it came to the rumba, the classic Latin dance, Sylvia simply despaired.

'We'll begin with the CPP,' she would instruct newcomers with as much patience as she could muster. 'Counter Promenade Position – make the usual V-shape in the space between your bodies: man's left hip in contact with the woman's right. No, Don – the left hip, not the right. Take it slowly. Dorothy, please remember the preparatory step to the side on the count of four-one. One, two, three, *four*, *one*, two, three, four!'

'Perhaps I'm not cut out for teaching after all,' she mentioned to Terry after an especially frustrating class.

'Sometimes I feel as though I'm speaking double Dutch, judging by the expressions on people's faces.'

'Don't say that.' Terry had assisted her during the session by demonstrating basic rumba moves, but now he was preparing to shoot off to rehearse routines for *Sleeping Beauty* at the Winter Gardens. 'It's hardly your fault if people don't know their left from their right.'

Sylvia gave a weary sigh. From here she must catch the tram to King Alfred Street and cover her mother's waltz session with Tommy and Joy and Eddie and Mavis: something she wasn't looking forward to. But Lorna had insisted and Sylvia had been backed into a corner. 'How are rehearsals going?' she asked as Terry changed his shoes and zipped up his windcheater.

'It's flippin' chaos,' he reported equably. 'We open in two weeks and the chorus still has two routines to learn from scratch. The good news is they've given me a three-minute solo. I'm a huntsman in the woods where Beauty falls asleep.'

'Bravo!' Sylvia was genuinely pleased.

'Are you having second thoughts about backing out of the auditions?' Terry wondered.

Sylvia didn't answer immediately.

'You are, aren't you?' Terry paused by the door to allow Cliff to enter. 'Sylvia needs a shoulder to cry on,' he reported before making himself scarce.

Preoccupied by his mounting money problems, Cliff paid little attention to Terry's parting shot and set down a pile of records on top of the gramophone. He was stylish as ever, in a patterned sweater and casual trousers, carefully teamed with brown brogues and a yellow silk cravat, but there were dark circles under his eyes and he had a careworn expression. 'I've had two cancellations for tomorrow's salsa class – that adds up to another four bob that won't be flowing into our coffers.'

'Let me carry on spreading the word.' Sylvia was well aware that her own living depended on them being able to drum up more custom. 'I'll persuade Mother to take leaflets for us.'

Cliff grunted. 'I doubt she'll allow it – we're the opposition, after all.'

Sylvia disagreed. 'Mother's refusal to entertain Latin leaves the door wide open for us on that front. All I have to do is convince her that people want to learn both styles of ballroom dance so there'll be no falling off of business for her even if they do decide to test the water with us.'

'Good luck with that.' Cliff didn't seem convinced. 'What did Terry mean, by the way? Why are you down in the dumps?'

'It's Mavis Thorne,' she blurted out. 'She and Eddie are a definite team now and Mavis enjoys rubbing my nose in the fact whenever she gets the chance.'

'Is that so?' Cliff cocked an eyebrow as he sorted through records.

'It's my own fault, I know.'

'You want my honest opinion?'

'Yes please.' Since starting to teach alongside Cliff, Sylvia increasingly relied on his advice.

'That ship has sailed, my dear. It's time to move on.'
Better to tell her straight; no point beating about the bush.

'I know!' she wailed. 'Joy has said the same thing. But what shall I move on to? I mean, there has to be more to life than teaching classes for you and Mother – no offence.'

'None taken.'

'Since Mr Burns's plan for me to move to London fell

through I feel as if I'm in limbo. Perhaps I should have gone anyway.'

'And done what, pray?' Cliff trained his full attention on her. 'Mitch Burns is one of many such men, ready to exploit naive young girls for their own advantage. To my everlasting shame I should have warned you earlier what Mitch was up to.' An introduction to London high society had been the lure – ostensibly dancing at the Ritz and Claridge's with well-heeled gentlemen willing to pay a fee to secure a professional partner – but the reality had been much more sordid. Cliff had revealed the truth just in time and Sylvia's dream had been shattered.

'I know better now,' she insisted. 'I'd be on my guard. And it wouldn't have to be London; I'd be willing to travel to Manchester or Liverpool to work in cabaret or musical theatre. What do you think?'

Cliff raised both hands. 'Whoa! Stop and consider. Of course you feel sore about Mavis taking your place and that's understandable, but is it a good enough reason for you to scarper?'

'Scarper?' she echoed faintly.

'Yes; what you describe sounds like running away to me. Why not stick it out here for a while and see what happens? I for one would be sorry to see you go. Truly, I would miss you.'

A lump came into Sylvia's throat so she simply nodded.

'Besides, you have friends here – Joy and Pearl, for a start. Have you asked them for their advice?'

'Not yet.'

'Then talk to them – sooner rather than later. And Blackpool is not so bad when you think about it; it's where people flock to in their thousands to escape the grim realities of rationing and air raids. The Tower Ballroom, the Palace, the Empress – our splendid dance halls are what draw the crowds, not to mention the circus and a dozen or more live shows across town, plus three piers, the Pleasure Beach, the Golden Mile . . .'

'Stop – I can't argue with any of that,' Sylvia said with a loud sigh.

'Good. And I mean what I said – I don't want you to leave. You were the one person who showed kindness to me and Terry when you first found out the truth about us. You could easily have sided with the likes of Mick Greene and Sam Grigg.'

'Never!' Sylvia's declaration was heartfelt.

'Talking of which, I have a confession of my own.' Cliff drew her into the alcove where the photographs from his time in Berlin and London were displayed – the one of a younger Cliff surrounded by a bevy of chorus girls dressed in corsets, fishnet tights, high heels and little else stood out from the rest. 'This is about Terry and me; I can't quite put my finger on it but something has changed. It's not the same as it was between us.'

'In what way?'

Cliff struggled to express his doubts. 'We've spent so little time together lately. Either I'm busy teaching or else he's dashing off to rehearsals – to be frank, we're like ships passing in the night. And I have a niggling suspicion that he's started to keep secrets from me.'

Sylvia shook her head in disbelief. 'Do you have any evidence?'

'No; it's merely a feeling. But I've noticed the way he brushes aside any questions I ask about the show routines and he rarely mentions the names of the people he dances with.'

'Are you sure you're not imagining it?'

Cliff smiled thinly. 'Perhaps I am. Yes, forget I said anything.'

'I'm sure if you asked Terry—'

'Quite.' He cut her off. 'Enough of my worries. Now, shoo. You're due to teach at King Alfred Street, if I'm not mistaken.'

'Oh Lord, yes!' A glance at her watch told Sylvia that she would miss her tram if she didn't get a move on, so she shoved her dance shoes into her bag and flung on her coat. 'Thanks for listening to my tale of woe,' she called over her shoulder as she headed off.

'Likewise,' Cliff said after the door had banged shut.

Determined to take Cliff's advice, Sylvia arrived at the Lorna Ellis Dance Academy hoping for another heart-to-heart with Joy before the evening's lesson got underway but she was out of luck.

'Tommy telephoned to say that he and Joy are unable to come to class this evening,' Lorna informed Sylvia with a disgruntled frown. She'd waylaid her daughter in the entrance to the empty studio. 'It's most unlike them, I must say. Joy in particular is so reliable.'

Sylvia's heart sank at the news. *Disaster – that leaves just me, Eddie and Mavis!* 'Did Tommy say why?'

'No, but I assume it was important.' Lorna was dressed up for an evening at the theatre with Eddie's father: a picture of elegance in the slim-fitting silvery-grey two-piece that she'd worn for Pearl and Bernie's wedding, teamed with mauve handbag, shoes and gloves. 'Ah, that must be Maurice.' At the sound of a car drawing up, she opened the outer door then departed with a hasty farewell to Sylvia. 'Edward and Mavis are here,' she called over her shoulder as the young couple stepped out of the car.

'Dad gave us a lift,' Eddie explained to Sylvia as he and Mavis entered the studio.

'Where are the others?' Mavis made a beeline for the bench behind the piano where she took off her coat and changed her shoes then checked her reflection in one of the tall mirrors.

'They can't make it.'

'That's a shame,' Eddie remarked with a questioning glance at Sylvia. He could tell from her tense expression and refusal to meet his gaze that she was on edge. Mavis, however, was determined to ignore any potential awkwardness.

'Ready when you are!' she declared, smoothing out the creases in her navy-blue skirt as she advanced towards the middle of the floor. Perky, smiling and eager, she waited for the lesson to begin.

Sylvia chose a record and placed it carefully on the turntable. All was familiar: the upright piano with Mavis's coat draped over it and the piano stool upholstered in green velvet, the stack of records on a shelf above the gramophone, the ballet barre that stretched the length of one wall, the floor-to-ceiling mirrors, the expanse of smooth, polished floorboards – these were things that Sylvia had known all her life, where she and Eddie had learned to dance. And yet today she felt estranged from her surroundings and unsure.

Mavis grinned at Eddie as he took her in close hold, his head tilted to the right, hers to the left, her left hand lightly touching his right shoulder, bodies in contact, feet together.

Sylvia went through the motions, speaking over the music. 'Shoulders down at all times,' she reminded Mavis. 'We'll begin by going through the twelve steps of the quarter turn, on the count of three.' She observed closely then moved on without comment. Now for the natural turn; six steps in all. And the reverse turn and the forward change in both directions in quick succession. Needless to say, Eddie was faultless throughout. 'More control,' Sylvia instructed Mavis during an exaggerated sway to her left. 'Head a little more tilted towards the ceiling. Smile.'

'Blimey, it's fast!' Relieved when she was allowed to take a break, Mavis fanned her face with her hand and plonked herself down on the piano stool. 'How am I doing?' she asked Sylvia, feeling that she'd performed to the best of her ability and anticipating praise.

'Very well as far as technique goes.' There was no denying that Mavis was an exceptionally fast learner. 'But competition dancing requires musicality and character-ization as well.'

'Come again?'

'In January's competition the judges will look at presen-tation as much as technique.' Sylvia warmed to her theme. 'They will award higher marks depending on how well you express your personality through the dance, how con-fidently you execute the choreography and so on.'

'Blimey,' Mavis said again, this time with an anxious glance in Eddie's direction. 'Maybe I should stick to netball.'

'Don't worry – you'll learn as you go on,' he assured her. 'Good presentation is easier to master if you think of it simply as showing off to the judges.'

'Rightio.' The penny dropped and Mavis was ready to go again. 'My ma says I'm a born show-off. She doesn't know where I get it from – she's a real shrinking violet. Dad says it comes of me being an only child.'

'That might explain it.' Sylvia allowed an edge of

sarcasm to creep into her voice, which she regretted when Eddie shot her one of his rare severe looks. *Only thirty more minutes of this torture to get through!* She began the second half of the lesson by demonstrating the finer points of spotting as you turn – vital in the Viennese waltz to avoid dizziness. Mavis copied perfectly while Eddie stood to one side. 'Excellent, Mavis,' he commented. 'Well done.'

Sylvia chose another record, one with an even faster tempo. Mavis and Eddie were poised to begin. Together they whirled around the studio without missing a beat, gliding and swaying, with Mavis's skirt flaring to reveal neat ankles, slim calves and lightning-quick feet. They were perfect together: Eddie a mere inch or two taller, leading his partner, sweeping her effortlessly across the floor, and Mavis graceful, slender and supple, without a hint of raised shoulders. Swan-like neck, long, slim arms, tapering fingers – you name it, she had it.

The session ended on an exhilarating high and Mavis gave a skip and a jump as she and Eddie broke out of hold. She held on to his hand and towed him towards Sylvia. 'How was that?' she demanded.

'Very good; you have every right to be pleased with your progress.'

'I am – I'm chuffed.' Mavis was all smiles as she ordered Eddie to get a move on. 'I've arranged a get-together in the Queen's Arms. Some pals of mine are dying to meet you. How about it?'

'You're on,' Eddie agreed, bending forward to finish changing into his outdoor shoes.

'And from there we could go on to the Odeon to watch a flick if you like.' Mavis was halfway across the room with him still in tow. 'Ta very much for the tips on presentation, Miss Ellis,' she cried as they departed. 'I've learned a lot.'

The door swung shut and silence descended. For a while Sylvia made no move but the sight of her reflection in various mirrors around the studio made her feel more isolated and sadder than ever. *If only, if only* . . . But the evening had proved yet again that the old days were gone for good. After switching off the lights and locking the door, she stepped out into darkness, to the inevitable sound of waves crashing against the sea wall and the sight of a full moon low in the sky, partially obscured by clouds.

'Yes, I'll marry you.' Tommy's proposal had come out of the blue and made Joy's heart swell and practically burst with happiness.

He'd thrown his arms around her and lifted her off her feet. 'Are you sure?'

'Certain. Tommy, put me down. Let me catch my breath.' He'd kept on hugging and kissing her until she'd grown dizzy and in the end she'd pushed him away. 'I've said yes and I mean it, but on one condition.'

'Anything you like – just name it.' Nothing could spoil this joyous moment. Tommy sailed high in the sky like a kite scarcely tethered to the ground.

'Wait – my head's spinning. There's one important thing we have to do before we get married.'

'Only one?' He knew how girls liked to fuss over details like wedding dresses and bridesmaids; it was all a necessary part of the build-up to the journey down the aisle. Joy had said yes; this was all that mattered. On he sailed in his version of heaven.

'I'm serious, Tommy. We can't marry until we've found out who's behind this horrid note.'

'Why ever not?' Feeling a sudden tug on his heartstrings, the kite plunged towards the ground.

'It's obvious, isn't it? I'm desperate to clear my name. I can't bear for people to think bad things about me – about us.' Joy was deadly serious. 'We have to put it right.'

Hold steady; find an upwards current. 'No one believes this rubbish,' Tommy tried to argue.

'That's not true!' she exclaimed. 'You saw for yourself how quickly rumours take hold – there was that man in the front row of the audience for a start. And there'll be a hundred more like him if we don't act.'

'But how much does it really matter?' he pleaded, with the plummeting feeling growing stronger by the second. 'Why not stand up to those idiots: get married straight away with a special licence, the way Pearl and Bernie did?'

'Because!' Joy kissed him and tried to explain. 'I can't bear it if a single person believes that there's a grain of truth in this horrid gossip.'

Finally Tommy had come down to earth with a bump. 'I get it; you want us to prove that Sam Grigg is the guilty party and get him to admit he made it all up?'

'Yes.' Joy had insisted that it was the only way forward. 'You promised to help me,' she'd reminded him.

'It won't be easy,' Tommy had warned. 'But if it means that much to you . . .'

'It does.'

'Then yes, we'll do it together,' he'd agreed.

Joy had shed happy tears. 'I couldn't love you more,' she'd murmured. 'Marrying you will be a dream come true. But we won't tell anyone what we've decided; not until we've sorted this out.'

'So you want to keep our engagement a secret?'

'Yes please.' Her eyes had widened when Tommy had said the word 'engagement' and she'd turned dizzy again at the thought of Joy Hebden soon to be Mrs Joy Rossi with a band of gold on her finger to prove it.

'Not even . . . ?' Tommy had rolled his eyes towards the ceiling.

'Your mother? No, not yet – please!'

'But I can buy a ring?'

Joy had agreed to this. 'Nothing too showy,' she'd pleaded. 'Remember, I'm not a flashy sort of girl.'

'You're the best, most beautiful girl in the world to me.' Taking her face between his palms, he'd kissed her tenderly. 'And once we've managed to kill off the nasty rumours, be warned: I intend to shout the news from the top of Blackpool Tower – "Joy Hebden has agreed to be my wife, Hallelujah!!"'

'Hush.' She'd kissed him – lips lingering, hearts beating fast. 'Your mother will hear.'

They'd laughed and hugged each other tight. 'As for Sam Grigg . . .'

'*If* it's him,' she'd cautioned.

'There's only one way to find out,' Tommy had insisted. The job now was to follow up their theory as quickly as possible. 'I have a night off later this week. No putting it off; we'll go to his house and have it out with him, make sure he never does it again.'

Which was the reason why, earlier that day, he'd telephoned Mrs Ellis with his sincere apologies: he and Joy were obliged to miss tonight's dance lesson. And here they were, walking hand in hand under a full moon towards Silver Street, with the Tower behind them and the Pleasure Beach to one side, the sound of the sea in their ears as they turned into the street where Joy had recently lodged.

Rat-a-tat-tat on the lion-head knocker of number 57;

Tommy took the initiative. Joy felt strangely calm while they waited for a response.

'Come on; we know someone's in there,' Tommy muttered. A chink of light seeped under the blackout blind in a downstairs room and he'd picked up mutterings from the back of the house. He knocked again then stooped to peer through the letter box.

A neighbour – a surly, middle-aged man in shirtsleeves and a waistcoat – came to his door to warn them that they were wasting their time. 'Stop that racket. Can't you see the "No Vacancies" sign in the window?' he'd grumbled. A ginger tomcat slunk between his legs and into the house.

'We're not looking for lodgings,' Joy started to explain.

'Wait a minute – don't I know you?' The neighbour took a closer look. 'Aren't you the floozy that lodged here not so long ago . . . and isn't that the Eyetie you shacked up with?'

Joy breathed in sharply while Tommy reacted too quickly for her to prevent him from leaping down the two front steps of number 57 and up those of the interfering neighbour. He pushed both hands against the man's chest, flooring him and leaving him spread-eagled in the hallway, to the consternation of the cat which, yowling at the top of its voice, shot back out of the house and disappeared up the street.

'What the dickens?' A sour-faced Iris Grigg opened the door to number 57. 'Oh, it's you,' she added when she saw Joy.

Before the landlady could slam the door in their faces Tommy leaped back up the steps and wedged his foot between the jamb and the door.

'What do you want?' Iris demanded through the narrow opening.

'We've come to talk to Sam.' Joy fought to remain calm.

'What about?' Snappy as a Jack Russell terrier, Iris refused to budge.

'That's between him and us,' Tommy told her.

'Not in,' Iris barked back.

Tommy showed that he didn't believe her by shoving the door with his shoulder to force it open. Then he yelled down the hallway, 'Sam? It's Tommy Rossi and Joy Hebden here. We'd like a word.'

'I'm telling you, he's not in.' Iris raised her voice as she stepped to one side. 'Go ahead – see for yourself. His room is second on the left. The door's not locked.'

Tommy and Joy rushed to investigate. Sure enough, Sam's room, containing a bed, wardrobe, bedside cabinet and little else, was indeed empty. A spare pair of crutches rested against the bed next to a solitary boot minus its lace.

'Told you so.' The landlady gave a thin, spiteful smile as they returned. She had no time for Joy, a lodger who had upped and left without notice, and even less for Tommy, who had been involved in the fight that had ended in Sam's near fatal accident. Any mother worth her salt would send the pair packing. 'And if you come back bothering Sam and me again, I'll call the police on you.'

'If she doesn't, I will.' Iris's neighbour appeared on the pavement, his jowly face red with fury.

'All right, we'll leave you in peace.' Joy tugged at Tommy's sleeve until they were safely out of the door. 'We only want Sam to stop spreading fibs about our living arrangements, that's all.'

Iris folded her arms and stood full-square on the doorstep. 'Are you calling my son a liar?'

Tommy's anger was still bubbling away as he seized on

her remark. 'So you're not denying that Sam was the one who wrote that nasty note?'

'I'm not saying that he did either,' Iris stonewalled. 'Anyway, you've only got yourselves to blame. To my mind, a decent girl doesn't shack up with the first chap who asks her; she waits until after they're married.'

'Shack up' again – the insulting phrase cut deep, but Joy swallowed back her anger. 'Come on,' she said to Tommy. 'We're wasting our time here.'

'And good riddance.' The neighbour watched them down the street. 'You heard Iris: we'll set the bobbies on to you if you show your ugly mugs round here again.' The wind whipped away his threat as Joy and Tommy retraced their steps towards the seafront.

'That's that, then.' Joy's heart sank. *What now?* she wondered.

Tommy wasn't ready to give in as they faced into the wind and walked on along the dark prom towards the lifeboat station. A tram rattled past, followed by a truck piled high with sandbags. 'I've an idea where Sam might be,' he confided.

'Oh, let's leave it,' Joy said with a sigh. Outside number 57 her anger had flared then burned itself out. Now she felt a strong urge to return home and act as though nothing had happened.

'He'll be with his pals at the Black Horse.' Tommy quickened his pace. 'It's their favourite watering hole. What do you say we take a look?'

Joy sighed again. Yes, she'd started this so they must see it through to the bitter end. Reluctantly she nodded and they pressed on together, down the side of the Tower building, across the deserted market square and on to the narrow terraced street beyond.

CHAPTER EIGHT

Dear Pearl, Just a quick note to inform you we'll be on the move tomorrow, sailing out of Greenock . . . Pearl sat in her chilly bedroom rereading Bernie's last letter for the umpteenth time, as if to wring more meaning out of the few short lines. She registered his mentions of Ernie, socks and Christmas cake, and noted with flat disappointment the yawning gap that would normally be stuffed with endearments and professions of love. Glancing up with tears in her eyes, she stared at her as-yet unaltered wedding dress still hanging limply from a hook on the door. Bernie's unit had been at sea for days, heading for unknown shores. For all Pearl knew, his flotilla had already been the target of an enemy attack in the Irish Sea or else was anchored off Gibraltar, awaiting safe passage into the Med. She shuddered at the thought of stealthy U-boats lying in wait on the seabed and of deadly torpedoes speeding silently through the clear blue water.

Then her thoughts switched to her last letter to him – had she made too little of the Tower Ballroom business? On the whole she regretted following Sylvia's advice to keep it brief – she felt now that she ought to have addressed the issue head-on and done more to reassure Bernie. As it was, she'd left room for his imagination to run riot.

I will explain it all next time I write, she promised herself. Today she would be busy at the arcade but tomorrow she would pressgang Ernie into taking over for a few hours, giving her time to make amends with a long, loving letter that would leave her new husband in no doubt as to how much she loved and missed him.

'Knock, knock.' Maria tapped on Pearl's door before opening it and peering in. 'Good Lord, girl – you're not even dressed. What's wrong? What does Bernie say in his letter?'

'Nothing's wrong. Bernie has received orders to join his regiment, that's all.'

'It was bound to happen before too long.' Maria lifted clean items from Pearl's chest of drawers – a vest, bra and pants – and laid them on the bed. 'Try not to worry too much. Keep busy; that's the main thing – especially in the run-up to Christmas; there'll be lots to do.'

Pearl was touched by her mother's unusual show of concern. 'Thanks, Mum – I mean it.'

'The red one or the green?' Maria held up two sweaters from another drawer.

'The green one, please. And I'll wear my brown corduroy slacks.' Pearl began to get dressed. 'My wedding day already seems like a dream,' she confessed.

'Yes, but your father's wallet can vouch for the fact that it did happen. He harps on about what he had to fork out for the reception.' Maria sat on the bed and patted the mattress for Pearl to join her. 'Listen to me – I was fourteen when the Great War started: too young to have a sweetheart serving on the front line. But my older brother was eighteen when he was called up and your poor grandmother lost a lot of sleep over it, especially if she didn't hear from him for weeks on end. She had to get used to the worry; we all did.'

'I know; I'm sorry.'

'Your uncle came home in one piece.' The reminder was accompanied by a sympathetic smile. 'And so will Bernie, fingers crossed.'

'Yes, then we'll find a little place of our own on the north side of town and Bernie and me will run the arcade together and we'll make a success of it and then we'll have lots of kids.' Pearl grinned as she envisaged a rosy future full of sunshine and laughter.

'That's the ticket.' Satisfied, Maria left her daughter to get dressed. 'One foot in front of another – it's the most any of us can do when there's a war on.'

'Are you busy?' Sylvia enquired when she dropped in unexpectedly on Pearl later that morning.

'See for yourself.' Pearl gestured around the almost empty arcade. The weekend rush hadn't materialized, thanks to the dreadful weather. Heavy rain and strong wind had driven even the pluckiest of day-trippers indoors, to the tea rooms and fish and chip cafés in streets set back from the exposed promenade.

'It's blowing a gale out there,' Sylvia remarked as she produced a flask of tea and two metal cups from her bag. 'I was at a loose end so I thought I'd call by.'

'And . . . ?' Pearl turned down the volume on the gramophone that played cheery music to entice the thin trickle of customers through the door. 'Strip Polka' by the Andrews Sisters provided a background to the girls' private conversation.

'And I wish I was dead!' Sylvia declared dramatically.

Pearl's expression didn't alter as she took a sip from her mug and she hazarded a guess: 'Mavis?'

'Spot on.' Sylvia nodded. 'I can't stand the girl. And

last night I was obliged to teach her and Eddie the finer points of the Viennese waltz – it was just them and me in my mother's studio.'

'What's wrong with Mavis, other than the fact that she's dancing with your Eddie?'

The Sisters warbled on about how much Queenie the cutie hated corny waltzes and preferred stripping her clothes off to the polka instead. Pearl smiled to herself at the risqué lyrics.

'Eddie's not mine; not any more.' Sylvia had been forced to swallow this unpalatable truth. 'But I ask you – Mavis Thorne of all people!'

'Stop right there.' It was time for Pearl to present Sylvia with a few cold facts. 'Mavis isn't to blame here. You're the one who pushed Eddie away in the first place, leaving him high and dry without a dance partner. And it was your mother's idea to choose Mavis, not his.'

'I know, I know!' Sylvia put her hands to her ears. 'But when I see them together I can't stop myself from thinking horrid thoughts about her.'

Queenie carried on stripping but never went too far – ooh-la-la! Across the room one of the slot machines paid out and coins tumbled into the metal dish.

'You and Mavis belong to different sides of the tracks,' Pearl pointed out. 'But that doesn't mean she's a bad person or that she's had an easy life. Quite the opposite, from what Joy tells me.'

This was news to Sylvia, who tried to set aside her own troubles and listen more carefully.

'Joy says that Ruby has taken Mavis under her wing since Mavis's dad fell ill.'

'When was that?'

'A week ago. He's had to give up his job at Vickers.

The family will struggle to make ends meet, so Ruby has offered Mavis extra cleaning hours at the Tower.'

'Mavis never let on – she seemed her normal self.'

'Yes; she tries to make the best of things.'

'I'll remember that in future,' Sylvia promised as she screwed the top back on to her flask. 'And thanks for putting me straight.'

Pearl patted her hand. 'It's what friends are for. You know something? You're not the only one who misjudges people. Take me; I used to watch you and Eddie queuing up for tickets at the Tower. Back then, I thought you were too stuck up for words, looking down your nose at the rest of us.'

'But now you know different?'

Pearl nodded. 'Feet of clay,' she joked.

'That's me,' Sylvia admitted, packing away the flask and mugs. 'But I'll do better from now on; you'll see.'

'When will I see?'

'Tonight, for a start. If Mavis and Eddie are at the Tower, I'll be nice as pie to them both. And you and Joy will be there to make sure I'm on my best behaviour.'

What to wear and when to meet – Pearl and Sylvia went on to make firm arrangements.

'I take it Joy already knows?' Sylvia said over the sound of another jackpot win.

'She does,' Pearl confirmed. 'We'll all meet tonight at half past seven, outside the main entrance. And don't be late.'

'Half seven on the dot,' Sylvia agreed as she stepped out on to the practically deserted pier.

'Queenie, queen of them all,' the Andrews Sisters harmonized. *Ker-ching!* Little Mickey finished paying out and one happy customer returned to his digs jangling a pocketful of coins.

*

117

Joy and Mavis polished the mahogany bar top in the Tower Ballroom until they could see their reflections.

Pleased with the effect as their shift came to an end, Mavis stood back, hands on hips, her face flushed from the effort. 'Look; I can see our ugly mugs in it.'

'Nice work, you two.' Ruby finished stacking glasses then took off her overall and checked her reflection in the mirror behind the bar. 'That's it; time to clock off,' she called to her crew of ten.

Without more ado, her girls stashed stepladders, stools, buckets, mops, dusters and tins of polish in the storeroom under the stage, chattering about their plans for the week-end – one arranged to borrow a blouse, another to lend her pal a couple of shillings until pay day.

'Will I see you two back here later on?' Ruby asked.

Joy was the first to answer. 'Count me in – Tommy and I intend to try our luck in the competition as usual.'

'Mavis?' Ruby prompted.

'I'm not sure. I'm strapped for cash right now.'

'But Eddie will pay for your ticket, surely?'

Mavis blushed bright red. 'He would, but I don't like to rely on him every time.'

Ruby tutted loudly. 'If you ask me, that's called looking a gift horse in the mouth.'

'I didn't ask you,' Mavis shot back with an impish grin. 'What do you think, Joy? Should I pay my own way or not?'

'That's a hard one. Normally I'd say yes you should, especially if you and Eddie aren't officially walking out together.'

'"Walking out"!' Ruby echoed with a laugh. 'What a quaint little thing it is!'

'Ignore her,' Mavis insisted.

'But,' Joy continued, 'this is a special case. There's only a couple of months to go before the Allied Championship. If you and he hope to do well there, you'll need all the practice you can get.'

'See!' Ruby crowed. 'Joy agrees with me. Anyway, I'm off to paint my nails and tart myself up. See you both later.'

Mavis and Joy took their time to gather their belongings and make their way through a side exit close to the stage, chatting as they walked down a plain, dimly lit corridor that was a world away from the sparkling chandeliers and frescoes of the ballroom.

'I fear I'm in Sylvia Ellis's bad books,' Mavis confided with a wicked wink. 'If looks could kill . . .'

'Best not to take any notice,' Joy advised. 'Sylvia has had a lot to deal with lately.'

'And she still holds a candle for Eddie – anyone can see that.' Mavis chattered on without brakes as usual. 'Except Eddie, of course; blind as a bat like most men.'

Reaching the exit, they prepared to go their separate ways – Mavis towards her home on Duke Street close to the North Pier and Joy in the direction of the bustling market square where she planned to buy vegetables for the evening meal – until one further thought popped into Mavis's head. 'By the way, I gave Howard Reynolds a piece of my mind on your behalf the other night.'

Joy's stomach lurched in anticipation of what was to follow.

'You know Howard: he works out at Squires Gate, building the hangars? Well, he was in the Queen's Arms the other night, spouting nonsense about you and Tommy Rossi, blackening your names – he and a couple of other layabouts.'

119

'Who else?' Joy managed to ask, though her heart knocked against her ribs.

'Fred Salter for one.'

'And Sam Grigg?'

'You guessed it. Nasty pieces of work, all of them. Are you all right?' Mavis noticed that Joy had turned deathly pale. 'Don't worry – I soon put them straight.'

'Yes, I'm fine – and thank you.' Joy's mind flew back to the previous night when she and Tommy had followed their hunch and sought out Sam Grigg in the Black Horse. It had proved a dead end – according to the barman, Sam and his gang had been drinking there earlier in the evening but Sam had had a skinful and at around seven o'clock his mates had bundled him into a taxi and sent him home to bed.

'Damn it; his mother was lying!' On learning this, Tommy had cursed Iris to kingdom come. 'She had him tucked away in Silver Street all along.'

'She didn't let us into the living room.' Joy too had realized that they'd been tricked.

Tommy had stormed out of the pub and taken out his frustration on a deflated leather football lying in the gutter. He'd kicked it against the rickety door of Mason's Yard where it landed with a heavy thud, rattled the padlock then rolled off down the street. 'Iris Grigg is as bad as her lousy, good-for-nothing son.'

Forced to accept defeat for the time being, they'd walked off the worst of their anger and arrived home to find that Lucia had already gone to bed.

'We won't let it drop – we'll try again tomorrow,' Tommy had murmured between soft kisses.

'Hush, don't talk about it now.' Joy had been relieved to shelve the problem for the night. What mattered most was that the anonymous note hadn't spoiled the affection between her and her sweetheart and their evening had ended in warm embraces and the usual goodnight kisses filled with love and longing.

'Well, as long as you're fine.' Mavis didn't sound convinced by Joy's declaration but went on her way with a cheery 'See you later', as Joy headed to the market for her spuds and carrots.

'Sorry, we're clean out of carrots,' Joe informed her when she put in her request.

The small square was packed with shoppers seeking bargains. Bartering was the order of the day for canny housewives struggling to feed their families on meagre rations, while a stall selling army-surplus overcoats seemed to do a roaring trade. 'That's just right for the winter,' the woman stallholder assured an elderly man trying on a double-breasted coat that was several sizes too big. 'You can wear a couple of jumpers under there and never feel the cold.'

'What about turnips?' Joy asked Joe.

'I've got plenty of them.' He jerked his thumb towards a dirt-encrusted heap. 'Choose a nice one and pop it in your bag. Since it's you, that'll be fourpence ha'penny for the lot.'

'Thanks, Joe.' She held out her bag to receive the loose potatoes. Then she fished in her purse for the coppers and counted them into his palm. 'I must dash. Will we see you later at the Tower?'

'If you're lucky,' he replied with a wink.

Joy turned quickly, only to bump slap bang into – of all people – Sam Grigg.

'Watch where you're going!' he croaked in a hoarse voice – the result of smoking too much and general self-neglect.

121

She stepped to one side, attempting to collect herself as Sam stuck out a crutch to obstruct her progress. He wore a nasty expression – eyes narrowed and lips curled into a sneer. 'Let me pass,' she demanded.

'What – too many airs and graces to say hello to an old pal?' Sam taunted. His frame had shrunk since the accident and he was skin and bones beneath a shabby overcoat. He was unshaven and wore his cap low over his forehead. 'That's a laugh, for a start.'

A few shoppers turned their heads out of idle curiosity. Aye, aye – Sam Grigg was busy stirring things up as usual.

'Not much to say for yourself without your Eyetie boyfriend to defend you, eh?'

The insult sent a hot flash of fury through Joy, burning through her customary reticence. 'That's not true,' she retorted. 'I have plenty to say off my own bat. In fact: everyone listen to me. I'm standing here, accusing this man of spreading nasty rumours about me and Tommy, none of which are true.'

'Take it easy.' Joe came out from behind his stall to place a restraining hand on Joy's shoulder. 'It's best not to tangle with the likes of him.'

'You hear that?' Sam invited onlookers to take his side. 'Joy Hebden might look like butter wouldn't melt but I know different – she's the hussy who's decided to shack up with an enemy alien, no less.'

Joy shook herself free from Joe's steadying hand. 'Tommy is no such thing. He was born in Blackpool and he's lived here all his life.'

'But his father's a rotten traitor, locked up on the Isle of Man for the duration. Stick that in your pipe!' Sam's resentment knew no bounds.

'Leave the girl alone,' someone muttered uneasily, while others fanned the flames.

'It's true – she's living at the Rossis' place.'

'She looks a decent sort but you can't always go by appearances.'

'You make me sick.' Fuelled by the drip-drip-drip of pent-up anger, Joy counter-attacked. 'Admit it, Sam – it was you who wrote that note.'

'What if it was? I never said anything in it that wasn't true.' He faced her head-on, the sneer continuing to contort his thin features.

'Yes you did – you told a bunch of lies because you want to spoil everything for other people, because your life has gone to pot and you're determined to pull everyone down to your level – that's why.' Joy's voice was strong as she had her say. 'I'm sorry about your accident; I truly am. But Tommy and I are doing nothing wrong and it's not fair to try to get your own back by telling lies.'

'She's right,' Joe said, this time putting his hand on Sam's shoulder.

'Get off me!' Sam pushed Joe away with his crutch then overbalanced against the stall, dislodging potatoes and sending them rolling across the cobbles. 'Bloody storm in a teacup – one little note, that's all.'

'Not very nice, though.' The woman selling army-surplus overcoats set off ripples of disapproval across the square.

'Look at the state of Sam Grigg – all washed up and nasty with it.'

'And you can't blame the girl for leaving his mother's boarding house. It's a cold, damp hole and Iris Grigg has the cheek to charge far more than the going rate.'

'I've never heard a bad word said about Joy Hebden. It's up to her where she chooses to live.'

Interest dissolved amidst dark remarks about Sam's drinking habits and the company he kept, while the man himself, sensing that he'd lost the argument, wiped the sneer from his face. 'Just you wait, Joy Hebden – I'm not done with you and your boyfriend; not by a long chalk.'

'Oh yes you are.' Joe came between the two of them. 'I for one will make sure that everyone knows what you've been up to. I have barman pals who work in pubs all along the Golden Mile – it won't be hard to get you banned from every single one of them, believe you me.'

'You wouldn't.' Sam gave a shifty laugh, realizing that Joe meant what he said.

'Try me.'

'All right, all right; you win.' What could he do but beat a retreat? 'It was only a bit of fun – nothing to get het up over.' Sam hobbled off in the direction of the Black Horse where a few beers would wash away the taste of defeat and then he would be ready to move on to his next target.

'You can't help but feel sorry for the bloke,' Joe commented as he stooped to retrieve stray spuds from beneath his stall. 'But bloody hell, Joy; what did *you* have for breakfast!'

Proud that she'd stood up for herself, she made an incoherent noise – something between a laugh and a sob. 'I've been desperate for Sam to admit what he did – and now, finally, he has. Honestly, I can't wait to tell Tommy the news.'

'Bloody well done.' Joe congratulated her as he took up position behind his stall once more. 'That took guts, Joy. I hope everything works out for you and Tommy – you deserve it.'

*

124

Eddie had followed through with his intention to join the first-aid branch of the Civil Defence team – either as a driver or in any other capacity. He'd applied and been accepted and was due to collect his uniform – dark blue battledress, greatcoat and beret – and to start his training the following week.

'It may be voluntary but it'll be no picnic,' Blackpool's controller had warned him at the Town Hall recruiting office. 'Your basic training will teach you how to deal with incendiaries and high explosives and you'll learn all about our anti-gas measures. This is obligatory for all passive defence sections. Afterwards there'll be specialist training in first aid, where the emphasis will be on teamwork. In the event of an incident, your team of first-aiders, ambulance drivers and stretcher bearers will be deployed by a coordinating officer who will report back to Central Control.' He'd handed Eddie a stack of handbooks issued by the local authority. 'Read the one called *Tactical Training for Wardens and Other Services* first.'

It had only been once Eddie got home that he'd taken on board the full seriousness of his new role. He'd learned from the handbook that he would be based in a North Blackpool first-aid post where he would take orders from a medical officer. When sent to an incident he would be issued with a helmet and a gas mask. His equipment would include a metal water bottle, haversack, dressings, rubber gloves, splints and scissors.

'Are you quite sure about this?' His concerned father had picked up one of the handbooks from the dining-room table. 'Blackpool might not be a major Luftwaffe target but a tip-and-run raid can occur at any time.'

'I'm well aware of the dangers, Dad.' Eddie had been

insistent. 'But I'll feel better about myself once I'm making a bigger contribution.'

Maurice Winter had presented a possible obstacle. 'What about this big dance competition in January?'

'I've already assured Lorna that the first-aid work won't interfere with my dancing – it'll only be two or three nights a week.'

'More importantly, are the Civil Defence people aware of your medical history?'

'You mean my asthma? Yes, Dad – they are. I convinced them that since I've had no serious attack in the last two years and I'm otherwise fit and healthy, I won't prove a liability.'

'Very good.' Maurice had reluctantly accepted his son's decision. 'As you wish.'

It was signed and sealed; Eddie would join Blackpool's Civil Defence team.

Now, as he headed towards the Queen's Arms to meet Mavis before they went on to the Tower, he felt confident that it was the right course of action. The role would give him the focus that he'd needed ever since he and Sylvia had broken off. Dancing without her left him feeling incomplete, like a gull with a broken wing, earthbound and no longer able to soar into a blue heaven. *Fool that I am, I let the girl of my dreams slip through my fingers.* Over and over he'd blamed himself for not fighting hard enough to keep her, until he'd realized the futility of such thoughts and had grown determined to move on.

As he entered the pub, he wondered why Mavis had suggested this early meeting. The lounge bar was crowded but he spotted her sitting at a table in a recess next to the fireplace and made his way across.

'You look nice,' he complimented her as he approached.

Her fair hair was swept back from her face and her cheeks were flushed from the warmth of the fire. Her sleeveless dress was dark pink with a paler pink corsage of felt flowers. A black jacket was draped across the back of her chair.

'Thanks. So do you.' Mavis couldn't help noticing the impact Eddie had made as he came in. Women's heads had turned in open admiration. Light brown wavy hair, pale grey eyes, broad shoulders and long legs were a winning combination in any girl's books.

'What would you like to drink?' he asked.

'Half a pint of shandy, please.' She watched with a knot in her stomach as Eddie ordered her beer and lemonade mix and a pint of bitter for himself at the bar then brought them back to the table. 'You're probably wondering why I asked to meet you here.'

He nodded and sat down opposite, glancing at the framed photograph above Mavis's head of Blackpool in its splendid Edwardian heyday, with women strolling along the prom in long dresses and enormous hats and men in striped blazers and straw boaters.

'The thing is, I thought I ought to give you fair warning . . .'

'About what?' Eddie picked up on her hesitation.

'After tonight you'll have to find a new dance partner,' she blurted out. 'I can't carry on dancing with you after all.'

'Good Lord above!' Eddie rocked back in his seat. 'Why ever not?'

'Because I can't afford to pay for lessons from Mrs Ellis, that's why not. And I can't let you pay for me every time we go to the Tower either. There, I've said it!'

Once he'd got over the initial shock, he slowly absorbed

the information. This required careful handling if he were to avoid offending her. 'I'm sorry to hear that. Might it be worth talking to Lorna before jumping ship?'

'What for?' Obviously a man like Eddie Winter didn't understand what it was like to be flat broke, so she must spell it out. 'My dad's out of work now and Mum will need most of my wage to help keep a roof over our heads. I'm sorry, that's just the way it is.'

'But if you were to point out that our success in January's competition will be good for the academy – that it will improve Lorna's reputation and bring in new pupils – then I'm sure an agreement could be reached.'

'Maybe.' This hadn't crossed Mavis's mind. 'But that still leaves me strapped for cash for dance shoes and dresses, not to mention practising with you at the Tower. And no, before you offer, I'm not happy about you paying for me every time. It means I'm not a free agent.'

'To dance with other people?' Eddie's eyebrows shot up for a second time.

'Yes, don't look so surprised. Sometimes I like to go off with my pals and have a lark. And sometimes I want to make new friends.'

'But I thought . . .'

'You thought I'd set my cap at you.' Mavis enjoyed his obvious embarrassment. 'So did a certain other person, mentioning no names.'

He swerved the oblique reference to Sylvia. 'No, I thought you'd set your sights on us winning the big competition. Was I wrong?'

'That would've been nice,' she admitted. 'A shiny cup to go next to my netball trophies.'

'So can't you swallow your pride for a few more weeks?' Eddie's powers of persuasion came into play. 'Let me talk to Lorna about payment for the classes – I'm sure I can make headway there. As for my buying your admission ticket at the Tower, don't you see that it's in my interest as much as yours?'

Mavis wrinkled her nose. 'I suppose so. But money's not the only thing. It's this blooming war – no, not the blackouts and the rationing; we all have to put up with that, worse luck. My cousin Bobby is in the Merchant Navy. We've just heard that his convoy was attacked out in the Atlantic and his ship went down. They've reported him missing. My Aunty Beryl's beside herself with worry. Mum wants me to go and stay with her – I don't know how long for.'

The blows fell one after another and this one was more difficult for Eddie to solve. 'Where does your aunt live?'

'In Llandudno. It's miles away. I haven't said yes yet, but I'll most likely have to.'

So there was no way around this one. He frowned and admitted defeat. 'I'm disappointed, of course – but if your family needs you . . .'

'Unless a miracle happens and Bobby turns up out of the blue.'

Mavis's sudden switch to childlike optimism made Eddie reach out and take her hand. It felt smooth and warm to his touch. 'There's always hope,' he murmured. 'I'm sorry for what you and your family are going through.'

Tears sprang out of nowhere. 'Mum, Dad and me used to go to Llandudno for our holidays when I was a kid. Me and Bobby played on the beach together, building sand-castles and paddling in the sea. Aunty Beryl gave us slices of apple dipped in sugar as a bedtime treat.'

Eddie squeezed her hand and tried to reassure her. 'Perhaps your cousin has been picked up by a foreign vessel; that happens sometimes. And in such cases it can take a while for the information to filter through.'

'Let's hope so.' Mavis used her free hand to brush away the tears then she pulled herself together and reached for her jacket. 'In any case, let's stick with tonight's plan and give it all we've got,' she resolved with a brave smile. 'This could well be our swansong, but Tower Ballroom, here we come!'

CHAPTER NINE

Joy idled away some time by examining more of the dazzling sapphire, gold and crimson mosaics that decorated the corridor outside Tommy's dressing room. She tilted her head to study the intricate plasterwork of the ceiling – complicated geometric designs combined with flowers and leaves – then lowered it to examine an Illuminations poster from pre-war days. *Brilliant Blackpool*, she read. Scarlet letters stood out against a glowing sunset. *Where the Full Summer Programme merges into a blaze of Autumn Glory*. Not any more, thanks to Herr Hitler.

There was still no sign of Tommy. With an impatient sigh, Joy walked a little way along the corridor to watch the circus finale. A dozen fountains rose high in the air, sparkling under the spotlights and cascading down around the lithe bodies of Irena and Alina; the two Polish girls were dressed in silver leotards, performing acrobatic feats on a podium in the centre of the ring.

All lions and tigers were safely back in their subterranean cages after their matinee performance. Vic Marsden, the elephant trainer, was down there too: dosing his animals with their daily cod liver oil before taking them out for their early-evening stroll along the beach. In kennels close by, Cavalini's Canine Comedians were taking a well-earned rest. But still no Tommy!

The clowns' dressing-room door opened and two of his fellow performers emerged in civilian clothes. Ted Mackie was small and thin while Leo Court was tall and fat – the Laurel and Hardy of the circus world, down to Ted's gormless stare and Leo's bristling black moustache.

Spying Joy, Ted offered to go back and put a rocket under Tommy for her but she said no, she was happy to wait.

'He doesn't know I'm here,' she explained. 'I want it to be a surprise.'

'A very tasty one too.' Ted winked as he darted by.

'Tommy won't be long,' Leo assured her against the sounds of splashing fountains and ripples of audience applause. 'Lucky devil – I hear he's got the night off to trip the light fantastic with you?'

'He has,' Joy confirmed.

'Well, I hardly recognized you in your glad rags.' Leo progressed along the corridor at a stately pace. 'Like I said, Tommy's a lucky so-and-so.'

She glanced down self-consciously at her 'glad rags' – a cream brocade dress nipped in at the waist with a peplum bodice over a mid-calf-length skirt. She'd finished it off with a double string of pearls borrowed from Sylvia and a spray of cream silk flowers pinned into her loose, dark locks. How was it that time limped along when you least wanted it to? *Come along, Tommy!*

'At last!' she cried when he finally appeared.

'Blimey, Joy – what are you doing here?' He'd taken his time getting ready because tonight was special. He'd put on a clean white shirt and a dark suit and he'd polished his shoes. Dark blue tie or the grey one with a thin red stripe? He'd held up both to his reflection in the mirror and chosen the former. 'I thought we'd agreed to meet at the main entrance.'

'We did.' Her brown eyes sparkled with excitement. 'I have some surprising news,' she teased.

Tommy patted his jacket pocket to feel for the small, square box that he intended to save for later. 'I like surprises,' he said as they walked hand in hand along the corridor then down the stairs into the entrance foyer, where a queue for the ballroom had already begun to form. 'So go ahead: shoot.'

'I went to the market for spuds after I finished my shift.'

'Fancy that.' Joy was obviously building up to something significant but he couldn't work out what. 'Was it busy?'

'Quite busy. Guess who I bumped into.'

'Let me think: Joan Crawford, Laurence Olivier, Mickey Mouse . . . ?'

'Don't be silly.' She tugged at his hand. 'It was Sam Grigg.'

Tommy stopped dead in his tracks. 'Seriously?'

'Yes, seriously. Oh Tommy, you would've been proud of me – I decided to have it out with him right there in the market in front of Joe and dozens of others. I accused Sam of writing the note – face to face and I didn't care who heard. He didn't deny it. And boy, did he make my blood boil when he called you an enemy alien. That was the final straw; I soon put him straight on that one.'

'Good heavens, Joy.' Tommy grasped both of her hands. He pictured her during the public stand-off: fierce and proud, unafraid to speak the truth. And he loved her more than ever for it. 'Then what?'

'I accused him of wanting to drag me and you down into the dirt for no good reason.'

He sat her down on a padded bench beneath one of the fan-shaped windows to allow her to catch her breath. 'And then?'

'Then I made it clear that not a single word of what he said in the note was true. Joe took my side, thank goodness, and other people joined in as well. They all believed me, not Sam. In the end he was forced to admit what he'd done then slink off with his tail between his legs.'

'Stop – breathe!' Tommy had never seen Joy so animated. 'So where does that leave us – you and me?'

'In the clear!' she exclaimed with a soaring sense of relief. 'Honestly, Tommy; I can't explain how it feels to know that no one will be whispering behind our backs from now on.'

'And we're free to announce our engagement?' His heart beat fast as he slipped his hand into his pocket and curled his fingers around the precious box. *Deep breath. Wait for her to agree.*

'Yes!' she cried.

Eureka! 'When?'

'There's no time like the present.' Aware that Sylvia and Pearl would be waiting for them outside the entrance, Joy jumped to her feet.

'No, wait.' Tommy caught hold of her hand and sat her down again. 'I was going to save this until after the dance but it turns out that now is as good a time as any.'

Trembling with anticipation, Joy watched him take a small, square object from his pocket. He placed it in her palm: a dark blue box with a small hinge, with the words 'Hartley's Jewellers' printed in gold.

'Aren't you going to open it?'

'It's a ring,' she murmured, scarcely able to breathe.

'I promised I'd buy you one.' Now that it came to it,

Tommy was suddenly a bag of nerves. What if Joy didn't like the ring? What if he'd chosen the wrong stones, the wrong size, the wrong moment, the wrong everything? 'I can always take it back to Hartley's if it's not right.'

'A ring,' she repeated as she lifted the lid and peered inside.

It was an oval sapphire surrounded by tiny diamonds, set in gold. The stones sparkled in the light cast by the chandelier above their heads.

'Do you like it? I thought blue was your colour,' he ventured.

'Like it? I love it!' Her heartbeat quickened as Tommy took the ring from its box and slid it on to her finger. She raised her hand and studied it from all angles. 'It's perfect.' The delicate stones shone bright as their smiles, bright as the future that had suddenly opened up for them.

The ring made it official – Tommy and Joy were engaged. 'Now can we go and tell the others?' he demanded.

'Where on earth has Joy got to?' Pearl stood with Sylvia outside the main entrance to the Tower. They'd arrived at the same time and had expected their punctual friend to join them soon after. 'She's never late – I hope nothing bad has happened.'

'Brrr! I wish she'd hurry up.' Sylvia wasn't dressed for a late November night – why break the habit of a lifetime? A short black evening jacket over a low-necked pale green chiffon gown offered little protection against the biting wind or the light drizzle that had begun to fall.

'Vanity, vanity,' Pearl teased, stamping her feet in an attempt to keep warm. 'I bet you're not wearing a vest.'

'A vest?' Sylvia pretended to be appalled as she and Pearl huddled under the glass canopy.

A tram stopped nearby and disgorged its passengers, all of whom headed straight for the entrance where Sylvia and Pearl sheltered.

'Hello, you two.' Ruby appeared out of the darkness in a cloud of perfume, high heels clicking, taffeta skirt rustling. 'You'll catch your deaths out here if you're not careful.'

'We're waiting for Joy,' Pearl explained through chattering teeth.

'Rather you than me,' Ruby commented as she swept by.

'You go in with Ruby. I'll wait here.' Pearl took pity on a shivering Sylvia.

'No; Joy will be here any minute. We'll wait together.'

More people streamed towards them, including a group of GIs in uniform, jostling and talking at the tops of their voices, taking up most of the pavement as they approached the Tower building.

'Gee, gals; why not come in out of the cold with us?' An American voice invited Pearl and Sylvia to join their gang. 'C'mon – let's have some fun.'

'No thanks – we're waiting for our friend,' Sylvia answered.

'Evenin', Miss Pearl.' Errol Jackson brought up the rear of the group. He tipped his cap respectfully then walked on by.

Before Pearl had time to react, Sylvia caught sight of two figures inside the building, going against the flow and having to push their way through the group of GIs to reach the entrance. 'For heaven's sake, Joy's already here!' she exclaimed with a touch of irritation. 'She's been in there with Tommy all along.'

Pearl followed Sylvia in out of the cold and waited for Tommy and Joy to reach them. She could tell that something was afoot, to judge by the elated smiles on their faces.

'What happened to our arrangement?' Sylvia demanded crossly.

Instead of replying, Joy held up her hand to display her new ring while Tommy hung back to allow Joy her moment.

There was a split second's pause before Pearl and Sylvia flung themselves at Joy. They hugged and smiled gleefully then hugged again.

'About time!' Sylvia beamed at Tommy. 'What took you so long?'

'When's the big day?' Pearl demanded details while all around them a continuous stream of people joined the queue for the ballroom.

'We haven't decided,' Tommy explained. 'I only proposed a few days ago.'

'A few days!' Sylvia echoed before turning to Joy. 'And you kept it from us?'

'It's true, I did.' Joy blushed. 'But now it's official.'

'Time to celebrate – let's take our place in the queue.' Pearl herded them across the vast entrance hall. Ahead of them were the Yanks, loud and flirtatious as ever, determined to make the most of their night on the town. 'Ruby, did you know that Joy and Tommy are engaged?' she called over the heads of the GIs.

'Yippee!' Ruby raised her hands above her head and clapped loudly. Then she passed the news to Mavis, who stood near the head of the queue with Eddie. 'Joy's beaten you to it,' she joked. 'She's only gone and got herself engaged.'

'Tell her congratulations from me.' Mavis ignored Ruby's jibe and smiled apologetically at Eddie. They shuffled forward towards the ticket booths.

'Yeah, congratulations!' The GIs added their voices and soon Tommy and Joy were the centre of attention.

'Say, you're one lucky guy!'

'He sure looks like the cat that got the cream.'

'So he should – she's real cute.'

Normally Joy would have wished for the ground to swallow her up, but tonight she rode high on a wave of excitement. She kept staring at her sparkling sapphire ring then at Tommy, who was beaming fit to burst.

'Get spliced as soon as you can,' Pearl enthused. 'Take it from one who speaks from experience.'

'Yes, why wait?' Sylvia agreed. 'You can do it before Christmas if you get a move on.'

'And Sylvia and I can be your maids of honour. You know us; we can run up the dresses on our sewing machines in no time.'

'Whoa!' Tommy held up his hands. 'We haven't even told my mother yet.'

'Then there are all the arrangements,' Joy reminded them. 'The church, the vicar, the licence, the invitations . . .'

'What licence? What invitations?' Cliff asked. He and Terry had joined the end of the queue and picked up on their friends' excitement.

Pearl beckoned for the two men to join them. 'You don't mind, do you?' she checked with the couple standing immediately behind. 'Hot off the press – there's going to be another wedding,' she explained to the newcomers. 'Lord knows, it's like standing at a bus stop – you wait for ages and then two come along together.'

'Congratulations!' Cliff shook hands with Tommy then planted an affectionate kiss on Joy's cheek. 'Here's to a long and happy marriage.'

'With lots of kids.' Terry too shook hands with the

groom-to-be. He seemed distracted and ill at ease, keeping a distance from Cliff as the queue moved slowly forward.

'Hold your horses, everyone – we haven't got a date yet.' Tommy was still coming to terms with the fact that Joy had agreed to announce their engagement to the world. 'We'll want to do it properly so I doubt it can happen that quickly.'

'At least you won't be called up.' Sylvia bit her tongue; it was a crass comment, given that Pearl was standing right next to her. 'So you can afford to take your time if you want to,' she added apologetically.

Finally they reached the front of the queue. Their money was taken and tickets issued.

'The drinks are on me,' Cliff volunteered as he took off his coat and he and Terry headed for the cloakroom. 'Come and find us at the bar.'

Joy and Tommy entered the ballroom with their arms around each other's waist. There they were surrounded by Ruby and Joy's cleaning pals, including Mavis – all rushing to add their congratulations.

'Tommy's a lovely lad,' Ruby assured Joy. 'A real family man.'

'I am here, you know,' an embarrassed Tommy pointed out.

'Yes and I've known you since you were knee high to a grasshopper and no one's ever said a bad word about you.'

'I love a good wedding,' Mavis enthused. 'Make sure you send me an invitation if I'm still around.'

Sylvia stood close by. 'Why would you not be around?' she asked with a puzzled frown.

'No reason.' Mavis batted away the question then rejoined Eddie at the far end of the bar.

Soon after, Pearl spotted Cliff. Spirits were high as her group joined him.

'So what would everyone like to drink?' he asked.

Beer for Tommy, sweet martini for Pearl – 'Make it a large one' – orange juice for Joy and Sylvia. Everyone put in their request then Sylvia stayed with Cliff to help order the drinks.

'Where's Terry got to?' she wanted to know.

'Sulking,' Cliff told her in a disgruntled tone.

'What about?'

'Search me – he went off in a huff; that's all I know.'

No more was said. The crimson curtains opened and the footlights lit up the stage with its sunny Mediterranean backdrop of blue sea and sky. The Wurlitzer rose from under the stage with Reginald Dixon at the keyboard. After his breezy signature tune, he began the evening with the popular Silvester number 'You're Dancing On My Heart': a snappy quickstep that soon filled the ballroom floor with excited couples while Joy and Tommy's crowd stayed drinking at the bar. After two Martinis, Pearl confessed to feeling distinctly squiffy but accepted a third from Terry, who had reappeared and seemed to be in a better mood.

'Polish off your drink then we'll show everyone how it's done,' he promised Pearl as the strains of a tango filled the hall and many less experienced couples drifted towards the bar, leaving space for the experts to show off their skill.

'What do you say – shall we give it a go?' Tommy held out his hand to Joy. 'After that, we could call it a night and go home to share our news with Mum.'

'Done!' She accepted gladly. Lucia would be thrilled – Joy couldn't wait to see her reaction. 'Just this one dance.' They joined Pearl and Terry and fifty other couples, all flinging themselves into the clipped, staccato moves of the passionate Argentinian dance.

'Shall we?' Cliff asked Sylvia. The music charged on as they took to the floor in close hold. Swish, swish; Cliff brushed his right foot between Sylvia's legs. Their knees touched then they sidestepped, rocked and turned in perfect synchronicity.

'I'm sorry that you and Terry aren't getting along.' Sylvia's concern was genuine.

'Thanks, but I prefer not to talk about it right now.' Cliff led her into a gliding promenade, all the while keeping contact at the hips.

'Right you are,' she murmured. Out of the side of her vision she noticed that Terry had guided Pearl towards a table under the balcony. Pearl looked unsteady on her feet and seemed glad to sit out the rest of the dance. Putting the disconcerting picture out of her mind, Sylvia suggested a heart-to-heart with Cliff once this dance was over.

'How many have you had?' Terry asked Pearl once he'd sat her down. 'Never mind; stay here while I fetch you a glass of water.' He cut back across the dance floor towards the bar.

'One too many?' Sylvia enquired over her shoulder as she and Cliff promenaded in tango prowl close to where Pearl sat.

'Don't worry – I'm fine.' A little dizzy, it was true, but to Pearl the evening seemed to be going swimmingly. Colours appeared more vivid and the chandeliers sparkled more brightly than ever. The harp-playing maidens depicted in the fresco high above her head seemed to sway in time to the music.

'Care to?' The GI asking the abbreviated question didn't wait for an answer but pulled Pearl to her feet and whooshed her on to the dance floor. He was bold and brash, smiling and handsome, completely sure of himself as the music changed from tango to loud, lively jive.

'The name's Charlie,' he informed Pearl in a nasal New York twang. 'Everyone calls me Chuck.'

'Hello, Chuck. I'm Pearl.' She found herself manoeuvred into a tight space close to the stage where her toes were trodden on by a group of enthusiastic local boys in search of partners. The clumsy idiots barged and pushed her off balance and she was caught and set upright by her new partner.

'You OK?' he asked as they found a quieter space.

'I'm a bit dizzy,' she confessed.

'No problem – I'll take good care of you.' Her partner seemed sincere as he waited for her to compose herself.

Pearl tucked her blouse more securely into the waistband of her skirt. 'Tell me your name again.'

'Chuck.'

'All right, Chuck – I'm all yours.'

She soon discovered that her Yank was an accomplished mover – of course he was; the jive was their dance, after all. Why, she'd seen American youngsters on Pathé newsreels, leapfrogging and somersaulting, pecking and kicking to kingdom come. Chuck swung her out then back in, rocked her and twirled her, all the while bouncing and sidestepping in time to the music. She followed where he led, glad that she was wearing a short, full skirt that allowed freedom of movement. Shimmy shimmy; she shook her shoulders and flapped her arms with abandon. Chuck grabbed her hand and swung her to arm's length and back; once, twice, three times, then pulled her to him and lifted her clean off her feet as he whirled her round.

'If you don't mind . . .' Terry reappeared out of nowhere, tapping her GI on the shoulder in a no-nonsense way then taking her by the hand. 'Pearl is with me.'

Instinctively Chuck squared up to Terry then thought better of it. Instead, he gave him the once-over, taking in his stylishly cut hair, open-necked shirt and blue cravat, then shoved his hands in his pockets and took a couple of steps back, continuing to glare at Terry. The MC for the night stood at the edge of the stage, keeping a close eye on the GI as he retreated.

'Spoilsport,' Pearl complained as Terry led her back to the table. 'I was enjoying that.'

'A bit too much, perhaps,' Terry commented as he pushed a glass of water towards her.

Pearl giggled. 'What's the matter – can't a girl have fun?'

'Of course she can,' Terry agreed. As the jive finished and a sedate waltz began, he noticed that a group of the GIs had gathered in a huddle by the exit. They were exchanging cigarettes and raucous remarks as they waved at a bunch of girls waiting to be asked to dance. The girls waved back and several of the Americans moved in on them. Pearl's erstwhile partner remained in the doorway with two others.

'How often will I get a chance to dance the jive with an expert now that Bernie's not around?' Pearl pouted. 'I wasn't doing anything wrong, was I?'

'Not a thing,' Terry acknowledged. 'It wasn't you I was worried about. I didn't like the look of your partner, that's all.' The chap had had his hands all over Pearl and had been flinging her about like there was no tomorrow. A couple of times Pearl had lost her balance and her timing had been off. And now he became aware that the three Yanks by the exit had decided to head their way, obviously intent on causing trouble. 'Come on; let's get out of here,' Terry suggested hastily.

'What for? Where to?' Pearl was slow to react and by the time she'd got to her feet, Chuck and his pals had surrounded their table.

'What do you want?' Terry stood his ground.

'Nothin'.' Chuck scarcely moved his lips when he replied. 'Just checkin'.'

'Checking what?'

'That the little lady was OK with you haulin' her off the dance floor.' Flanked by his friends, Chuck straddled the nearest chair then spoke directly to Pearl. 'Sorry to state the obvious, honey – you'll have a whole lot more fun with me tonight than you will with him.'

The underhand insult tore through Terry's already strained patience. 'You take that back!' He shoved at the table, upskittling the glass of water that spilled over his trousers and Pearl's skirt. Pearl gave a high-pitched shriek then shot to her feet to examine the damage.

The shriek attracted the attention of the MC, who purposefully fixed his microphone to its stand then came down the steps at the side of the stage.

'Gee!' Chuck gave a hoarse laugh before leaning over to stroke Terry's sleeve. 'You're a little touchy, ain't ya, darlin'?'

'Don't do that!' Terry pushed his hand away.

His friends thought this the height of hilarity. One dug Chuck's side with his elbow while the second doubled up with laughter. 'Yeah; he sure is touchy!' they echoed.

That was it; Terry took a wild swing at the nearest soldier. He missed then took a second swing: this time at Chuck who neatly sidestepped. Again Terry's fist met thin air.

'Stop it, for goodness' sake!' Pearl's befuddled brain couldn't make out why they were fighting. Now fists were flying in all directions and chairs and tables were being pushed over, glasses broken and voices raised. It was an out and out brawl.

The MC called for help from two brawny doormen whose job it was to keep order. Reggie Dixon kept on playing his waltz and couples whirled on through the fisti-cuffs – a common enough occurrence when men fought over dance partners and good behaviour went out of the window.

Crunch! Terry was socked on the jaw but sprang right back, grabbing one of his opponents by the tie and yanking hard. A doorman wrestled Chuck to the ground, knelt on his chest and held him there. That left two against one; a fight that Terry was sure he could win. He went in again with fists flying until the second doorman separated them and Cliff put in a belated appearance.

Seeing how out of control Terry was, he immediately took charge. 'That's enough. Terry, calm down.'

Still only dimly aware of what had happened, Pearl sank down on a chair and, with a creeping, hot sense of shame, bent forward to hide her face in her lap.

Terry raised his hands in surrender while the doormen herded the three sheepish GIs towards the exit. There would be trouble with their platoon commander if news of this incident got through. Straightening their ties and mustering what was left of their dignity, they agreed to leave the building.

'Really?' Cliff demanded of Terry after assuring the MC that he had everything under control. 'I mean, really?' He spread his hands in a gesture of disbelief.

'Don't start,' Terry retorted. His jaw felt tender – there

might be bruises that he would have to conceal when he went to his next rehearsal. 'You weren't here to witness what went on – I was provoked.'

Cliff turned to Pearl. 'Was he?'

'I have no idea. What's going on?' she wailed and shook her head. Her earlier feeling of elation had plummeted; all she could do was sit helplessly and watch her friends argue.

'Did you have to make such a display of yourself?' Cliff demanded.

'Oh, come off it, Cliff. You're talking out of your backside – I was sticking up for Pearl, that's all.'

'I don't care – your behaviour was unacceptable. Everyone was staring at you, for God's sake!'

Terry whirled round to face Pearl. 'Tell him!' he implored.

Once more she shook her head in bewilderment.

'Do you realize what this does to our good name?' Cliff challenged. He tingled with anger over the shameful display.

'Is that all you care about?' Terry retaliated. *Bloody Cliff and his good name!*

'Yes – it's taken me months to build it up. You know perfectly well how hard I've had to work since you and I got together. And now look.'

Back on stage, the MC took to his microphone to announce a break. After the interval there would be a foxtrot competition; all-comers were welcome. The floor emptied and queues formed at the bar.

'We got together, as you call it, because we both felt the same way – or so I thought.' Terry's anger made him blind to the small group of fascinated onlookers who had stayed to witness the lovers' tiff. Two men arguing

146

in public about their private lives wasn't something you came across every day. At this rate, the dodgy pair could get themselves arrested.

'Now I'm not so sure,' Terry went on rashly.

'Me neither,' Cliff fumed. 'It certainly seems I can't trust you not to draw attention to us in the worst possible way. So where does that leave us?'

'Nowhere!' Terry too had reached the end of his tether. 'If you really don't trust me, it leaves us with nowhere to go and nothing to build on. Well?'

'How can I trust you? I hardly ever see you these days.' Suddenly Cliff sounded deflated, defeated, broken. With doubt and suspicion mounting ever since Terry started rehearsing for *Sleeping Beauty*, there was no fight left in him.

'All right then; I'm off!' That was it; with a final angry flourish Terry made his decision. 'There's no point trying to change my mind. First thing tomorrow I pack my bags and leave.'

CHAPTER TEN

After the argument between Cliff and Terry, Pearl's head ached and her senses were dulled. She looked around for Joy and Sylvia but soon gave up on them and left the ballroom, desperate to step out on to the promenade for a breath of fresh air. The darkness was thick and cold – heavy cloud obscured both moon and stars. Invisible waves swirled around the legs of the pier and broke on the shore.

Unluckily for Pearl, Chuck and his two friends were skulking in the side alley leading to the market square. Their evening of fun had turned sour and now they must hang around in the cold and the dark until the platoon bus arrived at midnight to ferry them back to base.

'This place is a dump.' Chuck swivelled his foot over a spent cigarette. His shoulders were hunched and his hands shoved deep into his trouser pockets.

'Yeah; give me Vegas any day,' one friend agreed.

'Give me anywhere but here,' the other added.

There was general agreement before Chuck spotted Pearl walking unsteadily towards them and his interest was suddenly piqued. 'Look who it isn't!' he breathed before stepping out in front of her. 'Say, honey, where you headin'?'

'Home,' she replied. It was too dark for her to make out who was speaking but her instinct for self-preservation kicked in and she marched on past the trio towards the square.

The taller of Chuck's friends soon caught up with her. 'Hey, why so fast?'

'Yeah, the night is young.' Chuck ran ahead, walking backwards as he propositioned her. 'There must be somewhere for a guy to get a drink around here. Come on, Miss Pearl – name your poison.'

'Oh, it's you.' Recognizing him, Pearl relaxed and her pace slowed. 'Listen, I don't want any more to drink but I know a pub on Empire Street. I'm heading that way so I can point you in the right direction.'

'That's real friendly, ain't it?' The third man, not tall but heavily built, came alongside and slid an arm around her waist.

The smell of beer and tobacco on his breath made Pearl pull away but then she lost her balance and tottered forward. Chuck caught her and patted the top of her head as if she were a pet dog before linking arms with her. 'Steady, Miss Pearl. There, that's better. Walk with me, left-right, left-right.'

'Please don't – leave me alone,' she protested. The shadows grew darker as they crossed the square then entered the narrow street where she lived. All was silent except for a wind that whistled between chimney pots and rattled the lids of the metal dustbins lining the pavements. All doors were closed, all blackout blinds firmly pulled down.

'Like it or not, you're my gal for the night.' Chuck kept tight hold as he took in their surroundings, noticing a hardware store to one side of the street, opposite the arched entrance of a tradesman's premises. A stack of leaking sandbags barricaded the wide doors and he read a faded sign over the arch that told him that the derelict site had once been a stable yard.

'Let go of me.' Pearl struggled to free herself without success. 'I just want to go home.'

'You hear that? She wants to go home!' The dark-haired GI's mocking echo made the others smirk.

'Not yet, Miss Pearl.' Chuck's emphasis was on the 'Miss' and it was loaded with cruel sarcasm. His grip tightened again as he steered her towards Mason's yard. 'How about you and me get a whole lot more friendly, huh?'

The wind cut through her. Her head cleared a little and for the first time she recognized the danger she was in. *Fool!* She ought to have seen the warning flag before now. Should she put up a fight or pretend to give in? She decided that her chances were better if she agreed to go with them to the Black Horse after all. 'All right, you win; I'll have that drink with you.'

But Chuck's intentions had changed. 'Stay here. Keep a lookout,' he ordered his companions as he crossed the street with Pearl. He pushed her against the sandbags and wrenched at the padlock on the doors, intending to take her into the yard and out of sight. It was locked, but never mind; this wouldn't take long. It could happen in the open – he didn't care.

Alarm shot through Pearl's body. She could talk herself out of most situations but at this moment, as Chuck pushed himself up against her, words failed her. His handsome face took on a callous, mean look; this was an act that he would carry through to its conclusion whether she liked it or not.

Pearl was a girl with plenty of spirit; it was what had

made her stand out from the gaggle of eager local girls when he'd first set eyes on her. That and her short dark hair and, boy, those wide-apart, heavily lashed green eyes were quite something. But she was small and slight – no match for Chuck. Using his strength to quickly overpower her, he shoved her against the sandbag barrier then thrust his hands under her jacket: one against her throat, the other over her small, firm breast. Let her writhe and resist all she liked – he would go ahead with this regardless.

Pearl felt the pile of sandbags collapse beneath her. She reached out and caught hold of the heavy padlock to heave herself upright.

'Stay still, dammit!' Her flesh was warm and soft. He pressed his fingers harder against her throat.

She could scarcely breathe. With his free hand he ripped her blouse. Her own hands flew to her breasts to defend herself but he shoved her to the ground and stood astride her. Then he dropped to his knees and she felt the full weight of his body on top of her. The pavement was wet and slimy beneath her.

'Chuck!' A warning voice distracted him.

Pearl seized her chance. She shoved her attacker off balance and wriggled out from underneath him. Then she brought both knees to her chest and kicked out as hard as she could.

'Chuck, we gotta get out of here!' Panic had set in.

Too late. Footsteps approached. 'Stay right there, boys. I got your number.'

'No, no, no!' Pearl kicked again and again, grunting each time her foot made contact. She caught Chuck where it hurt. He bent double, clutching his groin.

'Stand up, Private Sanderson. You hear me; stand to

151

attention!' Sergeant Errol Jackson hauled the soldier to his feet. 'Don't move a muscle.'

Across the street, Sanderson's two accomplices fled the scene.

Thank God; it was over. Pearl closed her eyes and lay still for a few seconds until a hand gently raised her. When she opened her eyes she pulled her jacket across her exposed breasts and let out a long, shuddering breath.

'OK, I gotcha.' Errol had come between her and Chuck, who stood nearby, arms clamped to his sides, eyes rolling, teeth gritted, breathing heavily. 'He won't hurt you now.'

'Oh!' she sighed, shaking her head and sobbing with relief.

'You.' Errol addressed his subordinate in a clipped, severe tone that brooked no argument. 'Get your ass straight back to base; I don't care how. I'll deal with you later.'

Chuck's eyelids flickered shut. 'Yessir!' Caught red handed, he departed without a backwards glance.

'He won't get away with this,' Errol assured Pearl as Sanderson's cowed figure was swallowed by the looming shadow cast by the Tower.

'How did you know . . . ?' She struggled to pull together the threads and make sense of what had just happened.

'I saw the way the three of them acted, back in the ballroom. When they were thrown out they were still lookin' for a fight. That's the reason I kept them in my sights.'

'What will happen to them now?'

Errol's voice was calm and steady. 'We have a procedure to deal with violation of discipline. We act on a case-by-case basis. What Sanderson did constitutes a pretty serious offence, in my view.'

'What does that mean?'

'This ain't the first time he's been in trouble. We'll throw the book at him.'

The sensation of a strong hand throttling her, of being mauled and thrown to the ground lingered. She remembered with dread the feeling of her attacker's weight as he'd dropped down on her. 'Yes, he deserves it,' she murmured.

'I'm sure glad I got here in time.' Errol observed the dark look of shock in Pearl's eyes. He kept a respectful distance. 'You're pretty shaken up. Is there anythin' I can do?'

'No – thanks; I'm fine.'

'You're not fine. Let me walk you home.' He looked up and down the street, noting a sliver of light fall across the pavement as customers emerged from the Black Horse.

Pearl nodded her agreement. Her legs felt weak and the sense of her skin crawling with disgust threatened to overwhelm her. 'It's not far,' she whispered.

Errol dipped his head in acknowledgement, adjusting to her slow pace as she set off. 'I'll keep you informed about Sanderson's punishment,' he promised. 'If you want me to do that.'

She nodded. 'Yes, but I'd rather not be dragged in.' No one need know about this: not her family, not her friends and especially not Bernie. God forbid if news of the attack filtered through to him. 'I'm sorry.' She glanced sideways at Errol's profile and saw no reaction. Looking straight ahead, with his arms behind his back, he walked steadily along.

'Sure thing,' he said quietly. 'I'll keep your name out of it if I can.'

Every single thing about this man was solid, measured

and reliable. They reached the door to number six and Pearl thanked him again.

'You're sure you're OK now?'

'Yes; thanks to you.' Hoping that she could slip inside the house without being noticed, she took her key from her pocket. 'Dad will still be in the pub and with luck the others will already be in bed.'

'Ma'am.' Errol took a step back and watched her mount two worn stone steps before inserting the key in the lock.

She opened the door then turned to take one last look.

'Miss Pearl, I hope you know we're not all like Private Sanderson,' he assured her – upright, open and sincere. 'Some of us were brought up right.'

'I know it,' she replied. 'Thank you and goodnight.'

'Goodnight, ma'am.'

Taking a deep, juddering breath, Pearl stepped into the silent house.

An unexploded sea mine had been discovered on the beach at Fleetwood. Joy read about the latest local emergency in the *Gazette* as Lucia cooked up a storm. Onions were rapidly chopped, tinned tomatoes heated, a clove of garlic, grown in Lucia's allotment, was added to the pan. Stir well, bring to the boil then simmer on a low heat to reduce the mixture.

Joy switched her attention to the adverts. Zubes were apparently the best cure for coughs and Aspro should be taken for colds and flu. A cup of Rowntree's Cocoa was guaranteed to provide extra energy during the short, cold winter days.

'You taste, *carissima*.' Lucia offered her a spoonful of sauce from the pan. 'Is good?'

'Very good.' Joy saw that it was time to pull down the

blackout blind. 'The nights are really drawing in,' she said with a sigh as she completed the task then returned to her newspaper. 'Are you sure I can't help?' she checked.

'Sit!' Lucia wielded her wooden spoon like a conductor's baton. 'You and my Tommy work all day. Now I feed you.'

Steam rose from the pan and the smell was delicious. A fire in the old-fashioned range heated the room. What could be cosier? Soon Tommy would be home and the three of them would sit down at the table to eat a meal of spaghetti Bolognese.

Joy read that a pedestrian had been run over by a bus and killed during the blackout. It had been raining and visibility had been poor. Joy scanned more headlines. One article in particular drew her attention: apparently a pair of bloodstained gloves had provided vital evidence of a violent attack and robbery. A Canadian gunner based at Squires Gate had been arrested and charged.

She pushed the paper to one side. The week had flown by and there had been no repercussions following her confrontation with Sam Grigg. Joy had gone about her business with a lighter heart and a sparkling sapphire ring on her finger. Everyone she worked with and for had congratulated her and wished her well. When she and Tommy had broken the news to Lucia, Tommy's mother had covered her face with her apron and cried loud, happy tears.

'*Eccellente! Eccellentissimo!*' Breathless hugs had followed and rapid words in a mixture of Italian and English had poured from Lucia's lips. She would write a letter to her other dear Tommaso, forced to stay in a prisoner-of-war camp on a cold island, far away. Tommy's father would be happy, so happy. Of course it broke Lucia's heart that he would miss the wedding but she would write another letter describing every detail.

'Soon you will marry. But when?' had been the pressing question.

'Joy doesn't want to rush things,' Tommy had explained. 'You know what she's like: everything has to be perfect.'

'*Sì, sì, ma quando?*' Lucia had grasped Joy's hands and implored her to name a day.

'Perhaps in May?' Joy's dream was of a spring wedding, with blue skies and pink blossom in the trees – new life all around. Her dress would be white, of course. She hoped Sylvia and Pearl would have a hand in designing and making it. On whose arm would she walk down the aisle of All Saints church? Would it be too presumptuous to ask Eddie to give her away? There was a lot to discuss and meanwhile she and Tommy had to fit in dance lessons with Mrs Ellis and Christmas was fast approaching; presents had to be bought or made, cards written, cakes baked and trees decorated. Then in January she and Tommy must be ready to enter the Allied North of England Championship.

'In May?' Lucia had cast a dejected look at her son. 'Why this wait?'

'It's up to Joy,' he'd replied.

But why this wait? Tommy had repeated his mother's question to Joy more than once during the week. 'What's stopping us from having a Christmas wedding?' Sleigh bells ringing, snow glistening – what was wrong with a winter wonderland? He'd crooned the words of a popular Bing Crosby song into her ear.

She'd pushed him away and teased him back. 'You could charm the birds out of the trees if you wanted.'

'The bluebird may be gone away but there's a new

bird in town and he whispers in my ear, "The sooner the better".' Tommy had kissed her and tempted her with promises that they could be ready in time if they set their minds to it.

Just yesterday Joy had agreed to consider at least bringing the wedding forward to April and Tommy had been forced to accept this small shift in his direction.

Now she could hear his voice as he crossed the backyard, trilling away as he turned his key in the lock. "'In the meadow we can build a snowman . . ."'

'Here is my Tommy!' Lucia declared. 'He has nice voice – *bellissima*!'

After a routine matinee performance of tumbling and tomfoolery, of clowning around in his sequinned costume and playing the silver trumpet, still he arrived home singing in full voice about dreaming by the fire and never being afraid of what the future might hold.

Joy loved this man: his cheeky cheeriness and ability to see the fun in everything, the smile in his beautiful brown eyes. His kiss when he greeted her.

'Sit!' Lucia brought pans to the table and dished out the meal.

Tommy ate ravenously, sucking up the long strings of spaghetti then scraping a spoon across his plate to scoop up the last of the sauce.

'Seriously,' he said to Joy later in the evening, after their supper had been cleared away and Lucia had gone off to bed. 'I keep asking you until I'm blue in the face: what's wrong with us being married before Christmas?'

'It's so soon!' She faced him across the table, struggling to resist his smile.

He sat beside her, the low firelight flickering across their faces. 'But really; what's to stop us?'

'Nothing practical, as far as the ceremony goes,' she conceded. 'But have you thought about where we would live once we're married? Oughtn't we to find a place to move into first?'

Tommy reined in his enthusiasm. 'I hadn't actually thought about it.'

'What – you were thinking we could stay here with your mother?'

He shrugged. 'I'm sure she'd be happy with that.'

'And she's lovely, but . . .'

'But there's not much privacy, I agree.' Tommy shifted uncomfortably on his chair. 'It's just that in Italy . . .'

'Families stay together more?'

'Yes, but this is England,' he acknowledged.

Their future living arrangement was a stumbling block that neither had addressed until now. They talked it through softly in the semi-darkness as the glowing embers settled in the grate.

'Your mother would be lonely without us.' Joy recognized how much store Lucia set on cooking and cleaning for them, by making their nest comfortable.

'She's never lived alone. I would worry about her.'

'But we would still help her in the ice-cream parlour. We wouldn't move far away.'

'She wouldn't want to stop us from finding a place of our own. She wouldn't stand in our way.'

'That's true,' Joy agreed with a sigh.

They went round in circles until the room fell dark and it was time for bed.

'No need to remind you how much I want to get married,' Tommy murmured as he kissed her goodnight. 'And why.'

'Because,' she whispered. She felt it too: the longing to lie together as man and wife.

158

'Until it happens, it feels like we're not a real couple – I can't put it into words, but you know anyway.'

She kissed him back and caressed his face. 'Am I being unfair?'

'No. I understand.' Their voices were soft and low, their lips touching as they talked.

'Let's do it – let's make it a Christmas wedding,' she said suddenly.

'You've changed your mind?' It was as if a door had been flung open, allowing passion to enter. Tommy cupped his hands behind her head and kissed her long and hard.

Joy felt his lips on her neck and throat, his body against hers, her hands drawing him closer. 'And we'll carry on living here for the time being – until the war is over and your dad is allowed to come home and be with your mum.'

'Perfect,' Tommy murmured.

Saturday 19 December was the date they chose. Now it was all hands on deck to be ready in time.

Friday saw a newcomer at Sylvia's jive class at North View Parade. Ruby Donovan breezed in without prior notice, wearing high-waisted black slacks and an apple-green, short-sleeved jumper that showed off an enviably trim figure for a married woman approaching thirty.

'What are you doing here?' Ruby was the last person that Sylvia expected to see. After all, Ruby had grown up going to dance halls with her parents and had flung herself into the new dance styles that had gained ground in the years leading up to the war. Jive, jitterbug, lindy hop; you name it and the high-spirited teenager had been renowned for giving it an energetic go.

'What do you mean, what am I doing here? I've come to learn from the top expert in town like everyone else.' Ruby wiggled her fingers in greeting at people she knew: Doris Scaife from Barrett's shoe shop, young Arnold White who ran the dodgems ride at the Pleasure Beach and Geoff Baker who worked on the trams – all gathered by the gramophone waiting for the class to begin.

'I'm not sure I have anything to teach you.' Sylvia meant what she said. 'I've watched your jive at the Tower many a time and honestly I can't fault it.'

'Ta very much.' A chuffed Ruby showed that nevertheless she was here to stay by changing into her dance shoes. 'Let's just say I fancied a night out rather than sitting at home with my knitting.'

'Fair enough.' Sylvia chose a record from the rack. 'I'll partner you with Arnold. You can show him the ropes.'

Ruby seized the gawky fairground lad's hand and drew him on to the floor. 'Remember, we're not at the dodgems now,' she quipped. 'The aim is to steer clear of other couples, not barge into them and knock them flat.'

Arnold had the grace to laugh. 'Bloody hell, Ruby – you don't do a lot for a chap's confidence.'

'Ready?' Sylvia called above the swinging, big-band introduction. She noted that she had a total of twenty pupils: a full house for once. Cliff would be pleased. 'Jive is all bounce and energy; lively as you like. We'll start with the sidestep to the left.'

'Relax and live a little,' Ruby advised a worried-looking Arnold, whose trousers were two inches too short and whose bony wrists poked out from his shirtsleeves. 'Throw yourself into it, never mind how it looks.'

'Stand side by side, man on the right, lady on the left, and take a small sidestep to the left then bounce and feet together,' Sylvia instructed. 'Keep to the beat. Now the gentleman swings his lady round to face him then pushes her two steps back, releases her hand and lets her make a full clockwise turn. Clockwise, Doris. Try that again.'

'Buck up,' Ruby told Arnold, who had confused his left with his right and fallen behind the beat. 'This time I'll lead and you follow. That's right; and one, two, three, four – go!'

They battled through and by the end of the action-packed class Arnold had picked up the basics. Ruby praised his efforts. 'Great stuff – we'll soon have you throwing a girl over your shoulder with the best of them.'

Meanwhile, Sylvia drew the session to a close with encouraging words for everyone. 'Well done. Remember, there's no set sequence of steps to the jive. It's up to you to improvise.'

'She means you make it up as you go along,' Ruby explained.

'And I paid good money to learn that?' Arnold grumbled. 'I could have worked that out for myself.'

'Get away with you.' Ruby ushered him bossily towards the door then went in search of her belongings. 'Now where did I put my coat and bag? Would you believe that Arnold White?' she asked Sylvia, who was placing records in their paper sleeves. 'One lesson and he thinks he's the bee's knees. By the way, did you hear the latest on Mavis and Eddie?'

Certain that she wouldn't like what she was about to be told, Sylvia clutched the records to her chest.

'I got it from the horse's mouth – actually from Doris who works in the shoe shop with Mavis's mother. Mavis isn't going to Welsh Wales after all.'

'Good heavens – I had no idea she intended to.'

'Keep your hair on; her plans have changed anyway.'

'Explain!' Sylvia demanded.

'Mavis's mother wanted her to go to Llandudno to look after her aunt whose boy is in the Merchant Navy and whose ship had been torpedoed by a U-boat. Bobby is his name. Well, praise the Lord, hallelujah – the lad lived to tell the tale. He's been given a week's shore leave and all is well.'

'Goodness gracious,' Sylvia stammered.

'Yes, but on top of which, Eddie has sweet-talked your mother into not charging Mavis for lessons.'

'Are you sure?' It was the first Sylvia had heard of any of this and in spite of all previous good resolutions to mind her own business, she felt her heart sink down into her boots.

'Sure I'm sure.' Ruby was ready to depart. 'It's no secret that Mavis is permanently short of cash but Eddie seems to have solved that problem for her.'

'No. Yes – that's good.' Sylvia swallowed hard then concentrated on returning the records to the rack. 'Thanks for helping with Arnold, by the way.'

'You're welcome.' Ruby breezed out the way that she'd entered – blithe and confident, on top of the world.

'Why the long face?' Cliff asked Sylvia when she went upstairs to hand over the studio key.

'What do you mean?' she retorted. The flat was immaculate: not a speck of dust on the marble mantelpiece or the low occasional table, every sofa cushion positioned just so. Some of Cliff's dance trophies were displayed on a shelf behind the sofa, alongside books by Vernon and Irene Castle, pioneer teachers of modern dance, next to neat stacks of specialist magazines such as *Danceland* and *Popular Dancing Weekly*. 'I expect Terry's at rehearsal?'

162

'Don't ask me.' Shrugging off the question, Cliff offered to make Sylvia a cup of tea.

She trailed after him into the tiny but equally orderly kitchen where she shared Ruby's update about the Eddie–Mavis partnership. 'I don't know why I'm even bothering to mention it,' she added.

'Because it means there's now no chance of you stepping into the breach, dear friend.' Cliff's sharp reply put an end to the touchy topic. He frowned as he spooned tea leaves into the pot then waited for the kettle to boil. 'And before you poke your nose any further into my private affairs, Terry's moved out.'

'You don't say!' Sylvia exclaimed.

'I do say.' He carried on calmly pouring hot water into the teapot. 'Look around you – do you see any sign of his mess?'

'No.' It was true that Terry was more untidy than Cliff. He would kick off his shoes and abandon them in the middle of the room or hang his tie over a doorknob and his jacket on the back of a chair. The orderliness that she'd noticed when she came in was proof that Cliff was telling the truth.

'You might not have been aware at the time but he lost his rag and threatened to do it last Saturday night at the Tower and it turns out he meant every word. He packed his bag and was gone by Sunday lunchtime.'

'But where's he moved on to?'

Cliff arranged tea things on a tray then carried it into the lounge. 'He didn't say.'

'And don't you care?'

'Of course I care.' Cliff sat on the sofa with a weary sigh. 'I care very much.'

'I could find out for you,' Sylvia offered. She too was weary as she flopped down next to him. 'I can go along

163

to the Winter Gardens, to his next rehearsal, and ask him the question, face to face. Cliff?' she prompted after a long silence.

'What would be the point? Terry and I are all washed up.' He ran a hand through his light brown hair then rested his head against the back of the sofa. 'Like I said before: I've felt it coming on for some time.'

'I'm so sorry.' What else was there to say? Cliff and Terry had faced tough times and it had taken a lot of courage to stand up to the narrow-minded insults that had been flung in their faces. And all for nothing, it seemed.

'I miss him,' Cliff confessed. 'I even miss his scatter-brained habits. I was used to tidying up after him and making sure he wrote down his rehearsal schedule – things like that. I was proud of him, too.'

'I know you were. Perhaps he'll cool down and come back home when he's ready.'

'I don't think so for a minute.'

'Why not?'

'Because Terry's mixing with new people in the theatre world where morals are more . . . relaxed, shall we say?' Cliff raised a hand to stop Sylvia from interrupting. 'I speak from experience.'

'So you suspect there's someone else in the picture?'

'Most likely, yes. In any case, what's done is done and I've a lot on my plate, as you know.'

Sylvia took a deep breath. '*We* have a lot on our plates.' She made it clear that she and Cliff would continue to work together to make a success of the studio. 'Remember, the new sign above the door says "Learn to Dance with Cliff and Sylvia". Tonight I had twenty paying custom-ers. Tomorrow afternoon, seventeen people have signed up for my salsa class.'

'Onwards and upwards,' Cliff said with the ghost of a smile.

'Exactly. Eddie is gone from my life and now it seems Terry is gone from yours. What else do we have to do with our time, except put our backs into earning as much money as possible?'

Cliff grunted and sat upright. 'Appearances are deceptive – you're far more resilient than you appear, Sylvia Ellis.'

'I take after my mother. We may look shiny and ornamental on the outside but on the inside we're tough as old boots.'

'And smarter than you seem too,' Cliff admitted. He turned his head to look her in the eye. She met his gaze without blinking. 'You're right; we'll concentrate on the future and forget the past.'

'We can do it,' Sylvia vowed with missionary zeal. 'Terry might have left you in the lurch but I promise I won't.'

'Done!' He reached out and they shook hands. 'Make no mistake, the dream is alive and well.'

*

Dearest love, I'm sorry my last was so short.

Pearl sat behind the till in the entrance to her arcade, reading Bernie's latest letter for the umpteenth time. It had arrived that morning, just as she was leaving the house. Slipping it into her coat pocket, there'd been a spring in her step that had been missing for some time.

I'll make up for it by nattering on about everything that's been happening to me – so far as I'm allowed, that is. Boy, it's hot

165

*here. Scorching. You wouldn't recognize me – I look like a boiled
lobster from head to toe. Even my knees are sunburned. My
billet isn't bad and there's more than enough nosh to go around,
so no complaints there. Some of the boys don't do well in this
heat. A lot suffer from a gippy tummy. They keel over on parade
and get carted off on stretchers. Don't worry about me, though –
I drink plenty of water and so far so good. Blighty seems a
long way away, my Pearl. Believe it or not, I miss those cold
grey seas and the piers and the Tower and the Pleasure Beach
more than I can put into words. Most of all, I miss you, my
darling girl. I mentioned before that your photo looks the worse
for wear (creased and dog eared) because I take it everywhere
with me. Can you send me another when you get the chance?
Eh up – my sergeant is on the warpath, as per usual. I have
to stop now. Write back soon. Cheerio, Pearl, and look after
yourself. Say hello to everyone from me.*

    SWALK, Bernie

Pearl closed her eyes and tried to shut out the familiar
sounds of coins dropping into slots and metal balls rolling through mazes. She pictured Bernie clear as day in
his uniform waiting for her at the altar; the look of ado-
ration in his eyes as they'd exchanged vows. How could
her heart ache so much from missing him and not break
clean in two?

'Pearl, are you all right?' Joy broke into Pearl's remi-
niscences. She'd been on her way home from a cleaning
job on the north side of town and had seized the chance
to drop in at the arcade.

Pearl opened her eyes to the reality of rows of one-armed
bandits and Joy in a green hat and scarf peering anxiously
at her. 'I'm fine.' She held up Bernie's letter. 'This came
this morning.'

'Wonderful!' Joy clapped her hands with delight. 'What a relief!'

Pearl put the letter carefully back in its envelope. 'I've made a decision.'

'Oh?' Joy thought that Pearl had looked down in the mouth recently – ever since her squiffy episode at the Tower. That was part of the reason why she'd called in. The other was to let her know the revised wedding date. My, would Pearl be surprised!

'Yes. I've decided to stop going to the Tower on a Saturday night. No more tripping the light fantastic for me until Bernie comes home.'

'Are you sure?' Joy didn't hide her surprise. 'Is it because you had one too many last week?'

'Partly.'

'Well, why not decide not to drink in future? Then where would be the harm?'

Pearl stuck to her guns. 'It just doesn't seem right without Bernie. Mum had her doubts right from the start and now I see she was right.'

'If that's how you feel . . . but you'll carry on going to dance classes on North View Parade?'

'I haven't decided yet. If I don't, it's not the end of the world.'

'Oh, Pearl – Sylvia and I will miss you. It won't be the same.'

'You'll live,' Pearl said wryly. 'Now tell me what you're doing here on a cold Saturday afternoon when you should be getting ready for an exciting night out with Tommy.'

Joy's face lit up suddenly with the thrill of her surprise announcement. 'I've had a change of heart about the wedding. Put a date in your diary for the Saturday before Christmas – Tommy and I have decided to get married

167

on the nineteenth and I want Sylvia and you to be my bridesmaids. You'll do it, won't you?'

'I will,' Pearl promised with the broadest of smiles. For Joy, it was obviously the perfect end to a perfect day. 'And, hand on heart, I couldn't be happier for you both.'

CHAPTER ELEVEN

'We receive a fair number of early warnings,' the specialist instructor informed his recruits on Eddie's final day
of training for the first aid service. It took place in the
basement of the Majestic Hotel in a room stacked with
cardboard boxes containing supplies of hotel crockery
and cutlery. 'Nuisance raiders often stooge around over
the Irish Sea, looking to offload a spare incendiary or two
before they head back to base in Germany or France.
Control generally picks them up on the radar and the
Squires Gate boys leap into action before Jerry is able to
do any damage.'

Eddie's fellow trainees were a motley crew, ranging from
portly, elderly men in ill-fitting battledress to a couple of
wet-behind-the-ears schoolboys in Boy Scout uniforms
hoping to become messengers for the ARP. They'd all
started with the crash course in different types of bombs,
anti-gas measures and basic first aid, before splitting into
different sections. Eddie had been intrigued by the contents of a Ministry of Defence film about the gas vans
used to test the irritant effects of certain gases and to identify them by smell. After that, he'd taken part in a team
exercise involving fake casualties – volunteers had played
the roles of injured survivors of an enemy attack. One

woman in particular had executed her part with relish, groaning and crying out as Eddie and a fellow first-aider had attempted to lift her on to a stretcher.

'Each one of you will be assigned a party leader,' the instructor concluded. 'Your team will answer to an MO – a medical officer in charge of your post – whose job it will be to assess the level of injury and determine whether or not the patient needs to be transferred to hospital for emergency treatment.'

The trainees were left in little doubt that volunteering could be a hazardous business. After three sessions they were aware of enemy threats that government propaganda seldom disclosed. Now Eddie knew all about parachute mines that exploded like the lash of a whip even at a distance of fifty yards, ripping out roofs, windows and doors. He'd learned about flaring incendiaries that must be scooped up and disposed of during the few short seconds prior to explosion and about Junkers flying in low over crowded city streets, machine guns blazing.

'Let's hope we never need to put any of this into practice,' the bald-headed man sitting next to Eddie observed as the instructor handed out a final batch of instruction leaflets.

Recruits began to shuffle out of the dingy, unheated cellar, but Eddie sat for a while. He was in no hurry to join Mavis in the Queen's Arms, as arranged. Rather, he would take time to think through the implications of his new Civil Defence role. *Will I be able to keep calm in extremis?* he wondered. *If or when I come to deal with a genuine victim of Jerry's terror raids, how will I measure up?*

'Not having second thoughts, are we?' his instructor – a shrewd man in his forties with a clipped, grey moustache and steel-rimmed glasses – queried. 'You wouldn't be the first, believe me.'

'No, sir,' Eddie answered firmly as he put on his overcoat. 'Not at all – I'm ready to do my bit.'

'That's the ticket.' The instructor thrust leaflets into his hand. 'You're just the type we need: strong and nimble, with a good head on your shoulders.'

Eddie thanked him then filed out after the rest of his group. He walked a few steps up King Alfred Street before turning into the lounge bar of the Queen's Arms where Mavis was waiting. 'I'm sorry I'm late – the training session went on longer than expected,' he apologized.

'And here was me thinking you'd stood me up,' she teased, bright and perky as ever in her tweed outfit, complete with pheasant-feather brooch.

'Oh no; I'd never do that.'

'I know – I'm kidding.' She'd forgotten that Eddie took everything at face value. 'Anyhow, I had a nice natter with Joy and Tommy to pass the time.'

He glanced around the bar at the velvet-upholstered booths where couples sat drinking and smoking, taking in mine host behind the bar, resplendent in his crimson brocade waistcoat with a gold watch chain slung across his chest, deftly pulling pints of best bitter.

'They just left,' Mavis continued. 'It's all go as far as they're concerned. They were due to meet the vicar at All Saints, to make the final arrangements for their wedding.'

'I've agreed to walk Joy down the aisle,' Eddie informed her. 'She has no father to do the job so I told her it would be an honour.'

While Eddie went to order their drinks at the bar, Mavis took out her powder compact and peered into the small, round mirror. She dabbed her nose with the powder puff then popped the compact back into her handbag. 'What happened to Joy's father, by the way?' she asked as she accepted her shandy from Eddie.

'Sad to say, he died during an air raid on Manchester at the start of the war, along with her mother and sister. As far as I know, that was all the family Joy had.'

Mavis's expression grew serious. 'Oh dear, I had no idea.'

'Joy was fifteen or sixteen at the time. Her parents had decided to send her out of the city, to finish her secretarial training here in Blackpool, where they thought she would be safer.'

'It turns out they were right. But poor thing; to lose everyone at one fell swoop. This bloody war has a lot to answer for.' Mavis sipped her drink. 'To tell you the truth, I didn't think much of Joy when we first met – too straitlaced for my liking. But I saw a different side to her after Ruby persuaded her on to the dance floor. That's where she really blossoms.'

'Don't we all?' Eddie said. 'We pack up our troubles and smile, smile, smile when we dance.'

'True,' Mavis agreed enthusiastically. 'Off the floor, you and me are chalk and cheese, but when we dance, somehow I forget our differences. The music takes hold and that's it – we float across the floor as one.'

'I'm glad you didn't have to go to Wales to stay with your aunt.' His unguarded confession brought a rush of blood to his cheeks. He cleared his throat then proceeded to backtrack. 'I mean, it would have been disastrous as far as January's competition goes.'

'Yes; disastrous.' Mavis toyed with his embarrassment. 'Then again, perhaps Miss Ellis would've come to the rescue? Kidding again,' she added with a mischievous wink.

Eddie sighed and supped. 'I never know when to take you seriously.'

Mavis gestured with her forefinger to indicate that he had froth on his upper lip. 'The answer is never. I'm not a serious person.'

He wiped his lip. 'That can't be true.'

'Be warned; it is. I'm not the type to mope around, crying woe is me – I like going out and larking about, full stop.'

'But you also like winning,' Eddie pointed out. 'And that takes dedication, concentration, determination . . .'

'I'll give you that,' she conceded.

'Those are the things that I noticed in you from the start.'

Mavis gave a self-conscious laugh. 'What else?'

'Your natural ability, of course.'

'And . . . ?'

'The larking about, as you call it. I'm not used to that. It's refreshing.'

'Is it?' She took several quick sips of her drink.

'Most definitely. You make me feel staid by comparison.'

'Yes, you old fuddy-duddy – you should loosen up. How old are you anyway?'

'Twenty-two.'

'Ancient!'

'Why – how old are you?'

'Tut-tut; a girl never tells. Actually, I turned twenty on November the fifth – bonfire night.' Mavis threw back her head and this time the laugh was full throated. 'I don't care who knows it.'

'You have your whole life ahead of you,' Eddie countered. There were only two years between them, plus a wide ocean of upbringing and experience. 'I'm glad we've had this chat. Now, what do you say we take in a flick – spur of the moment? Your choice.'

'Now you're talking!' Mavis finished her drink then grabbed her handbag. 'Micky Rooney is on in a new Andy Hardy adventure. Look lively, Edward; we don't want the film to start without us.'

'Hello, dear.' Lorna gave Sylvia a peck on the cheek.

'I take it you're not going out?' Sylvia had popped in to see her mother – a regular occurrence these days – and had found her already in her dressing gown and slippers, though it was only eight o'clock in the evening. Her fair hair, threaded with grey, was brushed back from her forehead and held in place by a snood, and her face was scrubbed clean.

'No; I thought I'd have a quiet night in for a change.' Lorna produced sherry and glasses from the drinks cabinet. She sat Sylvia close to the fire then perched on the arm of the chair opposite and waited for her to say what was on her mind.

Sylvia kicked off her shoes then drew her legs under her. 'Why does life have to be so difficult?' she wondered.

'Is it?' Lorna noticed that Sylvia looked tired but thankfully not so painfully thin as she'd been in the autumn. However, she knew from past experience with pupils desperate to maintain a sylph-like figure that her daughter's preoccupation with her weight was something to keep an eye on both now and in the future.

'Yes; everywhere you look there are problems. If it's not more rationing, then it's landmines being washed up on the beach or people being run over by a bus during the blackout.'

'I see.'

'Luckily it doesn't seem to affect our business too much,' Sylvia continued.

'I'm with you there – learning to dance has never been so popular; I'm not sure why exactly.'

'Simple; it's because it bucks people up. Incidentally, did you know that Pearl has given it up? She says it's not fair on Bernie. Joy and I have both tried to change her mind.'

'But she won't?'

Sylvia frowned. 'Who knows? Pearl acts on impulse so it's hard to predict. For some reason she rushed away from the Tower early last Saturday and she hasn't seemed herself since.'

'Give her time to reconsider,' Lorna advised.

'Talking of learning to dance . . .' Sylvia circled back to the real reason why she'd come. 'Cliff and I would love it if you would hand out some of our leaflets.'

'Ah, Cliff.' Lorna cocked her head to one side, expecting more.

'We're busy but not quite busy enough.' Sylvia rushed on with her explanation. 'And our expenses have gone up recently. Mr Nicholson has put up Cliff's rent and Terry won't be making a contribution in the foreseeable future.'

'Oh; why not?'

'He and Cliff have parted company.'

'I'm sorry to hear that. They may not have been most people's idea of an ideal couple but I've always believed in live and let live.' Though a traditionalist, Lorna had been involved in the dance world long enough to learn tolerance towards relationships outside of society's norm.

'Terry's the one who made the break. Cliff may not show it, but deep down he's heartbroken. We've decided between us that the best way to cope is to throw ourselves into work.'

Lorna took note of Sylvia's use of 'our' and 'we'. 'You've decided to stay with Cliff, despite – you know . . . ?'

'Despite what, Mother?'

'Despite his past association with that dreadful man whose name will never pass my lips?'

Sylvia flipped aside the reference to Mitch Burns. 'Cliff admitted his mistake and is genuinely sorry. And yes, I'm in for a penny, in for a pound, so to speak. So will you help us to spread the word?' Sylvia produced a clutch of colourful leaflets from her handbag. *Live in Your Dreams* was splashed in imitation neon letters across the front, with a photograph of a glamorous couple in Latin dress below. The inside pages gave details of class times and prices, with a telephone number prominently displayed.

Lorna took the leaflets and examined the top one. 'These can't have been cheap to produce,' she commented.

'That's right, so don't waste them.' It was only recently that Sylvia had felt able to chivvy and tease her mother. 'Don't hand them out willy-nilly; take care to choose younger couples with a bit of get up and go.'

'Very well; I'll do my best.' Lorna put aside the leaflets then poured more sherry. 'I'm glad,' she added.

'About what?' The warmth of the fire and the comfortable glow caused by the sweet drink had left Sylvia feeling nicely relaxed.

'Glad that you didn't go to London – that goes without saying. And relieved that you and Cliff have hit it off. Most of all, I'm happy that you've found a new purpose in life since you and Edward parted company.'

'Oh Mother, don't start on that.'

Lorna ignored the plea. 'Make no mistake, Edward is a dear but he does lack a certain *je ne sais quoi*. Without a doubt he and I were holding you back, stopping you from developing your own style of dance. I see that now.'

Sylvia's eyes widened in astonishment.

'It's true,' Lorna insisted. 'Whilst I saw how devoted to you Edward was and how perfect you were together on the dance floor, deep down I think I realized that it wasn't enough, that sooner or later you would choose to break away.'

Oddly, Sylvia found herself springing to Eddie's defence. 'None of it was his fault. I was the one who behaved badly – blowing hot and cold, leading him on. And now I'm paying the price.'

'Don't look at it like that.'

'But I am, Mother. I didn't realize how much I would miss his company or how much I relied on him. Now there's a gaping hole at the centre of my life that no amount of teaching salsa and jive will fill.'

'Are you sure this isn't jealousy speaking?'

'You're not the first to think that – Cliff says the same thing.' Sylvia stood up and walked several times around the room before she spoke again. 'You're right – I am. I'm stuck in that rut, Mother, and I don't know how to get out of it.' She was sick to death of feeling this way, digging herself ever deeper.

'Off the dance floor, is there no way back for you and Eddie?'

'Not that I can see. As for them dancing together; Mavis has stepped into my shoes and she's perfect for Eddie and you. She's a blank slate for you to work wonders with.' Regret rose from the pit of Sylvia's stomach and threatened to choke her. 'I'm sorry,' she breathed. 'I don't feel well – I'd better go.'

Lorna watched her daughter retrieve her shoes then

pick up her coat from the back of the sofa. 'Take heart, dear,' she said as they hugged goodbye. 'The hurt will feel less sharp with the passage of time.'

Sylvia thanked her then made her way downstairs. She breathed in cold air as she opened the door.

'And remember how lucky you are.' Lorna saw her out on to the pavement. 'You have a talent to express yourself through dance. Be grateful that you will always have that in your life, no matter what.'

'My Tommy, he is working?' Lucia asked Joy, who sat at the kitchen table checking items on her list.

'Meet Reverend Inman at All Saints' – tick. 'Arrange to have flowers delivered to the house before ten o'clock' – tick. 'Finish writing invitations' – tick. There wasn't enough time before the event to have them printed and sent out so a handwritten version must do instead. 'Yes, worse luck,' Joy replied.

'But you go out to dance?' Lucia looked over Joy's shoulder at the list, speaking softly as she stroked the sleeve of her cream dress.

'Yes, with Sylvia.' Joy glanced up from her list. 'Tommy doesn't mind.'

'*Va bene.*' Lucia's tone was concerned.

'Really, he doesn't mind. And Sylvia has asked me to keep her company.'

'*Bene, bene.*' Lucia knew that her views were old-fashioned. Back in Milan, she would never have dreamed of visiting a dance hall without her fiancé at the time – Tommy senior – but she was willing to acknowledge that she was behind the times. '*Bellissima,*' she whispered proudly as Joy stood up from the table and smoothed away the creases in her dress.

Joy glanced at her watch. 'I must dash – it won't do to keep Sylvia waiting.'

Lucia watched her rush to put on her coat. '*Divertiti,*' she murmured as Joy headed for the door. Have a lovely time. Tomorrow would be soon enough to mention to Joy several letters that had arrived in today's post – most likely replies to wedding invitations. Oh, to be young again, with so much energy. Oh, to be so full of hope, with your whole life ahead of you.

Pearl had promised to babysit Elsie.

'I don't need a babysitter,' Elsie had protested with her bottom lip thrust out.

Their mother had disagreed. 'Your dad has asked a couple of his sidekicks to man the arcades while he and I enjoy a rare night out. You can't be in the house alone.'

'I'm staying in anyway.' Pearl had backed Maria up. 'So do as you're told. Brush your teeth and get ready for bed.'

'Bossyboots.' Elsie's capacity for sulking had increased ten-fold of late. She'd stormed upstairs and slammed the bedroom door.

'Thank you.' Maria, dressed in her best coat with its fox-fur collar, had made a hasty exit, leaving Pearl twiddling her thumbs in the kitchen.

Pearl picked up a magazine and flicked through it. There was nothing of interest. Perhaps a game of patience instead? She went through to the front room, pulled down the blind then found a pack of cards in a drawer. She laid them out on the small table next to the sofa but was distracted by noises from above of Elsie stomping around and making her presence felt. Pearl went to the bottom of the stairs. 'Go to bed,' she yelled. Receiving no reply, she drifted back into the front room. Patience had lost its appeal (it never had much in the first place) so she packed away the cards and took out pen and paper to begin a letter to Bernie.

She sat with her pen at the ready. When was the last time she'd stayed in on a Saturday night? she wondered. Months, probably. She pictured the scene outside the Tower – crowded trams would be dropping off passengers, each one excited by the prospect of moonlight and love and romance, as the song said. There would be the rapid chatter of girls greeting each other, the sight of uniformed men strutting their way into the foyer as usual and the first strains of Reggie Dixon's Wurlitzer as the dance began. And here was Pearl stuck at home, wondering and worrying about why she had received no letter from Bernie lately and not knowing what to write to him. Her page remained blank.

For the first time in her life Pearl realized that this was how loneliness felt: adrift, left out, resentful.

The wall clock ticked; apart from that there was silence. China dogs on the mantelpiece, polished brass fender, coal scuttle, round leather pouffe – her gaze rested on each in turn. Add claustrophobic to the list; adrift, left out, resentful, hemmed in.

Dear Bernie, she began. Her big news that she was yet to share with him was that she'd given up going to the Tower. She'd skipped her weekly dance class on North View Parade since the 'incident' too, had not breathed a word about it, not even to Joy and Sylvia. The page stayed empty as Pearl stared into space.

However hard she tried to keep painful memories at bay, they would flood back in. She had been Chuck Sanderson's chosen dance partner for the night and she'd noticed nothing in his manner to suggest how badly the

180

evening would end. Ought she to have registered alarm bells sooner? One thing was certain: Pearl had had too much to drink and for this she only had herself to blame. Terry had done his best to look after her but, no doubt about it, she should have taken responsibility for her actions. Then there was the scrappy fight between Terry and the GIs, her befuddlement followed by the rush of cold air as she'd stepped outside the foyer and seen three figures hanging around in the dark alley. Alcohol fumes on the men's breaths. 'Miss Pearl' – used as an insult, not as a mark of respect. Sanderson's strength as he'd thrust her against the pile of sandbags, the damp, rough feel of them against her bare skin. His hands, his weight on top of her. The certain, terrifying knowledge that she lacked the strength to fend him off.

A key turned in the lock and brisk, high-heeled footsteps came down the corridor.

'Who's there?' With a jolt, Pearl clicked back into the present.

'It's only me.' Maria stuck her head around the door. 'Have you seen your father?'

'No; I thought you'd arranged to meet him at the Black Horse.'

'He wasn't there,' Maria retorted. 'And no sign of him since teatime either, according to the barman. Trust him to let me down.'

Pearl followed her mother into the kitchen. 'That's too bad,' she sympathized.

Maria shrugged. 'I'm sorry I was short with you. You know what your dad's like – he's most likely chasing a new scheme that will make his fortune, which means our arrangement went clean out of his head.'

'But still . . .'

'I'm used to it.' Maria kicked off her shoes then sat down heavily. 'Every cloud,' she said with a sigh.

Not for the first time Pearl wondered why her mother put up with her father's unreliability. Then again, what choice did she have? 'What do you mean?' she asked as she put the kettle on and lifted the tea caddy down from the shelf.

'It means I'm here to look after Elsie so you're free to join your pals at the Tower,' Maria explained.

Pearl threw her mother a sideways glance. 'You've changed your tune since the last time we spoke about it.'

'Not really,' Maria argued. 'I only said you should write and tell Bernie what you were up to. You did tell him?'

'Yes, I mentioned it.'

'That's all right then. So off you go.'

'Oh, no – I'm happy to stay in. Anyway, it's too late now.'

'Nonsense.' Maria gave Pearl a long, hard stare. 'You've been moping around all week, waiting to hear from that husband of yours. It'd do you good to get out.'

'Would it?' Pearl's resolution faltered. If she got changed quickly she could reach the ballroom in time for the second half. She would seek out Sylvia and Joy and act as if everything was normal. Dancing might even take away her current blues.

'Believe me, it would.' Maria gave Pearl the benefit of her experience; knowledge that she'd gleaned from all the years of being married. 'It doesn't pay to sit at home brooding if things don't turn out the way you expect. You have to get out there and live your own life regardless.'

Pearl remained silent as she let the words sink in.

'Within reason, of course,' Maria added. 'You must take care not to overstep the mark.'

'I suppose I could go out for an hour or so . . .' Joy and

182

Sylvia would be there without partners; the three girls could take it in turns to dance together. Pearl would reject all invitations from strangers and could ask a friend such as Joe to walk her home.

'Do as you're told.' Maria adopted the hectoring tone that she'd used when Pearl was a young child. 'Your red skirt is freshly washed, starched and ironed. It's hanging up in the airing cupboard. Now go.'

CHAPTER TWELVE

The minute Pearl stepped under the glass awning outside the main entrance into the Tower building, she felt her mood lift. The evening was already in full swing, with strains of organ music reaching her from the ballroom, as well as laughter and snippets of conversation from the crowded bar area.

Right; this is it! One last check in the mirror on the stairway, one deep breath, then Pearl experienced the sheer delight of entering the ballroom and immediately being dazzled by the enormous chandeliers – six to each side, with three more overhead – of looking up at the tiered balconies, of crossing the sprung parquet floor.

'Pearl, you changed your mind!' Sylvia and Joy rushed to greet her with gleeful hugs and smiles. As the interval came to an end, her bright red skirt had attracted their attention and they'd recognized her straight away.

'Mum shooed me out of the house,' a sheepish Pearl explained. 'She said it would do me good to get out.'

'That's exactly what we said.' Joy took Pearl by the hand and led her to their table under the balcony. 'Sit here with us. The competition is about to begin.'

'It's foxtrot tonight.' Sylvia drew up a spare chair from the neighbouring table. 'Keep an eye on Eddie and Mavis – they should do well.'

'Yoo-hoo, Pearl!' A smiling Ida whirled by in the arms of an RAF man.

'We wondered where you'd got to.' Thora, who was dancing with Joe, gave her a jaunty wave. 'It's not like you to miss a Saturday night.'

Pearl placed her handbag under the table. She noticed several GIs inviting girls to dance. Making sure that Chuck Sanderson wasn't among them, she began to relax.

'How do, Pearl, what's your poison?' Terry soon joined them at their table. He stood out from the crowd in a crisp, striped shirt with gold cufflinks and stylish blue slacks – the centre of attention, as usual.

'Nothing, thanks.' After last week Pearl had resolved to stay sober.

'But you'll enter the foxtrot competition with me?' He offered her his hand.

Hesitating, she glanced at Sylvia and Joy.

'Of course she will.' Joy gave Pearl an encouraging nudge as the introductory notes of Gershwin's 'Fascinating Rhythm' filled the room and rose to the gilded rafters.

'Go along; we'll be scoring you – no rise and fall, lively as you like,' Sylvia reminded them.

'Ready?' Terry took Pearl in hold. 'We can add a few of our own variations if you want.'

He meant unexpected sidesteps and swift changes of direction. 'I'll follow you,' she agreed.

And they were off at a smooth, rapid trot to the opposite side of the floor, turning swiftly and skipping nimbly between competing couples who were eliminated one by one.

After five minutes of high-energy dancing, Sylvia's prediction proved correct – Eddie and Mavis remained on the floor to the end, along with Terry and Pearl and Ida and her RAF man, plus three other couples.

'You did well.' Eddie complimented Mavis on her rhythm and poise as they awaited the judges' decision. 'You made it look effortless.'

'Foxtrot is a doddle; I can dance it in my sleep.' Mavis didn't expect to win – not after going head to head with Terry and Pearl's more showy display.

But another couple took first prize: Nancy and Walter Mercer, who had travelled by train from their home town of Wigan. The elegant pair had danced with confidence and without Terry and Pearl's variations, which one of the judges had taken exception to, believing that standard rules were to be adhered to at all times.

'So much for our inventive sidesteps,' Terry muttered under his breath to Pearl.

'You can't win 'em all,' she acknowledged. 'The taking part was fun, though.'

Terry squeezed her hand then led her off the floor.

'The Mercers are very good,' Eddie acknowledged to Mavis. 'I expect we'll be up against them in the Allied Championship.' He nodded hello to Sylvia and Joy as he and Mavis walked past their table.

'We're a proper pair of wilting wallflowers,' Sylvia grumbled to Joy.

'Not for long.' Terry lost no time in inviting her on to the floor for a sedate waltz, leaving Pearl to pair up with Joy.

'I will if you will.' Pearl sprang to her feet, swiftly followed by Joy. 'There are plenty of spare men but I'd far rather dance with you.'

'It'll keep us out of mischief,' Joy agreed.

They swept smoothly across the floor, swaying into a reverse turn, with Joy, the taller of the two, taking the lead.

A couple of RAF engineers leaning on the bar, pint glasses in hand, wolf whistled as they waltzed by. 'Play your cards right and you two girls might be able to dance the next one with us!' one called after them.

'Not on your nelly.' Pearl's muttered response made Joy laugh.

They glided on towards the stage, eyes sparkling, bodies swaying. As ever, the dreamy smoothness of the waltz took away the knots and wrinkles of their everyday lives.

'That's better,' Joy declared as the waltz ended and they sat down. It wasn't long before Sylvia joined them. 'For a while there I forgot all about wedding guest lists and who should sit next to who.'

'Just what I needed: a girls' night out,' Sylvia confirmed and Pearl agreed.

'It's bucked me up no end,' she said.

'Uh-oh, look who's heading our way.' Sylvia gave Pearl a small kick under the table. 'It's your GI sergeant.'

Pearl frowned. 'He's not *my*—'

'Ssh!' Sylvia ordered.

'Howdy, Miss Pearl.' Errol Jackson approached with hands clasped behind his back and his gaze fixed firmly on her. 'Good to see you.' Behind him, new couples stood ready for the next dance: this time a quickstep that would present a tricky challenge for less experienced hoofers.

'Good to see you too.' Reluctant to meet his gaze, Pearl stared down at his highly polished shoes.

'Can we have a word?' he asked, shoulders back, no words wasted. 'In private.'

Joy and Sylvia shot concerned looks in her direction.

'It's all right – back in two ticks.' Overcoming an urge to flee, Pearl followed Errol out into the first-floor foyer.

He stopped next to an empty ticket booth. 'I sure am sorry to break into your evenin',' he began. 'You made it plain you just wanted to forget last week's . . . incident.'

'That's all right – please say what you have to say and let me get back to my friends.'

'Sure. About Private Sanderson; I thought you should know that somethin' new came to light a couple days ago. My platoon commander did some diggin' – he found that two women have brought charges against Sanderson for events that took place back in New York, prior to him joinin' the army.'

Pearl felt the blood drain from her cheeks. 'What kind of charges?'

'They're pretty goddamn serious. I can't give specifics – the information is hush-hush – but rest assured, the matter's in hand.'

Pearl absorbed the officially worded information then spoke quietly. 'What will happen to him?'

Errol leaned in closer to hear what she said. 'First off: dishonourable discharge. The criminal courts will take it from there.'

'Will he be sent back to America straight away?'

'Yes; you won't be involved.'

'Thank you.' She took a deep breath and felt the colour return to her cheeks. 'I appreciate you taking the trouble to bring me up to date.'

'It was my duty, ma'am.' He paused to consider. 'I feel kinda responsible; I knew trouble was brewin' but I failed to follow up.'

Pearl shook her head. 'Private Sanderson disobeyed orders about returning to base. It wasn't your fault.'

'Plus, I wasn't happy.' Errol's Southern civility made him choose his words carefully. 'You went through an ordeal back there, with no one to protect you. It's been playin' on my mind ever since.'

'Please don't worry – it'll take time but I'll get over it.'

'Did you tell anyone?'

'No.'

'Not even your husband?'

'Not a soul.'

'Why not?'

'Better not to dwell.'

He considered her answer. 'Gotcha,' he said without conviction.

'Bernie's been posted abroad. I haven't heard from him.' Pearl blurted out the words then immediately regretted it.

'Jeez,' Errol breathed. 'That's tough.'

'Yes, it is.' Tears formed in Pearl's eyes and threatened to trickle down her cheeks.

He drew out a neatly folded handkerchief and handed it to her. 'Sorry, Miss Pearl – I never meant to upset you.'

'Don't be sorry.' His kindness only made things worse. She dabbed her eyes then returned the handkerchief. 'I'd better go.'

He dropped his gaze and took a respectful step away. She hurried off – small, bright and birdlike – back to her friends. Errol sincerely hoped that at the end of the evening they would take care of her and see that she came to no harm.

As the night drew to a close, Terry made a point of taking Sylvia to one side. They climbed the stairs to the upper balcony, close to the arched roof with its painted maidens garlanded with flowers and playing harps.

'How's Cliff?' he began by asking her as they sat on the red plush seats. There was no one within earshot.

'He's getting by, I suppose.'

Her guarded answer failed to satisfy him. 'Tell me honestly. Has he talked about what happened?'

'A bit. He says that even before last week's scrap you had less and less in common; you were drifting apart.'

'That's news to me,' Terry muttered.

'Is it?' Sylvia gave him a sharp look.

'Well, all right; we weren't spending much time together. We were both so busy – him with getting his studio up and running, me with rehearsals. That blazing row we had in front of everyone was the final straw. If Cliff really thought he couldn't trust me, what was the point of carrying on?'

Wisely, Sylvia chose to bite her tongue. There was more to come from Terry once he'd taken a few deep breaths.

'Scratch beneath the surface and the truth is: Cliff was jealous. Don't laugh,' Terry went on. 'This may sound like two kids scrapping in the playground, but he was against me making new friends. Whenever I left the flat, he'd demand to know where I was going and what time I'd be back. In the end, it got me down.'

'But there are two sides to every coin,' Sylvia pointed out. 'Cliff's version is that you were prone to sulking when you didn't get your own way. He said you were secretive.'

'Did he?' Terry's features settled into a deep scowl. 'You and he talked about me behind my back?'

'Yes, we did. And you're doing it now: sulking.'

'Fair enough.' Terry had the grace to shrug then accept her comment. 'Really, though; how is he?'

'He's keeping busy but he misses you.' On the dance floor below, the last waltz took place under dimmed lights – soft and slow.

Terry breathed out through his nose – an exasperated sound ending in a soft grunt.

'Where did you move out to?' Sylvia asked.

'I'm back in my old digs on King Street, in Joe's house.'

'Shall I let Cliff know?'

'It's up to you. I probably won't be there long, though. I'm looking for something permanent, with more space.'

'I'll pass that on. And how are rehearsals going?'

'Still an absolute shambles. The stage manager and the scene painter have both been called up out of the blue – one by the Merchant Navy, the other by the RAF. Worse than that, the wicked fairy's caught laryngitis – she's lost her voice.'

A smile quivered on Sylvia's lips.

'This is serious – I'm her understudy.'

She raised an eyebrow. 'They think a man can play a fairy?'

'Yes, why not? Like Puck in *A Midsummer Night's Dream*. There's a chance I'll be asked to perform the role on opening night.'

'Oh, now that *will* be something to look forward to!'

'Not if it means I can't dance my solo.' Terry shifted sideways in his seat so that he faced Sylvia. 'I don't suppose you'd consider stepping in and playing the wicked fairy for us?'

'Me?'

'Yes, you. You're the haughty, high-drama type – the part wouldn't be much of a stretch.'

'I'll pretend I didn't hear that.' For a while Sylvia played along. 'I suppose I could work on perfecting my sneer.'

'I'm telling you, the director is desperate. There aren't many lines to learn. I'm sure you could do it.'

'But do I want to?' The ballroom was emptying rapidly. Lights were systematically being switched off and soon Terry and Sylvia would be left in the dark. 'Sorry; no – I can't leave Cliff in the lurch in the run-up to Christmas. I'll stick to teaching salsa, thanks.'

Terry accepted her rejection with a gracious, 'It was worth a shot.'

'I *will* tell Cliff we've had this chat,' she assured him as they headed for the door. The last lights were dimmed, with only the glowing red 'Exit' signs to guide them. 'Is there anything else he should know?'

'Like what?'

'Like any new friend whose name I could drop into our conversation?'

'No need to worry on that score,' Terry replied without missing a beat. 'I'm single and fancy-free, just like you.'

Next morning Tommy rose with the lark. The house was silent as he made his way downstairs to the kitchen. Yawning, he pulled up the blind then filled the kettle and placed it on the hob.

The previous night he'd arrived home late from the circus. Joy had beaten him to it and gone straight to bed but now he looked forward to them spending time together. They were both free all day and a glance out of the window told him that the weather promised to be fine enough for a long, leisurely walk on the beach. He wondered briefly whether or not to wake her for an early start (sunrise on an empty beach, complete with loving exchanges, had a definite appeal) but decided against it. A lie-in would do Joy good after the hectic week she'd just had.

Tommy moved quietly around the kitchen. His mother had left a note on the table asking him to fix a dripping tap on the kitchen sink – a task for later. Next to the note was a small pile of unopened letters that he sifted through with only half his mind on the job. A couple of bills – they could wait. A few letters addressed to him and Joy – most likely replies to wedding invitations. He took a knife from the drawer and sliced open the first; yes – a reply from Ruby saying she could come. The second was from Mavis – also accepting the invitation. The third was addressed only to Joy but he opened it anyway, expecting more of the same. The letter inside was longer than the others and it was signed 'George Hebden', a name that Tommy didn't recognize. Quickly realizing that this was none of his business, curiosity nevertheless overcame him so his gaze flew up to the top of the page and he began to read the contents.

Dear Joy,

   This is your cousin, George, writing with news that is bound to surprise you. Allow me to fill in the background. You might remember visiting us with your family here on the west coast of Scotland when you were little – I think you were around three or four years old at the time.

A frown developed on Tommy's face. He was confused; Joy had never mentioned relatives in Scotland. Ought he to read on or wait until she came downstairs? Once more, curiosity got the better of him.

   Soon afterwards there was a falling-out between our fathers. They didn't see eye to eye over money matters. To cut a long story short, my father, Henry Hebden, cheated your father out of a share in the family business: a knitwear manufacturer on the outskirts of Glasgow, with a warehouse in Manchester. He cut off all contact and it was only after my father's death earlier this year that a local solicitor, going through his papers,

193

discovered that your father, Charles Hebden, had been denied a legitimate claim to part-ownership of the company. There is a proviso attached to the claim which I will explain at a later date.

Great Scott! Tommy's head was flooded with confusing ideas. Did this mean that Joy was due to inherit some money? If so, how much? A history of a family at war was bound to cause complications as far as wills were concerned. How long might it take to sort out? Were there other Scottish cousins she didn't know about?

Forgive me; I know this must come as a shock.

The letter continued in George Hebden's small, neat hand.

Once I learned the truth, I felt duty-bound to make contact with your father at his last-known Manchester address, only to learn of his sad fate and that of your mother and sister. Please accept my condolences for your loss. Some months down the line, after persistent enquiries in the neighbourhood, I learned of your prior evacuation to Blackpool and, after further difficulty, was finally able to locate you at your present address.

Tommy sat down at the table. This was a lot to take in and noises overhead told him that Joy and his mother were both on the move. His heartbeat quickened and his hand trembled. He wished for the impossible – that he could stuff the letter back into its envelope and pretend that he hadn't opened it; that he could put it back in the pile and let Joy be the first to discover its contents. Instead, he continued to read.

The thing is, Joy – would you be prepared to meet with me so that I can explain the situation in more detail? It is a matter of some urgency so I could travel down to Blackpool on the train; perhaps next weekend?

What further details were there? Why the need for a meeting? Surely this George Hebden chap could inform Joy by letter how much money she was owed, if any? Panic set in on top of increasing confusion as Tommy heard his mother and his fiancée talking quietly on the first-floor landing. Damn it; he was shaking like a leaf.

With a vague notion that he could reseal the envelope to make it look as if had never been opened before handing it to Joy, Tommy shoved George Hebden's letter and its torn envelope into his pocket.

CHAPTER THIRTEEN

Eddie had been assigned to a first-aid post based in the grounds of the White Swan Hotel in the north part of town. Its old stable block had been converted for Civil Defence use and the yard also housed vehicles and personnel for the ambulance service: a total of twelve volunteers in all, including drivers, first-aiders, a medical officer and two nurses.

On his first night on duty Eddie was greeted by the doctor in charge, a brisk, middle-aged orthopaedic surgeon named Peter Sparrow, who shook his hand then offered to show him round the facilities. 'This is the storeroom for essential equipment – rubber gloves, bandages, splints, stretchers, and so on. Come along, old chap; keep up. And here is the treatment room for casualties brought in by ambulance for initial examination. We deal with minor injuries on the spot. These two Bedford vans are equipped with stretchers, blankets, larger splints and reserve haversacks containing dressings, card labels, indelible pens and scissors; a big step-up from the old unconverted bread vans and private cars that came to us on loan from the general public.'

'What are the card labels and pens used for?' Eddie enquired.

'To write down a casualty's name and the nature of the

injury. You tie the label firmly to the patient's lapel before packing him off to hospital.'

Just like sending off a parcel. Eddie repressed a shudder. He'd been doing his best to take everything in, but face to face with the reality of first-aid work, his brain, like the weather, seemed to freeze. Was he not up to it after all? En route back to the treatment room his MO exchanged friendly greetings with two young female drivers who sat smoking on a bench close to their ambulance. The women regarded Eddie with more than passing interest.

'Is your father Maurice Winter?' Peter Sparrow asked at the end of the high-speed guided tour.

'The very same,' Eddie replied.

'He's a good chap – known him for years. Marion, this is Dr Winter's lad, Edward.' Sparrow handed him over to the nurse in charge. 'Keep an eye on him for me.'

'Marion Cole – pleased to have you on board, Edward.' Officially retired from full-time nursing, Marion – a stout woman with tightly permed hair and an unflappable demeanour – had taken up volunteer work and had soon become the power behind the throne at the White Swan first-aid post.

'It's good to be here. Please call me Eddie.'

'Eddie, follow me.' With the introductions over, Marion assigned him the humdrum task of transferring rubber gloves from a cardboard box on the storeroom floor to the shelf directly above. 'There should be a hundred pairs of each size: small, medium and large. Write down any discrepancy then report back to me.'

Nurse Cole bustled off, leaving Eddie alone in the dimly lit storeroom. He was soon interrupted in his task by one of the female ambulance drivers, a chirpy girl with curly auburn hair and a ready smile.

'Want one?' She offered Eddie a cigarette, which he declined. 'I'm Eileen Shaw, by the way. You're Mavis Thorne's new dance partner, aren't you?'

'I am.' He continued to stack rubber gloves as they talked.

'I live two doors down from her, on Duke Street. She goes on and on about you: Eddie this, Eddie that – how you sweet-talked your dance teacher into giving her lessons for nothing. Honestly, to hear Mavis talk, you'd think the sun shone out of your backside.'

Eddie laughed. 'I'd take that with a pinch of salt if I were you.'

'She's not wrong about one thing, though.' Eileen forged boldly ahead. 'You're easy on the eye and no mistake.'

'Steady on.' He laughed again.

They were interrupted by Eileen's fellow driver, Sandra Turnbull, rushing into the storeroom to deliver a breathless message. 'No time for yacking, you two. Control reports lone Luftwaffe pilot hit by ack-ack fire, bailed out and landed in the drink. To the ambulance pronto!'

Eileen prodded a startled Eddie into action. 'Come along, sunshine; grab your haversack.'

Before he knew it, he found himself squashed between the two girls in the front of the ambulance. Sandra set off at speed, tyres squealing, as they left the yard and turned on to a narrow back street leading to the promenade, where they found other vehicles speeding towards the same incident – a fire engine and a Reserve Police car among them. Closer to the reported sighting, Eileen pointed out a Civil Defence messenger standing by with his bicycle at the entrance to the North Pier, as well as an Incident Officer identifiable by the blue cloth covering on his helmet.

'How do you rate the pilot's chances?' Eddie asked as they reached their destination and, grabbing their equipment, ran on to the beach. Light from the moon allowed them to make out a lifeboat circling the area beyond the end of the pier.

'It depends how quickly he bailed out.' Sandra shared her thoughts. 'By all accounts his Dornier went up in flames. Even if he got out in time he'd have to steer his parachute away from blazing wreckage. Then of course he'd have to be able to swim.'

Eddie didn't hold out much hope as they reached the water's edge. As his eyes grew accustomed to the dark, he was able to make out a white parachute floating on the black surface and he heard the loud voices of the lifeboat men above the sound of crashing waves.

'It sounds as if they've spotted someone,' Eileen muttered.

The first-aiders waited and watched with bated breath as activity at sea narrowed down to an area underneath the pier, close to the shoreline. The Incident Officer took out a pair of binoculars and reported a sighting of a person clinging to a leg of the pier. 'That's our man,' he said through gritted teeth. 'The lifeboat boys can't get close enough – I need a volunteer to wade in and get him.'

Without a moment's hesitation, Eddie sprang into action. Dropping his haversack, he sprinted into the bitterly cold water until the strength of the waves slowed him down. The stench of rotting seaweed filled his nostrils and he struggled to stay upright. Soon he was out of his depth and forced to swim, trying not to swallow saltwater as he made progress through the swirling waves. The enemy pilot still clung to the iron structure, crying out for help in a mixture of German and English.

At last Eddie reached him. To his surprise, the pilot – out of his mind with fear and fury – lashed out, kicking Eddie away and cursing him – '*Berühre mich nicht; no touch, Englischer bastard!*' Losing his grip on the slime-coated leg of the pier, he sank below the surface, still cursing.

Eddie steadied himself on the nearest iron strut, waiting for the stricken pilot to resurface. Sure enough, a head appeared at a distance of some three or four yards. A strong current pushed the man back towards the pier and soon Eddie was able to reach out and grab him by his collar. 'Don't struggle,' he ordered. 'I'm here to help.'

'*Hilfe,*' the pilot echoed faintly. His eyes rolled upwards and he slipped into unconsciousness.

Hearing a shout from above, Eddie made out the figure of Eileen Shaw leaning over the edge of the pier.

'Catch!' she yelled as she flung a lifebelt into the water.

Keeping the pilot's mouth and nose clear of the water as best he could, Eddie caught the belt and looped it over the German's head and shoulders before towing him towards the shore.

Sandra waited at the water's edge, watching anxiously while Eddie brought the enemy pilot ashore. The Incident Officer shone a strong torch beam in their direction, allowing them to assess the man's condition as Eddie dragged him closer. He was a dead weight; still unconscious. By this time Eileen had sprinted back along the pier and both girls wrapped their patient in blankets then laid him on a stretcher and carried him off the beach towards the ambulance with an exhausted Eddie staggering in their wake.

Inside the ambulance, still drenched and shivering from his midnight dip, Eddie helped Sandra to apply a tourniquet to the pilot's injured leg while Eileen drove at speed back to the White Swan post. The man groaned and began to come to, mumbling incoherently and lashing out with his fists as he attempted to sit up.

Sandra held him down. 'See, Eddie; that's what you get for your trouble.'

He tightened the tourniquet to stop the flow of blood. The exhausted patient slipped back into unconsciousness.

'I hope you weren't expecting a medal,' she added with a wry grin.

All that week Pearl went through the motions, rising early then helping to see Elsie safely off to school – 'Hat and gloves, don't forget your dinner money, good luck in your English comprehension test' – before setting off on a brisk walk along the prom to the North Pier. Saturday arrived and there was still no letter from Bernie.

'Give the chap a chance – he's got his hands full fighting Herr Hitler.' Her father's sarcastic mid-week comment had gone down badly with Pearl.

'Do you think I don't know that?' she'd snapped back.

Maria had been more sympathetic. 'There's most likely a logjam at the censors' office. Just you wait; two or three of Bernie's letters will land on the mat all at once.'

Pearl had penned two of her own and sent them off with fingers tightly crossed. She'd started her second letter by attempting to follow her mother's advice.

'Don't tackle anything serious and remember: no complaints,' Maria had cautioned.

'Am I allowed to say I'm missing him?' a peevish Pearl had asked.

'I wouldn't if I were you.' According to her mother, light and upbeat was the order of the day.

My dear Bernie, all is well with me, Pearl had begun.

Here at home we're getting ready for Christmas. I decided to make my cards this year instead of buying them from Woolworth's. I used green gummed paper cut out in the shape of a Christmas tree, with red decorations and a bit of silver glitter as a finishing touch. You'll be happy to know that the arcade is doing decent business for the time of year. Little Mickey is still a firm favourite with the youngsters while Spitfire is popular with the Yanks based at Warton, who get dropped off by the bus load and spend hours on the machines — which means good business for us!

She'd reread what she'd written and almost torn it up. Where would Bernie be when he read this breezy nonsense and what would he be doing? Why would he give a damn about Christmas cards and slot machines out there in the desert? To hell with it; she would write from the heart.

Dearest love; I long to see you again. Write to me please. Mum says your letters must be held up in the system but I don't know if that's true. Write as often as you're able and here's hoping that at least a few of them will get through. My heart aches for you. I think of you night and day. You're in my dreams; your arms are around me and our lips are touching. I wake up each morning hoping and praying that we'll be together again soon. I miss you, Bernie.
    Your ever-loving Pearl xxxx

Days dragged by and her lonely nights left her feeling more forlorn than ever, so she arrived at the arcade on Saturday morning with a heavy heart. *Still* no letter! Despite blue skies, a bitter wind blowing off the sea meant that few customers ventured as far as the end of the pier and as a result business had been slow all morning – only a few off-duty ground crew from the RAF base and the odd fisherman from the end of the pier had paid their entrance money then fed the machines.

Boredom set in. Though she'd tried to keep things positive in her recent letter to Bernie, she secretly wondered whether or not it was even worth opening at this time of year. Pearl's fingers were stiff with cold as she fumbled to place Bing Crosby's 'Deep In The Heart Of Texas' on the turntable and then – surprise, surprise – she glanced up to see a windswept Mavis approaching with her friend, Eileen Shaw from Duke Street, together with Eileen's three little brothers, bright as buttons in windcheaters and balaclavas. The rosy-cheeked boys made a beeline for the Little Mickey machines while Mavis and Eileen stayed by the door to chat with Pearl. Both were dressed for the weather in heavy coats, with woollen scarves and hats.

'I love this tune!' Eileen declared as she began to croon the words and tap her fingers on Pearl's desk in time to the music.

'I love everything by Bing,' Mavis agreed. 'My dream is to sail to America and see the sights, starting with the Statue of Liberty.'

'She has high hopes that a handsome GI from the Warton base will scoop her up,' Eileen confided. 'Mind you, don't we all?'

Pearl raised her eyebrows but said nothing.

'Not you – you're spoken for.' Eileen sifted idly through Pearl's pile of records, picking out 'Jingle, Jangle, Jingle' then 'Travellin' Light' to inspect their covers. At the far end of the room, one of her brothers hit the jackpot and coins rattled into the dish.

'I expect you heard about the hullaballoo here earlier this week?' Mavis drifted towards the nearest machine – a brand-new Dawn Patrol that Bernie had installed just before he left.

'You mean the Jerry pilot who landed in the drink?' Pearl had picked up fragments of gossip without paying too much attention. 'What happened to him in the end?'

'He's still in hospital with a couple of broken ribs, a gash to his left leg and burns to both feet,' Mavis informed her. 'They expect him to pull through, worse luck.'

'Don't say that.' Eileen gave Mavis a small shove. 'Your Eddie risked his life to pull Fritz ashore.'

'Really?' Pearl turned to Mavis. 'That's the first I heard.'

'Eddie signed up as a first-aider,' Mavis explained. 'It was his first night on duty and lo and behold, Jerry gets shot down in flames and Eddie's the hero.'

'Does Sylvia know?' If not, Pearl resolved to be the one to tell her.

Mavis blushed then shook her head. 'Eddie doesn't see much of Sylvia these days. He's too busy practising for January's championship.'

'With you,' Eileen added with a wink. 'Never mind those handsome GIs; you've got a real catch in Eddie Winter. You should've seen him on Tuesday night, Pearl. I was there on the sidelines, taking it all in. Talk about facing the elements – Eddie did front crawl and reached Jerry in no time at all, threw a lifebelt over his head and hauled him back to shore.'

'You don't say.' Pearl realized she would have to adjust her view of Eddie: from mild-mannered pen-pusher to action hero in one fell swoop. 'Who'd have thought he had it in him?'

'Uh-oh!' Hearing the jackpot pay out for a second time, followed by a noisy squabble between her brothers, Eileen hurried off to sort them out.

Meanwhile, Mavis shifted uneasily from one foot to the other. 'You know he's not *my* Eddie. He's just—'

Pearl cut her off mid sentence. 'There's no need to explain.'

Mavis sighed as she took off her knitted hat and let her fair hair fall over her coat collar. Without make-up she looked younger than her twenty years. 'Do you mind if I ask your opinion about Eddie?'

Pearl answered warily. 'Go ahead, though I'm not sure I'll be much help.'

'Him and me: what's it look like to you?'

The earnest, straightforward question took Pearl aback. 'It looks like Mrs Ellis made a good decision,' she answered evasively. 'You and he should do well in any competition you care to enter.'

'No, I mean – are we suited in other ways?'

Pearl's eyes opened wide in astonishment. 'Heavens above, how should I know?'

Mavis quickly checked that Eileen was still busy before continuing. 'I've been stewing over this for a while now and I can't work out what Eddie's thinking. I'm sure he likes me but he's a hard man to read. You know him better than I do – what do you think?'

'I agree – Eddie doesn't give much away,' Pearl confirmed.

'Is that what Sylvia used to say too?'

'She did.' Pearl's answer was abrupt, signalling that she'd say no more on the subject. 'Listen,' she went on, 'what Sylvia thinks isn't important; it's how *you* feel that matters.'

'That's just it – I don't know how I feel.' *Confused, out of my depth, scared, unsure.* 'Eddie's not my usual type, which is putting it mildly. I'm afraid of putting my foot in it with him. But sometimes when he looks at me in a certain way, I think there might be something there.'

A look, a gesture – Pearl remembered the early stages of her courtship with Bernie: that heart-racing, butterflies-in-the-stomach moment when friendship blossoms into romance. Her expression softened. 'I'm sorry I can't help you,' she murmured. 'Only you and Eddie can work that out between you.'

Over by the Little Mickey a stern Eileen gave the boys their marching orders. 'If you three can't play nicely without arguing over who wins what, it's time to leave.'

'Thank you anyway.' Mavis turned away from Pearl with a grateful smile. Then, with a sudden switch of mood, she led the way out of the arcade ahead of Eileen and her squawking brothers. 'Come on, you lot – I'll race you as far as the prom. Ready, get set, go!'

After the brief diversion of Mavis and Eileen's visit, the hours crawled by for Pearl and towards the end of the afternoon she was ready to shut up shop. She came out from behind her desk then stood in the doorway, stretching her arms above her head to ease her stiffness while gazing up at seagulls soaring effortlessly through a sky that showed small patches of blue between wispy white clouds. By the entrance to the pier a military bus stopped to unload a bunch of GIs who swung through the turnstile, obviously intent on playing the machines. Now Pearl would have to stay open longer than planned. And what if her attacker was among them? No; surely Sanderson wouldn't be allowed off base with serious accusations hanging over him? Still, she was on edge as the Americans approached.

They arrived with pockets full of loose change and a confident air, joshing among themselves, throwing around names such as Eugene, Earl and Leroy. After paying their entrance money they quickly chose their machines – Chip or Bust, Cigaretto and Defiant. 'Place coin in slot to release ball', 'Shoot ball into any tube to win'; after reading the instructions, pennies were inserted into slots before metal balls dropped and handles were flicked. Cigarette smoke soon filled the arcade as players stood with their backs turned to Pearl, giving full concentration to their game.

After a few minutes, she hopped down from her stool and went to change the record. When she returned to her desk she noticed Errol playing the Dawn Patrol machine by the door. Though unable to see his face, she recognized him by his sergeant stripes and upright posture.

He turned to greet her with a quiet, 'Howdy again, Miss Pearl.'

She dipped her head apprehensively as she returned the greeting. 'Hello, Sergeant Jackson.'

He approached the desk to pay his entrance money. 'I arrived a little late. And I'm here to tell you that Private Sanderson won't trouble you no more – in fact, he already shipped out.'

'That's good to know.' Pearl relaxed into a longer conversation with her knight errant. 'I take it you and your crew are in town for the night?'

'Yes, ma'am. You know how much these guys love to dance, so the ballroom is where we're headed after we're through here.' His direct gaze didn't waver. 'Will we see you there?'

'No, not tonight.'

'You have other plans?'

'Just a quiet night in with my sewing machine.'

Errol threw her a quizzical look, his dark eyebrows drawn together, his blue-grey eyes unblinking.

Pearl felt her cheeks grow warm. 'My friend is getting married soon. I'll spend the evening making my brides-maid's dress.'

'A wedding, huh? Seems everyone is gettin' hitched in a hurry these days.'

'You're right on that score. This war can whisk a couple down the aisle in the blink of an eye.'

'Sure, I get it.' He took out a pack of cigarettes and offered her one, which she refused. 'Mind if I do?'

'Of course not.' Pearl noticed his hands – they were broad and tanned, with clean nails that were clipped short.

'Same thing happened to guys back home,' Errol continued as he cupped one hand to his mouth to shield the flame from his lighter. 'I lost count of the wedding invitations.'

Pearl's curiosity got the better of her. 'What about you – you weren't tempted?'

He grinned. 'No, ma'am. I guess I wasn't lucky enough to meet the right gal. And maybe I fought shy for family reasons.'

'What would they be?' She was intrigued, as Errol surely intended. In the background, play went on and the air grew thick with cigarette smoke.

'Let's just say I was a kid who grew up watchin' his parents fight like cat and dog pretty much every day of the week.'

His frankness and the directness of his gaze drew her further in. 'That can't have been much fun.'

'No, but it sure taught me a lesson: don't get hitched unless you're certain.'

'I was certain.' For some reason Pearl trusted Errol with this snippet of personal information.

'Lucky you.' His cigarette glowed red as he inhaled. 'You got that letter yet?'

'From Bernie? No, I'm still waiting. Everyone says not to worry but I do.'

'You'd be the only gal in the world not to.' He flicked ash into the ashtray on her desk. 'How do you handle it?'

'You really want to know?'

'Sure.'

'Mostly I just stay busy. The nights are harder, though.'

'You can't sleep?'

'It depends. Sometimes I lie awake wondering where my husband is and what he's up to.'

'Bad idea.' Errol stubbed out his cigarette. 'That'll drive you crazy, for sure.'

'I know, but I can't help it.'

'You need somethin' to take your mind off it – like comin' to the Tower tonight.'

'Nice try!' Pearl's quick retort was accompanied by a laugh. Face it – Errol Jackson had plenty of cheek.

'Worth a shot.' He grinned back at her. 'Sure you won't change your mind?'

Pearl hesitated. Once upon a time she would have jumped at the chance to jive the night away with a good-looking GI who knew how to swing a girl around the floor.

'Sure?' he repeated, a smile still playing on his lips.

'Yes, I'm certain,' she decided. 'Thanks for asking but I've got a date with a Singer sewing machine and a deadline to meet.'

Pearl wasn't the only one who must adhere to a tight schedule. That same evening Joy had arranged for Sylvia to join her at the ice-cream parlour to run up her wedding dress out of surplus parachute silk purchased from the Army & Navy Stores. The pattern was pinned to the fabric laid out on Joy's bedroom floor when Sylvia arrived at dusk in a flurry of light snow.

'*Entra!* Come!' Lucia ushered Silvia in. 'Is cold tonight. Joy – she waits.'

'Upstairs?' Sylvia checked.

'*Sì, sì.*' Lucia's job for the evening was to stay in the kitchen and plan food for the reception. Tommy was working and wouldn't be back until late.

Sylvia tapped on Joy's door before stepping inside. 'I bring scissors, I bring silk thread,' she announced.

'Thank heavens you're here.' Joy knelt on the floor with flushed cheeks. 'I can't work out how to squeeze these last pattern pieces on to the material.'

Sylvia crouched beside her and offered expert advice, gleaned from years of helping her mother to sew elaborate ball gowns. 'Let me see . . . If we move the front bodice pieces an inch or two further over here, we can make room for pieces for the neck facing. *Voilà!*'

'Yes.' Joy breathed a sigh of relief as she pinned the repositioned pattern pieces in place. 'I was worried it wouldn't fit.'

Producing a pair of razor-sharp scissors from her basket, Sylvia proceeded to snip away. 'It's a fairly simple pattern – we'll have this done in no time. Here, take this reel, thread the machine. Stand by, ready for action.'

Joy followed instructions. She took freshly cut bodice pieces from Sylvia and sewed the shoulder seams. There was satisfaction in the whir of the machine and the rapid stabbing motion of the needle. Now it was time to sew the darts at bust and waist, followed by attaching strips of facing to the bodice neckline.

'The skirt will be nice and full,' Sylvia assured her as she set about running two rows of gathering stitches around the waist. 'There might even be enough material left over for a frill around the bottom.'

'No frill.' Joy decided that the dress would look better without.

They worked on in the yellow light cast by two bedside lamps, absorbed in their task, until Joy gathered enough courage to share what had been on her mind for days.

She lifted her foot off the treadle and spoke quietly. 'Sylvia, do you mind if I tell you something?'

'Feel free – that's what friends are for.'

'It might be my imagination but Tommy has seemed a bit off with me lately.'

Sylvia went on with her delicate hand sewing. 'How do you mean "off"?'

'Just not his cheerful self.' Joy found it hard to explain. 'You know Tommy – nothing ever bothers him – but all this week he's been in a bad mood. He even bit Lucia's head off when she asked him a perfectly innocent question about food for the reception.'

'That's not like Tommy.' Sylvia looked up from her work. 'Have you tackled him about it?'

'Twice. The first time he brushed me off with an excuse about Ted Mackie tearing him off a strip for making a late entrance into the ring. The second time he flatly denied anything was wrong.'

'Might it be pre-wedding nerves?' Sylvia suggested. 'Men tend not to show it but it's probably more common than we think; Pearl let slip that Bernie got a bad case of the jitters, remember?'

'It could be.' Joy wasn't convinced. 'But Tommy's the one who pushed for a Christmas wedding, whereas I'd have been happy to wait. Now he seems to have . . . not changed his mind exactly, but just lost interest in the details.'

'Again, that's men for you.' Sylvia's attempt to take the sting out of the situation fell on deaf ears. 'Look, I'm sure Tommy is as keen as ever to marry you. There must be another reason for his bad mood.'

'But what?' Joy had racked her brains and failed to come up with an answer. 'Why won't he talk to me about it?' She teetered on the brink of a further confession then stepped back. What good would it do to tell Sylvia that Tommy's kisses had been few and far between this past week and that every time she'd tried to embrace him he'd pulled away?

Sylvia placed the gathered skirt across the back of a chair then slid an arm around Joy's shoulders. 'I can see you're upset,' she murmured. 'What can I do to help?'

'Nothing, thanks.' Joy broke out of her misery when she glanced at the mantelpiece clock. 'Good Lord, look at the time.' Aware that Terry had given Sylvia two special passes to attend the dress rehearsal of *Sleeping Beauty*, she picked up Sylvia's jacket and thrust it into her hands. 'You'd better hurry if you want to get to the theatre on time.'

'Are you sure?' Sylvia was caught between staying to comfort Joy and fulfilling her promise to Terry.

'Yes – I'm fine; really, I am.' Putting on a brave face was second nature to Joy.

'I'll drop by again soon and help you to finish the dress.'

'Do,' Joy agreed, ushering Sylvia out of the room and hurrying her down the stairs. 'I'll let you out by the front door – it'll be quicker.'

The two girls crossed the unlit ice-cream parlour, careful to avoid upturned chairs resting on bare tables. Posters of Blackpool in summer were dimly visible, together with a framed list of prices for cones, sandwiches and tubs.

Sliding back the bolts, Joy opened the door on to the prom.

'Try not to worry too much,' Sylvia advised.

'I will and thank you again.' Joy watched Sylvia on her way. Snow lay an inch deep on the pavement. 'Mind how you go,' she called after her.

A tall stranger in an overcoat and a trilby hat attracted Joy's attention. He watched proceedings from a tram shelter ten paces from where she stood, seemingly uncertain about crossing the road to speak with her. Thinking that it was probably best not to linger, she closed the door and was halfway across the room when there was a sharp knock at the door.

Hearing the sound from the kitchen, a flustered Lucia joined Joy in the café. '*E tardi. Chi può essere?*'

'There was a man outside who I didn't recognize.' Joy was puzzled, though not especially concerned. 'Perhaps he's lost and needs to ask for directions.'

'*Sì, sì.*' Reassured, Lucia hurried to open the door. '*Buonasera, signore. Come possiamo aiutarla?*'

'How can we help?' Joy translated as she stepped forward.

The man was young, his slim face shaded by the brim of his hat. The crown was covered with a sprinkling of snow. 'Miss Joy Hebden?' he asked in a light, lilting voice.

'Yes, that's me.'

The visitor took off his gloves before offering to shake her hand. 'I'm very pleased to meet you. My name is George Hebden; your cousin from Glasgow – at your service.'

CHAPTER FOURTEEN

Lucia welcomed the stranger then ushered him into the kitchen at the back of the house, where a glowing fire offered both cheer and warmth. Taking his coat and hat, she offered him the seat closest to the fire.

For a while surprise robbed Joy of her powers of speech. She knew nothing about a cousin and yet she could see a family resemblance in George Hebden's dark hair and clean-shaven, fine-boned features. He was smartly dressed and she judged him to be a few years older than her.

'I take it you didn't receive my letter?' he said once he was settled.

Joy stood in mystified silence while Lucia fanned her face and sat down heavily at the table. '*Santo cielo, un'altra lettera!*'

Another letter! First the malicious note from Sam Grigg that had caused such ructions and now a non-existent missive from a well-dressed Scottish cousin that Joy didn't even know she had.

'It dealt with a sensitive matter,' George explained carefully. 'I posted it first class. When I didn't receive a reply, I decided that the best course of action was for me to come here in person.'

'I see.' Joy sat in the chair opposite. 'So this must be important?'

'Extremely. Let me begin at the beginning. Do you remember coming to Scotland on holiday when you were a small child?'

'I'm afraid not.' She had no memory of it whatsoever and felt increasingly confused.

'Hardly surprising – you were very young. But did your father ever mention the existence of an older brother: your uncle, Henry?'

Joy shook her head before glancing at Lucia for reassurance.

'*Calmati*,' Lucia whispered, showing Joy her crossed fingers. '*Va tutto bene.*'

'Yes, all is well.' The visitor displayed a knowledge of Italian before pausing to clear his throat. 'However, before we come to the good news, it's my duty to inform you that my late father, Henry Hebden, behaved very badly with regard to your father, Charles. He fell out with him over a business matter and subsequently cut off all contact.'

Mention of Joy's father brought memories flooding back: of how Charles had worked hard to provide for his family though his wage had never allowed for luxuries. However weary he'd been after an arduous day, he would take off his oil-stained overalls then play games with her and her sister. At weekends he would cycle with them into the countryside, teaching them the names of trees, flowers and birds. Then there'd been the attendance at chapel every Sunday, where the girls had been taught the importance of honesty and kindness. Not once had her father talked about a brother in Scotland. 'This business matter?' she prompted.

With a heavy sigh, George explained the details. 'In the early part of this century, our grandfather, Martin Hebden, began a business manufacturing high-class knitwear from materials sourced in Italy and elsewhere in Europe. He set up two bases – one in Glasgow and one in Manchester – and quickly became successful. When, sadly, Martin was killed during the Great War, provision was in place for Charles and Henry to take equal shares.' He paused to sigh again. 'But, as the older brother who felt he should inherit all, my father bitterly resented the contents of their father's will so he employed a solicitor, and together they cooked up a charge against his brother, your father.'

'What kind of a charge?' Jumping up from her chair, Joy began to pace the room.

'*Calmati*,' Lucia murmured again. She had picked up only fragments of what the visitor had told them.

'Of submitting false accounts and misappropriating funds.'

Joy was incensed. 'My father wouldn't do such a thing – *not ever*!'

'Quite. There wasn't a scrap of evidence but nevertheless the charge damaged Charles's standing with employees. My father also made everyday execution of business in the Manchester branch so difficult for your father that in the end Charles simply decided to close down the warehouse and walk away.'

'That does sound like something my father would do,' Joy confirmed. 'He didn't like to argue with strangers, never mind with his own brother.'

'The truth only came to light after my father passed away earlier this year. As I said in my letter, I found old, incriminating correspondence between my father and a firm of solicitors. The letters were locked away in a safe, together with more recent ones sent by your father attempting reconciliation.'

'I see.' In the cosiness of Lucia's kitchen, Joy began to absorb the implications of what she'd been told. 'So what happens now?'

'Wait – there's more. In those last letters, written three years ago – soon after the declaration of war – your father explained that his reason for re-establishing contact was to secure a better future for you and your sister. It was a heartfelt wish on his part – perhaps because war against Hitler brought home to him the fact that all our lives hang by a slender thread.'

Joy felt a tight band form around her chest. 'That was the reason Dad sent me to Blackpool – he believed I'd be safer here.'

'And he was proved right, as I discovered after much soul searching had led to my attempt to re-establish contact – too late, as it turned out.'

'Yes, too late.' A wave of grief threatened to overwhelm Joy but she held it at bay.

Her cousin's formal tone softened. 'To be plain, Joy, despite all the obstacles, I'm dead set on righting the wrongs of my father.'

Holding her breath, she sensed that a different wave was about to break and alter the shape of her world. Lucia too felt the mounting tension and rose unsteadily to her feet.

'Now that I've finally tracked you down, my aim is to hand over half of the Hebden Knitwear Company. It's rightfully yours, but there's one stipulation in our grandfather's original will, which I'm sure your father would have agreed to, were he still alive.'

'What is it?' Joy whispered. The wave roared in her ears as it crashed over her head.

'That, in order to inherit equally, all future heirs must

be on site to manage their part of the business. It follows that you will be required to live and work in our one remaining branch in Glasgow.'

'You mean I'd have to move away from Blackpool?'

'Correct,' George confirmed, calm and rational as ever. 'Your day-to-day input will only work if you're on the spot – surely you see that?'

Joy struggled to breathe. 'I do see it,' she gasped.

'But?'

'But I have a fiancé here. We're due to get married on Saturday.'

'*Sì, sì!*' The words 'fiancé' and 'married' brought a relieved smile to Lucia's lips. 'My Tommy, he loves this girl. Soon they marry – *saranno felice per sempre* – happy for ever; *capisci*!'

George Hebden had left without a firm commitment from Joy shortly before Tommy came home from the circus and found his fiancée and his mother sobbing their hearts out at the kitchen table. A flash of intuition told him that this was to do with the letter that he'd kept concealed in his jacket pocket.

Joy ran to him and collapsed in his arms. Her garbled account of her cousin's visit confirmed his fears. 'George says that in order to inherit my part of the family business I have to live in Scotland, but how is that possible? How can we leave Blackpool?'

Acute discomfort registered on Tommy's face. So this was the mysterious proviso that he'd read about. 'I don't know what to say,' he confessed.

Feeling the tension in his body, Joy took an instinctive step back to study his guarded expression. 'You don't seem surprised.'

Put on the spot, Tommy tried to bluster his way through. 'What makes you say that?'

'I can just tell.' Sixth sense prompted her next question: 'Did you already know about this?' Her voice rose in astonishment.

'No,' he muttered. 'It's news to me.'

'You did – you knew!' The realization that he was telling a lie shocked her to the core.

Crumbling under Joy's fierce gaze and not knowing what else to do, Tommy could only admit to what he'd done. Meekly he drew George Hebden's letter from his pocket and handed it to her without a word.

Joy's hands shook as she opened the envelope and scanned its contents. 'When did this arrive?'

'A week ago.' He'd endured six long days of doubt and fear about what would happen if Joy grew rich and he, Tommy Rossi, stayed poor. The notion had plagued him, entering his bloodstream like a deadly poison, preventing him from doing the honourable thing.

'My Tommy, you keep this from your Joy?' Lucia grew more distressed. 'My son, why?'

'It's all right,' Joy told her gently. 'This argument is between me and Tommy. You go up to bed.'

'I go, I go.' Reluctantly Lucia retreated, with tears still streaming down her cheeks.

'But yes; Lucia is right to ask – why hide it?' Joy was determined to drag the truth out of Tommy.

'I don't know why – I can't explain.' How to describe the panic he'd experienced at the notion of money creating a wedge between them; the shortness of breath, the churning stomach, the inability to think straight? 'I did intend to come clean but I just kept putting it off. I'm sorry.'

'Sorry!' she echoed in disbelief, clutching the letter in one hand. 'All week I've known that something was wrong and now I see what.'

'Please, Joy; I wasn't thinking straight.' He reached out to her but she backed away.

'I assume that you read it?'

He nodded miserably.

'So you knew how vitally important it was?'

'Yes – there's no excuse.'

'That's right; there isn't.' Now she approached him so that his face was only inches from hers. Her cheeks flamed with fury while his were white as a sheet. 'Tommy, I believed you when you said you loved me.'

'I do. You know I do. Please, Joy . . .' He reached out again, only for her to retreat for a second time.

'Love means being honest, not keeping secrets – that message was drummed into me by my mother and father.'

'Not keeping secrets; yes! But I could say the same thing about you – you didn't tell me about Sam Grigg's note.'

'That was different. I kept it a secret because I was upset and I knew that it would upset you too. I sat on it because I had no idea what else to do.'

'So it's the same.' Fearing that his defence didn't stand up to close scrutiny, Tommy was forced to back down. 'All right; your cousin's letter contained good news, not bad, and I ought not to have hidden it, but even so, you must know what it's like when your head goes into a spin and you can't see a way forward.'

Joy was in no mood to listen. 'My parents made sacrifices for me and my sister that you could never understand. It seems to me that they're the ones who truly cared.'

'Don't go on, please!' Tommy dreaded what was coming.

She put her hands over her ears. 'George believes that

Dad would have wanted me to accept the inheritance and move to Glasgow. There are letters from my father to that effect.'

Hope and energy drained from Tommy. What more was there to say?

Joy too ran out of words as she pictured her father swallowing his pride and writing to the brother who had wronged him, all for the sake of her and Margaret. 'Oh, Tommy!' She sighed, shaking her head in despair and turning from him before slowly mounting the stairs.

The dress rehearsal for *Sleeping Beauty* was open to specially invited guests, including Stanley Bishop, the theatre critic for the *Blackpool Gazette*.

From their vantage point in the front row of the upper circle, Sylvia and Cliff spotted Bishop, a small, dapper man with thick white hair and a prominent, beaky nose, who sat with other reviewers in the front row of the stalls. Cliff's heart sank: the *Gazette* man was known for writing harsh reviews. Sylvia, too, was ill at ease, remembering Terry's recent description of shambolic rehearsals.

'Why should I care what appears in the papers? What am I even doing here?' Cliff grumbled as the lights went down and the curtains opened.

'You came because I offered you my spare ticket,' Sylvia reminded him. 'And because you still care about Terry, however much you pretend not to.'

'You didn't tell him I was coming?' Cliff checked.

'Not a word,' she promised as they settled into their seats.

The performance began with a brightly lit castle interior showing an infant princess surrounded by a king and queen and their attendants, as seven fairy godmothers brought gifts to celebrate the baby's christening. The overture was brisk, the scene full of colour and movement.

'There he is!' Sylvia spotted Terry among the chorus in purple tabard and green tights, dancing the polka across the front of the stage as notes from the string section soared and presents of gold and jewels were laid beside the baby's cradle. Sylvia noted with relief that the wicked fairy, lurking behind the king's throne, had evidently got her voice back.

The first scene went without a hitch. The wicked fairy took centre stage and the lighting and music grew sinister. All was gloomy as she cursed the sleeping child. 'The prick of a spindle will mark her end. This much is certain: I will not bend!' With a melodramatic cackle the wicked fairy exited in a puff of smoke. Darkness descended.

'What's the verdict on Terry so far?' Sylvia whispered to Cliff as scene shifters went to work.

'Adequate.' The short, grudging answer hid a mix of emotions. Cliff's eyes had been glued to his former lover's every move and he hadn't been able to fault him – besides not putting a foot wrong, Terry had oozed confidence and given the impression of being perfectly at home on the stage.

'Don't be stingy; he's doing splendidly.' Sylvia had no more time to sing Terry's praises as a comedy section began, involving a new character: Simple Simon. The put-upon stable lad clowned his way through a scene with a pantomime horse until his mother, the palace cook and the show's Dame, came along and whacked him over the head with her frying pan.

Soon there was another scene change, during which twenty years passed in the blink of an eye. Beautiful Belle was now lovely to behold, waltzing her way through a charmed life with the chorus variously dressed as servants, peasants and courtiers. Girl dancers performed a high-kicking Tiller Girls routine, while the Dame and Simple Simon had more knockabout fun. But danger lurked in the tower, in a room containing a hidden spinning wheel. Disaster: Belle pricked her finger on the spindle and fell into the sleep that would last a hundred years. Terry was part of the sombre procession that carried her glass coffin deep into the forest.

'My nerves won't take much more of this,' Cliff confessed under his breath.

'Why? Terry's dancing really well.'

'Because!' *Because I wish we hadn't argued. Because I miss Terry every minute of every day and life without him is too much to bear.* For two pins Cliff would have got up and walked out.

'Stay for his solo, at least,' Sylvia implored in a whisper and Cliff gave in.

Enter Terry to a painted forest backdrop, dressed as the prince's huntsman in green jerkin, Robin Hood hat and long leather boots, to the sound of horns and the clip-clop of hooves from the orchestra pit. Terry's *grands jetés* were lithe and strong, his pirouettes were perfect, but the solo in front of a tangle of thorns that concealed Belle's coffin was over in a flash. Enter the handsome prince and his entourage, leading to the kiss that solved everything.

If only real life were that simple. Sylvia and Cliff descended from the upper circle exchanging similar thoughts. They emerged from the thinly populated foyer into the glass arcade, stopping briefly for a drink at the bar before stepping outside and attempting to flag down a taxi to take them back to North View Parade.

Competition for cabs was strong and Cliff hailed a few without success. 'Damn this blackout,' he muttered as he failed on his third attempt. 'It makes it impossible to work out which ones are already taken.'

As they stood and debated whether or not to catch a tram instead, two figures emerged from the side alley leading to the stage door of the Opera House. Despite the absence of street lamps, Sylvia recognized Terry immediately. He was with a friend and the two men seemed deep in conversation, though they were too far away to hear what was said. Terry's companion must have told a joke because Terry threw back his head and laughed long and loud. The companion elbowed him in the ribs, Terry clutched his side and pretended to be hurt then stood up straight and laughed again. The two men hugged.

'Let's take a tram.' Sylvia tried to turn Cliff in the direction of the prom.

It made no difference; Cliff had already spotted Terry and his companion. He watched them walk off in the other direction, flushed with success after the smooth dress rehearsal, arms linked and oblivious to their surroundings.

Cliff closed his eyes and swallowed hard. 'As I suspected.' With a deep frown he resisted Sylvia's attempt to steer him towards the prom. 'On second thoughts, I'll walk home,' he decided. 'You go ahead and catch the tram. Don't worry about me – I just need some air.'

Lorna made no effort to hide her disappointment. 'This is the second time Joy and Tommy have missed a lesson,' she complained to Mavis and Eddie as they began their Sunday-morning session. 'At this rate I'll be forced to withdraw them from the competition; they simply won't have had sufficient practice.'

'That's a bit harsh,' Mavis muttered under her breath as

Lorna placed a record on the gramophone. 'Doesn't she realize Tommy and Joy are getting married this coming Saturday? They're bound to have loads to do.'

'Lorna is a perfectionist,' Eddie reminded her. 'Besides, if entrants from her academy perform poorly, that reflects badly on her.'

'The pressure is on us then.' Mavis's competitive streak meant that she would rise to the challenge. During the next hour, every undulation, every sway and change of speed and every complicated step sequence received their full attention. Wintry sun shone in through the plate-glass window across the shiny studio floor. Dust motes floated in the air. Lorna's instructions drifted out through the open door and upstairs to the living room, where Sylvia sat leafing through magazines.

'Excellent, Mavis – keep up the good work!' Lorna's praise reached Sylvia's ears. 'That's the spirit, Edward – neatly synchronized. Mavis, remember to keep your feet perfectly parallel. Now let's try the tricky reverse turn one more time – that's right, Edward; beautifully done.'

'Phew!' Mavis exclaimed, dabbing at her forehead after Lorna had brought the lesson to a close then disappeared upstairs to keep Sylvia company. Muscles in Mavis's back, shoulders and neck ached and her heels felt as though they were developing blisters. 'I thought I was fit as a flea but it turns out I was wrong.'

'The Viennese waltz definitely takes it out of you,' Eddie admitted. 'It sounds simple: a change step with two rotational travelling figures; natural and reverse turns in six steps, not to mention the fleckerl, all at a hundred and eighty beats per minute.'

'You do love your facts and figures,' Mavis teased. 'I'm more of a relax-and-let-it-flow type myself.'

'Still, our partnership seems to work.' Eddie bent to tie the laces on his street shoes. When he looked up, Mavis's head was startlingly close to his as she too was changing her footwear. Her cheeks were flushed and the pupils of her brown eyes were dilated. When she blinked, he saw how her dark lashes curved and cast a shadow over her cheeks.

Mavis sat up abruptly and leaned against the mirror that ran the length of the studio. This could be a now-or-never moment between her and Eddie. True to form, she jumped in with both feet. 'Do you mind if I ask you something?'

He was tempted to brush back the strands of damp hair that strayed across her smooth forehead. 'Fire away,' he replied.

'You like dancing with me, don't you?'

'I should say so.' Eddie kept on studying details of Mavis's appearance: the way her eyebrows arched and her fair hair fell in waves, glinting gold in the sunlight.

'And is that all – you're happy with me as your dance partner?' Had she been too blunt? Would Eddie take to his heels and disappear in a cloud of dust like a Hollywood cowboy galloping off into the distance? Mavis held her breath.

'No.' His answer took them both by surprise. 'That's not all.'

'Then what else?'

'Then this,' he murmured. He leaned towards her and saw her mirror his movement. They tilted their heads in the same direction and smiled as their noses brushed. Then Eddie tilted his head further to the right and they moved closer and softly kissed.

Neither noticed Sylvia standing in the doorway. Lorna

had sent her to tidy up the studio and Sylvia had at first reacted with bad grace. Why must her mother treat her like a dogsbody? Didn't she deserve to put her feet up once in a while?

'I'm sorry, Mother,' she'd apologized immediately. 'Ignore me – I'm tired, that's all.'

'Then leave it for now.' Lorna had changed her mind. 'We can both do it later, after we've had a cup of tea.'

'No – you put the kettle on while I tidy up downstairs.'

And this was how Sylvia came to be standing in the doorway to witness Eddie and Mavis's first kiss. Their lips met, they drew back and stared into each other's eyes. Then Eddie drew Mavis to him and they kissed again.

The only way that Sylvia could cope was to try to obliterate the image from her mind. Sick at heart, she took the tram home from King Alfred Street, made herself a fish paste sandwich for lunch, forced it down and then sat down at her sewing machine to put the finishing touches to her bridesmaid's dress. Once this was done, she must iron two blouses and three pairs of slacks before polishing her shoes. Tomorrow she was due to teach five classes in all, standing in for Cliff while he touted for business further afield in Lytham St Anne's.

One foot after another was as much as she could manage.

The sudden ring of the doorbell made her jump out of her skin. Who on earth could this be?

There was a second ring – long and insistent.

Sylvia went to the first-floor window, parted the net curtains and looked down to see Joy, hatless and with her jacket hanging open, pressing the bell for a third time. She dashed downstairs and opened the door.

'Thank heavens you're in.' Joy stumbled across the threshold. 'I hope I'm not interrupting – I need to talk to you.'

'You're not interrupting.' Sylvia didn't waste time asking questions. 'Come on up.' She led the way to her living room and sat Joy down on the sofa, told her to take a few deep breaths to calm herself then sat down beside her. 'What is it? What's happened?'

Catching sight of the bridesmaid's dress on Sylvia's sewing table, Joy burst into tears. 'It's Tommy,' she sobbed.

'Is he ill? Has he had an accident?' Sylvia snatched likely explanations out of the air.

'No, it's not that. You know I told you that something felt off? It turns out I was right.'

'Why; what's happened?'

'He lied to me.' The words were out and couldn't be recalled. They turned the nightmare into a reality. 'Tommy lied to me!'

Sylvia waited for the sobbing to ease, patting Joy's shoulder and murmuring, 'There, there,' as if to quieten a child. 'Take your time.'

'I have a cousin called George.' Joy flew off at a tangent that at first Sylvia couldn't follow. 'He turned up out of the blue. Tommy already knew about him – he'd hidden a letter written by George and addressed to me then he lied about it.'

'Here; dry your eyes.' Sylvia offered a handkerchief from her pocket. 'This cousin . . . ?' she prompted.

'The thing is, Sylvia – he wants me to move to Scotland – to Glasgow.'

'Whatever for?' an incredulous Sylvia demanded. Glasgow might as well have been the ends of the earth as far as she was concerned.

'To work in the family knitwear business,' Joy explained. 'Years ago, after the Great War, there was a branch in Manchester that was run by my father but he was driven out of the business by George's father and they closed it down. Now there's only the one in Scotland.'

'Wait!' This was earth-shattering news indeed. 'Doesn't this cousin of yours realize you can't just up-sticks and leave? You have friends here and a job. You have a fiancé whom you're about to marry.'

'George knows all of that.' Gradually Joy's sobs subsided and she was able to take a few jagged breaths. 'I spelled it out carefully but that was before I learned what Tommy had done.'

'Slow down – take me through it step by step.'

'It's complicated: to do with my grandfather's will and some unscrupulous solicitors. The fact is, I've come into an inheritance.'

'But wait – surely that's good news. Doesn't coming into money mean you can give up your cleaning work and concentrate on dancing?'

'Sylvia, you're not listening.' Joy made an impatient, flicking gesture with her fingers. Her face was blotchy and her eyes red from crying as she gathered her thoughts. 'To inherit my share, I must move to Glasgow and get involved in the family business. Not that Tommy realized this when he opened the letter that George sent. He only knew that I was set to inherit some money and that's the reason he hid it.'

'But why?'

'Because!' Fresh tears flowed. 'Because it meant I would be rich and he wouldn't be – that's the way he explained it.'

'Hurt pride.' Sylvia's short comment summed up how Tommy must have felt. 'He's a traditionalist. He probably sees himself as the breadwinner looking after his wife, being the good husband.'

'That's all well and good. But I can't get over the fact that he deceived me. I trusted him and he betrayed me.'

'Betrayal is a big word,' Sylvia murmured.

'But that's how it feels.'

'Yes, and I'm not excusing it.'

A heavy silence enveloped them as they followed their own trains of thought. In Sylvia's opinion, it seemed that Tommy might have acted rashly and unwisely but had hardly committed a capital offence, while Joy felt herself stretched and tortured on the rack of distrust.

'I've told George that I'll seriously consider going to Scotland,' Joy said at last.

Sylvia gasped. 'No – surely not?'

'Don't you see? It's what my father wanted me to do – Dad made his wishes plain in letters he wrote before he died.'

'And how did Tommy react?'

'He pleaded with me, begged me not to leave.' Joy's words were choked by sobs heaved from deep within her chest. 'I thought my heart would break.'

'And you will at least let the dust settle before you make a final decision? Surely there's a way around this that you haven't thought of yet?'

'No.' *A broken heart doesn't mend. A betrayal as big as this can't be overcome.* Joy stretched out her left hand to show Sylvia that her ring finger was bare. 'I've already made up my mind about one thing: you and Pearl must pack up your sewing kits and put away your bridesmaids' dresses. The wedding is off and there's an end to it.'

CHAPTER FIFTEEN

Still no letter from Bernie. Not knowing where he was or how he was doing was torture for Pearl.

How could life go on as normal while she lived in a kind of suspended animation, her emotions strangled by constant worry? Her early-morning walk to North Pier reminded her how close to Christmas they were – shops selling cards and gifts displayed bright paper streamers in their windows while toy shops advertised special offers on dolls, teddy bears, Meccano sets and Hornby trains. A hoarding outside a newsagent's attracted her attention, informing her that British infantry had gained ground in the desert but reports of missing servicemen had increased. Repressing a shudder, she walked briskly on.

And last night, out of nowhere, had come this crushing news about Joy and Tommy. Sylvia had shown up un-announced at Empire Street to bring Pearl up to date. 'Hold everything – the wedding's off,' she'd reported breathlessly before she'd even stepped over the threshold. 'Poor Joy's in a terrible state – I left her in my flat, crying her eyes out. I promised to come straight here and tell you.'

The ins and outs had tumbled from Sylvia's lips over a cup of tea in the Scotts' kitchen. Apparently, Joy couldn't face going back to the ice-cream parlour so Sylvia had offered to let her stay overnight. 'She can sleep in my bed and I'll sleep on the couch, then we'll see how she feels in the morning.' From Pearl's house Sylvia had intended to go on to Rossi's to pick up a few of Joy's belongings.

Maria had listened in to Pearl and Sylvia's conversation, tutting and shaking her head before contributing her two penn'orth. 'What is the world coming to? One minute Joy Hebden and Tommy Rossi are head over heels in love, next minute it's all off. What about the vicar at All Saints – does he know the wedding's cancelled? And the best man and all the guests? What does Lucia Rossi have to say about it?'

Sylvia hadn't been able to provide any answers. Nothing was certain, everything was in flux.

How easily a dream was shattered – all those fragile hopes, those whispered endearments, were smashed to smithereens, their jagged shards scattered underfoot. Poor Joy. Poor Tommy. Pearl withheld judgement until she'd managed to talk it through with Joy face to face. Meanwhile, sticking to her resolution to concentrate on the next task in front of her, she pushed through the turnstile at the entrance to the pier and walked on towards the arcade. Through gaps between the weather-worn boards, seawater foamed beneath her feet and a persistent westerly wind tugged at her clothes. More snow was forecast and it was bitterly cold.

'I haven't given George my final answer yet.' Misery seeped from Joy's pores when she returned to the ice-cream parlour early on Monday afternoon. She'd chosen a time when she hoped Tommy would be working, intending to pack up the bulk of her belongings before her cleaning shift at the Tower. She'd expected to see Lucia and, sure enough, Tommy's mother greeted her with eyes that were red from weeping. 'My cousin has agreed to stay in town until midweek for me to make up my mind. Until then, nothing is certain.'

Lucia, dressed in a familiar green dress and striped apron, took comfort from this delay and made Joy sit down at a table in the empty ice-cream parlour. 'My Tommy, he is sorry,' she began before she was prevented from saying more by a fresh bout of loud crying.

Joy put her hand over Lucia's. 'I know he is.'

'His heart breaks,' Lucia sobbed after a long silence. 'My heart also – it aches *così tanto*.'

'An apology doesn't alter what he did,' Joy explained. 'Sorry is only a word.' She'd lain awake in Sylvia's bed, searching for a path towards forgiveness. This was a single betrayal that might never be repeated. Tommy had taken leave of his senses and acted out of fear. It had been completely out of character. She'd taken one tentative step along the road, then two, then three – but then she'd hit the brick wall of her beloved father's wish for her to go to Glasgow. Forgiving Tommy was one thing, but following her father's dream was another. The two were diametrically opposed.

'But he means it – he is sorry. He is good boy, true boy – he loves you *con tutto il suo cuore*.'

With all his heart. Tears came to Joy's eyes as she translated Lucia's phrase. 'Did he go to work today?' she asked.

'*Sì, sì*. I make him go.'

'Good. And you – you must keep busy too.'

'*Sì* . . . but the wedding . . . ?' Lucia's halting words hung in the air.

'It's off.' Joy was firm as she turned to practical matters. 'Sylvia has said that I can stay with her for as long as I want so I've come to collect my things. It won't take me long to pack.'

Lucia sat helplessly while Joy carried out her plan. She heard her run upstairs then listened to light footsteps moving quickly around the room above. '*No, no,*' she murmured. With a clumsy but determined movement she pushed back her chair then rushed up to the bedroom to plead with Joy one last time.

The suitcase lay open on the bed, spilling over with dresses, slacks, jumpers and shoes. All were carelessly thrown in and the room was cleared except for one item on the mantelpiece. Joy picked up the framed photograph of her, her sister and her parents at the fairground. 'Oh Boy!' read the sign on the roundabout behind them. Margaret wore white ribbons in her hair and a smile from ear to ear. Her mother, in a flowered cotton dress with white belt and sandals, stared shyly into the camera. Her father, in shirtsleeves, with neatly parted hair, looked happy and proud. Joy ran her fingertips over the smooth glass surface.

'*Mia cara ragazza,*' Lucia murmured on witnessing Joy's raw sense of loss. My dear girl.

Tommy timed his exit from the circus to coincide with the end of Joy's shift. 'I promised to pick up Mum's prescription from the chemist's before it shuts,' he explained to Ted Mackie, who sat at the brightly lit mirror in their dressing room, removing his make-up with cotton-wool swabs. 'Tell the boss I'll be back in time for tonight's show.'

'Prescription, my eye!' The little clown didn't believe a word. 'A quick kiss and cuddle in the broom cupboard, more like.'

How wrong could he be? Tommy felt the sting of the

jibe but seconds were precious if he wished to catch Joy before she left the building, so he rushed along the corridor that linked the circus to the ballroom then took the stairs to the balcony in time to see Ruby on the ballroom floor ordering her crew to pack away their cleaning gear. Joy was among them, her back turned as she stowed away her brushes and dusters in the storeroom under the stage then dragged out a bulging suitcase that he recognized with a piercing stab of remorse. Then he watched Ruby take Joy to one side and speak earnestly as the other cleaners hurried off. Joy kept shaking her head in response to Ruby's questions and the conversation ended with the supervisor giving her a quick hug before sending her on her way.

With his heart in his mouth, Tommy hurried back downstairs in time to intercept Joy on her way out through the main entrance, where she paused and dropped her heavy suitcase on the wet pavement. A sea mist had blown on to the shore, shrouding the prom in a thick grey mist. 'Please, can we talk?' he begged.

Overcoming the shock of him appearing out of nowhere, Joy picked up the case and carried on walking. 'What is there to talk about?'

'Can't we at least try?'

She stopped again to look him in the eye. There was no sparkle there; only dread. 'Tommy, it's no use.'

'But I love you,' he blurted out. 'I'll never love anyone else. And you love me – I know you do.'

'That's not the point.' Cold mist swirled around them, making it difficult to see the way ahead. A tram approached a nearby stop, a car horn sounded. A man pushing a wheelbarrow laden with holly and mistletoe emerged from the alleyway next to the Tower. 'Don't you see? My father's last wish before he died was to see me settled into a safe, secure future. Even if I could get over what you did, which I'm not saying I can, I still couldn't stay here and marry you.'

'But I'd look after you. I promise you'd be safe with me.' Tommy swore he would fight to the death for her, the love of his life. 'Your dad didn't know about us when he wrote those letters. If he'd met me, he would have changed his mind.'

'Oh, Tommy, please stop.' She saw the desperate hurt in those eyes, heard it in his voice, but still she wouldn't relent. 'I can't deal with what ifs; I can only go with what Dad wanted.'

He stared at her without speaking, no longer seeing the gay, dancing, laughing girl he loved but the lonely young outsider who had suffered the greatest loss of all. Joy's streak of self-reliance, independence, ability to survive – call it what you will – was what had set her apart in the first place, but now it created a gap between them that widened by the second.

'Say you understand,' she pleaded.

Tommy grew desperate. 'I do, but there must be a way for us to get through this. If I promise never ever to let you down again, if I say over and over that I wasn't thinking straight, that I'll do whatever it takes to put things right . . .'

'Tommy.' She spoke his name gently but with an air of finality. Another tram approached, as yet invisible but heading north along the prom in the direction she needed.

'Joy, please don't hate me,' he begged as they reached the tram shelter and she set down her case again.

'I could never hate you,' she promised. The looming tram materialized through the mist and rattled to a halt.

Passengers alighted, coughing and complaining about the weather. 'I'm sorry – I have to go.'

'Come on, love; are you getting on or not?' the impatient conductress leaned out from her platform at the back of the tram and called to Joy.

'I have to go,' Joy repeated in a faint whisper.

So Tommy, feeling the weight of the world on his shoulders, reluctantly lifted her case and slid it on to the platform. Joy stepped up after it. The clippie rang the bell and the tram departed.

Immediately on arrival at his first-aid post on Monday evening, Eddie was greeted by a report of an unexploded bomb found nestling in sand dunes at the northern end of the Golden Mile.

'No peace for the wicked!' Eileen yelled at him in her usual energetic manner as she climbed into her ambulance. 'Get a move on, slowcoach; grab your haversack. Let's go.'

Eddie collected his kit from the storeroom and was soon sitting in the passenger seat next to her. 'No Sandra tonight?' he asked as Eileen left the yard then drove hell for leather along the prom. Visibility was low due to a thick sea fret, but this didn't seem to bother the seasoned ambulance driver.

'No. It's just the two of us – lucky you!'

'Any reports of injuries?' he enquired.

'None so far. We'll be on standby, just in case.'

Eddie clung to the door handle as Eileen swerved wide of a parked car then careered on towards the scene of the incident. At this rate it would be him who required first-aid treatment. Through the mist he was able to make out the dark outline of the massive Norbreck Hydro to their right, which meant there were cliffs to their left and beyond that a stretch of dunes where the bomb had been found.

Sure enough, an Incident Officer soon flagged them down and updated them.

'The bomb disposal boys are on their way,' he reported quickly and efficiently. 'I've got two wardens standing by in case we need to evacuate nearby residents.'

'What's the score with the UXB?' Eileen tapped the steering wheel impatiently.

Their superior officer relayed the basic facts. 'Suspected Electron incendiary, one kilo variety; Jerry's favourite. Report came in from a member of the public – may be something, may be nothing. Bomb recognition warden is down there now, taking a closer look.'

'Good – we can't afford to take any risks,' she grunted.

'Stay where you are for now,' the Incident Officer ordered before flagging down the next vehicle to arrive – a rescue party lorry bringing searchlights to the scene.

'If it is an Electron, it could be a DA,' Eileen informed Eddie. 'A Delayed Action,' she explained as a party of men carried the searchlights across the dunes. 'The term is self-explanatory – they're designed to go off some time after they land, all the better to kill an innocent passer-by.'

Thrilled at being in the thick of things once more, Eddie wound down his window and leaned out. 'This damned fog,' he muttered. 'I can't see a thing.' He was about to open his door and jump down from the van to investigate when he remembered the order to stay where they were. It was a nerve-racking wait. Minutes ticked by without further news. Down on the beach, searchlights were switched on and were dimly visible from where he and Eileen sat.

A uniformed figure ran out of the dunes to speak to the Incident Officer then returned the way he'd come.

'Not much fun, is it?' Eileen picked up on Eddie's nervousness. 'Sitting here twiddling our thumbs.'

He was already aware that an incendiary, DA or otherwise, would fizz and send off a shower of bright sparks before exploding. 'If it is what they think it is, the trick will be to smother it in sand as soon as it starts to spark.'

Eddie and Eileen sat tight and waited . . . and waited. At last the same figure came up from the dunes, wielding what looked like a length of thick metal tube. 'False alarm!' he cried at the top of his voice. 'No bomb; just this piece of rusty old drainpipe.'

The Incident Officer backed this up with a call of, 'Relax – back to base, everyone.'

'Bloody hell.' Eddie felt a dull sense of anticlimax as he exhaled loudly and Eileen turned on the engine before making a wide U-turn.

'A pity there's no call for Superman heroics tonight,' she teased, driving at her usual breakneck speed back to the White Swan, with Eddie holding on to the door handle as before.

Nurse Marion Cole waited in the treatment room with a list of mundane tasks for them to complete. There were bandages and packets of cotton wool to unpack and the webbing straps on a Trigg lift to repair. Towards the end of Eileen and Eddie's shift, a civilian call came through – an ambulance was needed to take an elderly man to hospital. Eileen noted down the North View Parade address then Eddie joined her in the ambulance, preparing for yet another white-knuckle ride. He kept his eyes closed for most of the short journey, only opening them when Eileen squealed to a halt outside Ibbotson's tobacconist's.

'This is the place,' she declared as she applied the handbrake.

'Are you sure?' Of all the addresses that could have come up, it had to be this one. The elderly man mentioned in the telephone call must be Jack Ibbotson, owner of the shop beneath Sylvia's flat.

Eileen double-checked her information on a slip of paper provided by Nurse Cole. 'Sure as eggs,' she confirmed. 'Give them a knock, there's a good chap.'

Eddie obliged. A loud *rat-a-tat-tat* brought Ibbotson's shop boy to the door and a quick exchange of information established that the shopkeeper had fallen out of bed, landed on his head and knocked himself out. The lad had panicked. His first thought had been to telephone the first-aid post but now the ambulance was here it seemed that the old man had recovered.

'Let's check him over anyway,' Eileen decided.

Together she and Eddie followed the boy across the shop then into the dingy living quarters at the back, where they found old Mr Ibbotson sitting up in bed, his white hair tousled, his striped pyjamas wrongly buttoned.

'It's a lot of fuss about nothing,' he grumbled to Eddie, who examined a prominent bump on his forehead. 'I'll be right as rain come morning.'

Eddie took his temperature then felt his pulse. He shone a torch into his eyes to check for signs of double vision but found none. 'Right you are,' he decided. 'We'll be on our way and leave you to get a good night's sleep.'

Ibbotson's boy looked embarrassed as he showed them to the door.

'Better safe than sorry,' Eileen assured him. 'Don't worry – you did the right thing.'

Two anticlimaxes in one shift left Eddie feeling

deflated. Eileen looked at her watch and saw that their spell of duty had reached its end. 'I'll drive this old girl back to base – no need for you to tag along,' she suggested.

'Thanks.' Sensing that they were being watched, he glanced up to see a raised blind and the outline of a figure standing at the window. 'If you're sure.'

'Quite sure.' No sooner said than Eileen was roaring off in her ambulance, swerving around reserve water tanks all along the Golden Mile.

Back on North View Parade, the door opened again to reveal Sylvia in a blue silk dressing gown and slippers.

'Is everything all right?' She was obviously worried.

'Everything's fine,' Eddie replied awkwardly. 'We came to check on Mr Ibbotson. He had a fall but luckily he's none the worse for wear. Sorry to disturb you.'

'You didn't disturb me.' Looking down on the street from her first-floor viewpoint and spying Eddie in uniform had startled her and concern for her landlord had brought her downstairs in time to see the CD ambulance race off down the street. 'Have you finished your shift? Would you like to come in?'

He hesitated then said, 'No thanks – I'd better be off.'

Off where? Sylvia didn't speak the question but her quizzical look conveyed it. *Off to meet Mavis, perhaps?*

Eddie felt his heartbeat quicken inexplicably. Why did Sylvia still have this effect on him after all this time? 'Dad will be expecting me.'

'I see. Give him my regards.' Her unspoken question still hung in the air.

The dead-of-night conversation staggered on, as icy as the wind that cut through Sylvia's flimsy dressing gown. 'How's Mavis?' she asked pointedly.

'Ah.' Eddie stepped back again and adjusted his tone.

'She's well, thanks – naturally she's excited about the championship. Your mother may have mentioned how pleased she is with her progress.'

'She has,' Sylvia confirmed. It was clear from Eddie's evasive answer that mention of Mavis had thrown him off balance.

'Dash it, Sylvia – if there's something in particular that you want to know about me and Mavis, why not just ask?'

'There isn't,' she fibbed. The kiss in the studio had told her all she needed to know. 'It's none of my business,' she added hastily before swerving off in a new direction. 'By the way, I expect you've heard that Tommy and Joy have called off the wedding?'

The news hit Eddie like a thunderbolt. He stood open mouthed, unable to frame a sentence.

'You obviously haven't.' Sylvia waited for Eddie to draw breath.

'No, it's news to me. What on earth's gone wrong?'

'You'll have to ask them. All I know for certain is that Joy is the one who called it off.' Sylvia drew her robe more closely around her. 'She's staying here with me for the time being.'

Eddie shook his head at the sudden, unexpected turn of events. 'If you ask me, it's a damned shame. Can't you and Pearl talk some sense into her?'

'There are complications you don't know about.' Sylvia was adamant. 'All Pearl and I can do is provide a shoulder to cry on.'

'Complications!' Eddie sighed. He noticed that Sylvia was shivering – it was time to take his leave. 'I'll never understand the way a woman's mind works,' he confessed before departing.

'Best not to try.' Remembering how their own romance

had blossomed and faded, Sylvia gave the ghost of a smile. 'Talk to Tommy,' she said softly before she closed the door.

A boy stood on the step outside the house on Empire Street, building up the courage to knock. A cart loaded with empty barrels and pulled by two dray horses trundled over the cobbles, past an ARP warden who was busy pasting a recruitment poster to the battered door of Mason's Yard. An eagle-eyed neighbour spotted the lad and came out into the street, arms folded, waiting and watching.

This was the worst job in the world. For one thing, it meant an early-morning start in the dead of winter, when you slung the canvas satchel across your chest, left the post office and cycled through the traffic to the recipient's address. Then there was the knock on the door followed by a seemingly endless wait before the sound of footsteps in the corridor and finally the flash of fear across a person's face when they opened the door and saw who it was.

The boy took out the telegram and checked the address – number six.

The neighbour advanced towards him. 'Get a move on, sonny – what are you waiting for?' she asked sharply.

The boy took a deep breath and knocked on the door.

It was Tuesday and Maria was busy washing laundry at the kitchen sink, up to her elbows in soap suds. Henry was still in bed. Ernie was out delivering papers. Pearl, already running fifteen minutes late, had been roped into making toast for Elsie and Wilf.

'Get that, will you?' Maria barked at Pearl when she heard the knock.

'This toast is burnt.' Elsie turned up her nose and pushed her plate away.

'Eat up – it's all you're getting.' Rapping the bread knife down on the table, Pearl hurried to answer the door.

Here were the footsteps in the corridor. The short-sighted lad held the telegram close to his face, re-checking the address. A young, dark-haired woman with flushed cheeks opened the door wide.

Blind panic seized Pearl as, without saying a word, she snatched the flimsy paper from the telegram boy's hand. It was marked with the word 'Priority', next to the official Post Office stamp. 'No!' she breathed.

She read the typed message – *Regret to report that your husband, Private Bernard Greene, is missing presumed killed on war service* – followed by a series of numbers verifying Bernie's service number, signed by his commanding officer. The letters and numbers blurred. The telegram slipped from Pearl's trembling fingers and fluttered to the ground.

'I'm sorry, miss.' The telegram boy picked it up and handed it back to her. There it was: the look of panic, the gasp, the rapid collapse into despair. 'Angels of death' – that was the name they gave to lads like him.

'It's a mistake.' *Missing presumed killed*. Pearl clutched the telegram to her chest.

Maria came to the door, drying her hands on a towel. Over Pearl's shoulder she saw the delivery lad with his Post Office satchel, heard a dry sob from Pearl, spotted the crumpled telegram in her hand. 'No reply,' she told the boy, who picked up his bicycle and fled. 'Come inside,' she murmured to Pearl.

She led her daughter into the front room and sat her down, unfurled her fingers from around the telegram, smoothed it out then read its contents. *Missing presumed killed* . . . Maria was struck by the cruel brevity of a phrase that had already destroyed thousands of families across the land.

'Presumed . . .' Pearl clung desperately to the one word that offered a shred of hope. 'It means they can't be sure.'

'Hush.' Maria put her arms around her and rocked her gently. 'The telegram would say "missing in action" if there was any room for doubt.'

'But *how* can they be sure?' Sobs racked Pearl's body, dredged up from the pit of her stomach.

'I don't know, love. Hush, hush.'

'It's not true.' She was convinced that Bernie – so full of life and love – would surprise everyone by striding back into his desert camp, living proof that it was possible to survive the very worst the enemy could throw at him – bullets, bombs, shrapnel, blistering sun, parched thirst – the lot. That was what her brave Bernie was capable of. Because of his ordeal, the army would grant him a few days' compassionate leave. Soon he would walk through the front door of number six, large as life.

Maria allowed Pearl to cry. Hearing her sobs from the kitchen, Elsie and Wilf crept silently into the room, holding hands as they watched their mother comfort their sister. Henry came down the stairs barefoot, with braces dangling. A quick glance told him that the worst had come to pass: his son-in-law was dead.

CHAPTER SIXTEEN

Such news spreads like wildfire. Bernie Greene had copped
it out in the North African desert, poor sod. No surprise
there – anyone who read the newspapers knew that the
Eighth Army was still scrapping it out with Rommel at El
Alamein, despite the fact that the Yanks were now on board.
German ranks were swelled by the Vichy French and the
blasted Italians were building up troops in Tunisia, resulting
in stalemate in Algeria. Conditions out there must be hellish; if a British infantryman wasn't blown to smithereens
in battle, the poor bastard would catch dysentery or malaria
or dengue fever and that was that – his race was run.

Pearl was a widow at the age of twenty-one. The women
of the neighbourhood pegged out their washing and
exchanged opinions. Luckily she'd had the sense to marry
Bernie before he'd been shipped off to the desert so she'd
be due a pension – not much but it would help her to get
by. Her family would rally round and support her; redoubt-
able Maria Scott would see to that. But still, Pearl – the life
and soul of any party – had been dealt a dreadful blow.

By mid morning news of Bernie's fate had travelled far
beyond Empire Street. It explained why Maria's fish and
chip stall at the entrance to Central Pier had remained
closed, likewise the two Great Scott amusement arcades.

Madam Rosie sat inside her palmistry booth at the centre of the Golden Mile, letting it be known that she'd foreseen the event; an early break in Bernie Greene's life line had led her to predict as much. Had Bernie ever had his palm read? No one could be sure. Perhaps once, for a joke, soon after he'd left school. Over at the Pleasure Beach old-timers from the Great War remembered him as a cheerful, high-spirited lad who'd worked alongside them before going off to run the arcade with Pearl. Young Arnold White, who worked the dodgems, agreed that Bernie had always been up for a laugh, making the girls scream ever louder as he'd spun them on the waltzers until they were dizzy.

'It's always the good'uns who are the first to cop it.' The veterans from the trenches remembered all too well.

A clerk from the Department of Health shared the news with a porter at the Majestic who in turn told Lorna Ellis while she queued for light bulbs outside Loman's hardware shop on the corner of Regency Road and King Alfred Street. Lorna went straight home and telephoned Ibbotson's – would they please pass on the bad tidings to Sylvia?

Ibbotson's assistant raced up the stairs. 'Bernie Greene is dead!' he announced without preliminaries.

Four short words sent Sylvia reeling backwards into her living room, as though struck by lightning. She sat down on the sofa, scarcely able to draw breath. Joy came through from the bedroom to find Sylvia ashen faced. The explanation tumbled out – Bernie – dead – poor Pearl – she needs us.

'Drop everything – we must go to Empire Street, right now, this minute,' Joy agreed.

A tram ride later, amid the rush and crush of every-day life, Joy and Sylvia arrived at the door to number six, where the blackout blinds were down and neighbours kept careful watch from their doorsteps. Clothes lines were strung across the street from ground-floor windows, with frozen sheets and pillow cases pegged to them, stiff as boards. There was no breeze. Oppressive grey clouds hung low over the terraced roofs.

Joy knocked and waited. Maria, dressed in a wrap-over apron and with her sleeves rolled up, opened the door warily.

'How is she?' Sylvia asked.

Maria shook her head. 'Not good.'

'Can we come in?'

Another shake of the head as Maria stood her ground.

Joy put a restraining hand on Sylvia's shoulder. 'Mrs Scott, could you please tell Pearl we're here?'

'She doesn't want to see anyone.' Maria was adamant.

'Not even us?' Sylvia was bewildered.

'No one,' Maria repeated. 'Pearl's had a bad shock. She needs to rest.'

'We understand.' Joy stepped back from the door and persuaded Sylvia to do the same. 'But you will tell her that we came?'

'I will.'

'And if there's anything we can do to help . . .'

'There isn't,' Maria insisted more gently. 'Not right now. Give her time.'

Upstairs in the bedroom that she shared with Elsie, Pearl overheard Joy and Sylvia's pleading voices and her mother turning them away. It seemed to be happening a great way off, beyond a transparent barrier that Pearl made no attempt to break through. On the far side of that barrier a street sweeper whistled as he wheeled his cart along the pavement, a dog barked, the front door closed.

On Pearl's side there was a vacuum, a space and silence that could never be filled.

She took the box containing Bernie's letters from under her bed then sat with it on her lap, making no attempt to open it, staring straight ahead at the rose-patterned wallpaper, picking out each leaf and delicate petal, wishing with all her heart that she had died with him.

In sombre mood, Sylvia and Joy decided to walk home; the route would take them down Empire Street and across the market square, along the side of the Winter Gardens then through more narrow back streets until they arrived at Yates Wine Lodge before turning right up North View Parade.

Sylvia voiced the hurt that they were both feeling. 'We're Pearl's dearest friends. Why is she shutting us out?'

'I don't know. Perhaps she doesn't mean to. When I lost Margaret and my mum and dad, I didn't want to speak to anyone. I stayed in my room on Silver Street for days and refused to come out. In the end, Mrs Grigg ran out of patience. She fetched the vicar from All Saints and he sat with me for hours until I was ready to talk.'

'At least Pearl has her family.' Sylvia stood to one side to allow a man pushing a bicycle to overtake them as he approached the market. His heavy pannier, containing a sack of potatoes, knocked against Sylvia's shin as he squeezed through the gap. The culprit turned to apologize: it was Joe.

'Sorry, Sylvia – I'm a clumsy idiot. I should've looked where I was going.'

'No harm done.' She brushed earth from her trouser leg then glanced sideways at Joy. To judge by his carefree manner, Joe seemed to be the only person in Blackpool who hadn't heard the news.

'Anyhow, it's your lucky day.' Tilting his cap back from his forehead, he dug into the canvas pannier. 'Take some of these spuds, fresh from my allotment. I've been there since the crack of dawn.'

'No – Joe, really . . .'

'Go on; take 'em. Hang on a sec; let me put 'em in a bag for you.' Joe led the way to his stall, where he flipped a sixpence in the direction of the lad who'd been looking after it for him. 'Hop it, Eric – I'll take it from here.'

The lad caught the coin then darted off. Other stall-holders stared curiously at Joe as, whistling a merry tune, he produced a large paper bag and filled it with freshly dug spuds.

Joy stepped forward. 'Joe, there's something you should know.'

'There's lots I should know that I don't,' he answered cheerfully. 'Like, who exactly discovered the world wasn't flat and how many "t"s are there in "Mediterranean"?'

'Joe,' Sylvia said. 'This is serious.'

He frowned as he looked from Sylvia to Joy then back again. 'How serious?'

'Very,' she murmured. 'Pearl received a telegram.'

'To do with Bernie?' Instinctively Joe gripped the pole that supported the canvas awning above his stall.

'Missing presumed killed,' Joy confirmed. 'We're sorry, Joe.'

'Killed, you say?' His knuckles turned white as he held tight to the pole.

'Yes; according to what we've been told.' Sylvia took the fold-up canvas stool proffered by a neighbouring stallholder and made Joe sit. 'Pearl's taken it hard, as you'd expect.'

Joe sank forward with his face in his hands. 'Why him? Why Bernie?'

The sad truth was, why not Bernie? Joy put an arm around Joe's shoulders. 'Why don't I stay here and look after your stall while Sylvia walks you home?'

He shook her off with a rough jab of his elbow so that she fell back against the stall. 'Sorry . . . I didn't . . . sorry . . .'

'I know; it's all right.'

'I need to do my job.' Joe rallied and took up position behind his array of vegetables. 'Do we know how it happened?'

Joy shook her head then the helpful man in charge of the stall next to Joe's spoke up. 'No, son – but the family will hear more soon. There'll be a letter from his commanding officer – giving the when and where and how.'

Thank you. Sylvia mouthed the words as she picked up spilled carrots from the cobbles.

'I ought to know.' The man bent down to help her. 'My missis and me had one of them letters in the post a week after our lad's ship went down with all hands. "May I be permitted to express my sincere sympathy", blah-blah.'

'I'm all right,' Joe insisted to Joy meanwhile. 'How about you?'

'It's hard to believe,' she admitted, her voice breaking. 'Bernie was so full of life; he seemed indestructible. I'll never forget the sight of him on the dance floor, jiving along with Pearl.'

'Me neither.' Joe drew a sharp breath. 'It was an honour to be best man at his wedding, handing him the ring, hearing him say "I do". There's no pal in the world to match Bernie Greene and for me there never will be.'

*

Life went on – the phrase was trite but true. That same evening Sylvia prepared to lead a samba class with Cliff. Thirty pupils had signed up for a cut-price session, including a group of off-duty GIs from Warton, plus Eileen Shaw and Sandra Turnbull and a few of their ambulance driver pals intent on casting off wartime worries and entering into the carnival spirit of the Brazilian dance.

Before the class Sylvia had spent time selecting a record that suited the samba rhythm – two strong beats to the bar, with the accent on the second beat. The tempo had to be a fast-and-furious fifty bars per minute, featuring guitar and percussion. Eventually she chose her favourite: Carmen Miranda's 'Mamãe eu quero'. Cliff had approved her choice and now they sat smoking in the alcove at the far end of the studio, awaiting the arrival of their pupils.

'I don't usually,' Sylvia remarked wearily as she accepted a cigarette.

'Hard day?' Cliff asked as he lit up.

She nodded. 'Mostly the sad news about Bernie – such a blow.'

'Yes; I heard.'

'The shock knocked me and Joy for six. Lord alone knows what Pearl must be feeling.'

Wreathed in cigarette smoke, they were silent for a time then Sylvia picked up from where she'd left off. 'None of us thought that Bernie would be killed – we were convinced he'd come through the war unscathed. He just had an air about him; that big laugh of his, how he could talk his way out of any kind of trouble.'

Unable to find any words of comfort, Cliff sat and quietly smoked his cigarette, staring around the empty studio, remembering Bernie's boyish eagerness to learn samba, rumba and salsa so that he and Pearl could win prize money by competing at the Tower. 'How much?' 'Ten bob.' 'You're on!'

At six o'clock the first pupils arrived. It was the four ambulance girls, led by Eileen, who breezed in out of the cold dressed in a red jacket with military-style brass buttons over high-waisted slacks and a tight green sweater.

Cliff and Sylvia snapped out of their sombre mood.

'Come on in: hang your coats on those hooks − that's right. Change your shoes in the alcove behind the gramophone.'

The girls followed instructions as the GIs arrived − all first-timers except for Errol Jackson, whose role was to supervise his new recruits. He acknowledged Sylvia and Cliff with a brief nod and a low 'Howdy' before unzipping his leather windcheater and hanging it on a hook.

Had Errol heard the news about Bernie? Sylvia wondered. There was no reason why he should have, given that the American base was some miles out of town and the soldiers had travelled in by military bus. She recalled how keen he'd been to dance with Pearl that Saturday night at the Tower, how he'd made a beeline for her and jived the night away. They'd made a handsome couple: petite Pearl in her bright red skirt, Errol over six feet tall and casually dressed in shirt and trousers that emphasized his broad shoulders and slim hips. In other circumstances, it could have been a match made in heaven.

Within five minutes, the full complement of thirty pupils had crowded on to the studio floor, ready to begin.

'First things first, boys and girls.' Cliff clapped to gain their attention. 'We start without a partner, facing me and Sylvia, and listening carefully to the samba beat: one and two. Sylvia will put on the record then demonstrate.

253

Ready – step to the left on one, close with the right on two, transfer full weight on three.'

Sylvia was able to perform the simple steps practically in her sleep. She heard Cliff describe the samba bounce – flex the knees and push off from the standing foot. Again she demonstrated. Then Cliff gave the instruction to take a partner for the samba walk, initiating a mad scramble that resulted in Eileen claiming Errol, by far the dishiest man in the room. Tilt the pelvis forward then back. Bounce and tilt, bounce and tilt. Carmen Miranda's lilting voice filled the room – *'Mamãe eu quero, Mamãe eu quero.'*

'We'll take a five-minute break,' Cliff announced after half an hour of strenuous effort and varying levels of success.

This gave the go-ahead for some energetic flirting between the GIs and the ambulance girls.

'Where are you from?' Sandra asked her GI, a skinny youth whose white T-shirt was visible beneath his partly unbuttoned checked shirt. He sported the regulation crew cut and offered her chewing gum as they talked.

'Noo York,' was the laconic reply.

'Lucky you – I've always wanted to see the Empire State Building,' Sandra admitted. 'What's it like?'

'Pretty tall, I guess.'

'What about the Statue of Liberty – have you ever been up it?'

'No, ma'am; I never even been near it.' Her GI slid an arm around her waist and gave her a friendly squeeze.

Across the room, Eileen failed to make headway with her handsome sergeant, despite complimenting him on his dancing. 'You're pretty good at this Latin lark – I'd say you're an old hand.'

'Pretty much,' was his curt reply as he watched Sylvia change the record on the gramophone.

Eileen persisted. Where was he from? Was Fayetteville anywhere near Chicago? She had a cousin who had stowed away on the *Queen Mary* then gone to work in Chicago as a hotel bell boy. Wasn't that what the Yanks called them?

Errol supplied one-word answers with one eye still on Sylvia before abruptly ending the conversation with, 'Will you excuse me, Miss Eileen?' then making straight for Cliff's blonde assistant.

She was standing by the gramophone when Errol interrupted her reverie.

'You're friendly with Pearl, ain't you?' he began without any preamble, standing close and lowering his voice in a confidential manner. 'I've seen you with her at the Tower.'

'I've seen you too,' she replied cautiously.

'How's she doin'?'

Sylvia's heart skipped a beat. Was it possible after all that he'd heard today's tragic news? 'Why do you ask?'

'Cos last time I came across her in her amusement arcade – Saturday, if I remember right – she was frettin' over a letter that hadn't made it through.'

'She told you that?' Sylvia didn't hide her surprise.

'Sure – we got to talkin'. So, did she get the letter yet?'

Caught off guard, Sylvia blurted out the truth. 'No. Sadly, Bernie – her husband – won't be writing any more letters from North Africa.'

'How come?'

'A telegram came.'

This could only mean one of two things: Pearl's soldier husband was either dead or missing. Instead of pressing Sylvia to divulge more, Errol backed away in confusion, almost tripping over the gramophone cable in the process. The plug was pulled from its wall socket so he stooped to pick it up.

Sylvia bent with him. 'Bernie is missing, presumed killed,' she murmured.

'Gee, I sure am sorry to hear that.' He inserted the plug then stood up straight. 'Tell Pearl from me, will you?'

'I will,' Sylvia promised.

'Real sorry,' Errol insisted, shaking his head as he crossed the studio and left the building. Outside on the pavement, he stood in the dark street and lit a cigarette. Strains of music reached his ears. He blew columns of smoke straight up into the air, reassessing the situation. So in all likelihood the husband wouldn't be coming home. Pearl would need time to get over her loss, but nature had a way of healing a broken heart, especially one as young and healthy as Pearl's. It might take more time than he had, though – Errol's posting to Warton could end without warning and he might then be deployed to any air base in the UK that needed experienced engineers – maybe further south and closer to the action in Europe. Better to forget about her. Then again, if their paths did happen to cross, in this day and age things could gallop ahead pretty darn quick.

In the studio, Cliff instructed and Sylvia demonstrated an under-arm turn, first to the right then to the left. Eileen found herself a new partner. The key to the samba was to relax and enjoy – bounce and tilt, whisk and turn. Carmen Miranda had exactly what it took, so Eileen swung her hips and shook her shoulders to a new song: 'Chica Chica Boom Chic'. As far as she was concerned, this was all it took to chase the blues away.

'So far so good.' Cliff was satisfied with the way the class had gone. 'If we keep on with our cut-price offer, we should carry on pulling in more pupils.'

'Fingers crossed,' Sylvia agreed. The silence of the

empty studio after the noise and energetic activity of the previous hour made her realize how weary she felt. 'I have a headache. Do you mind if I leave you to clear up?'

'Not at all – you look done in.'

'Thanks. I'll see you tomorrow.' Intent on catching up with Joy over a cup of cocoa, Sylvia was surprised to find Terry lingering in Ibbotson's doorway. He wore a light mackintosh with his collar turned up and a checked woollen scarf looped loosely around his neck. 'What are you doing here?' she demanded. 'Shouldn't you be at the Opera House, getting ready for tonight's performance?'

'I've got half an hour to spare,' he assured her with a nervous smile before jerking his head in the direction of the studio. 'I thought I might catch up with you-know-who, but now I've got cold feet. What kind of mood is he in?'

'Good, as far as I know.'

'But?' Terry queried.

'But he saw you and a friend leaving the Opera House together after the dress rehearsal.' Feeling duty-bound to inform him, Sylvia put quotation marks around the word 'friend'.

Terry acknowledged the warning by raising his eyebrows.

'Good luck,' she said as she turned her key in the lock.

'Thanks – it sounds like I'll need it.' Thirty minutes was all he had. 'I'd better get a move on.'

They went their separate ways – Sylvia upstairs to find no sign of Joy and Terry to the studio.

Hearing the outer door open and close, Cliff thought that Sylvia must have forgotten something. He was taking a casual look around for her cardigan or her handbag when he glanced up and saw Terry.

'Hello, Cliff.' Terry stood with his hands at his sides,

trying to control his rapid breathing. Perhaps this had been a bad idea after all.

'What do you want?'

'To talk, that's all.' He thought that Cliff looked frayed around the edges – less groomed, more worn down by the stress of trying to make ends meet.

'There's nothing to talk about.' Cliff lowered the gramophone lid a touch too forcefully.

'I came to apologize.'

'What for?' Suspicion soured Cliff's words and he turned his back.

'For brawling in public. There was no excuse for embarrassing you and I'm truly sorry.' Terry waited in vain for a response. 'Do you hear me, Cliff? I'm apologizing for what I did and said.'

'Apology accepted. Now, if you don't mind, I'm busy.' With his back still turned, Cliff made a dismissive gesture then began to switch off the lights.

'Can't you see? I want us to be friends again.'

Cliff left on a single overhead light that shone directly on Terry. 'Friends,' he repeated with a hollow laugh. 'I'm afraid it doesn't work that way – not for me.'

'But I can't bear for you to hate me.'

'I don't hate you.' Cliff advanced slowly towards him. 'As a matter of fact, I have no feelings at all towards you, Terry.' He intended the remark to cut deep and, sure enough, he saw from his erstwhile lover's wounded expression that he'd succeeded. 'Now, as I said, I'm busy.'

Terry recovered in time to prevent Cliff from pushing past. He grabbed hold of his arm. 'Is this about Derek?'

'Derek who?' Cliff echoed scornfully. 'Ah yes; your latest "friend". Does he dance in the chorus line with you? Or wait; perhaps he's Prince Charming himself?'

'Cliff, you've got the wrong end of the stick.' Realizing that he was running out of time, Terry grew desperate. 'Sylvia said that you saw us together but, believe me, that doesn't mean a thing.'

'Really? You looked pretty cosy, hugging and walking along arm in arm.'

'Listen – Derek Evans is new to performing, like me. We often compare notes after rehearsals, that's all. Derek lodges with his girlfriend on King Street.'

Girlfriend? Cliff opened his eyes wide in astonishment.

'That's right.' Terry let the revelation sink in. 'I'm still renting a room from Joe so Derek and Cynthia live three doors down from me. She's a dancer too – the three of us often walk to and from the theatre together.'

Cliff put a hand to his forehead and rubbed his temples. 'It seems I've been a fool,' he admitted.

'That makes two of us.' A slow smile spread across Terry's face. 'I take it we've cleared up that little misunderstanding?'

Cliff replied with a low, grudging 'Yes', feeling himself weaken in the face of Terry's charm offensive.

'Look at what's happened to Bernie – doesn't it prove that life's too short for us to argue?'

'I suppose it does.'

Terry concluded his argument. 'Then we *can* stay friends!'

'Whatever that means.' Cliff's eyes narrowed. 'I'm not a complete push-over,' he cautioned. 'There will have to be a fresh understanding – we can't go on as we were.'

'I realize that. But let's at least meet and chat over a drink. You can come and watch me dance in *Sleeping Beauty* as often as you like – I'll give you some free tickets – and perhaps I could come here and lead a few tap-dance classes?'

'Don't rush me, Terry. Let me think it over.'

'Of course.' Satisfied by the progress he'd made, Terry backed across the darkened studio towards the door. 'Take all the time you need.'

Cliff watched him tie his scarf more tightly and brace himself for the cold before opening the door. He could read all of this man's expressions – the way he knotted his brows when he struggled to express himself clearly and the gradual smile that lit up the room.

'I know where to find you,' Terry said in his slow, deep drawl before disappearing into the night.

The sound of 'Chica Chica Boom Chic' had followed Joy along North View Parade. It was a silly song; not one of her favourites. Samba wasn't to her taste either – all that flirtatious tilting of hips and wild carnival racket.

She was on her way to see her cousin at the Norbreck, which meant a tram ride along the prom at a time when most sensible people were keeping warm by the fire, winding down after a day's work. The tram was almost empty and the conductress was a chatty type, telling Joy about her elderly dad who had landed in hospital with bad bronchitis. The clippie blamed the weather and the fact that her dad refused to wrap up properly – 'You'd think he'd know better at his age but he wouldn't be told.'

All Joy had to do was nod and sigh until the largest hotel in Blackpool hove into view and she was able to hop off at her stop.

Ding-ding – the bell rang and the tram rumbled on.

Entering by a side door – the main part of the building had been requisitioned by the civil service for the duration of the war – Joy approached a temporary reception desk and stated that a guest, Mr George Hebden, was expecting her. The prim receptionist looked Joy up and down, from her practical laced shoes, black trousers, thick brown overcoat to her beige felt hat, before informing her that Mr Hebden had left an instruction for Joy to join him in the hotel's premier lounge. Regretting that she hadn't dressed more smartly for the occasion, Joy asked timidly for directions – take the corridor on the left, follow the Sunshine Deck all the way to the Sun Circle and from there follow the sign to the Sun Lounge.

The hotel corridors were only dimly lit due to blackout rules, but Joy could make out that they were fashionably decorated in sleek art deco style, with stained-glass panels and arched doorways, leading to an impressive circular room with a glass cupola – the famous Sun Circle. She gazed around in amazement at the lavish decor. The Norbreck was steeped in glamour, the haunt of famous actors and actresses and of lords and ladies. Feeling completely out of her depth, Joy was on the point of turning tail when George appeared, dressed in a white dinner jacket and dark trousers. His hair was slicked back and neatly parted and she noticed a pair of gold cufflinks and a gold ring on his wedding finger.

'There you are.' He stepped forward to shake her hand then invited her to follow him to the lounge where he'd been waiting. 'This place is a rabbit warren. It's easy to get lost so I thought I'd better come and find you. Sit, please.'

Still flustered, Joy took off her coat and hat then sat in one of the low, crimson armchairs.

'Anything to drink?' George asked.

She shook her head. 'No, thank you.'

He sat down facing her, leaning forwards and pulling at his cuffs – evidently as nervous as she was. 'Well – have you reached your decision?'

Joy pressed her lips together. How many times had she

gone through the ins and outs of this situation? Should she or shouldn't she join her cousin in Glasgow? And now that it had come to the moment of truth, she felt unable to give George an immediate answer.

'Perhaps you need more information,' he said hastily. 'The Hebden Knitwear Company remains profitable despite the war. Our customers are generally well-heeled people who are willing to pay high prices for quality knitwear, and although war with Germany has cut off supplies of yarn from Italy, we've been able to source our materials more locally, albeit for a higher price. However, there's very little risk of us going under.'

'I understand – thank you.'

'That's not the main reason you're hesitating,' George surmised. 'You have your fiancé and his mother to consider.'

Joy's heart jolted to a standstill then restarted with a sickening jerk. 'I've cancelled the wedding,' she admitted. 'It turns out that Tommy – my fiancé – withheld your original letter.'

George absorbed the information with raised eyebrows but without comment.

'He was behaving oddly so I guessed something was wrong. In the end I forced him to admit what he'd done.' Tears blurred Joy's vision. 'I'm sorry – I promised myself I wouldn't get upset.'

'Did Tommy say why he'd done it? No; that was tactless of me. You don't have to answer if you'd prefer not to.'

George's considerate manner prompted Joy to divulge more details. 'It was before Tommy learned that I'd have to leave Blackpool to take up your offer. It boiled down to him being afraid that any inheritance would drive a wedge between us.'

'As well it might,' George conceded. 'Coming into money can have that effect. But there's a warm welcome waiting for you over the border if you do decide to make a fresh start. My wife Mary shares my sense of fair play and is keen for you to join us. Our first baby is due in March. As for accommodation: our house on the outskirts of Glasgow is big enough for you to have your own wing, with as much privacy as you choose.'

A tempting picture formed in Joy's mind of a comfortable future where she was surrounded by a growing family, with new places to explore and the challenge of finding her feet in a business that was rightfully hers. 'It's not that I care so much about the money,' she tried to explain. 'It's more that I'd be following my father's wishes.'

'Even if it means giving up on Tommy?' George presented the choice in deliberately stark terms. 'You have to be absolutely sure that it's the right thing to do.'

'I am,' she said quietly, remembering her dad's proud smile in the black-and-white holiday snapshot, her mum in her flowered dress and Margaret with white ribbons in her dark hair, grinning like the Cheshire Cat. How happy they would be for Joy to expand her horizons. 'I'm willing to move to Glasgow,' she decided.

'George leaned forward and grasped her hand. 'Are you sure?'

'Certain,' she said. 'I'll join you and Mary soon after Christmas, once I've had time to say my goodbyes.'

CHAPTER SEVENTEEN

Doubt was the worst possible state of mind. Once Joy had given George her decision, relief set in and she returned to North View Parade with renewed energy, taking the stairs up to Sylvia's room two at a time. There was much to do and so little time in which to do it.

Sylvia greeted her with a one-word question: 'Well?'

Joy quickly put her out of her misery. 'I've made up my mind to go.'

Sylvia put aside the jar of cold cream that she'd been massaging into her face. She was in her dressing gown and had been waiting on tenterhooks for Joy to return. 'You're certain?'

'Yes; think about it – how could I possibly turn this down? George is a thoroughly decent person. He has a wife and is soon to be a father. They have a lovely, big house which he says I can share. The work will be an exciting new challenge—'

'Stop!' Sylvia raised both hands. 'It's not me you have to convince.'

Flinging her hat and handbag on to a chair, Joy took off her coat. 'It wasn't easy for me to decide,' she continued at the same breakneck speed as before. 'I'm all too aware of what I'm giving up – being around you and Pearl and my other pals at the Tower. Then there are my dance lessons with Mrs Ellis. I intend to see her in person to explain my reasons for leaving.'

'It'll be a big disappointment,' Sylvia predicted. 'Mother had high hopes for you and Tommy. She says you have exceptional talent.'

Joy raced on. 'And there's Lucia to consider; I owe her a full explanation too. And Tommy,' she added with a frown.

'Yes; Tommy,' Sylvia echoed sadly.

'So you see how much I have to do before I leave? First thing tomorrow, after I've waved George off at the station, I'll hand in my notice at the Tower. No; before that, I'll drop in on Pearl and hope that she's up to seeing me. I don't want to leave without explaining to her face to face. And afterwards, I'll call at All Saints vicarage to make sure that Reverend Inman has received official notice that the wedding is off. That can't be put off any longer.'

'It makes me weary, just thinking about it.' Sylvia drew Joy towards the glowing embers of the fire and sat her down. 'You're shivering.'

'I'm not cold,' Joy protested weakly. Her heart was beating like fury and her head was spinning. What on earth was the matter with her?

'Tommy.' Sylvia repeated the name. 'When will you tell him that you're leaving?'

'Tomorr—' The answer stuck in Joy's throat so she tried again. 'Tomorrow, after his matinee.' Then she collapsed forward in floods of tears, sobbing her heart out. She cried and cried her dream away – there would be no wearing white, no bridesmaids, no walk down the aisle, no wedding night. She, Joy Hebden, would never be Tommy Rossi's wife.

*

That night Joy didn't get much sleep. Rising before dawn, she fulfilled her promise to wave her cousin off from his platform at North Station.

George looked pale and drawn when she met him: a sign that he too lacked sleep. He stood out from the crowd of flat-capped workers in his camelhair coat and trilby hat, careful to obey a porter's warning to watch his back when a cart stacked high with postbags trundled by. The smell of smoke filled their nostrils and Joy and her cousin spoke over the scrape of firemen's shovels stoking the furnace and the slamming of compartment doors as they parted.

'It's good of you to see me off.' George noticed how young and slender Joy seemed in the grey light – scarcely out of girlhood, with her long, straight hair loosely tied back by a red ribbon and an innocent, wide-eyed look that made him reach out with his gloved hand to touch her shoulder protectively. 'You have my telephone number. Call me any time you wish.'

Joy thanked him. Billowing clouds of white steam rose to the wrought-iron and glass roof, obscuring the face of the enormous station clock.

'Try not to worry.' He tapped her shoulder. 'Mary can't wait to meet you. Come as soon as you can.'

'I will,' she promised. 'Have a safe journey.'

'Thank you and Happy Christmas.'

Joy felt the lightest of kisses on her cheek and then George was gone.

He stepped up into the train, closing the door behind him, then leaned out of the window to the sound of the stationmaster's whistle and the slow shunt of wheels. He waved. She waved back. 'I'll see you soon!' he called again; mission accomplished. Carefully placing his hat and small, monogrammed suitcase on the luggage rack above his head before settling down with a newspaper for the long journey north, George Hebden hoped with all his heart that Joy had made the right decision.

Next stop for Joy was Empire Street. She approached the Scotts' house with little hope that Pearl would be ready to see her. Still, she was determined to try.

'Yes?' Henry Scott demanded when he answered Joy's knock on the door. He was unshaven and dishevelled, collarless and with the top buttons of his shirt undone. 'What do you want?'

'Don't you recognize me?'

'No – I don't know you from Adam.' Henry was all for slamming the door in her face but was prevented from doing so by his wife, who had followed him down the corridor.

'It's all right, Henry.' Maria quickly took over guard duty and Pearl's father shuffled away barefoot. 'Don't mind him,' she said to Joy. 'Bernie getting killed has come as a shock. Henry was banking on him and Pearl taking over the arcades as soon as Bernie got demobbed. Now he won't be able to retire until Ernie and Wilf are old enough to step forward.'

Of all the reasons to mourn the death of a son-in-law, this seemed to Joy to be the least deserving of sympathy.

Maria read her thoughts. 'Yes – typical bloke. But don't be too hard on Pearl's dad – he never was one for wearing his heart on his sleeve.'

'How is Pearl?' Joy was full of apprehension, awaiting the answer.

'The same.' Maria had sat up with her eldest daughter for most of the night, waiting for her to accept what had happened. Pearl hadn't spoken but by morning she'd stopped crying, as everyone must. Maria knew from experience that there were only so many tears a person was physically capable of shedding. 'She's reached the stage of staring into space, not saying a dicky bird.'

'Will she see me this time, do you think?'

Maria narrowed her eyes to study Joy's anxious face. The girl seemed to have a lot on her mind. 'Probably best not.' She closed the door a fraction.

'It's all right, Mum.' Pearl stood on the landing, still dressed in the clothes she'd been wearing when she'd answered the door to the telegram boy. 'Ask Joy to come up.'

Maria grimaced, one arm braced against the door jamb to stop Joy from entering.

'Mum, I said to let her in.'

So Maria stepped aside with bad grace. 'Try not to set her off again,' she muttered as Joy climbed the stairs.

Back in her room, Pearl sank on to her bed, making space for Joy to sit beside her.

'We don't have to talk if you'd rather not,' Joy said gently. She recognized the hollowed-out look that Maria had described and she remembered how grief felt – fierce and sharp at first before an aching emptiness set in.

'What is there to say?' Pearl turned her face away. 'He's not coming back, is he?'

Joy placed her hand over Pearl's. 'Have you eaten or drunk anything?'

'Endless cups of tea – Mum's remedy for everything. Joy, do you think Bernie got my last letter before . . . ?' Pearl was unable to go on.

'We'll never know for certain – let's hope he did.'

'I told him I missed him and couldn't wait to see him again. I said I loved him.'

'I'm sure he knew that.'

Pearl leaned her head against Joy's shoulder. 'I could tell from one of his letters that he didn't like me going dancing without him. Now I wish I'd never done it.'

'Sylvia and I egged you on – you didn't mean any harm.'

'But I wish . . .'

'Bernie knew that you loved him and no one else,' Joy insisted. 'And vice versa.'

Her words drifted through the door that she'd left open on purpose, guessing that Maria would be on hand if needed. Sure enough, it wasn't long before Pearl's mother came in with two cups of freshly brewed tea.

'What did I say?' Pearl sat up straight and took a deep breath. 'Tea is Mum's cure-all.'

'No arguments – drink it down.' Maria cast Joy a grateful glance before disappearing from the room.

'I have some news of my own,' Joy ventured.

Pearl's mind suddenly shifted gear and she sprang to the obvious conclusion. 'You and Tommy are back together.'

'Wrong,' Joy said with a sigh.

'Why not? What's stopping you?'

'Sylvia told you some of the reasons – remember: my cousin's letter and Tommy's big lie? I came to give you a proper explanation of why I can't marry him and why I have to go.'

'Go where?' Life had come knocking, dragging Pearl back into the present.

'To Glasgow, to work with my cousin.'

'Without Tommy?' *Of course without him! There's no way on earth that Tommy can leave the circus or his mother. Anyway, the wedding's off.*

'Yes, but you and Sylvia have to promise to visit me

whenever you can. Scotland is famous for its beautiful mountains and lakes.'

'Lochs,' Pearl corrected her. Another strong tie was being stretched to breaking point; Joy was about to embark on a new life and good luck to her. 'Up there you'll have to drop the Viennese waltz and take up Scottish dancing, och aye!'

'Let's wait and see.' Joy gave a wan smile. 'But we three can still be friends, can't we?'

'I sincerely hope so.' Pearl's heartbeat faltered. Hadn't she looked up places in Scotland on the map when Bernie had been sent to the primary training centre in Perth? You were talking hours and hours on the train, and how would she and Sylvia ever find the time to visit?

Joy took Pearl's cold hand and squeezed it. 'Promise that we three ballroom girls will stay in touch.'

There would be exchanges of Christmas and birthday cards, phone calls, long and chatty letters dwindling to postcards and then to nothing as life pushed Joy, Sylvia and Pearl down different paths. Pearl squeezed back. 'I promise,' she said.

Soon after Joy's departure, Pearl retreated into deep silence. She sat on the edge of the bed, her hands in her lap. Time dragged. At midday Maria tapped on her door and informed her that she had to go out.

'Fish and chips won't sell themselves,' she said in her no-nonsense way. 'Your dad's downstairs if you need anything. Pearl – did you hear what I said?'

She nodded.

'Will you be all right?'

'Yes.'

The box containing Bernie's letters sat unopened on

Pearl's bedside cabinet next to her hairbrush and alarm clock. Elsie, Wilf and Ernie were at school, not expected home until half past four. At three o'clock she heard her father leave the house to head who-knew-where; probably to the betting shop, knowing him. Pearl lay down on her side, curled into a ball and let herself drift into a light sleep.

A sharp sound brought her back to consciousness. She opened her eyes but didn't move. Lethargy rendered her limbs heavy and unresponsive. The sound was repeated – *knock, knock, knock* on the front door. *Go away!* More knocking. *Trust Dad to slope off and leave me to answer that.*

Pearl stood up slowly and went to the window to peer through the gap in the curtain. It was already dusk – later than she'd expected – and in the half-light she made out a figure in khaki battledress. *Bernie?* She gasped and flung open the curtain. *No, how could it be?* This man had a similar build but his features were sharper. He wore his left arm in a sling.

The visitor glanced up at the first-floor window then knocked again.

Moving at half her usual speed, Pearl descended the stairs and opened the door, turning the knob with a hand that trembled alarmingly.

'Mrs Pearl Greene?'

'That's me,' she whispered. Her throat felt dry and rough as sandpaper.

The man took off his beret to introduce himself. 'I'm Private Arthur Allen. Can I come in?'

Bewildered, Pearl shook her head.

'I'm Bernie's pal,' he explained. 'Home on leave. I served alongside him in the Western Desert. I promised

271

him I'd look you up if . . .' The soldier's sentence trailed off in a helpless shrug.

'Yes, yes; come in!' Her mind was a blur as she led the visitor into the front room.

Arthur sat down awkwardly in a seat by the window. The fading light fell sideways across his face, emphasizing his hollow cheeks and the shadows under his eyes. 'I recognize you from the photograph that Bernie carried. He never went anywhere without it – we all took the mick at training camp cos of that.' He lifted the flap on his top pocket and pulled out a cigarette, allowing Pearl to help him when he struggled to light it one-handed.

'What did you do to your arm?'

'Not my arm – my fingers. I got two blown off by one of Fritz's booby traps.'

Pearl shuddered then braced herself to face up to the reason for Arthur's visit. 'I take it you're here to tell me more about what happened to Bernie?'

The visitor nodded. 'Like I said, we made each other a firm promise.'

'All I know is what was in the telegram.' *Missing presumed killed.*

'Rightio; I won't pussyfoot. We all found it tough going out there in the desert, though the worst of the fighting was over when we arrived.' Arthur inhaled deeply before breathing out a thin spiral of blue smoke. Pearl was a good-looking girl – even better in the flesh than in her photo: small and neat and well put together. According to Bernie, she was a good little dancer too. Arthur didn't relish the task ahead of him; but hell, a promise was a promise. 'Well, we first saw action on the twentieth of November. Our boys had pretty much sent Rommel packing by then, knocking him for six like

272

Monty said we would. All that was left was to clear up the mess.'

'Yes, we read about the victory in the newspapers.' Pearl clung to every stuttering word her visitor said. 'I'm sorry, I didn't mean to interrupt – carry on, please.'

'Easier said than done, as it turned out.'

'What do you mean?'

'Fritz has a nasty habit of digging holes in the sand and filling them with landmines as he retreats.'

She closed her eyes in a vain effort to shut out the picture that Arthur had created.

'Still want me go on?' he checked.

'Yes – it's better to know.'

'Last Thursday the tenth, fifteen hundred hours – Bernie and me were in the back of an American truck, in charge of a twenty-five-pounder. We were advancing on a town called Sirte, keeping our eyes peeled for those damned booby traps, but two lads in front of us drove their Jeep over one and that was it – their time was up. First thing I knew, there was an almighty explosion; bits of Jeep and bodies flying in every direction, flames and thick black smoke and God knows what.' Arthur took another deep drag on his cigarette. 'I was thrown up in the air and knocked clean out. When I woke up I was on a stretcher on my way to a field hospital. There was no sign of Bernie – nothing.'

Flames, smoke, shrapnel flying through the air. The image would stay with Pearl for ever.

'It was quick,' Arthur told her in a scarcely audible voice. 'He would have wanted me to tell you that.'

'Yes. Thank you.' She could scarcely speak.

'And he was a good lad – none better.' He looked around for an ashtray and Pearl offered him one. He would keep it simple – no point using fancy words like courage and honour and victory; not when you'd been through hell. 'And well liked, too. We're all sorry he's gone.'

A landmine. Lives lost in a flash. This terrible war.

Arthur stood up, ready to leave. 'I'm sorry it's bad news, Mrs Greene. But I've done what I said I would.'

'Thank you.' Pearl's voice seemed to belong to someone else.

'I'll let myself out.'

'Thank you.'

The visit ended in a series of scarcely audible murmurs. Arthur Allen left the house and walked swiftly down Empire Street, his duty done. He crossed paths with Henry, hurrying home from William Hill's betting shop. Noticing that the living-room light was on, Pearl's father made a blustering, bad-tempered return.

'There's a bloody warden heading this way,' he berated Pearl, who stood in the window staring into space. 'Pull that blind down, for God's sake. And don't tell your mother I slipped out to place a bet. I'll never hear the end of it if you do.'

'What do you mean, he's not here?' Joy stood at the door to Tommy's dressing room in a state of high anxiety.

'What I say: young Tommy didn't show up for today's matinee.' Ted Mackie, still in his clown's outfit of baggy trousers, black jacket and bowler hat, studied Joy's worried expression. The girl was white as a sheet, so slender and insubstantial that a stiff sea breeze would knock her clean off her feet. 'Do I take it that there's trouble in paradise?'

Ignoring the question, Joy tried to peer into the dressing room.

Ted stepped aside obligingly. 'See for yourself.'

274

The cluttered room was empty and Tommy's sequinned costume hung from its hook. His trumpet and other brass instruments had been pushed carelessly into a corner. 'Have you any idea where I might find him?'

'Not a clue.' Ted took off his hat and flung it on to an empty hook with practised ease. 'I'll say one thing, though – him going AWOL upset Gerry Martin no end, so I wouldn't fancy being in Tommy's shoes when he does turn up.'

Persuaded that Ted was telling the truth, Joy trailed off down the corridor.

'Do you want to leave him a message?' Ted called after her.

'No; no message.' She went on her way with her head down: from the Tower to the vicarage to make sure the wedding had been cancelled and then on to the Lorna Ellis Dance Academy, to face the music there.

Lorna was quietly preparing for an evening session with Eddie and Mavis when Joy arrived. The studio lights were on and the blinds down, the space as immaculate as ever with its highly polished wooden floor and sparkling mirrors.

Joy stood in the doorway, clasping her hands in front of her. 'Mrs Ellis, please could we have a word?'

'Ah, the wanderer returns.' Lorna put down the sheet music that she'd been studying and gestured for Joy to join her by the piano. 'Come. I have a few minutes to spare, no more.'

'Thank you.' Joy's nerves were in tatters as she began her explanation. 'Sylvia might have given you forewarning of what I'm about to say.'

Lorna nodded. 'She tells me that you're leaving us to start a new life? Yes, and I can't pretend that I was glad. I had such high hopes for you and Thomas in January's championship. Of course, you have your reasons – Sylvia intimated as much.'

'I'm truly sorry to let you down, Mrs Ellis.'

'And I'm sorry too.' Joy's evident distress made Lorna soften her tone. 'Poor child; you look exhausted. Sit here, on the piano stool.'

'I wanted to thank you in person for everything you've done for me.' This studio was where Joy's life had been transformed, where she'd slowly emerged from her drab chrysalis and learned to express her emotions through dance – from the romantic swoon of waltz to the elation of foxtrot to the sensuous drama of tango. 'I started here as your cleaner, never for a minute dreaming of anything else.'

'Yes; you were a shy little mouse, creeping about with your dustpan and brush, your mops and your dusters. Now look at you – one of the most accomplished ball-room dancers that I've ever had the pleasure to teach.'

Joy's heart was full to bursting. 'Thanks to you. Everyone knows that you're the best teacher in town.' She glanced around the room, at the row of framed Imperial Society certificates on the wall and copies of *Popular Dancing Weekly* in a rack by the door. 'I'll miss coming to this studio,' she confessed. 'I've had some of my happiest times here.'

'You'll be welcome back whenever you choose.' Time was pressing so Lorna drew the conversation to a close. 'And before you go, I'd like you to make me a promise.'

'Anything.' Battling back tears, Joy responded with a brave smile.

Lorna took her by the hand and stared intently into her troubled eyes. 'You have a rare gift. Wherever you go and whatever you choose to do with your life, please don't turn your back on the ballroom.'

*

'My heart wasn't in it tonight,' Mavis confessed to Eddie as they lingered outside the academy after their lesson.

'We were all a little lacklustre,' he admitted. 'Even Lorna.'

Their teacher had emphasized the importance of flow in the Viennese waltz; that and confidence were the keys to success. She'd seemed distracted, however, and had ended the session ten minutes early.

'Perhaps it's the bad news about Bernie Greene,' Mavis suggested. 'Everyone I know is feeling down in the dumps about him. Ruby, Ida, Thora; none of us can believe we'll never see him again. He's been a fixture on the Golden Mile for as long as any of us can remember.'

Eddie commiserated by linking arms with her and setting off towards the Queen's Arms. 'Perhaps a drink would cheer us up?'

'No, ta. I'm worn out.' And sad and fearful that, as far as the war was concerned, there seemed no end in sight.

'Then let me see you home.' Eddie walked her on, past a row of trees whose trunks were painted with horizontal white stripes as part of the town's blackout measures.

'I thought you had a first-aider shift tonight?'

'I do, but not till later. It's not right for a girl to walk alone at night.'

'Ever the gentleman,' Mavis teased. 'Well, kind sir, you can walk me as far as my street corner.'

'Right you are.' Reaching the prom, they went on past the entrance to North Pier, with the boating pool and the miniature golf course visible under a bright moon.

'Here will do.' Mavis came to a halt beside a bus shelter and gestured towards a side street running at right angles to the main thoroughfare. 'Duke Street's only a stone's throw from here.'

277

Spying a bunch of rowdy men standing outside a working men's club, Eddie was reluctant to let her walk on alone. 'I'll happily escort you to your door.'

'No,' she insisted hotly. 'I'll be fine.'

Surprised by her tone, he made her stop and look at him. 'Why so keen to get rid of me?'

'I'm not. I'm sorry – I have to go.' Unaware of an approaching taxi, Mavis stepped into the road without looking. The driver braked suddenly, wound down his window and swore at her before driving on.

Eddie pulled her back on to the pavement. 'That was too close for comfort.'

'My own fault; I should've looked where I was going.' Drat; now Eddie would see she was upset and would probably insist on keeping her company all the way home. Home for Mavis was a shabby two-up two-down terrace with no front garden and an outside privy at the back, while Eddie lived with his father in a brand-new detached house on the edge of town. 'I can manage from here,' she insisted again.

He took her arm. 'Come along; let me walk with you – no arguments.'

'Eddie, no!' Pulling away again, Mavis burst into tears and fled. 'Don't you see?'

'See what?' He followed her into the bus shelter where he sat with her and waited for her to calm down.

'My house – it isn't what you're used to.' Ashamed of feeling ashamed, Mavis failed to express herself clearly.

Ah, so that was it: Mavis viewed him as a snob who would look down his nose at her once he saw where she lived. 'I don't mind,' he said simply.

Startled, Mavis brushed away her tears then spoke angrily. 'How can you not mind? Everyone minds what other people think of them. I wish I lived in a lovely big house with a lovely big garden that I could invite you to but I don't. And I didn't pass any exams so I don't have a job I can be proud of either.'

'Mavis, I know and I don't care.' Eddie couldn't be plainer than this.

Did he mean it? She stared at him in disbelief. The men outside the club dispersed, leaving a solitary dog walker among them to cross the prom and pass close to the shelter where they sat.

'A big house doesn't bring happiness,' Eddie tried to convince her.

'But not having to worry about paying the bills helps,' she shot back.

'*Touché*.'

'Too-shay?' There he went again, throwing in posh foreign words. With a toss of the head she stood up and went to lean on the railing overlooking the beach. Silver ripples stretched far out to sea, glimmering in the moonlight. How many millions of stars were sprinkled across the night sky?

Eddie came to stand beside her. 'I'm saying I agree with you – money does help but it's not everything.'

'I never said it was.'

Sticking his hands in his trouser pockets, he looked up at the clear night sky. 'Do you always have to have the last word?'

'Yes.' Smiling, she turned her head to look directly at him. 'Dad says it's a bad habit, learned at my mother's knee.'

Eddie smiled back at her. The wind blew her hair across her face and he brushed it gently back. 'You're funny – you know that?'

'And you're too serious by half, Eddie Winter.'

'See – you did it again.'

'What?' Mavis felt his warm breath on her cheek as he moved closer.

'The last word; you can't help yourself.' He held her and kissed her so that she couldn't talk back. And she didn't resist.

'You cheat; you stole it from me,' she whispered when they drew apart.

CHAPTER EIGHTEEN

Christmas was bound to be different this year as the war raged on in Tunisia and in Russia, Italy and throughout Europe. Further afield, America had pushed the Japanese out of New Guinea, yet in other regions closer to home German resistance was strong and cruel. The Luftwaffe flew in supplies to their besieged troops in Stalingrad, and Hitler pressed ahead in his mission to exterminate all Jews. The names Treblinka and Auschwitz began to feature regularly in chilling news reports.

Such headlines made for sombre reading. It seemed to many people that tinsel and tree lights were better left in their boxes and that energy and effort should be put into making up parcels to send to British troops instead. Socks and balaclavas were knitted, food coupons clubbed together to make cakes and biscuits for the brave boys fighting for their country.

But still, the urge to celebrate survived. In their dimly lit, strictly rationed homes, families wrapped presents: a hand-knitted scarf or artificial flowers fashioned out of melted wax and twigs. Groups of Boy Scouts did the rounds of Blackpool's streets, defiantly belting out carols. In spite of everything, Good King Wenceslas still looked out on the Feast of Stephen.

On Empire Street Pearl heard the carol singers as she watched Ernie help their mother to put up paper streamers. 'I'll hold the bottom of the ladder and pass you the drawing pins. Mind you don't fall.' It was the normal run-up to the big day.

'Can you spare a tanner?' Pearl opened the door to a round-faced, rosy-cheeked boy and a tuneless rendition of 'While Shepherds Watched'.

Pearl handed him the sixpence and a handful of toffees, doing her best to ignore splutters from Wilf and Elsie huddled in the corridor close behind.

'"While shepherds washed their socks by night, all seated on the ground,"' they crowed in hilarious mimicry.

Roused from his fireside doze, Henry rolled up his newspaper and threatened to use it as a truncheon. 'You're not too old for a good hiding,' he warned.

Yes, it was the normal run-up and yet nothing could ever be the same again for Pearl, who went through the motions like a robot, devoid of emotion. On the morning after Arthur Allen's visit she was up before anyone else and out of the house before dawn, drawn towards the deserted Pleasure Beach where Bernie had worked. She slipped in, unnoticed by the half-awake security guard, then wandered from ride to ride in search of a memory – anything that would bring her closer to the man she had loved and lost. The Big Dipper's network of interlocking wooden struts and steel track dominated all. It rose to vertiginous heights then swooped sickeningly to ground level. Ignoring it, Pearl walked on past the doors of the Fun House, whose distorting mirrors and mazes held no interest either. The Side Winder attracted her attention – the dive-bomber ride had been one of Bernie's favourites, though he'd never worked on it. On she walked towards the waltzers.

This was more like it. Pearl mounted two broad wooden steps to the garishly painted roundabout and sat down in the nearest teacup-shaped carriage. It rolled on its axis: a half-turn then back again. 'Yell if you want to go faster!' She heard Bernie's voice, saw his grin as he leaned in and spun the cups with his strong arms. He spoke to her when no one else was around, in the grey, cold light. And again, at the entrance to the Ghost Train, daring her to give it a go – spiders and skeletons, whoo-hoo! – laughing then urging Pearl on towards the dodgems. 'Come on, Miss Slowcoach – keep up!'

Tommy had ruined everything. The knowledge made him want to crawl into a hole. He hadn't the heart to cavort around the ring in glittering pantaloons and a dunce's hat, to juggle balls and turn somersaults, much less to face Joy and her cleaner pals. So he'd lain low, faking illness when his boss had telephoned to demand where he was.

'Why, what's up with you?' Ringmaster Gerry Martin – a sergeant-major type who didn't suffer fools – had grilled him down the phone line. Then, without waiting for an answer: 'Never mind – unless you're at death's door, I expect to see you back in the ring Saturday afternoon at the latest.'

Tommy had even avoided his mother, much to her dismay. 'My son, why you not eat? Why you hide from me?'

He'd kept to his room overlooking the backyard and when, on Thursday afternoon, he heard Lucia answer the door to Joy, his heart had lurched to a standstill.

'*Entra*, come in. You want to see my Tommy?' Lucia greeted the visitor eagerly.

'Yes please, if he's in.'

It was Joy's voice and no mistake. Tommy waited until he was sure that his mother had taken the visitor into her back kitchen before nipping downstairs then out through the café, leaving the front door open in his haste. It was by no means his finest hour.

'Wait. I bring Tommy,' Lucia told Joy before disappearing upstairs.

Holding her breath, Joy had no idea how she would feel when they came face to face at last.

Lucia returned without Tommy. 'He goes,' she announced tearfully. 'No one is there.'

Joy let out a groan. 'I had no luck at the circus either. I really need to talk to him.'

'You change your mind?' Lucia's expression lightened; it seemed there was a glimmer of hope after all. 'You come to say I love you?'

'No. I mean yes; I still love Tommy but everything is different now.'

'How different?' In Lucia's eyes, love was the strongest bond on earth, able to overcome all obstacles.

'I can't marry him.' Joy tried to explain in words that Tommy's mother would understand. 'He knows why not.'

'So why you come?' Lucia's mood changed again to one verging on accusation as she moved restlessly around the room, rattling cups on the draining board and placing knives into the cutlery drawer. 'My Tommy, he knows he does wrong. He is sad.'

'And so am I, Lucia – very sad. But I came here to tell him something important.'

'*Importante?*'

'Yes – I wanted him to hear it from me, not from other people. I believe I owe him that. But Tommy is avoiding me so I'm forced to tell you instead.'

'What is this – *importante*?' Lucia's ever-changing expression settled into a deep frown as she sat at the table next to Joy. 'Say to me.'

'I will go to Glasgow.' Five simple words, leaving no room for doubt. 'This is what I've decided. Please tell Tommy.'

Lucia gave a startled gasp. 'You will go away? He will not see you again?'

'That's right,' Joy confirmed with a racing heartbeat.

'Never?' Lucia feared that her son's wounded heart would suffer a fatal blow when she passed on this news.

'A complete break is for the best, Lucia. It will be a fresh start for us both. I'll be in Scotland with my cousin and Tommy will be here with you.'

Tommy's mother made a last desperate plea. 'My son does wrong to hide the letter. He is sorry and you cannot forgive?'

'Perhaps I can in time. But by then I'll be a long way away, living a different life, doing what my father wanted me to do. You understand this?'

'*Sì, capisco*.' Gradually the frown eased as Lucia took in the implications of Joy's last remark. 'Your father, your cousin – it is what they wish.'

'That's right. So you will tell Tommy for me?'

'*Sì*. It is family. Your father wishes this for you.' Lucia reached for Joy's hand. 'My Joy; now I see. You must say yes.'

'Thank you.' The cold fear in Joy's heart melted away at the feel of Lucia's broad, warm hand over hers. She took one last look around the room at the pristine display of blue plates on the dresser and the shiny copper pans hanging from a row of hooks over the cooker. 'I was alone, with no one in the world to care about me, when you and

Tommy welcomed me here with open arms. I'll always remember that – *sempre.*'

'I cry.' Lucia dabbed her eyes with her apron. 'You go now. I cry *ancora.*'

'Thank you,' Joy repeated in a whisper, standing then leaning over to kiss Lucia's damp cheek before leaving Rossi's for the final time. 'Thank you for everything.'

Joy left the ice-cream parlour and hurried to the Tower for another farewell at what was to be her last cleaning shift in the ballroom. When she arrived the girls were full of their usual bustle and chatter. The talk was of Christmas gatherings. Ruby's mother-in-law had invited Ruby for Christmas Day dinner at her house, along with her husband, Doug's sister and family. Ida was going to her brother's in Bradford – worst luck, according to Ida, who would rather stay in Blackpool with her innamorata. 'Innamorata!' Thora scoffed at her friend's misuse of the posh word.

Choosing not to join in with the lively exchanges, Joy quietly whisked a feather duster over the ornate plaster-work that framed the speaker at one side of the proscenium arch. Mavis was nearby, sweeping the stage with Doris, a small girl with a loud voice, curly red hair and a fiery temperament to match.

Doris rested on her broom and demanded Mavis's full attention. 'So, Miss Thorne, what's the latest?'

Mavis used a hand-brush to sweep confetti into her dustpan. 'This damned stuff gets everywhere,' she grumbled. 'Lord knows why they keep on using it.'

Doris gave her a knowing nudge. 'Come on; don't be coy.'

'The latest on what?' Mavis decided to toy with her cleaning companion for a while longer.

'Not on what – on *who*! On the devilishly handsome Edward, of course.' Doris was bursting with curiosity. 'Has he made his move?'

Picking up the drift of their conversation, Joy's duster hovered over a plaster frieze of vine leaves and grapes.

'Wouldn't you like to know?' Mavis teased.

'Yes, that's why I'm asking. Have you two kissed yet?'

Mavis snatched Doris's broom and used it to sweep the front of the stage. 'Yes, if you must know.'

'Hurrah!' Doris gave a round of applause and Mavis curtsied. 'You hear that, everyone? It's official: Mavis and Eddie Winter are more than just dance partners.'

'About time too,' Thora and Ida chimed from the ball-room floor.

'Tell us more,' Doris cried. 'How many times have you kissed? Has Eddie declared his undying love? What's the next step for you two lovebirds?'

'As if I'd tell you.' Mavis worked on with a secretive grin, basking in the memory of the previous night's tender embrace. In fact, she and Eddie had done much more than kiss in the moonlight; they'd shared confidences and swept away misunderstandings. In the end, she'd been happy for him to walk her all the way up Duke Street.

'This is it: my humble abode.' She'd pointed at the house whose front door was peeling, whose darned and patched net curtains had seen better days. 'Would you like to come in?'

It had turned out that yes, he would. Eddie had met her mother and they'd got on like a house on fire, chatting about the importance of a well-made pair of shoes and how, though she worked at Barrett's, she would always recommend Clarks' shoe-fitting system for children. Quite right, Eddie had agreed.

'He met my ma and charmed the pants off her,' Mavis reported to Doris.

'He met your mother?' Doris was astonished. 'Listen, you lot – Eddie has met Mavis's mother; talk about a fast mover!'

Joy took it all in without comment. It made her sad to think of Sylvia left out in the cold.

Mavis dropped the nonchalant act and shared her giddy excitement with anyone who cared to listen. 'It's early days,' she admitted, 'but I'm beginning to think that Eddie has real feelings for me and that we might have a future together.'

'Steady on,' Ruby warned from the floor. 'Don't run before you can walk.'

'Ignore her.' Doris brushed aside the voice of reason.

'There's no side to him,' Mavis chattered on. 'That's how Mum put it. Scratch the surface and Eddie Winter is the same as you and me.'

'Only, with more money,' Doris shot back.

Mavis threw back her head and laughed. 'Yes, there is that,' she agreed.

'What's it to be tonight: jive or jitterbug?' Cliff consulted with Sylvia about their next class. Thanks to their recent leafleting campaign, they were expecting an influx of new pupils: a mixture of civil service clerks and more workers from the Vickers Armstrong factory.

'Neither is straightforward for beginners – not everyone has the necessary natural rhythm.' Sylvia had a sudden, vivid memory of the time when she and her mother had gone to the Odeon to watch Gracie Fields in *Shipyard Sally*. At the point where the Lancashire lass had danced to 'I've Got The Jitterbugs' – kicking and gyrating her way across the enormous screen – Lorna had walked out of the cinema. 'As far as my dear mother is concerned, there are a dozen good reasons why they call it dance madness,' she reminded him.

'And that's why you're here with me and not still teaching the Veleta and the military two-step with her.'

'Point taken.'

'So which is it to be?' Cliff busied himself by pulling down the blinds and switching on the lights. As he did so, he saw Terry striding towards the studio with his old, characteristic swagger. The sight unnerved him and he retreated to the alcove without mentioning it to Sylvia.

'Jive,' she decided. 'Let's start with the basic swing-out step then move on to under-arm turn.'

By the time Terry breezed in through the door, Cliff had regained his composure. 'Hello, Terry. I wasn't aware that we'd arranged for you to drop by,' he said coolly.

'Nice to see you too, Cliff. And you, Sylvia.' Terry's confidence had returned with a vengeance. 'There was no arrangement but I happened to be in the neighbourhood.'

'And we happen to be busy preparing for our next class.' Cliff's sniffy tone was intended to remind Terry that he couldn't sail blithely in and take up from where they'd left off. Any reconciliation had to be on terms which they'd both agreed. 'So, if you don't mind . . .'

'This won't take long,' Terry assured him. 'And it's actually Sylvia I want to talk to, not you.'

'Feel free,' Cliff muttered as he studiously sifted through discs for the evening session.

Terry rolled his eyes in Cliff's direction. 'What's up with his lordship?'

'Hush; lower your voice.' She saw that it would be

diplomatic to keep Terry by the door. 'We *are* busy,' she insisted. 'So you'd better make it quick.'

'I've had an idea, that's all.' Terry's teasing, throwaway style that had drawn the girls to him like bees to a honey pot when he'd first come to town was also back. 'Don't you want to know what it is?'

'Terry, I said get a move on.'

He removed his hat and smoothed down his hair in an unhurried manner. 'I hear it's all off between Joy and Tommy Rossi.'

Sylvia bridled at the seemingly random, unfeeling remark. 'For heaven's sake, what's that got to do with anything?'

'So it's clear they won't be going to the Allied Championship after all, leaving just Eddie and Mavis for your mother to send.'

Sylvia felt an irrational urge to grab Terry by his nonchalant lapels and shake him. 'Please get to the point,' she muttered.

'Keep your hair on. What I'm thinking is – we could ask Lorna to pair us up and enter us alongside Mavis and Eddie.'

Nothing could have been further from Sylvia's mind. 'You and me?' Her raised voice carried across the studio to Cliff's alcove.

'Yes; why not? Your mother's a good teacher and I'm a quick learner.'

'There are lots of reasons why not. What about your job at the Opera House, for a start?'

'That's an easy one – I'm signed up there until the middle of January but after that I'm free as a bird. The competition isn't until the twenty-fifth. Yes, it's a lot to learn in a short space of time, but I'm game if you are.'

'With Eddie and Mavis?' she repeated uncertainly as Cliff joined them.

'Forgive me if I'm wrong,' he challenged Terry with forced politeness, 'but did I just hear you attempting to tempt my assistant back into the ISTD fold?'

'Come off it, Cliff; I wouldn't do that to you. No; this wouldn't interfere with my theatre work and it wouldn't overlap with Sylvia's teaching here either. She and I would practise in our spare time. It would be her chance to demonstrate that she can still out-waltz anyone for miles around. As for me; it'd be a way of working my way up the ladder by proving how versatile I am.'

Cliff turned to Sylvia to gauge her reaction. 'It's up to you – I wouldn't be against it if it's what you want to do.'

'Think how thrilled your mother would be,' Terry added with his most persuasive smile.

'Oh, I don't know,' she said with a groan. 'Eddie and I have done well in the Allied Championship in the past and I've always enjoyed the challenge, but—'

'But there's a sticking point.' Cliff jumped in quickly. 'Could you bear to go up against Eddie and his new partner?'

Sylvia sighed. 'I'm not sure that I could.'

'It might be good for you.' Terry gave her hand a squeeze. 'It would be a question of you looking forward, not back. And I know you, Sylvia; once you take to that dance floor, you're in your element. You won't give another thought to what Eddie is up to.'

'Terry has a point,' Cliff agreed. 'I've watched you struggle to get over your old sweetheart. Competing against him could be a real signal that you've put the past behind you.'

'But have I?' Sylvia wondered out loud. 'Eddie and I

291

grew up dancing together. And yes, we've had our ups and downs – who doesn't?'

'Stop,' Cliff interrupted gently. 'Isn't there someone else whose name you've both left out of this scenario?'

'Mavis.' Terry hit the nail on the head; it was common knowledge that Eddie Winter and Mavis Thorne were in harmony both on and off the dance floor.

'Quite.' Cliff insisted that it was time for Sylvia to acknowledge the truth. 'You must see that Eddie's ship has well and truly sailed?'

'I do.' Yes, and it was fast disappearing over the horizon, charting a new course, putting an ocean of new experience between them. 'All right, I'll be your partner,' Sylvia said to Terry at last. 'Starting tomorrow – I'll telephone Mother and let her know.'

CHAPTER NINETEEN

The following morning, Sylvia was moving quietly around her living room, relieved that Joy was having a rare lie-in, when Ibbotson's lad clattered up the stairs with a message.

'Telephone call for Miss Hebden,' he reported in his squeaky, half-broken voice. 'Girl on the switchboard says it's come all the way from Scotland, from a Mr George Hebden.'

'Say that Joy will call him back as soon as she's able,' Sylvia decided.

'Rightio.' The boy disappeared as quickly as he'd come, back to the tobacconist's shop where his employer sold two packets of Player's Navy Cut and a box of matches to the man who sold newspapers at the corner of North View Parade.

Upstairs, Joy emerged from the bedroom in her dressing gown. Despite the strain of recent events, she looked rested. 'Did I hear that George was on the telephone?'

'Yes. I considered taking it on your behalf but then I said you would call him back.'

A look of alarm flashed across Joy's face. 'You don't suppose George has changed his mind?'

'About your going to Scotland?' Sylvia left off tidying

magazines and newspapers scattered across the rug. 'Oh Lord, that never crossed my mind. Shall I come down with you and find out?'

Joy nodded and they descended the stairs together. Old man Ibbotson was still speaking to the caller and when he saw Joy, he motioned for her to join him behind the counter. 'She's here now,' he said into the phone.

Sylvia hovered by the window display, breathing in the sweet smell of loose tobacco, until Joy beckoned her across then tilted the receiver so that Sylvia could listen in to the conversation.

Joy began nervously. 'Hello, George – it's me.'

'Hello, Joy. It's good to hear your voice,' he said pleasantly.

'How was your train journey?'

'It went very smoothly, thank you. I was back in the office yesterday, informing staff about our exciting new plans.'

So he hadn't changed his mind. Joy put her hand over the receiver and murmured a few words to Sylvia. 'You heard? Everything is fine.'

'Joy, are you still there?' George's voice crackled down the line.

'Yes, I'm here.'

'Excellent. I'm calling to reassure myself that this hasn't all been too much of a shock. In other words: you haven't changed your mind?'

'No, as a matter of fact I was afraid that it was the other way around. I wondered if you and Mary had talked it through and reached a different conclusion.'

'No, no – I'm a man of my word. The offer stands; you'll have what's rightfully yours. How are arrangements going at your end?'

'Well, thank you. I've handed in my notice to my employers and started to say my goodbyes.'

Sylvia pulled a miserable face – *boo-hoo!* Ibbotson's boy shyly offered her a Mint Imperial from a crumpled paper bag: a love token for the blonde beauty whom he worshipped from afar.

'So you're making good progress.' George wanted to ask how matters stood with Joy's fiancé but delicacy held him back.

'Meanwhile, my friend Sylvia has offered to let me stay with her for as long as necessary,' Joy went on unprompted. 'Tommy is doing his best to avoid me but his mother is aware of my decision.'

'That can't have been easy. But on the positive side, the news here is that Mary has employed a housekeeper for the wing of the house where you'll be staying and I'm in the process of interviewing candidates for a secretary's position: someone to assist you with shorthand and typing. I've also arranged for Alan Henderson to show you around the factory. Alan has worked for us for many years. We moved him up from Manchester when the warehouse closed down. He knew your father and I'm sure you'll like him.'

Joy listened and nodded, occasionally raising her eyebrows at Sylvia. This was a lot to take in.

'And one last thing,' George continued swiftly. 'Mary and I would like you to join us for Christmas. It will be a quiet family affair – just the three of us – but you'd be most welcome.'

Overhearing this, Sylvia shook her head vehemently and mouthed a silent, *No!*

Joy hesitated.

'It would give you a chance to settle in before the start

of the new year,' George continued. 'To get your feet under the table, so to speak. Of course, it would mean taking the train up here a few days earlier than planned.'

No! Sylvia mouthed again. Every hour that Joy remained in Blackpool was a bonus as far as she was concerned and she was sure that Pearl felt the same way.

'I'm not sure if I can be ready in time,' Joy told him. There were people she still wished to see, including Ruby who had nagged Joy to join her and the girls for one last whirl around the ballroom floor.

'Of course,' George said more briskly. 'Sleep on it and telephone me when you decide.'

The call ended with an exchange of brief but friendly goodbyes and as soon as the receiver clicked into its cradle, Sylvia whisked Joy back upstairs. 'Sit down on the sofa while I make us breakfast,' she ordered.

Flopping back against the cushions, Joy watched Sylvia cut into a fresh loaf then light the gas with a pop and slide two slices of bread under the grill.

'By the way, you're not the only one to receive a proposition lately,' Sylvia dropped in casually.

Joy sat up straight and gave Sylvia her full attention. 'Do tell.'

'Terry has asked me to enter the Allied Championship.'

'You and him together, as partners?' This was surprising news indeed.

'Yes. And if Mother agrees to put us forward as representatives of the Lorna Ellis Academy, it would mean going there with Eddie and Mavis.'

Now Joy was on the edge of her seat, staring at Sylvia's back view. 'And what did you say?'

Sylvia took the toast from under the grill then turned to face Joy. 'I said yes,' she replied with a brave smile. 'With you as my example, I decided it was best to go full steam ahead with never a backwards glance.'

Memories of Bernie continued to drift in and out of Pearl's head, more vivid to her than the here and now. First there was the Pleasure Beach – 'Yell if you want to go faster!' – and now, several days later, on this cold December morning, she stood inside the entrance to the North Pier arcade, staring along aisles of one-armed bandits, at the shiny glass and metallic machines in which Bernie had taken such pride. She left the 'Closed' sign in place as she shut the door behind her and brushed her fingers over the smooth surfaces of the Spitfire, Dawn Patrol and Chip or Bust. Bernie with his ready smile, inviting hopeful lads in short trousers and plimsolls to try their hand at the Little Mickeys or convincing a coachload of tightly permed ladies from the Women's Institute that today would be their lucky day. Bernie in faded overalls tinkering with machines that had gone wrong – a bent penny jammed in the slot, a steel ball that had been swallowed up in the innards. Bernie standing up to her dad and demanding prompt payment of the money that he was owed. His rapid-fire jokes, his special smile – tender and slow – reserved for her alone.

Despite the 'Closed' sign, there was a light tap on the door and when Pearl went to open it she found Errol standing there, bare-headed but with the collar of his brown leather jacket turned up against the wind.

'OK if I step inside?' he asked.

'We're shut,' she pointed out. There were no lights on, no bright and cheerful tunes blaring out of loudspeakers above the door.

'Sure, but I'm not here for the slots. I was playing a

round of mini-golf with a couple of guys when I spotted you.'

Pearl saw that he was out of uniform, dressed in a casual blue sweater and matching slacks. 'You followed me?'

'Yeah, I guess I did,' he confessed without embarrassment. 'I just wanted to say I'm sorry for your loss.'

Pearl took a sharp intake of breath. 'How did you know?'

'Miss Sylvia told me. I'm real sorry, Pearl.'

She stood to one side. 'You'd better come in.'

He stepped past her then took a long look up and down the aisles. 'Back home, Mills is the big name for slot machines – Castle and Century were my favourites. Growin' up in Georgia, there wasn't a whole lot to do except play the slots and listen to the jukebox.' There was a long pause before he turned towards her with a frank gaze. 'How are you doin'? Tell me for real.'

Pearl shook her head helplessly. 'I keep expecting him to walk through the door.'

'Gee, I hear you.' He saw and felt the depth of her sorrow.

'I had a visit from Bernie's comrade who was there when it happened, so now I know for certain that he won't be coming back.'

'Was it an air attack?' Errol prompted quietly.

'No – a landmine buried in the sand.'

Errol frowned deeply then strolled a little way down the nearest aisle. 'Liberty Bell was another of my favourites, and Page Boy.'

Pearl stayed where she was. 'Why are we talking about slot machines?'

He walked back towards her. 'I guess it was my ham-fisted way of tryin' to ease your pain a little. But if you want me to leave . . .'

'No, you can stay. And you're right – let's change the subject.'

Errol leaned back against the Dawn Patrol with his hands in his pockets. 'OK, what do you want to talk about? I can tell you about Thanksgiving back home and how it's way bigger than Christmas – how about that?'

Pearl shook her head. 'That's worse than slot machines.'

'Or I can give you the latest news on Private Sanderson?'

She took a deep breath then nodded.

'Last I heard, he made a run for it on the way to court in New York – damn near succeeded. A prison guard shot him in the leg to stop him.'

Pearl's stomach twisted into a tight knot and she felt a surge of anger replace the black hollowness of recent days. 'Thank goodness he didn't get away.'

'Yes, ma'am.' He studied her suddenly flushed cheeks. 'Sanderson deserves a good long stretch behind bars.'

'So, what else? Tell me, is there someone back home who sends you letters – a brother or a sister?'

'My sister, Jeanie. She's the reason I stuck around in Fayetteville so long. Without her, I'd have taken work a million miles from where I was born. But Jeanie, she's a sweet girl who needed lookin' after. Now she's plannin' to get hitched to a good friend of mine. I'm sad to miss the wedding but boy, I sure am happy for them. Before you know it they'll have a clutch of cute kids for me to visit.'

A smile flitted across Pearl's face. 'What do you tell Jeanie about your life in Blighty?'

'I say it rains a hell of a lot. I say Blackpool has a tower like the one in Paris. I say the gals here can jive and jitter-bug just as good as the gals back home; I'm thinkin' of a little dark-haired one in particular . . .'

'But she's off-limits.' Pearl looked directly into those blue-grey eyes to make sure he understood.

'Yes, ma'am – I tell Jeanie that, too.' Errol was the first to flinch. 'I promise my sister I'd never make a move unless this gal wanted me to.'

'Good – I'm glad that's clear.' Pearl's gaze still didn't waver. 'And you can tell Jeanie from me that she has the best brother a girl could wish for; will you do that?'

'Sure thing.' Errol sighed, recognizing exactly where he stood.

'The very best,' Pearl insisted. 'And tell her how you were there to stop something horrible from happening to that girl and that she will be thankful for that for the rest of her life.'

'I'll write it in my next letter.' Face it; the timing was bad as could be and there was a whole heap of regrets that Errol would carry away with him – but yes, Pearl was right to set the record straight. 'You take care,' he murmured as he broke away and strode out on to the pier where, way below his feet, dark water swirled and overhead the underside of seagulls' wings stood out as white curves against the leaden sky.

Lorna was unsure how the first session with Terry and Sylvia would go. Sylvia had done her best to convince her that there was no ill feeling between her and Eddie but Lorna knew her daughter through and through; like a swan gliding across a lake, she could seem cool, calm and collected while at the same time paddling frantically below the surface. Besides, Terry Liddle was an unknown quantity as far as ISTD standards were concerned and it remained to be seen how well he would take to the Viennese waltz.

Eddie and Mavis were the first to arrive; Mavis obviously on edge and chattering ten to the dozen to hide her nerves. She'd also made a special effort with her appearance: she wore her hair up in a neat chignon, with a flick of mascara to emphasize her wide brown eyes, and carefully applied lipstick in an attractive coral shade to complement her short-sleeved sweater and flared skirt.

'Mum saved up her clothes coupons and sewed this skirt for me,' she informed Lorna while standing in the centre of the studio and turning on the spot. 'She did all the embroidery by hand.'

'Very nice.' Lorna paid scant attention. Sylvia and Terry were five minutes late and she let her irritation show.

'The roads are icy and the traffic was bad,' Eddie informed her diplomatically.

'But you and Mavis thought to make allowances for that.' Lorna drummed her fingers on the top of the piano, wondering whether to start the lesson without them.

After another minute or two, a flustered Sylvia burst through the door with Terry in tow and a quick excuse. 'Sorry, Mother – bad traffic.'

The new arrivals rushed to change their shoes while Lorna put on a record.

'Apologies to you too,' Sylvia mentioned to Eddie, who responded with a self-conscious shrug.

'Is everyone ready?' Lorna took up position next to the piano. 'Now, Terry, you must forget everything you've learned about theatre and Latin dance techniques – there will be no freedom of expression or outlandish steps here. Always remember: the English style is all about standardisation.'

Terry dipped his head in acknowledgement while Mavis, standing in hold with Eddie and with her back turned to their teacher, whispered out of the side of her mouth, 'Don't worry, Terence – Mrs Ellis's bark is worse than her bite.'

'Your head position is vital.' Lorna moved forward to adjust Terry's posture. 'You must look forward over Sylvia's right shoulder. Your left arm is raised to her eye level. Right arm is placed lightly under her left shoulder blade; just so.'

Sylvia stood patiently while Lorna worked on further details with Terry. She happened to be directly in Eddie's line of vision and when their eyes met he gave her a faint smile and a look that seemed to say, *Well, here we are, making a brand-new start.*

She smiled back at him. *How strange this feels!*

I know – but it's time for us both to move on.

Sylvia nodded. *I'm happy with that if you are.*

It was a conversation that they might never have, but the frank exchange of glances was enough.

Then Lorna gave the instruction to begin – a quarter turn followed by a natural turn then a reverse turn on the count of three.

Sylvia and Terry and Eddie and Mavis glided across the floor – feet parallel, heads tilted just so. Lorna praised the perfect V-shape made by the upper bodies of both couples. Soon all four dancers forgot their initial awkwardness and relaxed into the smooth, swooning rhythm of the dance, accepting praise and criticism, aiming for perfection.

'Well done, everyone.' After an hour, Lorna drew the lesson to a close. 'Terry, that was a very good first effort – we'll make a decent dancer of you yet.'

'You see?' Mavis winked at him as they collected their belongings. 'Mrs Ellis isn't half as bad as they make out.'

Meanwhile, Sylvia drew her mother to one side for a quiet word. 'Well, will Terry be ready in time for the competition?'

'Possibly,' Lorna replied. 'If he applies himself and doesn't fall back into slovenly habits.'

'So it's a risk worth taking?'

'I think so.' Lorna studied her daughter's eager expression. 'Entering this competition means a lot to you, doesn't it?'

'Yes, it does. For one thing, it will prove that Eddie and I are free to live our own lives from now on.'

'And you really don't mind about Mavis?'

Sylvia looked towards the corner of the room where Mavis chatted gaily with Eddie and Terry. Mavis laughed at something Terry had said while Eddie put her dance shoes in her bag for her to hurry her along. 'No, I don't mind at all,' she told Lorna without a shred of jealousy or spitefulness. 'In fact, good luck to her.'

'Very well.' Satisfied, Lorna patted Sylvia's cheek and gently smoothed her hair. 'Let's enter you and Terry into the championship. But be warned: you must work extra hard if you wish to beat some talented rivals to the trophy – Eddie and Mavis included.'

Anything was possible. Buoyed by the success of their first lesson as partners in the Viennese waltz, Sylvia bade farewell to Terry then caught the tram home to North View Parade. Solving any problem, however knotty, was simply a question of breaking free from old habits and seeing the world in a completely different light.

Her feet scarcely touched the ground after she'd alighted at her stop then hurried up the dark street, past the newsagent's and the greengrocer's then in through the entrance that she shared with Ibbotson's. She ran up the narrow stairs two at a time and into her flat, where she found Joy sitting at the table with a fountain pen and a blank sheet of paper in front of her.

'Who are you writing to?' Sylvia kicked off her shoes and flung her bag down on the floor.

'No one – I'm making lists.' Joy had divided the paper into two columns – one for and one against spending Christmas in Glasgow. She'd sat for ages without writing a thing.

Sylvia snatched the paper away. 'Stop what you're doing and listen to me.'

'Sylvia, don't!' Joy snatched it back. 'I'm trying to decide about George's offer for me to share their Christmas.' All day she'd considered the pros and cons, in between dithering over a small Christmas gift for Mary in Debenhams (eau de cologne or stockings; so hard to decide when you didn't know a person's tastes) and ironing shirts and slacks before packing them in her suitcase.

'Sit down here with me.' Sylvia dragged Joy to the sofa. 'Let me explain my latest brilliant idea.'

'Another one?' Joy was sceptical but gave way to her friend's obvious enthusiasm. 'All right, I'm listening.' What was this about and why was Sylvia so animated?

'Let's go right back to the beginning, to what your father had in mind for your future.'

Joy held up her hand. It was painful to be reminded of the letters to his brother that had been so cruelly ignored. 'Why drag this up?'

Bursting with confidence, Sylvia rushed on regardless. 'Your father wanted you to have what's rightfully yours and that's what brought your cousin to Blackpool – better late than never. And since he made the offer we've all been assuming that this means your moving to Glasgow, but what if it doesn't?'

'How can it not?' Joy was mystified. 'I can't break the stipulation in the original will – it states that all heirs must be on the spot. I have to work with George and learn how to manage the company hands-on.'

'Yes – those are the terms. But I've been thinking through what George said on the telephone this morning. He mentioned a man called Alan Henderson.'

'Yes. He's a manager who's worked for the company for a long time, starting in Manchester when Dad was alive.'

'In Manchester – exactly!' Sylvia waited in vain for Joy to follow her train of thought. 'Hebden Knitwear Company only gave up their warehouse there because your father was forced out. So why don't you suggest re-opening it with you as the boss and with Mr Henderson moving back to Lancashire to guide you?'

Joy took a deep breath to steady herself – though it had come out of the blue, this didn't strike her as the most outlandish notion she'd ever heard. 'Do you really believe it would work?'

Sylvia had had time to think it through and was now on a mission to convince her friend. 'Anything's possible if you believe in it enough. Look, the factory is making a profit in spite of the war. Present this plan to George as a way to expand the business.'

'Manchester.' Joy began to turn over the possibilities in her mind. Not an actual factory but a warehouse importing supplies and helping to distribute the finished article. There was a regular train service between Manchester and Blackpool . . .

'That way you wouldn't be breaking the original

agreement.' Sylvia sat back and waited for the penny to finally drop. 'And it means you won't have to move away.'

'I could stay down here and run things.' Joy's face lit up at the prospect of not having to turn her whole life upside down; of not being forced to leave her friends behind. At that moment she didn't spare a thought for the impact on Tommy; this would come to her later. Right now, all she could think about was still being able to walk along the beach at sunset and go dancing at the Tower.

Sylvia grasped Joy's hands and held them tight. 'All you need to do is find the right warehouse – somewhere with access to roads and railways – and employ the right people. You could travel up to Glasgow occasionally for board meetings. You see – I've thought of everything!'

'Except for one thing.' Joy brought her down to earth with a bump. 'What if George says no?'

CHAPTER TWENTY

Sylvia's brainwaves kept on coming. Her head was still bursting with ideas when she joined Cliff in his studio next morning to discuss more ways of promoting their classes.

'First of all, we should take photographs of you teaching the jive,' she suggested. 'Let's have them enlarged as much as possible – then we'll pin the prints on the wall at the back of the studio to create an exciting, modern atmosphere. And we could use the same pictures in our leaflets. Plus, we can have posters printed for display in shop windows and bus shelters – wherever we can think of to let people know where we are and what we do. Your face and name will be everywhere.'

'That's not a bad idea.' Cliff looked long and hard at the new, profit-driven gleam in Sylvia's eyes. She was wearing a bright blue blouse and white capri pants, with white canvas pumps, even though it was the dead of winter. 'Who do we know who could take the photos?'

'Me!' she insisted. 'There's nothing complicated about pointing a camera in the right direction and clicking away. Then, as well as the pictures, we should expand our special offers.'

'Such as?'

'For a start, let's advertise a reduced rate for block

bookings of six lessons or more. And we could charge under-fourteens half the adult rate. Oh, and how about going out to local schools and offering to teach lessons in their gymnasiums?'

'I see – if the mountain won't come to Muhammad . . .' Cliff murmured.

'Exactly. What's to stop us?' Noticing that Terry had slipped into the studio while she and Cliff were talking, she drew him into the conversation. 'We're thinking of ways to get rich,' she explained.

'Stand well back unless you want to be flattened by this steamroller cunningly disguised as Sylvia,' Cliff added wryly. Once again Terry had dropped by without prior notice, but this time Cliff didn't resent it. In fact, he felt a faint glow of pleasure mixed with his surprise. 'In her present mood she's unstoppable.'

'Yes, I can see that.' Terry was amused by what he'd heard. 'I caught the bit about going out to schools, which strikes me as an excellent idea. And Sylvia, have you thought of following your mother's example and entering star pupils into local competitions?'

Cliff spread his hands, palms upwards, in a gesture of defeat. 'Why don't I resign on the spot and hand over the reins to you and Sylvia? By the way, how did you two get on last night?'

'Not too badly.' For once Terry chose not to blow his own trumpet.

'Don't listen to him,' Sylvia objected. 'He impressed Ma no end with his undulations and fleckerls. It only took a minute to persuade her to enter us into the championship.'

'Hmm, that should prove interesting.' Cliff glanced approvingly from Sylvia to Terry then back again. 'Eddie and Mavis will take some beating,' he predicted.

'You think so?' Terry scooped Sylvia into hold and waltzed her across the floor with flawless footwork and perfect aplomb. 'How about that for a start?'

'I'll give you eight out of ten.' Cliff's score took into account the slight lack of power in Terry's body swing on the first beat of each bar. 'Pretty good, considering last night was your first proper stab at it.'

'So, we're all agreed?' Sylvia skipped back across the room, her loose hair swinging, her slim body full of optimistic energy as she seized Cliff and waltzed him towards Terry. 'We'll go ahead with my ideas to make this the premier swing dance studio in the whole of the North West?'

'Steady on!' Cliff laughed at the sheer scale of her ambition then capitulated with, 'Yes, why not?'

'Excellent. But boys, I have things to attend to – I'll leave you two to mull it over.' She was gone from the room in a bright flash of blue, like a kingfisher darting upstream in the sunlight.

'What things?' Cliff wondered aloud.

'Search me.' Terry casually drew a cigarette from a packet lodged in his shirt pocket.

'There's no smoking in here,' Cliff reminded him. 'Why not come upstairs?'

So they went up to the flat together, where Cliff made tea and Terry pushed aside the colourful sofa cushions before sitting down and taking in the impressive row of dance trophies on the marble mantelpiece. Then he picked up a recent copy of the *Gazette*, open at a review of *Sleeping Beauty*. There was praise for Hazel Forster as Beauty and Kenneth Beaumont as the Prince, though Stanley Bishop was less enthusiastic about Simple Simon and the Dame. Finally he picked out two newcomers: Ada

Masters as the wicked fairy and outstanding male dancer Terry Liddle, both of whom showed real promise.

Terry glanced up from the review to see Cliff watching him carefully.

'You show promise.' Cliff raised an ironic eyebrow. 'From Bishop that's high praise.'

'I couldn't have done it without you.' Here – sitting on Cliff's sofa surrounded by his possessions, his framed prints of stills from Hollywood musicals on the wall and his copper ashtray on the coffee table – felt right; Terry felt sure that this was where he belonged. If only Cliff would see it that way too.

Cliff seemed to key into Terry's mood. Studying his face for what felt like an age, eventually he spread his arms wide. 'Welcome home,' he said. 'I must say, it's good to have you back where you belong.'

There; the words were spoken, the gesture made and the bridge over the chasm mended. 'It's good to be back.' Terry gave a long sigh before patting the sofa and inviting Cliff to sit down next to him. 'I reckon we've both learned a lesson the hard way. If I swear to avoid future punch-ups, will you promise not to be jealous?'

'It's a deal,' Cliff agreed with a rueful smile. 'Now shut up and kiss me.'

It was time to put away the box of Bernie's letters. Anyway, Pearl knew their contents off by heart. She stowed them under her bed then calmly went downstairs to the usual disorder. Toast was burnt and porridge stuck to the bottom of the pan, while Henry stood at the sink and scraped away with his razor – slicing the blade through foam and tough bristles in swift, short strokes.

Maria acknowledged Pearl's appearance with the

briefest of smiles, taking in her Aran sweater and green corduroy slacks.

'How do you spell "presume"?' Elsie rushed to finish her comprehension exercise at the kitchen table.

'P-r-i-' Wilf began with a mouth full of toast.

Pearl quickly corrected him: 'P-r-e-s-u-m-e.'

'"Dr Livingstone, I presume?"' Elsie wrote laboriously in her exercise book.

'I need you to take delivery of a new Allwin later today,' Henry informed Pearl as he continued to shave. 'I say "new" but, to be honest, it's seen better days – I picked it up cheap from a pal of mine who works at the Fun House.'

'What time?' Pearl asked as she buttoned up her jacket.

'Around midday.'

'I'll be there,' she promised.

Maria followed her out into the corridor. 'Wouldn't you rather stay at home for a while longer? Your dad can get Ernie to look after your arcade.'

'No, thanks. I called in a few days ago to see what it felt like and it was fine. Anyway, I'd rather keep busy.'

'I'd probably feel the same,' her mother admitted. 'But don't stay out too long. Once you've taken delivery of the Allwin, why not shut up shop and come straight home?'

'I'll see how it goes,' Pearl promised. On with her scarf and gloves, on with her red beret, pulled firmly down over her forehead. Out into the cold.

Maria returned to the kitchen where Henry was patting his smooth jaw with a towel.

'Should I look in on her later?' He asked his wife for her opinion; a once-in-a-blue-moon occurrence. 'Or do you think she'll cope on her own?'

'What are you more worried about: our daughter or the new Allwin?' Maria challenged.

'Pardon me for breathing.' He glowered into his shaving mirror. 'Actually, I'm thinking of Pearl – how's the poor lass going to get on without Bernie?'

Maria put her hand over her mouth to suppress a groan. 'Lord only knows,' she said in a muffled voice.

'I'll look in on her just in case,' Henry decided as he put away his shaving kit.

Nodding and pressing her hand harder against her lips, Maria escaped through the back door. Elsie and Wilf would have to see themselves off to school this morning while their mother stayed out in the yard and had a good cry.

Was it even possible? All night Joy tossed and turned, questioning Sylvia's plan. Was it hare-brained or entirely reasonable, a pipe dream or something that she could seriously propose to an unsuspecting George?

At three in the morning she could bear it no longer so she got out of bed and started to refold the clothes that she'd already packed into her suitcase then stopped to run her fingers over the smooth satin of Sylvia's half-finished bridesmaid's dress that hung from a hanger on the back of the door. Glancing at the bedside table, she saw the box containing her sapphire and diamond ring. Opening it with a sigh and seeing the small jewels glimmer in the low light of the table lamp next to it, she felt her heart skip a beat. It must be returned to Tommy; but the prospect of it was too daunting so she closed the box with a click, shelved the problem then went back to bed, only to lie awake and endure more endless hours of leg-twitching uncertainty. When dawn finally filtered in as chinks of grey light to either side of the blackout blind, Joy still hadn't decided what to do.

There was no sign of Sylvia when she got dressed then went through to the living room – simply a hastily scribbled note saying that Joy should help herself to breakfast and asking her to fulfil her promise to come along to the Tower with Sylvia later on. *Remember that Ruby and the girls will be looking out for you. It will take your mind off things and do you good*, the note concluded.

Joy felt in no mood for dancing – or for eating breakfast, for that matter. George's pressing invitation weighed heavily – apart from anything else it was impolite to keep him and Mary wondering if she would join them for Christmas. She decided to make a telephone call and tell him her decision on that score at least.

So she went downstairs to the shop and asked Ibbotson's boy if it was possible for her to make the call. 'I'll pay for it,' she promised.

'Wait here – I'll ask the boss,' he croaked before disappearing into the old man's living quarters and giving Joy time to change her mind half a dozen times before he reappeared. 'He says go ahead but make it snappy,' the boy reported back.

Joy held her breath as she leaned over the counter and picked up the receiver. Gathering her courage, she gave her name and George's number to the operator, who asked her to hold the line. There were clicks and buzzes, followed by a ring tone then eventually George's voice.

'Joy, is that you?'

She jerked out a reply. 'Yes, it's me. I hope it's not too early to ring you.'

'No, not at all. You sound breathless; are you all right?'

'Yes, thank you. I'm sorry that it's such late notice but I

313

won't be joining you for Christmas after all. I've decided to spend it here in Blackpool with my friends.'

'But you'll join us for Hogmanay?' George asked.

'Yes, please – I'd like that very much.'

'Excellent – I'll let Mary know.'

This was the easy part; now the moment had come for Joy to settle the doubts that had flitted bat-like through her brain during the dark hours. Without planning what she would say and screwing her courage to the sticking place, she forged ahead. 'George, I have a new proposal to put to you.'

'Oh?' He expressed surprise then waited.

Joy began tentatively. 'It involves thinking again about me coming to Glasgow long term.'

'Oh dear.' Envisaging the whole scheme on the verge of collapse, George couldn't conceal his disappointment. 'I thought you understood that this was central to the terms of our arrangement.'

'Yes, but hear me out,' she pleaded. Suddenly her head was clear: she must explain the practicalities of the new plan and focus on its advantages. 'I'm eager to contribute to Hebden Knitwear Company's success, but what if I were to do it by reopening a warehouse in Manchester?'

There was a long pause then, 'Wait a moment – let me consider what this would entail.' This course of action hadn't entered his mind. 'You mean that you would be willing to take on your father's old role?'

'Yes, with Mr Henderson's help. I wouldn't mind how hard I had to work. We could set up an office and a warehouse which I would oversee. I'm a quick learner – we'd be up and running in no time.' There was another silence during which Joy closed her eyes and prayed.

'I have to admit, I'm in two minds,' George said at last.

'On the personal level, I confess to considerable disappointment that you wouldn't be here on the spot. I feel we got on well when we met and I was looking forward to having you around. Then again, with my business hat on, I can see the advantages of cautious expansion, leading to a better distribution network.'

Don't push too hard, let him make up his own mind. Joy held her nerve and let the seconds tick by.

'And you'd be happier to stay in Lancashire?' George checked.

'Yes,' she answered with quiet certainty.

'I see that it might work if you were prepared to come up here for regular meetings. Of course, it would depend on finding the right premises and on Alan agreeing to move down from Glasgow.'

As if by magic, pieces of the jigsaw slotted together to form a new picture. *Say yes!* Joy pleaded silently.

'I suppose there would be ample time for us to thrash it all out while you're up here for Hogmanay.'

Please, please say yes! More seconds passed and Joy prayed with all her might.

'It's a good deal of responsibility for one so young,' he cautioned. 'But, as I told Mary, you seem to have a wise head on your shoulders.'

'I promise I won't let you down.'

'Alan knows the business inside out.' There were risks and advantages to think through in more detail but George allowed instinct to guide him. 'I believe in you,' he told Joy. 'And I do wish to make the business work for both of us.'

'So you'll let me try?' If she held her breath for much longer she felt sure she would pass out.

'Yes,' he said. 'The idea has merit; I agree to give it a go.'

Yes – one short word that transformed Joy's future. She breathed out and let her head sink on to her chest.

'Watch out!' Ibbotson's lad ran forward to retrieve the receiver that she'd let slip from her hand. It dangled from the cradle, swinging like a pendulum while she steadied herself on the glass counter. 'What's happened? What's wrong?'

'Nothing's wrong,' she replied breathlessly. It was only that her whole world had shifted on its axis. Now only one doubt remained.

Tommy's job was on the line. Unless he showed up for today's matinee he might as well kiss goodbye to the Tower Circus and a career as a professional clown.

'Tommy, why you don't eat?' For days his mother had plied him with appetising plates of home-cooked food. 'Tommy, why you no go to work?'

After Joy's last visit and his run-away-like-a-scared-rabbit act, he'd stayed in his room and moped, obsessively running through events that had led to his current misery, starting with hiding the damned letter. If only he'd stopped to think. And after having made his fatal mistake, how come he hadn't had the courage to own up? He lacked backbone; that was why. Equally, if Tommy took a step back from all the hurt, he saw that Joy's view of the affair had been too black and white. After all, he'd been right to point out that she'd found herself in a similar situation, acting out of sheer panic when she'd burned Sam Grigg's note. Couldn't she see that fear made you keep secrets and do things you would later regret?

Lucia knocked on his door to remind him that time was pressing. 'My Tommy, you have one hour. I make sand-wich before you leave.'

'Not hungry,' he replied.

'But you work today?'

He gathered his willpower to give the answer she longed to hear. 'Yes, I will.'

'*Bene, bene,* my Tommy!' Relieved, Lucia hurried off to carry on serving in the café.

When she got there Lucia found that Joy had entered by the front entrance and sat at a table, quietly waiting. There were only three other customers – a Merchant Navy sailor home on shore leave, treating his two small children to ice cream, all muffled up in thick coats, hats and scarves.

Once more, Joy had had plenty of time to change her mind. What if Tommy wasn't here again? Worse still, what if he was but refused point-blank to see her? She'd been on the point of flight when Lucia appeared.

Seeing Joy, Lucia threw her hands up in shock and squealed, 'It is Joy – you come!'

The sailor and his children turned to stare, their spoons held immobile above their ice creams.

Joy joined Tommy's mother at the counter and spoke in an urgent undertone. 'Is Tommy in?'

'*Sì, sì!*' A flustered Lucia didn't know which way to turn. 'Wait – I fetch him. No – this time you come with me.'

Joy followed her into the living quarters and up the stairs. Halfway up, Lucia stopped suddenly. 'You will not be angry?' she begged.

'No,' Joy promised. 'I only want to talk.'

'Talk – yes.' Lucia urged Joy to go on alone before quietly retreating to her café.

That's Joy's voice. Inside his room, Tommy froze on the spot. *Or is it my imagination? Am I going stark, staring mad?*

Joy knocked on his door. 'Tommy, it's me.'

So he wasn't hearing things. He opened the door to find her standing there with a pale face and a strained expression, clasping her hands in front of her. 'Come in,' he murmured.

It was the strangest thing; despite having lived here, Joy realized that this was the first time that she'd stepped inside Tommy's room. It wasn't the least like she expected a man's room to be: there were no clothes strewn over chairs, no unmade bed or wardrobe door hanging open, no overflowing drawers. Instead, she saw order: a music stand in one corner with an open musical score, a trumpet on the window sill, a framed photo of his parents on the cast-iron mantelpiece and a small bookcase with a dozen or so books neatly arranged. 'There's been a change of plan,' she began.

Tommy noticed Joy's uncertainty; the way she kept her hands tightly clasped and then the absence of her engagement ring. Her voice was low as she shifted from one foot to the other.

'I thought you should know that I'll be staying in Blackpool after all.'

Maybe he'd misheard. 'You're not going to Glasgow? But Momma told me that you wanted a clean break.'

'I did, but I've changed my mind. George and I have decided to reopen a Manchester branch. It means I can stay where I am and catch the train to work.'

Tommy took two wary steps back towards the window then shook his head. 'And why are you telling me this?' The clumsy question didn't come out right. 'Damn it; I mean, how does it affect us?'

'I'm not sure. You deserve to know; that's all.' Seeing his doubt, Joy felt adrift in unknown waters, pulled by currents this way and that.

'I'm glad of it,' he ventured. 'Am I allowed to say that?'

Joy nodded. 'You've been avoiding me so I wasn't sure how you'd take it.' She stood here in his room, seemingly waiting for him to speak.

'I didn't know what to say to you; that's why. You already knew how sorry I was for being such a fool and I understood why you felt let down. But listen, did you come here to say we can still be friends?' Perhaps there was a flicker of light at the end of the long, dark tunnel?

'I hope so.' 'Friends' was a tame little word for the wave of emotion Joy unexpectedly experienced. 'I wanted to say I'm sorry too.'

'For what?'

She went on in a scarcely audible whisper. 'For being unkind – for not understanding how you felt or being prepared to listen to your reasons.' The realization came to her in a flash that though honesty was at the heart of what she'd been taught as a child, so were kindness and forgiveness. 'We were both in the wrong – I was too hasty, too harsh.'

'Oh, Joy . . .' All Tommy wanted was to close the small gap that separated them and to hold her; not just in this moment but for ever.

'I wish I hadn't broken off our engagement.' Love swept her towards him and almost without knowing she was in his arms, her cheeks wet with tears.

'It's all right – we can begin again,' he promised. *Walk on the beach together, love each other, laugh again.*

'Can we?' She leaned in towards him, her head on his chest, feeling the warmth of his body and his strong embrace.

'Yes, it's not too late to put everything right.'

'Are you sure?' She raised her head and with trembling

lips she spoke from her heart: 'I didn't stop loving you –
not for a single second.'

'And that's all that matters.' Tommy held Joy more
tightly and kissed her over and over. 'I love you and you
love me.'

CHAPTER TWENTY-ONE

Pearl was surprised that anyone wanted to feed coins into one-armed bandits so close to Christmas. Surely her trickle of Christmas Eve customers had better things to spend their time and money on.

'Cheer up, love,' a threadbare old chap remarked as he pocketed his jackpot winnings then headed straight to the pub, coat-tails flapping as he was propelled along the pier by an icy wind.

'Don't tell my missis,' a worker from the Vickers factory said with a sly wink as he paid his sixpence to enter. 'She thinks I'm working overtime.'

A young couple stood for most of the morning beside a Little Mickey machine, occasionally inserting pennies into the slot. In reality they were there to listen to Tommy Dorsey records and to spoon.

Pearl stood by the door, gazing out to sea then up at shredded, iron-grey clouds driven swiftly inland. As ever, gulls shrieked and rode air currents overhead. Two hunched men in sou'westers and oilskin capes fished from the end of the pier with little hope of a catch. She glanced at her watch: any moment now she expected to spot a delivery man pushing her father's latest acquisition along the pier. She stamped her feet to bring some circulation back. *Come on – the sooner you get here, the sooner I can shut up shop.* There was no sign of any delivery so she decided to close anyway.

The last of her customers – a pair of regulars who were night porters at the Norbreck Hydro – managed to lose a week's worth of tips on Dawn Patrol. They trudged out past Pearl's ticket desk, swearing that the machine was rigged. 'Daylight robbery,' one grumbled, while the other vowed never to darken her door again.

'I'll see you in the New Year,' Pearl called after them as she turned off the record player and slipped 'Imagination' into its paper sleeve. Noticing a small ball of fluff on the gramophone needle, she bent to blow it off. Her back was to the entrance but she sensed a presence. 'Sorry, I'm about to close.' She turned round to see a figure in uniform silhouetted in the doorway.

Time stopped. The man stood motionless. Pearl closed her eyes. When she opened them again Bernie was still there. *No, it's not possible.* She shook her head. Her mind was playing tricks, willing him back to life – just as it had at the Pleasure Beach.

'Hello, Pearl,' Bernie said. 'I came straight from the train station.'

His voice had altered. It was slower and more serious. Anyway, it simply couldn't be.

'Pearl; it's me.' He took an uncertain step towards her.

He was dressed in his soldier's battledress, bare-headed and with a kitbag slung over one shoulder. And now she could make out his features – the same Bernie but different.

He swung his bag to the floor. 'I can see it's come as a shock. Didn't you get my telegram?'

'What telegram? Is it really you?'

He offered his hand. 'Here; feel.'

His palm was warm. Overcoming her terror, Pearl forced herself to look him in the eye.

'Now do you believe it?'

'No – no!' If this was a trick of her imagination and he vanished as suddenly as he'd appeared, then her heart would surely fail her. She would fall to the floor and never recover. 'How?' she breathed.

'Here – sit down. I'll explain.'

They were Bernie's brown eyes but without the light that had always shone in them, beneath straight brows and thick, dark hair with its severe soldier's cut. He was the same height, the same build, but his lips were cracked and his skin was darkened by the sun.

'They gave me two weeks' compassionate leave,' he told her. 'Are you sure you didn't get the telegram?'

'Not one telling me you were alive, only the one saying you were presumed killed.' Pearl gave a loud sob. Was she still dreaming? If she looked away would he fade and vanish? 'Private Allen,' she managed to whisper. 'He came to see me. He told me there was a landmine and afterwards you were missing.'

'I was but I made it back – and here I am.' The army doctor had diagnosed him with a mild case of shellshock. They'd awarded him leave and shipped him across the Med and out via Gibraltar then north, clinging to the west coast of the Iberian peninsula and finally into the English Channel – all a bit of a blur. He'd sat overnight on the train all the way from Southampton, thinking only of Pearl, of how a lifetime ago, he'd travelled south on a different train to marry her.

'How?' she said again in a faint whisper.

'It's true; Arthur and I did get blown sky high. The two lads in front of us never stood a chance. Somehow

I was flung clear and saw it all – bits of truck, broken bodies, flying rocks, sand everywhere and bloody Messerschmitts flying low to finish off any survivors.' The *ack-ack-ack* rattle of enemy guns, the roar and whine of engines and the whir of propellers would haunt Bernie's dreams for as long as he lived. He kept from Pearl the worst of the horrors, and this would prove to be the only time he talked about events in the North African desert. 'I scrambled under what was left of our truck until everything went quiet.'

Pearl clutched his hand in cold terror.

'I came through without a scratch,' Bernie insisted. 'But by the time I crawled out into the open there wasn't a living soul for miles – just wreckage and bodies, the sun beating down and a silence I'll never forget.' The silence and stench of death and a fierce heat under an azure sky and rolling sand dunes in every direction. No landmarks – not a single tree to shelter under. No water. Nothing. 'I hadn't a clue which way to walk and on top of that there was no way of knowing where the landmines were buried.'

Her whole body trembled. 'For how long?'

'I was out in the desert for two days before a platoon of Yanks on reconnaissance came across me and drove me back to base. I've no memory of it but they said I was off my head, ranting and raving like a lunatic. That's the reason I was granted leave. And all this time you thought . . .'

'That I'd never see you again.' His hand was warm and real. *Really* him, *really* Bernie returned from the dead. Tenderly Pearl touched his cheek with her fingertips. 'That I'd never be able to tell you how much I love you and always will.'

*

Pearl and Bernie turned to Joe for help. They hurried straight from the arcade to the market, where they found him dismantling his stall. There was the usual bustle as traders closed down after a busy morning and few people glanced in their direction. Those who did stopped in their tracks – could that be Bernie Greene hand in hand with Pearl Scott? Wasn't he supposed to have snuffed it?

Joe was busy loading leftover vegetables into his barrow. He would donate the spuds and turnips to the WI – they could turn them into soup and put hot food in the bellies of families in need. His neighbours' cries of astonishment made him look up.

'Bloody hell, I must be seeing things!'

'Stone me – it can't be!'

Bernie waited for his old friend to recognize him. He watched Joe's eyes widen and his jaw drop. A crowd had begun to gather when he spoke his first words. 'Wotcha, Joe – it's me. I'm back.'

His best pal staggered backwards then quickly recovered. Grinning from ear to ear, he launched himself at Bernie and hugged him, squeezing the breath out of him until Pearl managed to prise them apart. Then Bernie was swallowed up by an unruly crowd of well-wishers who piled in with hefty back slaps and expressions of wonder. Some even pinched him to prove he was real.

'Stand back, everyone,' Pearl pleaded.

Joe backed her up. 'Yes, stand back – give the bloke a chance.'

Bernie emerged, abashed and shaken. 'Blimey – who'd have thought I was this popular?' he asked with a touch of his old spirit as he straightened his battledress and smoothed down his ruffled hair.

'It's him, all right.'

'Here's me thinking he was a ghost.'

'No, the jammy bugger is alive and kicking.'

Gradually the comments died down and people started to drift away. Meanwhile, Joe collared a lad to wheel his barrow along to the WI kitchen then whisked Pearl and Bernie off to his house on King Street, asking no questions until the door was firmly closed behind them.

'Well?' Joe demanded after he'd sat the pair down at his kitchen table.

Bernie turned to Pearl. He was weary to the bone, still emerging from the nightmare of the last few weeks. 'Go on; you tell him.'

So she related the basics – the landmine, the days lost in the desert, Bernie's compassionate leave.

Joe hungrily took in every detail, grunting 'bloody hell' every now and then, his eyes glued to Bernie's face. 'We were convinced we'd seen the last of you,' he muttered.

'You know me – the proverbial bad penny.' Bernie managed a smile. 'Pearl and me – we're here to ask you a favour.'

'Anything,' Joe vowed.

'Pearl wonders if your spare room is going begging – the one I stayed in after me and my brother parted company.'

'It soon will be. Terry and Cliff have kissed and made up, so Terry's packing his bags as we speak. You two can move in as soon as you like, for as long as you like.'

Bernie reached over the table to shake his friend's hand. 'I've got two weeks.'

'It'll give Bernie and me precious time to ourselves over Christmas,' Pearl told him. 'We wouldn't have that on Empire Street.'

'No need to explain.' Joe kept hold of Bernie's hand. 'You know I don't have any family to speak of,' he said quietly. 'You've always been the closest thing I've had to a brother. Remember how we used to lark around in the Fun House when we were kids, how we played footie on the beach or nipped through the turnstiles at the open-air baths without paying . . . So this is me saying how . . . glad I am . . . you know . . . glad that you're back.'

Bernie and Pearl both felt tears well up at Joe's stumbling confession. Bernie roughly wiped his away with his cuff while Pearl was content to let hers fall. Now was the time for happy tears if ever there was one. Footsteps along the landing and down the stairs told them that Terry had finished his packing and then the man himself appeared in the doorway, loaded down with a heavy suitcase and a duffel bag.

'I'll be off,' he told Joe hastily. 'Thanks for every—' He stopped mid-sentence when he registered Bernie's presence. 'Crikey!'

'I know – would you credit it!' Joe laughed as Terry rushed at Bernie and gave him yet another bear hug.

'Go on – put him in the picture while me and Pearl take a shufti at our new room,' Bernie said to Joe as he extricated himself. 'Terry, I hope you left it in decent order,' he added with a wink.

'Spotless,' Terry promised. 'What the . . . ?' Still incredulous, he sat down at the table.

Pearl followed Bernie upstairs, her heart bursting with happiness. 'Spread the word,' she called over her shoulder to Joe and Terry. 'Tell Sylvia and Joy the good news. Make sure the whole world knows that Bernie is back in town.'

Although Joe's spare room was at the front of the house, sounds of traffic were surprisingly faint – just the occasional low rumble of tyres over cobbles and the warning ring of a bicycle bell. Bernie looked round the sparsely furnished space. It was as he remembered it: a narrow single bed, a small cabinet, a rug and an old-fashioned washstand with a water jug and basin.

'Will it do?' he asked doubtfully. 'If not, we could splash out on a hotel.'

'It's perfect,' Pearl told him. This was where they had first made love. 'You, the room, Joe, everything – just perfect.'

'Then here's where we'll stay.' He lowered his kitbag to the floor, uncertain what to say or do next. 'The old place doesn't change. Not just this room – I mean the market, the Tower, the Pleasure Beach. When I was away, I found it hard to picture, even though I knew it like the back of my hand.'

'Was it hard to picture me?' Pearl asked gently.

'No. I had your letters and this to remember you by.' Bernie took his treasured photo from his top pocket and showed it to her: a studio picture of her head and shoulders with her brilliant, beautiful smile. 'Sorry; it's like me – a bit the worse for wear.'

There were more tears. 'I keep your letters in a box under my bed. I read them so often that I know them by heart.'

Bernie took her in his arms and kissed her. 'These two weeks will fly by.'

She refused even to think of him leaving her again. 'We'll make every minute count.'

He led her to the bed and they lay side by side, looking up at the ceiling.

'The place doesn't change but I have,' Bernie warned.

'We all have.' She longed to soothe the worry from his brow, from his scorched body and his splintered heart.

'It's the war that does it. No one gets off scot-free.'

'Don't talk.' She kissed him to show him that there was a still, calm centre holding steady in the midst of whirling chaos. 'You're here with me now.' They lay quietly together, taking in the enormity of what had taken place.

Eventually Pearl and Bernie made gentle, tender love then slept. They were woken by a sudden cacophony in the hallway.

'Where are they?'

'Are they here?'

'Is it true; Bernie's come home?'

Pearl was the first to sit up and reach for her clothes. She struggled into her slacks and jumper while Bernie lay with his arms behind his head, watching her. 'Quick, get dressed – it's my lot, by the sound of things.'

Downstairs, Joe led Maria, Henry, Elsie and the boys into the front room and frantically fielded their questions. Yes, Bernie was alive. No, not a scratch. A fortnight's leave. Yes – upstairs with Pearl. Wait a sec; he would go and fetch them.

Racing upstairs, Joe found Pearl already on the landing and Bernie not far behind. 'Thank God you're decent.'

'Are they all here?' Pearl wanted to know.

'Yes – it's us!' Elsie screeched from the bottom of the stairs, jumping for joy, soon to be pushed aside by her father who took the stairs two at a time to pump Bernie's hand, up-down, up-down. 'By jingo!' he exclaimed. 'By jingo, you're back!'

Pearl rushed down to her mother. Neither said a word, only smiled and sobbed through their tears. Ernie and Wilf stood with their backs against the wall, watching the flood of emotions with bashful grins.

'In here.' Joe ushered everyone back into the front room while he answered another knock on the door.

'Is it true?' Joy demanded from the doorstep while Sylvia hovered on the pavement. 'Terry told Cliff and Cliff told Sylvia who told me. Is Bernie really here?'

'Come in and see for yourselves.'

Soon the room was bursting at the seams. Henry declared that he would put his son-in-law in sole charge of both arcades when he came home from the war for good since he, Henry Scott, intended to set up a business buying and selling Romany horses; he had the right contacts, the market for the piebald beauties was strong and there was lots of lolly to be made. Maria shrugged then dished out the orders – 'Elsie, stop pestering Bernie. Boys, nip back home and fetch those bottles of beer from under the kitchen sink. It's time for a celebration.'

Sylvia and Joy drew Pearl to one side; they couldn't be happier for her and now Joy had decided to stay in Blackpool, they could all continue to battle through the rest of the war together, arm in arm, dancing their cares away.

'Let's make a start by meeting up at the Tower tonight,' Sylvia suggested as she got ready to depart. 'It's a Christmas special, so no arguments – outside the main entrance, half past seven on the dot.'

Joy chose to wear the pearl-grey silk dress that had once belonged to Lucia. They'd altered it together when Joy had taken her first steps into the world of ballroom dancing and she'd left it behind when she'd fled in haste to Sylvia's flat. Now she was back in her old room above the ice-cream parlour, studying her reflection and counting her blessings.

'All is good?' Lucia had asked when Joy and Tommy had come down to the kitchen. One glance at their glowing, joyful faces had told her everything she'd needed to know. '*Sì, sì – bene, bene!*' She could write to Tommy's father and tell him that her prayers had been answered.

'But don't take your wedding outfit out of mothballs just yet,' Tommy had quipped.

He'd translated and Lucia's face had fallen. '*Perché no?*'

'Because this time we don't want to rush it.' Joy had squeezed Lucia's hand.

'*Quando, allora?*'

'We'll stick to the original plan and get married in the spring,' Joy had promised. Hopefully, that would give her plenty of time to find the Manchester warehouse and learn the ropes of her new business venture before she and Tommy walked down the aisle.

'Just what the blushing bride always wanted,' Tommy had reminded them with a nudge of his elbow and a rueful grin. 'Anything, anything!' he'd declared, once his feet were back on the ground and before they'd come downstairs to share the good news with Lucia. 'I promised Joy we'd do it her way – a spring wedding with sunshine and flowers and as many bridesmaids as she likes.'

Lucia had beamed and clapped her hands. '*Sì – nella primavera!*' What could be better than seeing Joy in a beautiful white dress and veil, next to her handsome Tommy in a dark suit, posing for photographs in the church porch with the sun on their faces and blossom in the trees?

And now Joy must make haste if they were to get to the Tower by half past seven. The sweetheart neckline of her dress was decorated with hundreds of pearl beads and the flowing hem was trimmed with thousands more – the effect was sophisticated and elegant.

'How much longer are you going to be?' Tommy called from the bottom of the stairs. 'It's almost seven.'

331

'Coming.' With one last twirl in front of the mirror, she grabbed her outdoor things then rushed to join him.

Joy and Tommy left the ice-cream parlour to cries of '*Bella!*' from Lucia. Tommy flagged down a taxi – hang the expense! – and they made it to the Tower building for half past seven by the skin of their teeth. Stepping out of the cab, they joined the throng that shuffled towards the main entrance where they found a magnificent Christmas tree, reaching almost to the ceiling and festooned with silver tinsel and shiny glass baubles.

'Where have you been?' Picking them out from the crowd, Sylvia tapped her wristwatch. 'I've been here ages.' In fact, she'd arrived two minutes earlier. 'Joy, you look marvellous. Tommy, why not go and order some drinks?'

'Aye aye, captain!'

As Tommy gave a spritely salute, the two girls stepped to one side to allow free passage to a bunch of GIs making their usual showy entrance into the foyer where they joined the queue for tickets.

'You must be freezing,' Joy mentioned to Sylvia, who was dressed in sparkly turquoise from head to toe. Her hair was up in a pony tail and her arms and legs were bare.

'I am, but why break the habit of a lifetime,' she joked. 'Where have Pearl and Bernie got to, I wonder?'

Eager young locals jostled for position in the entrance, preening and swaggering, calling out greetings to friends and grumbling about the length of the queue. This was their last chance to let their hair down before the family festivities began and they intended to make the most of it.

'Perhaps they've changed their minds.' Joy wouldn't be surprised. 'Bernie's been through a lot – he might prefer a quiet night in.'

'Let's hope not.' Sylvia crossed her fingers.

'For goodness' sake, you'll catch your death.' Without further ado, Joy bundled her vain friend inside then glanced anxiously up the alleyway beside the Tower. She was prepared to give it ten more minutes then, if Pearl and Bernie hadn't shown up, she would follow Sylvia into the foyer.

'We can always change our minds?' Pearl sensed Bernie's reluctance as they reached the deserted market square.

He'd stopped on the corner to light a cigarette. 'Just give me a second,' he said as he flicked his spent match to the ground. He knew every cobble of these back streets, every worn doorstep and polished knocker – so how come he felt so out of it, so . . . detached? Yes, that was the word. From here he could hear faint strains of music issuing from the ballroom and made out the outline of the Tower itself, stretching skywards, with its gigantic pepper-pot shape and its viewing gallery topped by a small steel dome – Blackpool's pride and joy.

'I mean it – we don't have to join the others if you'd rather not.'

Bernie drew hard on his cigarette. 'I don't know what's up with me.'

Before Pearl had time to offer words of comfort, footsteps hurried down King Street towards them. 'There you are. Come on, you two; step on it.' It was Joe, chatting as he whisked them on across the square. 'I lost track of the time. I had to look everywhere for a clean shirt then when I found one, it needed ironing. We'll miss the start if we don't get a move on.'

Bernie and Pearl couldn't fit a word in edgeways. Shrugging and giving in to the whirlwind that was Joe, they let themselves be bowled along.

'Mind you, I just ironed the front and the cuffs. They're the only bits on view. What do you think, Pearl – does this tie go with this jacket? Never mind; it's too late to change it now.'

Ahead of them, at the end of the alley and spilling out across the prom, was the usual cluster of people outside the ballroom entrance. 'You're sure?' Pearl whispered to Bernie, who nodded.

'Seeing as we're here,' he muttered to himself as much as to Pearl.

'Don't laugh but I'm thinking of asking Sylvia to step out on the floor with me,' Joe confided. 'She was forced to dance with me at your wedding reception because she was a bridesmaid and I was best man, but I haven't dared to ask her since.'

'What a dilemma!' Pearl's lips twitched.

Daunted by her unsympathetic response, Joe slowed his pace. 'You're right – Sylvia's way out of my league. Forget I mentioned it.'

'No, Joe – I was surprised, that's all. Actually, I think you *should* ask.'

Bernie agreed with Pearl. 'If anything, it's the other way around – Sylvia should be so lucky.'

'Now you're definitely taking the micky.'

It was Bernie's turn to propel Joe forward towards the magnificent Christmas tree at the entrance to the Tower. 'Sod it – just go ahead and do it.'

'Yes, nothing ventured . . .' Pearl spotted Joy gesturing for them to hurry. 'Ask Sylvia as soon as you see her, before anyone else nabs her – I bet you a tanner she says yes.'

Tommy stood on the balcony overlooking the foyer, waving a fistful of tickets at Joy, Sylvia, Joe, Pearl and

Bernie. He'd wangled a special deal with the girl at the cash desk who was a friend of his. 'No need to queue – come straight up.'

'It's all right for some,' Ida grumbled as the excited gang passed her and Thora on the stairs. The two girls had been giddily flirting with half a dozen GIs. 'I'm kidding. We're perfectly happy where we are, ta very much.'

Seeing Bernie's army uniform and sunburned face, the Americans fired brief questions at him – where had he served? Was North Africa as hellish as they said? How much leave had he got? God-damn; two whole weeks!

Sylvia led the way, squeezing past Eileen Shaw and Sandra Turnbull, who were regaling two RAF pilots with their recent ambulance escapades – a UXB that turned out to be no more than a length of old lead pipe and an ungrateful Jerry pilot who had to be pulled out of the drink. Ahead of them, at the front of the queue and in the process of buying their own tickets, were Mavis and Eddie.

'Oh, look who's here!' Sylvia felt only the mildest prick of regret as she exchanged greetings with them.

'No Terry and Cliff tonight?' Mavis kept her arm linked through Eddie's as she made small talk with Sylvia.

'No, Terry has a performance and Cliff has gone to watch him.' Not friendly exactly, but perfectly civil. And good luck to Mavis, who looked as glorious as ever in a simple white blouse and plum-coloured slacks. She could wear a sack and get away with it. 'I'll see you both in there,' Sylvia commented as she moved on.

Joining Tommy, the large group of friends entered the ballroom just as the crimson and gold curtains parted and the Wurlitzer rose through the stage trapdoor. The whole place was decorated with colourful balloons and patriotic red, white and blue banners spelling out the words *A Happy Christmas to One and All!* Mr Blackpool himself sat at the organ in black tie and white tuxedo – 'Where the brass band plays tiddly-om-pom-pom!'

Tommy led the way to the table that he'd reserved.

'Now's your chance!' Pearl gave Joe a sharp prod as Sylvia sat down, shiny and bright as a peacock in her satin dress.

'Sylvia, will you do me the honour?' The words were out and Joe's palms sweated as he waited for her answer.

'Why, yes, Joe – thank you.' She'd never thought of him as her type exactly but what did she have to lose? 'I'd like that very much.'

'You owe me sixpence,' Pearl hissed as Joe gulped down his beer.

And Christmas Eve was off in a whirl of waltzing and a flurry of foxtrots, in a glitter of crystal chandeliers and gilded plasterwork – all woes forgotten in chassés and lock steps, in whisks to the left and natural turns.

Tommy stepped out on to the crowded floor with Joy. It was plain for all to see that they'd found a way through their recent difficulties as they swayed and turned in perfect harmony. Look, everyone: she's wearing her engagement ring so there's the proof.

'Shall we?' In blind panic, Joe offered Sylvia his hand. What in God's name had he been thinking?

'One-two-three, one-two-three,' Pearl reminded him in a whisper as she and Bernie took to the floor at the same time as Sylvia and Joe.

The notes of the organ filled the vast space. They rose to the rafters and floated out through the wide doors, down the stairs, past the Christmas tree and out into the dark night. Joe held Sylvia in his arms, breathed in her perfume as they counted themselves in – one-two-three. He led, she followed in a quarter and then a half turn, smoothly swooping and gliding on a diagonal without putting a foot wrong.

'Would you look at that dark horse!' Pearl declared. 'Joe's a natural.'

'What did you expect?' Bernie grinned. 'There's more to my mate than meets the eye.' The music soared. Pearl smiled up at Bernie and he remembered in a sudden flash that this was where he'd first found happiness – here on the ballroom floor, jiving and jitterbugging with Pearl. 'All right, Mrs Greene; are you ready to be swept off your feet?'

'Yes, whenever you are.' *With you – always and for ever.* He swung her on the first beat (one) then swayed her (two-three) towards the centre of their first turn – natural as you like. Their bodies flowed as he wove Pearl between a hundred other couples, smoothly finding the spaces.

From time to time she caught a glimpse of turquoise and saw Sylvia smiling in pleasant surprise at Joe. Moments later, Bernie would waltz Pearl past Joy in a swirl of shimmering grey silk – Joy in a heavenly trance as she rested in Tommy's arms.

'Happy?' Pearl asked Bernie as the slow waltz ended and a swing number began.

'Remember, you asked me that once before – at our wedding reception? And my answer was . . .'

'"Need you ask?"' she murmured tenderly. 'Yes, I remember.'

'I was over the moon then and I'm over the moon now – here with you; knowing that I'm the luckiest man alive.'

All of a sudden thousands of balloons were released from the upper balconies, drifting down in colourful confusion. Dancers leaped to catch them or bat them away. The jive music swelled and filled the vast space. Unable to resist, Bernie broke hold and began to bounce on the spot and click his fingers to the new rhythm. Grabbing Pearl's hand, he swung her out to the side then pulled her close, rocking her in one direction and then the other, kicking with his left foot then with his right.

His grip was tight and he was laughing – actually laughing out loud, swinging his hips and shaking his shoulders. His eyes lit up in the old way. 'Happy Christmas!' he cried.

'Happy Christmas to you too.' Pearl laughed back at Bernie as the music quickened. 'Let's jive until we drop. Now swing me out and spin me again; fast as you can.'

ACKNOWLEDGEMENTS

None of this could happen without the support of my amazing agent and friend, Caroline Sheldon, and my supportive editor, Francesca Best and her brilliantly professional team. Heartfelt thanks.

After *The Ballroom Girls* and *The Ballroom Girls: Christmas Dreams* comes the dazzling third book in the series by Jenny Holmes:

The Ballroom Girls Hit the Big Time

Book 3 in *The Ballroom Girls* series

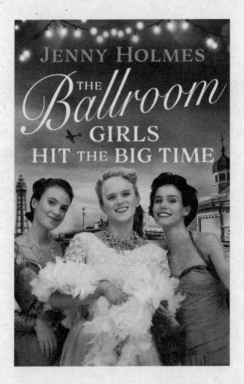

Available in 2024

Have you read the other wartime trilogies by Jenny Holmes? They are *The Air Raid Girls*, *The Spitfire Girls* and *The Land Girls*, out now in print and ebook.

The Air Raid Girls

Book 1 in *The Air Raid Girls* series

May, 1941

Connie's life has taken an unexpected turn since her husband died – she's living at home and working in the family bakery – but night shifts as an ARP Warden give her a firm sense of purpose.

Her younger sister **Lizzie** is eager to play her part too, perhaps as an ambulance driver. Her fiancé refuses to support her decision . . . but does he really know what's best for her?

Twenty-year-old **Pamela** has led a sheltered life, but when her family's home is destroyed in a raid she must learn to stand on her own two feet – helped by new friends.

As bombs fall and fires rage, the young women face the destruction of everything they've ever known. Can their fighting spirit prevail?

Available now

The Spitfire Girls

Book 1 in *The Spitfire Girls* series

'Anything to Anywhere!'

That's the motto of the Air
Transport Auxiliary, the brave
team of female pilots who fly
fighter planes between bases
at the height of the Second
World War.

Mary is a driver for the ATA
and although she yearns to fly
a Spitfire, she fears her humble
background will hold her back.
After all, glamorous **Angela** is
set to be the next 'Atta Girl' on
recruitment posters. **Bobbie**
learned to fly in her father's private plane and **Jean** was
taught the Queen's English at grammar school before
joining the squad. Dedicated and resilient, the three girls
rule the skies: weathering storms and dodging enemy
fire. Mary can only dream of joining them – until she
gets the push she needs to overcome her self-doubt.

Thrown together, the girls form a tight bond as they face
the perils of their job. But they soon find that affairs of the
heart can be just as dangerous as attacks from the skies.

**With all the fear and uncertainty ahead – can their
friendship see them through the tests of war?**

Available now

The Land Girls
at Christmas

Book 1 in *The Land Girls* series

'Calling All Women!'

It's 1941 and as the Second
World War rages on, girls
from all over the country are
signing up to the Women's
Land Army. Renowned for
their camaraderie and spirit,
it is these brave women who
step in to take on the
gruelling farm work from the
men conscripted into the
armed forces.

When Yorkshire mill girl **Una** joins the cause, she
wonders how she'll adapt to country life. Luckily she's
quickly befriended by more experienced Land Girls
Brenda and **Grace**. But as Christmas draws ever near,
the girls' resolve is tested as scandals and secrets are
revealed, lovers risk being torn apart, and even patriotic
loyalties are called into question . . .

**With only a week to go until the festivities, can the
strain of wartime still allow for the magic of Christmas?**

Available now

SIGN UP TO OUR NEW SAGA NEWSLETTER

Penny Street

The home of heart-warming reads

Welcome to **Penny Street**, your number **one stop for emotional and heartfelt historical reads**. Meet casts of characters you'll never forget, memories you'll treasure as your own, and places that will forever stay with you long after the last page.

Join our online **community** bringing you the latest book deals, competitions and new saga series releases.

You can also find extra content, talk to your favourite authors and share your discoveries with other saga fans on Facebook.

Join today by visiting
www.penguin.co.uk/pennystreet

Follow us on Facebook
www.facebook.com/welcometopennystreet/